THE

Christmas Mustang

To Judy

Merry Christmas

THE

The Christmas Mustang

PHILIP M. REPPERT

The Christmas Mustang

Copyright 2021 by Philip M. Reppert
Sweetwater Press

ISBN: 979-8-7636217-5-4

To contact the author email:
Philip.Reppert.SweetwaterPress@outlook.com

Follow the author on Facebook:
PhilReppertNovels

Editorial development and creative design support by Ascent:
www.spreadyourfire.net.

DEDICATION

To my mother and father, Marion and Miles Reppert,
who encouraged me to pursue my dreams and reminded me
that God has a plan for my life.

CHAPTER

1

*B*rooke jerked and sat straight-up in bed as electricity surged through her body. Her eyes were wide open with confusion dancing in her brain. The loud crash outside not only shook the house, but it also rattled her nerves. Her knees shook as she bolted to the bedroom window. She blinked and rubbed her eyes, trying to remove the haze that clouded her vision as she peered into the black blanket spread by the moonless night. *What caused that noise? Are the horses okay? Why are they running?* She had to know.

The howl of a truck engine along with the distant pounding of hooves cut to her soul as the sound pierced the night air. Her heart skipped with a second booming noise. Then the roar of the diesel engine faded into the night, only to be replaced by the distressed neighs of a lone horse. She screamed and vaulted sideways as a hand grabbed her shoulder. "Mom, what's going on? What was that noise?"

Brooke sighed as she waited for the effects of the adrenalin surge to dissipate. A measure of relief was written on her face as she looked at Kasey and motioned to the darkness outside. "I don't know, something's not right." Brooke's head swung back toward Kasey; they locked eyes as the sound of stampeding horses drew closer. "Get your boots on, we need to get out there."

They flew out of the house, pausing to slip on their cowboy boots before racing for the pasture, missing half of the back-porch steps along the way. They were halfway down the driveway when Brooke's burning lungs turned her run into a desperate walk. She pushed on as the distant neighs and now heavy breathing drew her closer.

Not another accident. She couldn't shake that thought.

Doubled over Brooke grabbed her side and then pushed on. Where would the sounds coming from the injured horse take them? The beam of her portable flood light bounced off the fence in front of them, casting long shadows into the distance. "Mom, look. The fence is in pieces." Kasey ran toward the gaping hole only to stop dead in her tracks. "It's Zoomey! He's down!" Her voice quivered.

Brooke's heart stopped and her legs shook. *O Lord please don't let it be. . .* She clenched her teeth and pushed through the pain as she made her way toward the injured horse. "Here, take the light." She thrust the lamp into Kasey's hands and moved next to Zoomey. His slow labored breathing was sporadically punctuated with moans that echoed in the night air. A chill went down Brooke's spine as she moved closer. "Kasey, keep shining the light on him so I can check him out." She carefully navigated from his hindquarters toward his head, and then froze in her tracks. "Shine the light over here on his chest." Brooke's voice went an octave higher.

"Mom, watch out!" The large horse surged forward, struggled to stand, and then crashed towards Brooke with a loud thud that not only took the air out of the horse but Brooke too. She dug deep and summoned her inner strength and forced herself to examine the injured horse. Visions of the owner and liability claims flooded her mind as the light illuminated the front of Zoomey's sorrel body.

"Hold the light still." She fought the urge to run.

"Mom, is he going to be alright?" The handlamp shook in Kasey's hands.

"I don't know sweetie; part of the fence is stuck in his chest." The blood-covered white board dripped crimson liquid on the ground.

"What are we going to do?" Kasey now used both hands to hold the light still.

"We'll try to keep him still and stop the bleeding. We need to get the vet out here, now! We'll also need to get the sheriff." The initial shock had started to fade, action was needed.

The blue and red flashing lights went dark as the deputies and fire department pulled onto the road. The first responders had been a distraction that kept Brooke and Kasey from focusing on the realities that loomed in front of them. Kasey's boots moved in unison with her mother's as they slogged back to the house, the sound of gravel driveway crunching beneath their feet rippled through the still night air. No longer would they be able to hide from the questions that pierced their minds. "Mom, why do bad things keep happening to us?"

"I wish I knew." Brooke's voice trailed off, "I wish I knew." *How much more can I take?* She moved closer to Kasey and put her arm around her for the remainder of the walk home.

Brooke collapsed into the kitchen chair next to Amber Moreno who was sipping a steaming cup of coffee. Brooke and Amber had been best friends since being in 4-H together in high school. "Thanks for coming over to keep an eye on Shane while we took care of things with the Sheriff and the vet."

"No problem." Amber motioned toward the hot pot of coffee. "You look exhausted, would you like a cup? It's still warm."

"Thanks, that'll be nice."

"Me too." Kasey mumbled as she slid into another chair at the table.

Brooke glanced at Kasey and then at the bedrooms. "Shouldn't you get some sleep?"

"I can't sleep right now, and school doesn't start for another week." That was only a partial truth. She was afraid of what might occur when she did fall asleep.

Amber placed two cups of coffee on the kitchen table. "Now that you two have that settled, can you fill me in on what happened with the sheriff and the vet?"

Brooke leaned forward and wrapped both hands around her cup. She hoped the heat would do more than warm her hands, maybe mend her soul. "We tried everything." Her voice cracked. "The vet ended up having to put Zoomey down." A tear ran down her cheek.

Amber's jaw dropped. "How'd this happen? You've got the safest pastures in the county."

"The Sheriff thinks someone was speeding down the road and lost control at the turn and crashed through the fence. They must have panicked and drove off. The spooked horses ran through the opening and Zoomey impaled himself as he went through."

"That's terrible. . . He was such a good horse."

"He was." Tears now trickled down both of Brooke's cheeks.

"Have you found the other horses yet?"

"Yeah, they made their way back to the barn on their own." She paused to wipe her eyes. "They're all okay".

"Does the Sheriff think they'll find the person who did this?"

"They don't know. They said they'd keep checking the body shops to see if a vehicle with the right kind of damage shows up."

Amber jumped up. "That's all they're going to do? What about looking at vehicles for white paint from the fence or what about the tire tracks that were made?"

"They said it will be like finding a needle in a haystack, and there's no other evidence for them to work with." Brooke let out a long deep breath.

"That just doesn't seem right. How badly was the fence damaged?"

"Two posts are gone, one where the truck went into the field and one where they went out. Plus, a bunch of broken fence boards."

Amber reached over and touched Brooke's arm. "I'll get some men from the homegroup to come by and help with the repairs."

"No, they've done too much over the past two years."

"But they enjoy helping out."

"We've gotta stand on our own. They've helped too much."

Kasey lifted her eyes. "Mom, their help would be nice."

"No! We can handle it." Brooke snapped back.

Kasey looked back at her cup and shook her head. A few minutes later she pushed her mug to the center of the table. "I can't keep my eyes open; I'm going to bed." Exhaustion overpowered her fear of what sleep might bring.

"Thanks for your help out there tonight." Brooke forced a tired smile.

Brooke sat quietly and stared into her coffee until Amber broke the silence. "How'd Kasey handle what happened tonight?"

"She's trying to be tough, but I can tell she's hurting inside. It has to bring back memories."

"I can only imagine. . . What about you?"

"It was rough out there, but I had to be strong for Kasey." Was it just for Kasey that she had to be courageous?

"Do you always have to be so tough?"

"Yes, I do."

Amber started to clear the table. "What about the ranch, this latest accident has to affect your business."

"Zoomey was a client's horse. I'll definitely lose that income. We'll see what happens with the other owners."

"You've done such a great job getting the ranch going again after the accident. But this bad luck you've been having; how much longer can you keep it going?"

Brooke shook her head. "Bad luck, that's an understatement. It's almost as if these accidents aren't really accidents."

Amber's brown eyes opened wide. "Do you think someone's behind them?"

"You tell me. One thing's for sure, I'll do whatever it takes to keep this ranch. Losing this ranch will be like losing a part of Cory." Brooke's thoughts drifted to her husband and then she softly touched her cheek. *I wish I had paid more attention to that last kiss from Cory.*

The August monsoon storm clouds had started to form off in the distance as Brooke put away the last of the lunch dishes. There was a knock at the backdoor, a slimly built man stood in the shadows.

Brooke cracked the door slightly. "Yes?"

He lifted his silver-belly Stetson to reveal a clean-shaven face except for a thick, dark mustache. "Good afternoon, Mrs. Anderson. I'm Hal Greer and I work for the Double-A Land Company." He offered his business card. "Can I have a few minutes of your time?"

Brooke examined his card as she blocked the door with her foot. No strange man was going to get into her house. *I wonder if this is the company I've been hearing about?* "I have some chores to do, would you mind talking to me outside while I do the afternoon feeding?"

"That'll be fine. I'll just follow along."

"Can you wait over there by the gate," she motioned toward the driveway, "I'll be out in a minute." She closed the door, leaned against the wall. *Now what Lord?*

She noticed Greer taking several pictures of the ranch. As she approached the gate, he stopped and refocused his attention on Brooke while he slowly canvased her from head to toe.   The way he looked at her made her skin crawl. "Okay Mr. Greer, I don't have a lot of time, so why don't you just tell me what the AA Land Company wants with me?"

"This is a beautiful place you have here, Mrs. Anderson. The view of Mount Humphreys is spectacular."

She headed to the barn at a brisk walk as Hal trailed a few steps behind. The way he walked and carried himself, he definitely was not a country boy. The soft-looking hands indicated he seldom did physical work. He tried to look the part of a local, but his creased and starched jeans didn't work. Brooke looked back over her shoulder. "To the point please, Mr. Greer."

"Do you mind if I call you Brooke?"

"You can call me Brooke."

"How many ponies do you run here?"

Brooke rolled her eyes. "We're set up to hold about twenty horses in the barn and another five to ten horses in run-in sheds. As I said, Mr. Greer, I have a lot of chores to do, so could you please get to the point?" They reached the hay barn where Brooke loaded a bale of hay onto a cart.

Hal took off his Stetson and wiped the sweat from his forehead. "My company is always looking for opportunities to acquire land holdings that may be beneficial to us in the future. The other week I heard that your ranch may be going on the market. To be perfectly honest, I did some checking on properties in the area and saw that your tax bill is quite overdue. Rumor has it that you're struggling to keep the ranch going. If you wait too long to make a move, you could be forced to sell. The selling price for the property will be much better if it's sold while you're still controlling it rather than when the bank or the county takes control."

Brooke's face turned red, her hand clenched the hay knife—she glared at Hal and took a long deep breath before placing the blade down. "Mr. Greer, I think I have heard enough. I don't know where you're getting your information, but I have no intention of selling this ranch to you or anyone else. My husband and I bought this place and built it up, and I plan to keep it. Tell your company, I'm not going to sell. Please see yourself off my property. . . Now!"

"Okay, Mrs. Anderson. Just remember the closer you get to foreclosure or a tax sale, the lower the price will be. We're prepared to make you a fair offer right now, but it won't last forever. You have my business card if you change your mind."

With his vehicle out of sight Brooke leaned against the barn wall and shook her head. For a moment, she almost laughed. *Take my ranch?* But in the next moment tears formed, she slid to the ground and put her face in her hands. There was some truth in his words. *I can't lose this place. I can't. It's our home.*

Tyler Alexander leaned back in a well-cushioned Italian leather club chair drumming his fingers on the armrest. Los Angles was visible through the wall-sized window of his plush office. Next to him in an identical chair was the president of AA Land Company who waited for a reply to the news he'd just delivered.

Tyler's eyes went from the skyline to Bob. "I'm not needed in Arizona. They can handle things out there. I've got too many accounts here that need my attention."

Bob leaned forward in his chair. "I'm not convinced of that. The Flagstaff Project is *major*, with many sensitive negotiations that need to take place during its initial stages. There are some serious holdups, and the project is not going as planned."

"What do you mean? Nothing was said at the meetings."

"In the past two months, the locals have staged several protests against our proposed development. I've made it clear to our people in Flagstaff that they're to do whatever it takes to get the job done, and I still haven't seen any results. I need you there to find out what's going on."

"But. . ."

Bob shut Tyler down. "You're to report back directly to me. If there are any missteps it could ruin the whole damn thing and cost us millions."

"I know what's at stake; I've been following the project at the staff meetings."

"You're my best man for this. I need you there to protect our interests and to babysit it until all the details are worked out and construction has started."

"Wait a minute. *Babysit*? How long are we talking?"

"For at least the next year."

The hair on the back of Tyler's neck stood up, but he kept his voice in-check. "There are others you can send. You don't need a lawyer there. What about Barbara? She's managed similar sized projects." Distance was needed, Tyler stood up and moved toward the window. "Level with me. What's the real reason you want me to go?"

"You're our best lawyer, but since your divorce you've buried yourself in your work. Now that your ex is engaged to Dale, the tension in this office has become palpable. For the well-being of the office, one of you needs to take a break." Bob crossed his arms.

"Why me and not Dale?"

Bob motioned for Tyler to sit down. "You're both partners in the firm, but you're the one not dealing well with the situation. I also think getting you away from L.A. for a period of time will do you some good."

Tyler's neck became red, but he knew there was no point in arguing any further. "Okay, I'll go."

Bob reclined back into his chair. "I want you to keep a low profile for the first couple of months. While you're checking out the situation, don't let anyone know who you work for. Don't let any of our Flagstaff employees know you're there. A lot of them are friendly with the locals and they could blow your cover."

"Cover? What are we up to that I need to be all cloak-and-dagger about being there?"

"I need you to find out why we are having problems getting the locals on board. It's a college-town community with a fair percentage of the people being 'Sierra Club' minded, you know what I mean. They're not getting the picture of how great this development could be for the local ecosystem. You could even say some of them are environmental activists. Get yourself plugged into the community, gain their trust. Find out what we need to do to change their thinking."

"Who will take care of my accounts and cases while I'm gone?"

"I told you, don't worry about that. You've taught Holly, she can pick up your load. Besides, you'll only be a phone call away if she has questions." Bob softened. "You know Tyler, your divorce was two years ago. Since then, you've had no social life to speak of. The only thing you do for yourself is run. While you're in Flagstaff, I want you to slow down and get some perspective on your life. Getting away from here will be good for you. You'll thank me."

Bob stood up. His agenda was complete, except for—"I want you in Flagstaff by Labor Day." The meeting was over.

Great, Labor Day. That's only two weeks from now. . . .

CHAPTER

Brooke was ambushed by Amber and the Homegroup when they showed up unexpectedly to repair the fence. Since the accident the other year, they had already done more then she could repay. Brooke's stomach turned at the thought of getting more help. Was it guilt for taking up so much of their time, or was it her pride? She always had to make it on her own.

The men made quick work of the post and rails and took care of a few other chores before the day wound down. As evening approached and the mission completed, the men and their families started to head home. The exodus was momentarily delayed when an afternoon monsoon barely grazed the ranch and slightly dampened the ground. The scent of fresh rain hung in the air as Brooke walked Amber to her car. All afternoon Brooke had tried unsuccessfully to corner Amber. Her jaw tightened as she replayed the previous day's confrontation with Hal Greer. His words still burned inside of her, she needed answers. Finally, alone with Amber, Brooke exploded. "You won't believe what happened yesterday. Some guy from a land development company tried to get me to sell. He knows I'm behind. . ." Amber's eyes lost contact with Brooke, she let out a deep breath as she slowly shook her head. "Yes, Amber, I'm still behind, way behind in my taxes and mortgage. Anyway, this guy knew. And how did he know that? Where did he get that information? A bank wouldn't give out that information—would they?"

Amber looked back at Brooke. "The tax information is public record, but. . ." She gritted her teeth. "I don't know how he'd get the mortgage information unless he has a contact inside the bank. That would be really frightening because that information is private and shouldn't be given out."

Brooke looked away from Amber. "I know I should have told you sooner about how far behind I'm on my taxes and mortgage. But I kept hoping I could bring in more clients."

"Maybe you need to learn how to market yourself. Get some new ideas and help getting the word out about your operation. There are several good businesspeople at church. Why don't you call them?" Brook slumped her shoulders and slowly nodded. "Talk to Slim and Martha—they've been successful marketing their business for years."

Brooke stiffened. "I'd prefer not to involve them."

Amber zeroed in. "What's with you? They were like grandparents to you, and now you won't even mention them. The accident wasn't their fault."

"They shouldn't have been there. They're too old to be driving that big team of horses. Slim was having more and more little accidents around their ranch and Martha kept making excuses for him. I tried to get him to stop driving that chuck wagon before they or someone got hurt—now it's too late." Brooke's voice quivered.

"The investigation showed there wasn't anything they could have done. The horses were spooked. . . ."

"Slim shouldn't have been driving that team. A younger man could have controlled those horses." Brooke's tone stung.

"Brooke, you don't know that." Brooke's eyes narrowed and she pursed her lips. Amber changed the subject. "How's Kasey's doing?"

Brooke slowly exhaled as her face relaxed. "The nightmares are less frequent, but she still struggles with having lost her father and Sidekick on the same night. Also, most of the strength has finally returned in her leg. Now it's just getting her lots of saddle time."

"Will the injury have any effect on her riding?"

"The doctor is confident she'll be one-hundred percent."

"I bet she's excited to be back on a horse again with no restrictions?"

Brooke leaned against Amber's car. "She seems excited, but in the past, she'd be planning out her competitions for the year. The fact is, she still hasn't mentioned entering a single show. I can't put my finger on it, but something is wrong, and she won't tell me what."

"Maybe she's waiting to see how her riding goes."

Brooke shook her head. "I don't think so."

As they were saying goodbye, Ray pulled into the driveway with a cloud of dust close behind. Ray was a childhood friend of Brooke and her late husband; he is now her farrier. He stopped next to them and smiled at Brooke. "I'll be done resetting the shoes on the two horses in a couple hours. Then I can do any chores you have for me."

"Thanks, Ray," Brooke called back as he continued to the barn.

Amber muttered. "He's so pompous, why do you keep encouraging him?"

"Stop it, Amber. You and Ray have always butted heads. He's been a friend for as long as I can remember. Since the accident he's been here whenever I've needed him."

"You have your feeling that something's going on with Kasey. And I have my feeling that something's going on with Ray."

Brooke shook her head. "Well, please keep it to yourself around me. He's a friend—and a good one."

"I bet he wants to be more than a friend."

Brooke glared. "Amber!"

Amber gave Brooke a goodbye hug. "I'll see you at church tomorrow."

As twilight approached, Brooke walked to the barn to check on Ray before she started dinner. He was nearly done with the first horse when she got there. "Ray, after you're packed up, can you come over to the house? I'll have your check ready for you."

He looked up from the hoof he was rasping and wiped the sweat off his brow. "No need for that. It's on me. Cory told me to take care of you."

"No! I insist on paying." She wasn't going to accept charity.

Ray stood up and faced Brooke and put his hands on his hips. "You can write a check, and you can push it into my hand. But I don't have to cash it."

"Ray!" Brooke shot back.

"Brooke," he smiled through his thick mustache, "you know how pig-headed I can be." Arguing was a lost cause. Ray was in fact very pig-headed.

"Okay, I'll back off if you stay for dinner."

Ray's smile broadened and he laughed. "You got yourself a deal, lady. I'll be in as soon as I finish the other horse and throw my tools in the truck."

Brooke sat across from Ray as they sipped their coffee after dinner while the kids watched TV. Ray gazed softly at Brooke. "How ya holdin' up?"

"I'm holding up and we're getting by," her monotone reply hinted at the exhaustion that came every day. *Why is he looking at me that way? I hope that's not pity in his eyes. . . .*

"You know Brooke it's been goin' on two years; Cory would not want you to wait forever to start getting on with your life."

"I know."

Ray hesitated for a moment. "I think it is time for us to start seeing each other—you know, more than just here at the ranch. Go out some place together. Cory wanted me to take care of you."

Amber's warning flashed in Brooke's head; she had not seen this coming. Her eyes widened as Ray reached across the table toward her. When his large, callused paw brushed against her, she quickly pulled her arm close to her chest. Brooke couldn't look at Ray, she focused on the cup in front of her. Finally, she lifted her eyes and broke the awkward silence. "Ray, I'm not ready. I don't know if I'll ever be ready."

"Take all the time you need," he gently replied.

Her muscles slightly relaxed. She'd never seen this softer side of Ray, was there a deeper side that he kept hidden? It caught her off guard, as did his surprise advance.

Bob had given Tyler little time to prepare for his move to Flagstaff. Maybe Bob just wanted him out of the office—things had been awkward—but why was it so urgent that he be in Flagstaff by Labor Day. *What's going on in Arizona? Why the rush, and why all the secrecy?*

His last few days in L.A. were spent making sure most of the loose ends were tied up on his other projects. Little time was spent preparing for his trip, he only took enough clothes to last a couple of weeks; sufficient time to find an apartment and get settled into Flagstaff.

The buildings in Flagstaff cast long shadows by the time Tyler arrived. With the remaining daylight he explored his surroundings and found some takeout before settling into his room for the night. He searched the Internet for athletic clubs, and some local churches. If he was going to be successful, getting connected to the locals was important. The High Desert Community Church caught his interest with a picture of the congregation standing in front of their building. Other pictures showed a warmth and sense of family that caught his eye. The photos drew him in, maybe it was the down-home friendliness of their faces. He decided to visit it on Sunday. Getting tied in with a local church was part of his and Bob's plan. *I bet this is going to be different from the megachurch I go to back in L.A...*

Just before going to bed, Tyler got around to opening the package that had been waiting for him when he arrived. After reading several documents he placed them back in the box and put them in the closet. *So, that's why Bob wanted me in Flagstaff by Labor Day.*

On Sunday morning, with the church's address in his GPS, Tyler drove to the north side of Flagstaff and pulled into the parking lot just off US 180. *Is this a good idea? There may be a lot of questions. And I don't want to lie at church.* At the mega-church, back in L.A., he was one of 10,000 people and could blend into the crowd. Here, it might be a different story. Since his meeting with Bob, his life had been a blur, and he hadn't given much thought about what to tell people when they asked who he was or what he did—which were standard questions. Lying was a bad option, a vague reply was better. *I'm a lawyer, and I'm here doing research for my company. Then I'll ask, what do you do? If they press on the type of research I do, I'll just tell them I specialize in contract law. It's truthful and will bore anyone who thinks being a lawyer is exciting.* Turn the conversation back on the other person, people love to talk about themselves. The strategy was set.

Tyler walked into a large foyer in the center of the building and picked up several pamphlets about the church and their activities. With some of the Sunday school classes ending, Tyler made his way toward the sanctuary. He was greeted by an attractive woman, who offered him a bulletin and a smile. "Good morning, I'm Brooke. Is this your first time visiting us?"

Tyler returned the smile. "Yes, this is my first visit." He took in Brooke and her lean form. *She's an attractive lady, too young, but definitely pretty.*

"Are you from the area?"

"No, I drove in from L.A. the other day."

"Are you visiting, or will you be staying for a while?"

The questions were starting. "Not sure yet," Tyler replied while focusing on Brooke's dark blue eyes. Something about them captivated him, they were mesmerizing in a way. And, behind the smile, something else. Sadness maybe?

Something about Tyler caught her attention; he was different than the other men at church. Was it his Southern California tan, or his clothes, maybe it was something else? Whatever it was, the fact remained that something primal was awakened inside of Brooke. Her eyes darted to see if anyone noticed, then she realized the bulletin was still in her hand. "Oh—sorry—this is for you. I'm glad you decided to visit this morning, I hope you enjoy our service and your stay in the area—One last thing, can I get you any information about our church?"

Tyler glanced back at the tables. "I picked up the information that was in the foyer."

"I hope you enjoy the service."

Sadness. Definitely sadness behind her eyes.

The service was over, and Tyler looked at his watch. Had an hour passed that quickly? The music was great and the pastor's message thoughtful. "Blessed are those who mourn, for they shall be comforted"—from the Gospel of Matthew. Appropriate for his frame of mind and spirit since his wife had abandoned him. Maybe he'd been in mourning the past two years, now that someone put a word to it.

He started to make his way back to the lobby. But someone grabbed his hand, and asked his name, where he was from. . . . And every time he turned again to head for the door another person would offer a congenial greeting. They seemed genuinely friendly, thanked him for visiting and asked how he enjoyed the service. Finally, he made it to the door where he was greeted by the pastor with a firm handshake. "Hi, I'm Scott Sena."

"I'm Tyler Alexander, and I appreciated your sermon."

"I noticed that."

He's forward. "What do you mean?"

"Your face. I could see by your expression that you seemed to be thinking about something that had brought you deep grief."

Okay, he's good. Tyler squirmed as it got personal, it was time to deflect and change the subject. "The singing in your worship service was exceptional. I've always enjoyed a good choir."

"Thank you, the choir is a blessing to all of us. . . . You're new here? I haven't seen you at the church before. If there's anything I can do. . . If you find that you want to talk with someone, don't hesitate to call me."

Tyler was about to balk, but the pastor had genuine interest—coming from L.A. he could read a phony at a hundred yards. This guy wasn't making an idle offer. "You know," Tyler replied, "some things are so deep it just takes a while to deal with them."

"Of course."

"But if I do need to talk with someone while I'm here in Flagstaff, I'll call you."

"The church is having a Labor Day picnic tomorrow. We love to have visitors join us, there's always plenty of food. If you don't have any other plans, it would be great if you could attend."

He'd come here to connect with locals. But now, given the depth at which Pastor Sena had read him, was there an increased risk of his cover being blown? It was a risk he'd have to take.

"I don't have any special plans for tomorrow. I might be able to join you. Is there anything I can bring?"

"No, the church is taking care of everything. Just wear sneakers for the activities."

Tyler pulled out of the church parking lot. *There is something special about this place and these people. What is it? I've never felt a connection this quick before.* He suspected there would be more questions.

*L*aughter was in the air as children played with frisbees under the cloudless sky. Teenagers played their instruments on a portable stage as the sound crew adjusted the volume. Other teens hauled chairs from inside the church to put in front of their make-shift amphitheater. Tyler made his way to the pavilion where most of the adults had congregated. He searched the grounds for long sand-colored hair and his heart sank every time he didn't recognize the face. Something about the attractive blond he met the day before drew him in. Before he knew it Tyler was greeted by several people who remembered him from the previous morning. Then, someone gave him a friendly slap on the shoulder; he turned; it was Scott Sena.

"Hey, glad you showed up. You play any sports—Volleyball? Softball?"

"Whoa, it's been a while. . . ."

"This is a friendly bunch, don't worry. We sure could use you on the volleyball court. The teenagers challenge the adults every Labor Day. Somehow, they won the last couple of years, and we can't let them beat us again."

"Well. . . ."

"I'll take that as a yes."

In the next moment Scott was gone. *No more questions. Good.* If he could keep things simple and superficial for the rest of the day that would be great.

In the pavilion Amber greeted Brooke, who was holding a large plastic bowl. "That better be your famous three-bean salad."

Brooke chuckled. "What else would I bring."

"What do you do to your dressing? I love it."

"You're probably the only one who does," She glanced over her shoulder to see that Shane had already abandoned her for the Frisbee field and Kasey had made a dash to the stage where her friends were rehearsing their music.

Amber stepped back to get a full view of Brooke. "Look at you!" Amber chortled. "Your hair looks fantastic."

"You're kidding? It's just pulled back into a ponytail."

"What are you talking about, your hair always. . . ."

Just then Scott Sena's voice boomed over the loudspeaker. "TIME FOR THE ADULT-TEEN VOLLEYBALL GRUDGE MATCH. ALL PLAYERS PLEASE COME TO THE COURT NOW."

Amber teased Brooke. "Are you going to let those teenagers beat you again this year?"

Brooke laughed. "Not if I can help it. I had to listen to Kasey gloat about last year's victory for two months. I don't want to deal with that again."

After taking off her boots and socks she stepped onto the warm sand court where she heard a voice. "Hi—it's Brooke, right?"

She turned and, stretching out his hand in greeting was—a man she recognized but couldn't place his name. "Yesterday at church," she offered.

"Right, Tyler Alexander. I'm the new guy."

In the time it took him to say those words, he shook her hand, and electricity went up her arm. She took him in, with his wavy dirty blond hair that danced lightly in the summer breeze. A soft smile formed on her lips; his California beach town fashion was not often seen in Flagstaff. "My daughter is on the other team." Men who dressed like Tyler tend to put her off. But there was a genuineness about him that threw her. Brooke blushed slightly, "I—don't know why I thought you needed to know that, but—well, anyway, I guess we're on the same team today."

"I hear the teens won last year and this is a grudge match."

"That pretty much says it. That's my daughter over there with the blonde hair and the pink tee shirt"

Tyler looked twice and then at Brooke. "You mean the pretty one that looks like you?" *Hmm, she may be older than as she looks.*

Brooke blushed again and before the pink on her cheeks had faded, she responded. "We need to take these teens down."

Tyler laughed. "Does that mean you want to do harm to that pretty daughter of yours?"

"Only on this volleyball court." Brooke's smile broadened.

"I'll see what I can do to help." They laughed together.

It didn't take long for the adult team to realize Tyler Alexander had definitely played this game before. He wasn't overly aggressive and didn't try to hog the ball, but when one of his teammates missed, Tyler was there to back them up and bring the ball back into play.

"Man—those are incredible saves," Pastor Sena complimented him.

"Just doing my part."

Three plays later, the ball was deflected, and headed straight toward Brooke's feet. Tyler instinctively dove to dig the ball out of the sand, at the same time Brooke dropped toward the ball faster than he anticipated. It wasn't a bone crushing collision, but the impact took them both to the ground with Brooke landing on top of Tyler.

Tyler stood, offered Brooke his hand, and hoisted her up. In that moment, their noses almost touched—and for an instant their eyes locked on each other. Tyler quickly backed away. "I'm so sorry. I didn't think you were going for that. It's my fault. Are you okay?"

"Yeah—sure."

"No. Your lip is bleeding."

Brooke sucked on her lip and gave a polite smile. "It's nothing." But that was not the full truth.

By the end of the match the teens were harassing Pastor Sena for bringing in a ringer, because the adults had fairly slaughtered them. Scott approached Tyler, who had just wiped the perspiration off his face and was guzzling a bottle of water. "When I asked you earlier, you said you played *some*. Level with me—how much and where? Were you a pro?"

Tyler shrugged. "I went to UCLA on a volleyball scholarship."

Brooke overheard. "Why didn't you tell us that in the beginning; we could have gotten coaching from you."

"I've learned from past pickup games that sometimes people want coaching during the match, and that distracts me from playing, or they get self-conscious playing in front of me. I just do what I can and try to be part of team." The lunch bell rang over at the pavilion. *Saved by the bell.*

The main dishes were devoured, and everyone had swarmed the

dessert stand, Amber noticed that Tyler was sitting alone at the end of a long picnic table. She seized Brooke by the arm and guided her over to him. "May we join you?"

Amber maneuvered Brooke onto the bench across the table from Tyler. He smiled politely; what was it about her that kept drawing his attention? Was it simple sweet goodness—or maybe he was just imagining that? After all, she was unknown to him. "So, has this group always been this warm and friendly to strangers like me?"

"Just the good-looking volleyball stars." Amber laughed.

"Oh, please. . ." Tyler protested.

Amber throttled ahead. "What brings you to Flagstaff?"

The questions. This time he was better prepared. "I'm an attorney and was sent here on business. I'm doing some legal research. Boring stuff trust me. What about you two—what do you do for a living?"

Amber jumped in. "I'm an administrative assistant for a Vice President at the Flagstaff National Bank."

Tyler looked at Brooke.

"I own Sweetwater ranch and train horses."

"She doesn't just train horses," Amber thrust herself into the exchange. "She's an amazing trainer." She nudged Brooke. "Why don't you give him a business card and see if he wants riding lessons." Amber looked at Tyler. "Or do you already ride?"

"Well, I have in the past, but just a little."

Brooke laughed. "Is that like you played *a little* volleyball?"

Amber pushed on. "She gives really good riding lessons." Brooke quietly elbowed her.

"A riding lesson or two would be a great way to break up the monotony of my work. Do you have a business card?"

Brooke searched deep into her pockets and found a crumpled one which she smoothed out before handing it across the table—only to knock over Tyler's full cup of lemonade. He leapt up to avoid the yellow tidal wave but wasn't fast enough. Most of it landed on his lap.

"I'm so sorry!" Brooke's cheeks turned bright pink as she lunged across the table to offer him a wad of napkins—and knocked her own drink into her lap.

"*Brooke!*" Amber shouted. "You're gonna drown us all."

Tyler grabbed some napkins, handed them to Brooke whose jeans were as soaked as his. "I hope you're a better riding instructor than waitress." Tyler winked as a grin spread across his face.

Amber started to laugh—and in a moment, so did Brooke and Tyler.

"Hey, I was just kidding. I'll call about those lessons. Really."

"After *this*?" Brooke pointing to the mess, "I wouldn't if I were you. How do you know you can trust me?"

"I can tell a lot about people, you'd be surprised."

Oh, can you really? Brooke dried her hands and Tyler's eyes were drawn to the thin gold band was on her left hand. *That's one lucky guy.* "I see you're married. Does your husband go to this church?"

"He did, my husband was killed in an accident almost two years ago." Brooke's voice trailed off as she gazed at her ring.

"I'm sorry."

Pastor Sena arrived at the table. "Ladies, can I take Tyler from you for a little while? I have some people I would like him to meet, and we could use a fourth in our horseshoe match."

When the men were out of hearing distance, Amber turned toward Brooke. "I didn't see him wearing a wedding ring, did you?"

Brooke fidgeted in her seat as she rolled her eyes. "No, and I wasn't checking. How old are you? The fact that he isn't wearing a ring doesn't mean anything. He's from *out of town*—you know? He probably has a girlfriend."

But the fact was, Brooke had noticed Tyler wasn't wearing a ring. And of course, she'd noticed he was handsome and charming. And in the next instant, Cory came to mind and a wave of guilt overwhelmed her. Guilt that she was being unfaithful.

Amber talked about how Tyler played volleyball while Brooke sat and nodded. She stared into the distance and touched her sore lip, the volleyball crash flashed through her mind. She pictured his light blue eyes.

Amber continued to ramble on until Martha stopped by. "I hope you ladies enjoyed the barbeque today; I don't know how many more of these Labor Day picnics Slim and I have in us."

"Martha, the food was as good as ever. And, if you and Slim retire, you won't know what to do with yourselves." Amber stood and gave Martha a friendly hug.

"She's right Martha, your cooking is as good as ever, and you'd go stir crazy if you retired." Brooke was cordial but cool.

Martha continued with a touch of sadness hanging on her words. "Slim has lost his enthusiasm. . . . Brooke, if you'd talk with him you might be able cheer him up; you always brightened his days."

Brooke stiffened and her face became flushed. "Slim should have retired from driving that chuck wagon years ago, before someone got hurt. I don't have anything to say to him. I have to go find Kasey." Brooke hastily left, leaving Martha and Amber staring at each other. A tear formed in Martha's eye. "When is she going to get over the accident?"

"She's been dealing with a lot ever since then. I shouldn't be telling you this, but she could lose the ranch."

Martha slowly shook her head. "I hope Brooke learns to deal with her bitterness and unforgiveness. They can take a toll on the body and a life. Just look at her mother."

The day drifted on until just a few diehards still played games while the other picnickers talked in small groups. Brooke rounded up her children; with everyone in the car and buckled-up, she announced. "Okay kids, there are two stops to make on the way home. We've got to get some gas and then we have to stop in and see Grandma."

An irritating whine came from Shane. "Do we have to go? It always stinks there."

Talking over Shane's last words, Kasey lifted out of her seat. "Mom, there's nothing to do there. Grandma doesn't even know who we are; what good does it do for us to go?"

Brooke bit her tongue and tightened her grip on the steering wheel as she pulled out onto the highway. "I've heard all of this before, but there are some things in life that are hard to do, and this is one of them."

They raised their voices in unison for one last time, but with less energy. "But Grandma doesn't even know we're there."

"We don't know that for sure. Her mind and her soul may not know we are there, but her spirit knows."

At the nursing home they found Grandma sitting in the chair next to her bed, aimlessly staring at a television. Grandma's eyes showed no recognition as the kids gave her a peck on the cheek. After Brooke gave her a kiss on the cheek, she asked. "Do I know you?"

"Yes Alice, I'm your daughter Brooke." Brooke weakly smiled as her shoulders rounded.

"Oh, which one?"

"Your only one Momma."

The kids plopped on the end of the bed while Brooke sat on the chair next to Grandma and updated her on all the activities of the kids and the goings on at the ranch. She read out loud from one of Grandma's favorite novels. Then Grandma asked Brooke if she knew

Mary, one of Grandma's childhood friends. She reminisced about their time together while growing up. Thirty minutes later Brooke got up from her chair and gave Grandma another kiss on the cheek. "I have to go home and take care of the horses. I'll stop by to see you later in the week."

"Will you ask Mary to stop by and visit?"

"I will if I see her." But Mary's been gone for ten years.

While leaving, Brooke spotted a nurse in the office. "How long will my mother have her long-term memory? She still remembers her childhood friends."

The heavy-set middle-aged nurse placed her clipboard on the counter, her bright floral scrubs seemed to brighten the room. "Some Alzheimer patients keep their long-term memory until the end. There are even some rare occasions when they become cognizant of their current surroundings and may even have a lucid conversation. This is not as common with early onset Alzheimer's like your mother's, especially when they are in the later stages."

"Should I look for more pictures and memorabilia from her childhood to show her? Will it help her?"

The nurse picked up the chart from the counter. "It can't hurt, and it may provide something to talk about." Brooke thanked her for the information and headed to the car with the kids. She had settled into a routine with these visits and the lack of acknowledgment from her mother no longer stung. Brooke smiled as she thought about being able to visit on a regular basis and making a difference.

Tyler had skipped his normal morning run and spent the time researching the Flagstaff area. He then reviewed the new documents Bob had sent him and wrote down some notes before putting them away. *Can I get the realtor to take me past the AA offices late in the afternoon, or do I need to cut the apartment hunting short and get there myself? I have to be there.*

The day of apartment hunting with Cindy Keating had been productive and he'd narrowed it down to two apartments. As Tyler planned, they were driving through the north part of town when he noticed a large gathering of people had spilled out onto the street. "Cindy, what's this—a protest?" Tyler pointed up the road.

"I have no idea."

"Would you mind stopping for a few minutes?"

"Why?—we still have the last apartment to see."

"I'm pretty well decided on the apartment I want, and I'd like to see what's going on here, if you don't mind. I'm trying to get to know the community. What better way to see what goes on around here than to observe what looks like a protest?"

His plan had worked perfectly. *Great opportunity to pump Cindy for information about AA without making her suspicious.* "Any idea what this is all about?"

"Well, it's right in front of the AA Land Company's office. My guess is the local environmentalists are trying to stop their project again."

Cindy pulled over and they got out of the car just as the local TV news crew started to setup their equipment. Tyler pressed Cindy for more information. "Do you know why these people are protesting? What are they trying to stop?"

"I only know what I've read in the paper and heard from other realtors. They're upset about plans to build a new community at the base of Mt. Humphreys on the north side of town. They claim it will destroy the ecosystem and increase the risk of wildfires for everyone in the area."

"What do *you* think about the new community?" Tyler probed deeper.

"I don't have any facts to go on about the development. What I do know is the AA Land Company hasn't made friends in the area or with local landowners."

"Why?" Tyler's eyes widened.

Cindy's voice became tense. "They've done what the locals consider to be some shady deals, and they've used legal shenanigans to have some people forced into foreclosure."

"I take it you don't think too highly of them?"

"No. Not really."

Tyler had heard enough and fought to maintain his neutral

expression even though his hands were clenched. He didn't want to dig much further at this point or seem too interested in the AA Land Company. He'd gather more information by watching the evening news.

Later that evening, Tyler went through his email as he watched the local news only to find that the protest at the AA offices was the lead story. The news anchor reported that several protestors threw rocks and bottles at the office windows—but the majority of the two to three dozen protestors were peaceful. *That must have happened after I left.* The news correspondent interviewed one of the leaders, Amy Jones, a thirty-something environmentalist. The anchor seemed sympathetic to her views and only showed things about AA Land Company that put it in a bad light. *This is not good. . . We'll end up with a public relations nightmare.*

Before the newscast was over, Tyler had looked at Amy's Facebook page and her blog. He thrust the tablet away to the other side of the bed. *So, she's preparing to file legal actions against AA Land Company and is planning to get assistance from the Environmental Protection Agency. That's all we need. It could delay the project for years. I need to learn more about her issues. I've got to get up to speed on this. Fast.*

As discussed during the horseshoe match, Tyler arrived at the church at 6:45 pm on Wednesday evening. As he entered the building, he looked for the blonde who spilled lemonade on him at the picnic, he saw her sing in the choir and handing out bulletins. There was something about her that pre-occupied his thoughts. What was it about their encounter at the picnic that drew him in?

Inside the sanctuary, the pianist, Brian Edmonston was flipping through sheet music with Juan Torres, the director, peering over his shoulder. As Tyler walked toward them, Juan called out, "Glad to see you came."

Tyler made his way to the piano and Juan continued. "Do you read music?"

Tyler shrugged. "Some."

Brian laughed. "Is that *some*, like the way you play a *little* volley-ball? Man, you sure helped us cream the youth team for once."

Tyler shot back a grin. "I'm not a professional musician if that's what you mean."

Juan took them back to the task at hand. "Is there any song you'd like to sing?"

"How about, 'Our God' by Chris Tomlin?"

"Water you turned into wine, opened the eyes of the blind—that one?"

"Yep."

"Brian, you know that one—Tyler what key do you want to sing in?"

"How about F."

Tyler moved closer to the piano and, as Brian played, he began to sing.

The Anderson family rushed into the church to avoid the thunderstorm that just started to drench the area. Brooke's stomach was in knots due to the ranch's financial situation, tonight's choir practice was going to provide a respite to her internal turmoil. Having sent the kids off to youth group she noticed someone was singing, a pure tenor voice, one she didn't recognize. It drew her into the sanctuary, and she sat down in the back row to listen.

Into the darkness You shine,
out of the ashes we rise,
there's no one like You, none like You!

Our God is greater, our God is stronger,
God, You are higher than any other.
Our God is Healer, awesome in power,
Our God! Our God!

How she needed to believe the message of this song. She did—but what about in the depths of her heart? Her attention went to the singer. *Tyler, so he can sing too.* A smile slowly formed on her lips.

When the melody ended the three men up front started to jam on some contemporary songs. Brooke remained in the back listening, she leaned back in her chair and closed her eyes, basking in the touch of comfort the lyrics had given her. Warmth enveloped her soul as she soaked in the new harmonies emanating from the trio. She was jolted back to the present when a man with a strong stocky body slid into the seat next to her.

"Brooke," he said in a loud whisper.

Her eyes widened and jaw dropped—to see Ray in the church. Brooke's heart began to race. Was it more bad news from the ranch? What else would bring Ray to church?

"What is it?" Brooke's voice quivered.

Ray tried to whisper, but his voice thundered out. "I just saw that there's a new mustang competition for teams of two, and I thought we could enter together."

With no emergency at the ranch, Brooke exhaled as her body re-laxed—but only for a moment. "You scared me half to death—for that?" A vein in Brooke's neck bulged, then she looked at Ray's head. "You're in a church. *Take off your hat.*"

Begrudgingly, Ray slowly removed his dark brown Stetson, and held it with both hands on his lap. "But what about the competition? Do you want to do it?" he pressed Brooke as he twisted the brim of his hat.

"You came to church for the first time since Cory's funeral to ask me this?" Brooke hissed.

"Well, I've meant to get to church, but. . . This competition, it's a great opportunity to work together. Cory was going to enter you both in a competition before he. . ."

"You knew about that?"

"Yeah, Cory told me."

Brooke huffed out a deep breath. "I don't have the time it will take to get ready for that. And I'm too busy trying to keep the ranch going."

"But.. . ."

She cut him off. "Ray, I mean it. I don't have the time, and I need to get started with choir practice."

Ray saw that several choir members had entered the sanctuary. He turned away from them and stood up as he glanced around the room to see who might have seen or overheard their conversation. Everyone was focused on the music that was coming from the stage. And then, as quickly as he came in, he slipped out of the sanctuary. Brooke stood, and shook her head. *I was scared half-to-death that something had happened to one of the horses or the ranch. Ray does a lot of good things for me and the kids, but sometimes he just doesn't think. He can be so frustrating, just like most men.*

The choir had assembled, and Brooke went to the front of the church. After Ray's surprise visit her heart had now started to slow down, along with her thoughts. But a new one started to grow. *A Mustang competition. Could be interesting if I could only find the time. But Ray as a training partner—it would bring back too many memories of Cory. . . . Cory why did you have to go and be a hero?*

Juan started to make introductions. "Brooke, this is Tyler."

"Yes, we met at church on Sunday and at the picnic the other day."

She turned toward Tyler. "I didn't know you were coming to choir—or that you could sing."

"It didn't come up." Tyler smiled at her.

"Will you be joining?" Her eyes lit up.

"It looks that way. At least for a while, until I have to go back to L.A. . ." Brooke's relaxed smile sent a warmth a through Tyler's core.

After practice, Tyler stuck around and got to know several of the members as they had coffee in the kitchen while waiting for the youth group meeting to end. He gravitated toward Brooke and then stopped next to her, there was more to know more about her. "Hi Brooke, are you originally from around here?"

"Sort of. I was born about two hours east of here in Gallup, New Mexico. We came here when I was five so my mother and I could be closer to her parents."

"What about your father?"

"That's a sore subject," Brooke said, as her smile momentarily disappeared. She generally avoided that topic. He like most men in life had become a disappointment.

"Oh,—Sorry to hear that." *Note to self, avoid that subject in the future.*

"Since you've been in this area most of your life, do you know how Flagstaff got its start?"

"Well, I'm not an expert, but in the late 1850s a road was built across northern Arizona for the pioneers to use on their trek to California."

"You seem to know a lot. Guess I asked the right person."

Brooke smiled and continued. "On July 4th, 1876 a group of settlers, who were taking a rest in the area decided to honor the centennial by flying a flag. They stripped the bark off one of the tallest pines and put the US flag on its top. They moved on but the stripped pine remained as a landmark which gave the area its name, Flagstaff."

"Do they know the location of the pole?"

"I doubt it. I've been told the town center has moved at least once, back when the railroad came through the area. One of the area's earliest claim to fame is that the Lowell Observatory was built here in the 1890s and that's where Pluto was later discovered." Brooke's face lit up when she talked about Flagstaff's history.

"If you're only going to be here a short time, what makes you so interested in knowing all about this place—and getting to know us?" Brooke posed.

"Oh, I just like history." Tyler focused on his cup for fear that his eyes might reveal the full truth. He changed the subject. "Say, my cup's almost empty and I'm going to warm it up. Would you like me to add some coffee to your cup too?"

"No thanks. I'll just get some water."

They had just finished refreshing their drinks when the youth group let out. Two boys raced for the iced tea and clipped Brooke's back knocking her forward toward Tyler. He was able to prevent her from falling but he couldn't elude the full cup of water that drenched his side and arm.

"I'm so sorry!" Brooke exclaimed, her blue eyes staring at Tyler's wet side,

"Are you alright?" Tyler asked at almost the same instant as he helped steady Brooke on her feet.

"Yes, but I got you all wet." Heat rushed through Brooke's body with some pink showing on her cheeks.

"It wasn't your fault."

"But you're all wet." She stepped back and took in the whole flooded scene.

"I'll dry off. Let's get some paper towels and dry up the floor."

While drying the floor their eyes met as they exchanged warm smiles. *She's really nice; maybe she could show me around and help me understand the heartbeat of this community.* By the time they cleaned up the wet floor, Brooke had to take her kids home. As they drove back to the ranch, Kasey asked, "Mom, why are you so quiet tonight?"

"Just thinking Kasey, just thinking."

How could I have spilled water on him again? But it did feel nice when he held me in his strong hands. She tried to think about the ranch; but her mind drifted to those secure hands stopping her fall, it was like being held by Cory. Then a shiver went down Brooke's spine. Was it spilling water on him or the emotions she just tried to suppress? What about Cory? Then came the guilt.

Brooke had stayed up late that night, trying once again to figure out how she was going to make ends meet. No matter how many times she looked at the figures she got the same result. *There's not enough money to pay the mortgage or the taxes.* The repair bills were still mounting, consuming her resources and energy. She threw her balance sheet down and paced the floor before sitting back down. With no progress being made on the finances, she started to clean her desk. In the middle drawer was Cory's mustang training application, the one she found the other year. Training horses with Cory always brought them closer together. *If Kasey and I train a mustang together, maybe, it might help her.*

Brooke pulled up the competition's website and studied the details. It was a good idea, but she wanted to look at it with a fresh perspective the next morning. Fighting to keep her eye open and her mind on task, she placed the old application back in the desk and went to bed well past midnight.

She was roused by the noise of the kids in the hallway as they got ready for school. A morning film blurred her vision as she groped for her barn clothes in the dark bedroom. In the kitchen and only half-awake, she was starting a pot of coffee when both kids appeared.

Shane looked surprised. "Mom, what are you still doing in the house? You're usually outside feeding by now."

"Don't ask." Brooke poured some coffee. "Kasey, I won't have time to make breakfast. You and Shane are going to have to take care of yourselves this morning. I should be back in before you leave."

"What did you pack us for lunch?" Shane asked.

"Peanut butter and jelly, carrot sticks, and chips."

He moaned. "Peanut butter and jelly *again*?"

Muscles tightened in Brooke's neck and she snapped. "I don't want to hear it. I'm tired, and not in the mood to hear your whining. You know we have to cut back on expenses."

Shane lowered his head, went to the cupboard and took out a box of cereal. She watched him slowly pour his cereal as a tear formed in her eye. Brooke's shoulders sagged under the heavy weight. She wanted to give him a better lunch, but every day there was a new financial burden. What sleep she got was restless, each day she snapped more at the kids. The downward spiral was going faster; she didn't know how to make it stop.

After Kasey and Shane left for school, Brooke went to the barn to start the day's training routine. She had four horses to work for clients and one of her own. At the barn she started with Scout, a 15-hand, gruella Quarter Horse gelding that Brooke had raised from a weanling. He nickered to her as she approached. When she entered his stall, Scout pushed his forehead into her hands while she braced and pressed back.

He continued to rub his face in her hands until Brooke moved to his side where she gently rubbed his withers. During his massage, Scout arched his head back toward Brooke and gently started to groom her shoulder with his lips.

"Scout, I'm at my wits-end. It seems every time I'm able to make some progress against the bills, something else happens that takes me two steps back. What's going on? It feels like I'm being punished. What did I do to deserve this?"

Tears trickled down her cheeks as she threw her arms around his neck and cried. Why did Cory have to die? Why do all the men in my life abandon me? After a minute or two, with the stream of tears now only a trickle, she tacked up Scout and got started on his training. At the end of her ride, she looked down at Scout and sighed, he understood her as well as she knew him. Brooke leaned forward in the saddle and wrapped her arms around Scout's neck. *Buddy, I don't know what I would do without you. You're the only one I can really share with. I can't lose the ranch And I can't lose you.*

CHAPTER

5

Brooke wiped her face trying to remove the damp smell that tickled her nose as the horse and rider moved through the faint haze of dust. "Keep him loping on the circle one more time, then bring him across the middle and do a flying lead change," Brooke instructed as she watched Amber in the arena.

"My legs are done. I can't take it anymore." Amber screamed.

"Push though it! You're almost finished." Brooke ordered, as Amber clenched her teeth and completed a circle at the far end of the indoor. She then came down the middle and executed a clean lead change. "That's the way. Bring him back to a walk and cool him out."

"Thank God!" Amber collapsed in her saddle. "I don't know if my thighs could take it any longer."

"But you did it, and it was a great ride. That was your best flying lead change I've seen yet."

"Thanks."

"I mean it. You two sure worked up a good sweat."

"I don't sweat, I glow." Amber laughed as she slid down from Danny and wiped beads of perspiration from her brow. She started to hand-walk him in a circle around Brooke. "How's Kasey been doing? Has the phycologist been making a difference?"

"Definitely better. The nightmares are much less frequent. The doctor said they could keep happening for years, but less and less each year."

"What about her riding?"

Brooke blew out a slow breath. "I'm not sure. The actual riding is better than ever; she's a natural. But something's still not quite right."

Amber paused for a moment and turned towards Brooke. "What makes you say that?"

"Mother's intuition. That, and she still hasn't asked to show."

"If she hasn't asked to show, you're probably right."

Brooke stared at the ground as she swirled a circle in the arena dirt with her boot. "Last night Ray asked me to team up with him in the Mustang Holiday Challenge."

"You're not going to, are you?" Amber shot a look at Brooke.

"No, working with him will bring back too many memories." Brooke shook her head.

"You had me worried for a second."

Brooke rolled her eyes. "Come-on, I know better than that. But I am thinking of entering it with Kasey. It might help me to connect with her. And maybe it will help with whatever is bothering her."

"I like the idea. Didn't you tell me the other year that you found an application for a mustang competition that Cory filled out for you?"

"Yeah—that's right." Brooke looked away, a million miles away.

"I bet Cory would want you to enter this one."

"Maybe you're right." She touched her necklace that Cory gave her. A tear beaded in her eye.

"When and where is it? Brooke, do you hear me?"

Brooke twitched. "Oh, I looked it up, they ship the mustangs by the end of September and the competition will take place over the New Year's Holiday, at the Los Angeles Equestrian Center."

"When are you going to ask her?"

Brooke sucked in a deep breath and slowly let it out. "That's the problem; the application has to be postmarked today and I can't wait to talk to her."

Amber tightened her lips. "Oh, I see. That is a problem."

"I'll have to enter today. Keep your fingers crossed and say a prayer that it goes well when I tell her."

"When's that going to be?"

"I think I'll tell her during her lesson tomorrow. I may also ask her to help me show some of the horses. It will be good for the business to have a teenager show and compete on them instead of it always being me."

"That makes sense." Amber led Danny outside to finish cooling him down.

Later, as Amber was putting Danny in the crossties to untack him, Brooke poked her head into the wash stall. "Do you need any help getting things into your trailer?"

Amber removed Danny's bridle and handed it to Brooke as she slid his halter on. "Sure, if you have the time. . ." She then guided the conversation a new direction. "Anything new from the sheriff on the accident?"

"No! And it's frustrating, I want answers." Brooke's voice echoed in the barn.

"Any impact on your clients?"

"So far no one's bailed except Zoomey's owner." That was only a partial truth. Brooke had to convince the other owners that Zoomey's accident had nothing to do with the safety of the ranch.

"Speaking of your business, have the guys from church helped you come up with any more ways to get the ranch back on its feet?"

"They've given me a couple of ideas, but their biggest concern is getting my maintenance and repair costs down. Doing that and getting a couple more clients could take care of most of my problems. They're suggesting a preventive maintenance program to catch problems before they get worse and become more expensive."

"That makes sense."

Amber drew out her words at a high pitch as she winked at Brooke. "Do you think we'll see that cute new guy at church again?"

Brooke hesitated. "Probably."

"What do you mean *probably*? What do you know?"

Brooke turned away from Amber. "He came to the choir practice last night."

"Why didn't you tell me sooner?" Anticipation hung on Amber's words.

"There's nothin' special to tell." *Other than I just about drowned him again.*

"Can he sing?"

"He has a very nice voice."

"Did you talk to him?" Amber moved closer to Brooke.

"Well"—Brooke nodded as a hint of pink showed on her cheeks—"I spilled a cup of water on him."

"*You didn't!*"

"I did. Some boys ran into me and knocked my cup on him."

Amber laughed. "Let me get this straight, lemonade at the picnic and water at choir practice. He'll be steering clear of you."

"He was very good about it. Seems to be a nice guy." Brooke hoped Amber could not see her inner soul. She had struggled throughout the day to suppress the images of Tyler that flashed into her head. Visions that hinted at Tyler being more than just a nice guy.

Amber finished loading Danny into the trailer when Ray's truck flew down the road. It turned into the driveway, with a dirt contrail kicking up behind. "Typical Ray. Thinks speed limits are for everyone else but him," Amber muttered.

The truck continued up the driveway and stopped next to Brooke and Amber with the dust cloud close behind. "Howdy, Brooke," Ray sported a large grin as the cloud drifted over them. Clearly, he didn't notice. Looking toward Amber, he mumbled, "Amber."

Brooke smiled, as she fanned the dirt away from her face. "Thanks for stopping by Ray."

Amber blurted between coughs. "Show some consideration Ray. Not everyone wants to breathe your dust or wash it off their truck."

Ray grinned. "Amber, when you're a runner-up, you're always going taste somebody's dust. Brooke is there anything you want me to look at besides your trailer?"

"Maybe Scouts feet. Why don't you get started on the trailer? I'll catch up with you later."

Ray parked next to Brooke's trailer as the women finished their conversation. Amber hissed in a whisper. "I can see it in his eyes, he wants more out of you than just a friend. When are you going to put some distance between you and him?"

"We're just good friends. He just wants to fulfill his promise to Cory."

That wasn't quite true, he had tried to take her hand. Brooke looked over at Ray and then back at Amber, "When are you two going to get over that rift you had a couple of years ago?

After Amber left, Brooke went to check on Ray. "Is everything okay on the trailer?"

"Yeah, just a loose connection. . . Do you know what time it is?"

Brooke looked at her watch. "Going on five-thirty."

"No wonder I'm gettin' hungry."

Brooke picked up on the not-so-subtle hint. "Would you like to stay for dinner?"

Ray's chapped lips formed a half-grin. "I don't want to impose."

Brooke put her hands on her hips. "Then what was the hint for?"

"If you're sure it ain't no problem."

Brooke shook her head and started to walk away and then called back to Ray. "You take care of Scout, and I'll get dinner started."

When dinner was finished and the dishes cleaned up, Ray struggled to ask, "hey do you want to take a walk around the ranch? It's a beautiful night."

"Not this evening, maybe another time. I'm beat, and still have to help Shane with his homework." Brooke replied not pausing from her clearing the table.

"Ah come on, Brooke. Take a break. Kasey can help him this time."

"Only if we want a disaster on our hands. And besides, I'm really tired."

"Okay, maybe next time," Ray stared deep into his cup of coffee and didn't look up until Brooke headed to Shane's room.

She called back to Ray. "You'll find some oatmeal cookies in the cookie jar if you want some dessert. Help yourself, and whenever you're ready to go, just let yourself out. See you tomorrow. And thanks again."

She could feel his eyes follow her out the kitchen. *I feel bad putting off Ray like this. He's helped so much around here. He just asked on the wrong evening.*

The day had been full of dead ends, and Tyler pounded on his laptop's keyboard as he replayed the day's events to see if he had missed any opportunities. Progress was slower than expected, Bob wasn't going to be happy. His cellphone rang and a small smile appeared as he looked at the incoming number and answered the cell using the speaker.

"Hey, Ryan, what's up? Why are you calling at this hour?" He continued to enter information into his laptop.

"Just called to say hi, Dad, and let you know that there is a beach volleyball tournament this weekend. I thought you might be interested in coming."

There was a long pause and then, "sorry, this weekend is booked. I have some work to do here on Saturday before flying to Seattle for a Monday morning meeting with some architects. I wish you'd let me know sooner." Tyler continued working on his laptop.

"I tried earlier but kept getting your voice mail."

"I'm really sorry about not making it. Do you need anything? Do you need some cash for the entry fee?"

"Dad, I've got the entry fee covered and I don't need any cash. I just thought you might like to see the volleyball tournament."

"I would, just not this weekend."

"Seems like every weekend. I don't know when you last saw me play."

"This past summer at the Huntington Beach tournament."

"No, Dad, that was the other year."

"Are you sure?"

"Yes, Dad."

"Oh."

"Dad, could you please stop working on the computer and focus on our conversation? Hearing the keyboard clicking in the background is really annoying."

Tyler stopped typing and sat back in his chair. "Okay, you've got my undivided attention. What else is on your mind?"

"I won't be around for Thanksgiving this year."

"What do you mean? You're supposed to visit me on Thanksgiving."

"I figured you'd forgot. Mom's getting married that weekend. They're doing the wedding in Hawaii, and then taking a month to honeymoon in the South Pacific."

Tyler shifted to the front of his chair as his voice got louder. "I didn't forget. I put it out of my mind."

"They want me to join them in Fiji over the Christmas holiday."

Tyler's blood pressure rose as he picked up the phone and put the microphone closer to his mouth. "They're taking you for Thanksgiving and wanting you for Christmas. Whatever happened to sharing the holidays?"

"I'm a senior in college—I can make my own decisions."

"Is there anything I can do to convince you to stay here for Christmas?"

"Don't try to manipulate me, Dad. It doesn't work anymore."

"It sounds like you've made up your mind."

"No, I haven't. Just don't try to make up my mind for me."

Tyler sat and brooded, he wasn't going to respond until finally Ryan asked, "Will I see you on your next trip to L.A.?"

Tyler sunk back into his chair as if someone had sucker punched him in the gut, his fist clenched as he thought about the holiday. Finally, he forced out the reply, "If I can fit it in." The phone call ended, and Tyler leaned forward in his chair and rested his head in his hands.

Why am I being so childish and punitive? Why can't I adapt to the fact that he's almost an adult? How could Ashley have left me? I worked myself like a dog to buy her everything she wanted. I did my best to provide for her. Then she had the gall to divorce me and take my son away. She said I was never there for her. Now she's marrying, of all people, Dale, who I have to see every day at work, reminding me of what I lost.

Kasey squinted as she swiftly moved in and out of the long shadows cast by the tall ponderosa pines. Brooke shivered as she supervised the final minutes of Diablo's training while butterflies danced in her stomach. Will she be able to get Kasey to help show the horses? Would the exciting news about the mustang competition go well?

"Let's do one more stop along the rail. If this one is good, we'll start building up to a sliding stop."

"Okay Mom."

"One more thing. I think you can start being more subtle with your cue. He's gotten good enough that we need to start making his signals smaller and smaller."

Kasey and Diablo picked up an easy lope, as they went down the far side of the arena. At the predetermined spot where she had always asked for the stop, she asked once more and got an immediate response, they came to a quick halt. Smiling with a sense of accomplishment, she relaxed in the saddle, and gave Diablo his head. "He felt really responsive. How did it look?"

"Nice job, he looked smooth and balanced. Now let's try it down the middle of the arena and ask for the stop when he doesn't have the que location to aid him."

Kasey rocked her pelvis position forward slightly, and Diablo started to walk. She then transitioned him into a lope and made a large circle at the far end of the arena before coming down the middle and asking for the stop at the center. Her cue was precise but barely noticeable and Diablo responded quickly.

"Great job! Call it quits with that. Let's make sure we end on a positive note."

Kasey got off Diablo and started to hand walk him around her mother. Brooke looked at her daughter and smiled. *That girl of mine sure is a natural. Her position and cues couldn't be better. She's got a connection with the horses that can't be taught. I could really use her help in the show ring.*

"Kasey, your riding has improved so much over the past several months. You're at the point where you need to be seen by some judges, and I could sure use your help showing some of the horses."

Kasey's body stiffened. "No, you don't need me Mom! You ride better than me."

"If I do, it won't be for long. Besides, it's one thing to have a professional compete and win on a horse; it's another thing to have a teenage non-pro do well on the horse. To have you riding in some of the competitions would really help prove that the horses I turn out are well trained."

Kasey stopped walking and turned toward her mother. "I'm not ready. I still need to work on my body position and my communication with the horse." Her resistance was deep.

"You're being too much of a perfectionist. You're getting more out of some of the horses than I do. I really could use your help."

"I don't want to compete. I just want to have fun at home."

"We have to pay for the horses somehow. Showing them is part of the business."

"I'll help with the training and barn chores, but I won't compete." The urge to run was building inside Kasey.

Her parental authority was challenged and instinctively she prepared for the battle. "If you're going to ride the horses around here, you're also going to ride at the shows. And that is *that*."

Kasey's face went pale. "I'm not ready to ride in front of all those people."

"What do you mean? We will start with small practice shows; they don't have many spectators."

Kasey started leading Diablo on the circle again. "But they're still strangers." Fear clung to her words.

"What do you mean? What's going on?"

"*I won't ride in public!*" Kasey said, on the verge of tears.

"I don't understand. Why wouldn't you want to ride in public? You always loved to go to competitions."

"The *accident*. I'm afraid something is going to happen when strangers are around my horse." Tears now flowed from her eyes.

Brooke bit the inside of her lip. *How could I have missed this? What kind of mother am I? She needs to be guided through this, not forced.*

Walking over to Kasey, Brooke took Diablo's reins with her left hand, and slipped her right arm around her daughter. "We'll get through this."

Kasey wrapped both arms around her mother and relaxed into sobs. "I really want to help you Mom; I really do. I just don't think I can."

"It's okay. Let's get Diablo untacked and back in his stall. We'll figure this out later." As they walked side by side Brooke added. "Have you mentioned these fears to your psychologist?

Barely audible, Kasey replied, "No."

Brooke had to know more; a mother's instinct is to help. "Is there a reason you haven't mentioned it to her?"

"I don't think I really realized it until just recently. It was only when we started talking about showing again that I realized I don't want to ride around strangers."

"Talk to her about it at your next appointment. See what she has to say."

"Okay."

They walked in silence the rest of the way back to the stalls. This was not the right moment to tell Kasey about the mustang competition. She wasn't ready for the news. Was this what's haunted Kasey, or was it something deeper?

Later that evening, Brooke sat at her desk and threw down her pen. *How could I have missed this?* Kasey would have to be helped through her fear. Brooke would have to move carefully and not push too much. Maybe the mustang would help. Maybe the psychologist would be able to give her some guidance on how much to urge and encourage. *What a tragic waste it would be, to have all that natural talent and not be able to let the world enjoy it.*

CHAPTER

The traffic was lite compared to what he was used to back in L.A. and Tyler arrived at church early. A smile appeared across his lips as he walked through the parking lot. *I hope she's here today. There's something about her; she's easy to talk to.* As he approached the main doors, his smile disappeared. How long would the questions to the newcomer continue? His gut tightened as he considered playing semantics with people who might become his friends.

Searching for Brooke he scanned through the swarm of people indulging in refreshments. When he spotted her, she was helping Shane get a snack. *She has a simple elegance. Maybe that's what it is about her.* He worked his way toward her and then gestured toward the food on the table. "Good Morning Brooke. What do you recommend?"

Shane looked up, with a white ring of powdered sugar around his mouth. "The donuts are *good*."

Tyler grinned at Brooke. "Yours?"

Brooke smiled. "Guilty as charged. Powdered donuts are his favorite. If you have a more refined palette, you might want to try some of the homemade banana bread." She pointed to the far end of the table.

Tyler looked down at Shane. "I think I'll have a powered donut and try a small slice of the banana bread." Shane's smile broadened. When had Tyler lost connection with his own son? It was years since he had the time to do anything with Ryan. But something inside him still hungered for that bond.

Brooke laughed. "Spoken like an attorney who keeps his options open while exploring all of the evidence. I'll get your banana bread if you could get another small powdered donut for Shane."

"Mom, I can get my own."

"I know you can, but I want to make sure you don't take too many."

Tyler studied Brooke as she walked away and then grabbed three donuts with his napkin. "I'll share the third donut with you if you don't tell," Tyler whispered to Shane.

Shane took his donut and broke off half of the other. "Deal." He shoved his half of the donut in his mouth to get rid of the evidence just as Brooke returned with the banana bread.

"I hope you like it."

With a full mouth and a cloud of white dust around his lips, Shane divulged, "You'd better, she made it."

"*Shane Anderson,*" Brooke whispered as a nervous smile crossed her lips.

Tyler smiled. "Then I'm sure I'll like it."

Tyler took his first bite and then a quick second. "This is really good." Brooke blushed slightly. "I'm getting a cup of coffee; would you like some?" Tyler offered.

"No, not me. I'm staying away from drinks when I'm near you."

Her eyes sparkled.

Tyler wiped his lips with a napkin as he moved toward the coffee pot and said, "I've got a question for you."

"Yes."

"Back in L.A., I attend a really large church where most everyone keeps to themselves. But, from the conversations I've overheard this morning it seems that most people know what everyone else is doing. Is that normal here?"

Brooke thought for a moment. "At a certain level, yes. People in this church tend to be pretty open with their lives."

"I've noticed." *Man, this could make it tough to keep a low profile for the next couple of months. I may have to rethink my level of involvement, at least for a while.*

Brooke continued. "People aren't nosey, they don't push to know your business; they wait for you to offer information. Of course, there are gossips just like everywhere else. But there are also some very private people."

Tyler nodded. *If that's the case, maybe this can work.*

"Why do you ask?"

"It's just so different from what I'm used to back in L.A.; I'm trying to understand the dynamics."

"How big is your church there?"

"Over 10,000. Rarely do you see the same person from one week to the next."

"Wow. That's a lot different than here."

Tyler took his place with the choir and waited for the service to begin. *I am really going to have to be careful. If I don't want to deceive these people, I'll have to walk a fine line between truth and deception. I'm a good attorney. I should be able to do that with no problem.* But, did Tyler truly know where that line was?

During the Andersons' drive to youth group, Kasey leaned against the passenger door and stared out the window. *What should I do about mom and her wanting me to show? Should I tell the whole youth group about my fear of riding in public, or just share it with Lisa and Daniel? They're the leaders, they'll be supportive. But what if they're not and they tell me my fears are just my imagination and I should suck it up and do it?*

Brooke glanced at Kasey. "You're awfully quiet. Everything okay?"

"Just thinking."

Kasey fidgeted the rest of the way to church. As soon as she would make up her mind about what to do, a different scenario invaded her mind that caused her to start all over again. No firm answer was in sight, she wanted the car to turn around and head home.

Maddie was already there when she entered the meeting room. "Did you get your homework done yet?" Kasey asked.

"Most of it. How about you?"

"I got everything done but two chemistry problems. I'm not sure if I can figure them out."

"Maybe Josh can help you." Maddie began to tease.

"I guess that could be nice, him sitting next to me and showing me how to work through the problems. . . Wait!. . . Then he'd see how I stink at chemistry, that won't work."

"You and your weirdness. Haven't you ever pretended to be stupid to get close to a boy?"

"Why would I want to look stupid for a boy?"

"Like I said—*to get close to him.*" Maddie pushed her dark curls away from her face.

Kasey rolled her eyes, hesitated, and then changed the subject. "You know that I haven't wanted to ride in shows, right?"

"Sort of. . ."

"Well, my mom found out but still wants me to help her show the horses. Things are really rough around our place. My mom just can't seem to get ahead."

"So. . . does that surprise you that she wants you to show?"

"I guess not. But I don't know if I should share it with the youth group so they can pray for me. And, I don't know if I want the boys knowing. I don't want to get teased."

"Why not just share it with the girls during our breakout time?"

Kasey paused, and then nodded. "Good idea."

"Sorry to hear about your mom's business still having problems." Maddie added.

A familiar voice interrupted them. "Hi Kasey, hi Maddie."

Kasey's heart pounded a little faster. "Hi Josh."

Daniel and Lisa West, the youth leaders, came into the room right behind Josh. Maddie got up and winked at Kasey. "I need to talk to Lisa before we start."

"Hey," Josh said, as he sat down. "I'm planning on joining the varsity rodeo team. Since you're riding again, why don't you join the team this year? You'd be great at barrel racing."

"I don't have the time. I've got to help out around the ranch, you know."

"Oh yeah, I forgot—Don't let your mom tie up all you time. It's your life."

"But I don't want to disappoint her. She really needs my help."

Just then Daniel announced, "Okay let's get started."

When the breakout period was over, Daniel made a surprise announcement. "Our activity for tonight is going to be a little different.

We're going to have a water balloon tossing contest. Boys against the girls."

"Cool."

"Awesome."

What followed was an explanation of the rules, and before he finished his last sentence the bag of water balloons was emptied along with a mad dash to get outside.

Choir practice had ended, and most of the adults were huddled around Seth Miller who was showing off his new guitar. Brooke hung back in the kitchen to keep herself busy. There was still something about that new guy that stirred her soul. But their previous encounters had her nervous about being near him.

Tyler was finishing up his conversation with Juan Torres. "I'll let you know if I won't get back from my business trip in time for choir practice next week."

"Thanks," Juan said as he and Tyler made their way to the coffee.

After doctoring his java, Tyler spotted Brooke in the kitchen and made his way over to her. "No kids to run into us today. That should make it a little safer for me." Tyler grinned and then they both laughed as Brooke started to relax.

"This might be our first conversation where I haven't gotten you wet."

"The evening isn't over."

"Very funny." Brooke, smiled.

"How's your week been?"

"Nothing's broken on the ranch yet. It's been one of those years with repairs and equipment breaking."

"That bad?"

"Don't get me started. Anyway, I don't want to bore you with my problems."

Shane ran into the kitchen excited and out of breath. "Mom, the teens are playing a great game. Can I join in if they let me?

"Sure, if they let you." Shane charged off as quickly as he came.

"That's a nice boy you've got there," Tyler commented, as he took a sip of his coffee.

"Thank you. He's the spitting image of his father and. . ." For a split-second she saw Cory's face. *At least I'll always have a piece of him in Kasey and Shane.*

"Are you okay?"

"Yes, our conversation just took me back."

"I understand. I've had my own losses." Brooke studied Tyler as an inquisitive expression came across her face. She never thought of him having experienced troubles. He seemed so together. Tyler sighed as he continued. "It's a long story better left for another time."

After a few minutes of helping Brooke clean and store the coffee-maker and cups, Tyler walked outside with her into the soft light of a full moon as they carried their jackets. Brooke smiled. "We did it. We made it through the evening without me getting you wet!" They both laughed.

In the well-lit ballfield next to the parking lot, the water balloon contest had deteriorated into a full-scale war, a battle that most of the preteens had now joined. "Mom!" Kasey ran towards Brooke as Shane chased her with his arsenal of balloons. Just before she reached the sanctuary of her mother, Shane launched one as Kasey ducked, and so did Brooke. Tyler didn't see it coming and was hit squarely on the shoulder.

"Oh no!" Brooke cried as she fought to hold back her laughter.

Shane and Kasey both stood still, wanting to run but too afraid. Their eyes and jaws were wide open as they looked at their mother and then at Tyler. Water dripped from him onto the sidewalk and pieces of a red balloon clung to his arm. Expressionless, Tyler scanned the pandemonium in the field and then looked at Shane, then Kasey, and then finally at Brooke. They expected the worst.

He shrugged and looked at Brooke as a grin grew on his lips. "We *almost* made it. Maybe next time."

Brooke laughed as she whispered to him, "Thank you." He smiled back, as Kasey and Shane flashed bewildered looks at each other.

"Okay kids gather your belongings. We'd better get out of here before Mr. Alexander decides to sue us or retaliate with water balloons."

Tyler smiled again. "Maybe next time."

Amber arrived early for the home-group meeting to help Brooke put together some snacks for the evening. As they filled trays with homemade brownies and cookies, Amber got personal. "So, what's with the rumors I hear? It seems that ever since Tyler showed up at church, you two always find each other."

Brooke's stomach jumped. "Who's telling you these stories?" Did Amber hit a nerve?

Amber finished filling a platter. "People notice things."

"I'm not interested in a relationship, and there's nothing between us. Anyway, he's a city boy and I'm just a country girl."

"I've heard that one before."

"We've just crossed paths a couple of times, so what?"

"Well I, and *others* have seen how he looks at you."

"What do you mean?"

"You know what I mean. The way a man looks at a woman when he's interested in her."

"You're imagining things."

Amber went to the stove and started to mix the marshmallows into the melted butter. She turned toward Brooke. "Come to think of it, the one or two times I've seen you with him, your face lights up."

"It does not." Brooke blushed.

"*Afraid so.*"

Amber finished with the marshmallow treats. "Do you want me to fill some cups with lemonade?"

"Sure, thanks."

Amber hesitated. "What about Ray?"

"What do mean, *what about Ray*?" Brooke's reply was sharp.

"I mean—I really think he wants to be more than a friend."

"I've told him I'm not ready to have a relationship and probably will never be ready."

"That's not the same as saying you're not interested."

"He's a good man. But, dating him will bring back too many memories of Cory."

"Brooke, he's a man. He won't understand the signals." Uneasiness danced in Brooke's stomach as the events of the other evening flashed through her mind. Maybe there was some truth in Amber's words.

Once the refreshments were set out, Brooke and Amber tried to relax at the table while waiting for the others to show up. Kasey came into the kitchen. "Mom, I'm going to the barn to do the final check on the horses."

"Can you take a look at Scout? He seemed a little off his feed earlier."

"Sure thing." Kasey yelled back as the kitchen door banged behind her.

Amber ventured in a new direction. "Have you talked to Kasey yet?"

"No, the timing just hasn't been right."

"You can't keep putting it off."

Brooke sighed. "I know, I'm just trying to find the right time."

"You'll never have the perfect time. You're just gonna have to do it. In another week or so the mustang will be here." Brooke nodded as she sunk lower in her chair. Amber continued, "I talked to Martha the other day at church. She said Slim is backing off his activities at the dude ranch."

"It's about time."

"Is that all you can say? He hasn't been the same since the accident and it's been over two years."

Brooke stood up and marched to the counter where she slammed down her oven mitts. "If he had retired before the accident, we wouldn't be where we are now. Would we?"

Amber looked straight into Brooke's eyes. "They miss you, Brooke. They want to make things right."

"It's kind of late for that. In fact, *way* too late."

After the home group meeting was over, Amber lingered. "How's the prep work going for your meeting with the bank?"

"I'm pretty close to having everything organized to show them. Thanks for your advice to meet with them before they send a foreclosure letter."

"I work with these people. If you can show them you have a plan to get caught up with your payments, they'd rather work with you than deal with the hassle of a foreclosure."

Brooke showed Amber her papers. "Looks good Brooke. Let's keep our fingers crossed." She put down the papers and focused on Brooke. "Have you heard anything from the Sheriff?"

"Nothing yet, I'm still waiting."

CHAPTER

7

The morning had been productive, and the horses were worked for the day. Brooke should have felt a sense of satisfaction as she was on schedule for the day, but her heart was unsettled. The previous night's conversation with Amber still nagged at her. *How can I forgive Martha for letting Slim drive that wagon, and Slim for driving it? I have good reason to be angry with them. Amber's wrong. Maybe God can forgive them, but I sure can't. They've destroyed my life. . . . It's not been the same since that day.*

Brooke had just closed the barn door when an SUV with darkened windows pulled into the driveway. She paused and watched; it continued past the house and toward the barn. *Who could this be?* The car stopped thirty feet from her. She started toward the vehicle when the driver's door opened and out stepped Hal Greer.

Brooke stiffened. "What do you want Mr. Greer?"

73

Hal adjusted his Stetson and a smug smile formed on his lips. "Have you had a chance to think about my offer."

Brooke crossed her arms and glared at him. "As I said the last time, there's nothing to think about. *I'm not selling!*"

"Mrs. Anderson, I urge you to reconsider."

"Absolutely not! Besides, I'm working with the bank to renegotiate the terms of the mortgage and provide more time to get the ranch back on its feet."

Hal leaned against his SUV and removed his sunglasses. "That's a futile effort Mrs. Anderson. Banks can be persuaded to change their minds. Also, the County is interested in my company's development. They may want your land for the project." His narrow eyes focused on her; she saw evil in them.

Brooke's face turned red, and her heart raced. "How dare you! I want you off this property right now!" She pointed toward the road as anger pounded in every vein. After his vehicle disappeared out of sight, Brooke stormed into the house and slammed the door. She tried to focus on her paperwork but couldn't. Hal Greer's smug, contemptuous look haunted her. She should have dismissed the encounter, but there was some truth in his words. *Banks are fickle and they might change their mind. Is Greer insinuating that his company will try to keep the bank from working with me?* She slammed her pen down on the desk. The paperwork would have to wait.

Neither Brooke nor Tyler would admit they were looking forward to seeing each other at choir practice. During the rehearsal Brooke casually looked up from her music and let her gaze drift toward Tyler. When she accidentally made eye contact with Tyler, her focus jumped back to the music and then to the rest of the choir, hoping no one noticed the hint of pink forming on her cheeks. When the group was done singing, they drifted towards each other; it was as if they were caught in a fast-moving current that pulled them into its powerful flow. How much longer would they struggle against it?

Tyler tried to maintain a safe distance from Brooke as he enjoyed his usual cup of coffee. But something pulled him closer to her. "Hi Brooke," he smiled. "Is the weather always this delightful around here? It's been gorgeous this week." Tyler studied Brooke and tried to understand what drew him toward her. Yes, she was attractive, but there was something deeper.

"Yes, most of the time," She noticed Tyler was apprehensive when she moved past him to get her own coffee. She laughed. "So, you're afraid to get close to me? Scared of getting soaked again?"

"Who me?" Tyler grinned as he backed away and slightly raised his hands in jest. Unfortunately, he didn't see Juan Torres behind him. The collision was minor, but big enough that his cup of coffee spilled on his hand and arm.

Brooke bit her lip to keep from laughing. "Are you all right? Did it burn you?" Then she couldn't contain her laughter any longer.

The surprised look disappeared from Tyler's face as he placed his now half full cup of coffee on a nearby table. "Yes, I'm fine—and it wasn't too hot." He shook his head and smiled as he joined in the laughter. "I just can't seem to stay dry around you."

"Now that your drenching is out of the way, you should be safe for the rest of the evening." Brooke reached for some napkins and helped clean up the spilled drink. "I'm partially responsible; is there anything I can do to make it up to you?" She continued to chuckle.

Tyler's eyes brightened. "So, you think this is funny." Brooke nodded, and smiled. "Well. . . let me think. Ah. . . I know—you've demonstrated an expert knowledge of the area and its history."

"I wouldn't go that far."

"You've done pretty well. Your knowledge of the region could help me learn the area. Why don't you give me a tour and fill me in on everything I should know about Flagstaff and the surrounding area." *Understanding the heartbeat of this community could really be useful. And being taught by a pretty lady whose company I enjoy is a nice addition.*

"Are you sure it's safe?" Brooke laughed.

"If we stay away from anything liquid—especially big bodies of water—I should be fine."

She hesitated for a moment. Was this an invitation to show him around the area? Or was it a, *I want to get to know you better* invitation? She did a quick calculation. . . *He's a decent guy and as Amber would say, "What can it hurt?"*

"Sure, I can give you a tour," she answered. "No guarantees on the historical accuracy."

"I'm sure it'll be excellent," Tyler got another cup of coffee, and they compared calendars and chose a day. Brooke suggested. "Why don't we meet at my ranch. Give me your cell number, and I'll text you the address."

Butterflies danced in Tyler's stomach as he pulled into Brook's driveway. *Calm down Tyler. Just a day of sightseeing. You know you're not ready for anything more.* He knocked on the kitchen door and called. "Are you ready?"

"Just need to grab my water bottle."

"*A water bottle!*"

"Just kidding." Brooke laughed.

Inside Tyler's SUV, Brooke began the tour. "I thought we'd start at the Snowbowl; it's the local ski area at the base of Mt. Humphrey."

"Okay, how do I get there?"

"Go back to US 180 and turn right. I'll tell when to make the next turn."

After a picturesque drive that ended on a Ponderosa Pine lined road, they arrived at their destination and took a short walk to the Scenic Chairlift. The scent of pines needles filled the air as Brooke motioned to the lift and then to the San Francisco Peaks. "If we take it to the top, you'll get some of the most spectacular views in Arizona."

"I'm game if you are." Tyler drew in a large breath of the scented air.

Brooke reached into her small purse to retrieve her wallet. "Let's go get our tickets."

"Please put that away. This is my treat. It's the least I can do when you're taking the time to show me the area."

"I can pay for my ticket; this isn't a date or anything?"

"I insist it's the least I can do. You're helping me out."

"Okay, if you insist." Brooke reluctantly put her wallet back in her purse.

Twenty-five minutes later they were at the top of the mountain with a brisk breeze chilling their skin. They were met by a US Forest Interpretive guide who was there to answer any questions visitors may have on the biology, geology and history of the region.

At the first vista, Tyler stopped dead in his tracks and gazed into the horizon. "Wow!"

"I thought you'd appreciate it."

"You were right. . . . Is that the Grand Canyon I see to the northwest?"

"Yes, it is." Then Brooke pointed to the south. "Over here is the Kachina Peaks Wilderness Area. It extends half-way down the mountain toward Flagstaff."

The Forest Guide introduced himself. "I'm Jack Slater; do you have any questions?"

Shaking his hand with a firm grip, Tyler asked, "Could you explain the difference between the National Forest and the wilderness areas?"

"Sure."

Jack explained in great detail about the Kachina Peaks Wilderness Area—its importance to the region and the differences between it and other parts of the National Forest. Tyler took in everything. When the guide moved on to another group Tyler took a long look at Brooke, smiled, and then returned his gaze to the scenery. *The trip up here was worth it just for the beautiful views.* He glanced again back at Brooke as her long blond hair danced in the wind, he liked what he saw. Something stirred inside of him, she was refreshing. *I'm glad I asked her to show me around.*

They hiked several paths that led to different vistas and soaked in more gorgeous views. "It's hard to believe we're walking on a volcano." Tyler commented.

"I know, and to think Sunset Crater, just a few miles from here, erupted less than a 1,000 years ago."

Tyler stood with his hands on his hips while he took in the scenery. "I still can't believe we're only14 miles from downtown Flagstaff. It's so peaceful here."

Brooke turned to answer him and was taken by the way he looked, as the sunlight fell across his tanned face. Her heart skipped a beat. *No! Just, no.* She willed herself back to tour mode. "The peacefulness here can disappear quickly. Sometimes storms blow into the area with hurricane strength winds. But even that has its own type of beauty."

Brooke gazed out over the green landscape which melted into different shades of brown and burnt orange as it faded into the horizon. She turned toward Tyler. "We have more to see and probably should get going. Are you hungry?"

"I've been so captivated by what I've seen that I didn't realize what time it is. But come to think of it, I am getting hungry. What do you have in mind?"

"We can get something here, which is a little touristy, or we can head back toward town and stop at Nancy's. It's a local diner in Hollister that's known for its chili and burgers."

"Nancy's sounds good, I'm ready if you are."

Forty-five minutes later they were back in Tyler's 4-Runner heading to Nancy's with Tyler prying Brooke for information on local folklore and rumors; both useful information to have when you're trying to understand the heartbeat of a community. As they pulled into the parking lot, Tyler pushed a little further. "While we were driving here, I noticed several signs for AA Land Company. I also saw them being protested on the evening news a couple of weeks ago. What do you know about them?" The peaceful look on Brooke's face vanished as she stiffened. "Are you okay?" Tyler asked.

Brooke relaxed a little. "You struck a nerve."

"About what?"

"AA Land Company."

Okay, be careful. Find out what you can, but don't let on that you work for them. "How do you know them?"

"I'll explain once we're seated inside. This could take a while." The last visit by Hal Greer flashed through Brooke's head as she clenched her jaw.

They found a window booth and ordered two bowls of chili.

Brooke noticed Tyler focused on her glass of water and smiled. "Don't worry, I'll be careful," she grinned.

Tyler smiled back. "I was hoping that would get you smiling again—you were so serious a few minutes ago."

"It's that company you mentioned, AA Land Company. They've been after me to sell." Frustration resonated in her words.

Tyler let out a deep breath. "Is that all?"

Brooke shot him an angry look. "What do you mean, *is that all*."

She's touchy on this subject. "Sorry if my comment seemed insensitive. I was just implying that's their business, to buy and sell land."

She looked deep into Tyler's eyes. "Is it their business to harass and threaten property owners?" Her frustration had moved to anger.

"They're doing that?" Tyler leaned back in his seat. That was information he wasn't expecting.

Brooke nodded. "Their agent suggested that he'll try to keep the bank from working with me on the renegotiation of my mortgage. . . . Can he do that?"

"Are you asking me as a friend or as an attorney?"

"Both, I guess."

Okay, be very careful how you answer this. "As a friend, they shouldn't be doing this. As an attorney, it depends. As long as they aren't getting inside information from the bank, it's probably legal. They can present options to the bank that make it seem more profitable to go one direction with a loan as opposed to another direction."

"He seemed to know about my mortgage problems. That makes me so angry. And frankly, scared."

Now he was on thin ice. Time to avoid responses that could later be construed as a conflict of interest. *Change the subject.* "Ask the bank if there is any way he could have gotten that information. . . Ah—here comes the chili."

Two steaming bowls of chili, with a side of cornbread and honey butter, arrived at the table. Tyler was relieved and inhaled the scent rising from the bowls. He then looked at Brooke. "Is it really as good as you say?"

Brooke had relaxed, but only a little. "Try it and see for yourself."

Tyler took a spoonful and savored the aroma before tasting. "This is really good. One of the best chilies I've had."

"I told you."

Tyler had gotten some valuable information. *No more questions about AA today.* He was sad and troubled that Brooke was involved with AA dealings.

After lunch, they returned to the tour. They visited the Lowell Observatory, Northern Arizona University, and Historic Route 66, as they maintained a low-key banter. While driving down Route 66 Tyler asked, "This seems to be a pretty eclectic community, the ranchers, the University, and all the activities associated with the National Forest; is there one topic that gets everyone united?"

Brooke looked out the passenger window and studied the area as she pondered Tyler's question. "I'd have to say it's the environment."

"Why, in what way?"

"Well, the ranchers need to protect it for their livelihood. Many of the local businesses depend on recreational tourism. Then there are the environmentalists, many of whom are associated with the University. They all want to look after the environment; mind you it's for different reasons, but they want to protect it just the same. It makes for an unusual coalition."

"I can imagine."

Brooke looked at her watch. "*Oh wow,* it's that late already? I need to be getting home."

"Okay, get me going in the right direction."

Neither Brooke nor Tyler paid attention to the light traffic on the way home, they focused on their conversation, which drifted to the choir and music. Twenty minutes later Tyler pulled into Brooke's driveway. "Thanks for the great tour and all the information you gave me. I had more fun than I've had in a long time."

"I should be thanking you. I've been so focused on the ranch these past couple of years that I forgot what it's like to just take a day off. I can't remember when an afternoon went by so fast."

Brooke entered her house with a broad smile, her heart was light with excitement on how much she enjoyed the day but also sad that the day had to end. Whatever feelings had tried to arise, were put aside; she needed to refocus her energy on the kids and the ranch. Time to push Tyler out of her mind. Or almost. *He's really nice; I think I've made a friend, even if he is a city boy.*

Tyler drove away with a satisfied grin. He knew there was something special about her. *I think I've got one friend here. I need to find out where her property falls in the development plan. I hope it's not a critical piece of land. And what is that Hal Greer up to?*

The next morning arrived quicker than Brooke would have liked. She forced herself out of bed and headed to the kitchen to make her morning pot of coffee. She flipped the faucet handle up, but no water flowed out—just a sputtering of air.

"Oh-no, not *this.*"

She went to the master bath and then the kid's bathroom, still no water. Next, she went to the barn and found the water didn't work there either. Back in the house she roused Kasey and Shane. "Time to get up and get ready for school" She yelled from the hallway, and followed with "But, we have one minor problem."

"WHAT?" came from both bedrooms.

"We don't have any water."

"I have to shower and wash my hair." Kasey exploded. "I can't go to school with dirty hair."

"No shower—yay!" Came from Shane.

"You're going to school, Kasey, and you'll shower later. We'll just have to be creative about how to get ready."

With some cowgirl ingenuity Brooke helped the kids get cleaned up and off to school. She then called Ray who promised to stop by and look at the water pump. *Oh Lord please don't have this be an expensive repair. I don't know how to pay for it.*

An hour later Ray was at the back door. "Thanks for coming. We aren't getting any water and I checked the pump's circuit breaker." Brooke wasted no time detailing the problem to Ray.

"I'll see what I can do."

"Please fix it. I can't afford a new pump, and I don't have the time or energy to haul water for the house and barn."

Ray gave Brooke a small hug. "I'll do my best."

A short time later while Brooke was cleaning stalls, Ray showed up in the barn wearing a broad smile. "Brooke, try your water; see if it works."

Her eyes brightened. "You fixed it?"

Ray puffed out his chest. "I think so, let's find out. There was a loose electrical connection which I fixed."

"How'd that happen?"

"That's a good question. Come to think of it, it could have burned out the pump if I hadn't found it."

Brooke turned on the cold-water faucet in the tack room. After it groaned and moaned for several seconds, spritzes of water started to appear, followed by a steady stream.

Brooke wrapped her arms around Ray as she gave him a kiss on the cheek. "Ray, thanks so much for coming. You've saved my day. What would I do around here without you?"

Ray smiled and looked down in embarrassment. "I've told you that I promised Cory I would look after you; maybe you need a man around here full time."

Brooke gave an uneasy smile as Ray laughed and seized the moment. "Have you had a chance to think about entering the mustang competition with me?"

"No, I haven't had a chance. . . But I really don't think it's the right time to do it with you. . . Thanks for thinking of me." *I really should have told him I've entered the mustang competition with Kasey.* Was it the timing or the fear of old memories being brought to the surface?

CHAPTER

A dust cloud drifted over Amber's car as she swung the door open and rushed straight into the kitchen. "Have you heard anything from the loan officer yet?"

Brooke turned from the stove and waved her hands. "No, and it's killing me."

"If they don't call soon, you won't hear anything till Monday."

"That's what I'm afraid of and I don't think I can wait that long."

Amber savored the aroma in the kitchen. "What smells so good?"

"Sloppy Joes and fries—You'll stay for dinner, won't you?"

"Wouldn't have it any other way." Amber moved to the stove and took a closer look at the meal. "Fill me in on what happened during this morning's meeting."

"Sure, it will help keep my mind occupied while I wait."

Brooke explained all the details of the morning's meeting while she worked on dinner. Her eyes drifted toward the clock to see if the bank had closed. It was ten minutes before the bank would close when her phone rang. She hesitated and bit her lip, was it going to be good news?

Amber watched and then burst out. "Answer it!"

"Hello, this is Brooke."

"Hi Brooke, this is Alan Ramos from Flagstaff National Bank, and I have some good news for you."

"Good news?" Brooke repeated. A deep breath escaped her lungs and she smiled at Amber, who gave a thumbs up.

Alan continued. "There are some conditions though."

"Conditions?" She repeated as her heart sank, and Amber's smile faded.

"Yes Brooke, there are a few conditions."

"What are they?" Brooke's knees became weak, and she sat down at the table.

"The biggest one is, because we've temporarily reduced your monthly payments you can't miss any of your payments. If you do, we'll immediately start the foreclosure process. Also, we will periodically inspect our investment to see if the property is being maintained and keeping its market value. If it's not, we'll have the option to immediately start the foreclosure process—Do you understand?"

"I think so."

"Okay then, if they're acceptable to you, please stop by my office on Monday to sign the paperwork. I hope to see you then and have a nice weekend."

"Thanks, you too." Brooke stood and started to pace while she tried to digest this new information.

Amber couldn't remain quiet any longer. "Well, what's the news?"

"I think it's good. But I'm not sure about the conditions."

Brooke went on to explain the stipulations to Amber, who stood nodding her head. "I see what you mean. But the fact is if you don't take this offer, you'll be in foreclosure in a short time anyway. At least this way you have a chance. Tyler is an attorney; why don't you get his opinion?"

Tyler arrived at church just in time to slip into the back of the choir as they climbed the risers and took their place upstage. A smile grew on Brooke's lips as she spotted Tyler, she had looked for him earlier during the social time, she wanted to ask him about the conditions on the loan but couldn't find him. *Darn it. . .* Her smile faded at the realization she had to leave right after the service and wouldn't have time to talk with him. While watching Tyler, she played with her wedding band. Then self-condemnation followed, was she treading a thin line? *He's a friend. That's all. Nothing wrong with having an interesting friend, plus I have a question for him.* Her justification fell short. *Yes, but would I be befriending this man if Corey was still alive?* She knew what Amber would say, in her loving but straightforward way. *"Brooke, Cory's not here."* Her heart jumped, as Tyler's eyes met hers. The she came to a resolution. *I'll try to catch him after the service to see if I can meet with him later in the day to get his opinion on the bank's offer.*

The service was over, and Brooke made her way to the foyer hoping to see Tyler. By the time she got there, Amber had him cornered and was flirting, she twirled her long brown hair, smiled, and pandered to the male ego. She heard Amber ask, "So—Tyler do you have any plans for lunch? Would you like to join me at Anita's for some Mexican food?" Brooke wasn't surprised by what she saw or heard; her rising blood pressure is what caught her off guard. Her heart raced and she bit her lip to keep from making any remarks. *Why am I feeling jealous? Especially of Amber who treats all men the same. Plus, he's not her type.*

Tyler glanced at Brooke while he fished for a polite response. "I would love to Amber, but maybe another time. I have some commitments this afternoon."

Amber smiled like a cat not ready to let the mouse escape. "I'll count on that rain-check."

Tyler stepped toward Brooke. "Sorry I didn't make it to the social time. It's been one of those mornings."

"I completely understand—I have to leave right away to meet with some clients. I was wondering if later this afternoon I could get some legal advice from you on my mortgage re-negotiation. I met with the bank on Friday, and they've put some conditions on the deal. If you're busy, though. . . ."

Tyler hesitated and cleared his throat. *How can I help her? I don't mind giving her advice. But, if it turns out badly for her, it doesn't matter whether my advice was good or bad, I'll be accused of conflict of interest. On the other hand, the company will not like it if I help someone keep a property we're going after. Perception is everything. The only thing I can do is avoid the subject. Thank goodness for my trip.*

"Brooke, I'm really sorry, I'd love too, but I have to catch a flight this afternoon. Can one of the businessmen from church help you?"

"I guess so—but they're not attorneys." Her heart sank, was it because he couldn't help or was it the fact that he couldn't stop by the ranch?

Guilt, an emotion Tyler was not accustomed to, crept in as he started toward the door. His conscience won the battle. "Can we talk while I go to my car? I have to keep moving so I don't miss my flight. . . Most of it is common sense and if it's not, the men from church can point you to a local attorney."

"Okay, I'll talk to them—So, where are you traveling to?" *Why do I feel so disappointed? His suggestion is sound.*

"Seattle. For some meetings."

"Have a safe trip." A wave of disappointment flooded over her as she turned to look for Kasey and Shane.

Tyler drove to his apartment and finished packing. *I made the right decision, so why do I feel like such a bad guy?*

Brooke was at peace with her decision and was ready to accept the bank's offer. A euphoric state replaced the doubts and questions that had nagged at her all morning long. That is, until the emergency alert notification sharply sounded on her cell phone shortly after dinner. A knot formed in her stomach, the realization grew that she was not out of the woods and there were still many challenges. She checked the message and bolted to the family room and stared at the TV.

Brooke abruptly changed the station to a local channel. Kasey shot a look at her mother. "What is it, Mom?"

"Severe storms are coming into the area. I want to see what the weatherman has to say." Banners ran across the bottom of the screen: **Severe Thunderstorms With Damaging Winds And Hail Are Moving Across Western Coconino County Toward**

Flagstaff. Be Prepared To Take Shelter. Stay Tuned For Breaking Information. . . .

Shane ran to the window. "Can I watch the lightening from the porch? Can I, Mom?"

"You're sick." Kasey snapped at him as she rolled her eyes. "Mom, are we going to be okay? You know how much I hate thunderstorms."

"Yes, Kasey, we'll be fine. You stay in the house; I'll go check on the horses and make sure the barn is secure."

Brooke was about to head outside when the meteorologist came on with a live Doppler Radar report. "A huge super-cell—this big mass of red, with damaging winds is tracking between Flagstaff and Mt. Humphrey. Anyone in its path should take shelter now. Stay away from windows. Go to an inside room or a basement. . . ."

"Mom is it heading for us?" fear shot from Kasey's eyes.

"Yes, it is, and I've got to check the barn, now!"

Shane was already at the door. "Can I come with you, *please*?"

"*No!*" Brooke tried to hide the fear in her voice. "You and Kasey stay inside and keep away from the doors and windows."

She dashed to the barn as the wind lashed her hair into her face. *How did this come up so quickly? Earlier the sky had been clear.* Her heart pounded as she ran from stall to stall checking to make sure the horses were okay. They were all agitated and paced in their stalls except for Cowboy, the old timer who stood quietly. With the barn doors secured, she looked at the sky and sprinted back to the house. *I don't think I've ever seen an angrier sky.* The blackness and the violently swirling clouds scared her.

In the space of a few steps, the wind seized her and push her sideways. Blowing pieces of gravel stung her face as she raced to the house. Terror grabbed her just like the wind had done. Fear for the kids, horses and now herself took hold. Never had she experienced this much fury in a storm. A gust of intense wind tore the door out of her hand and slammed it against the siding—the glass panes smashed into shards that blew against the house. With the remains of the door closed behind her she leaned against the wall and struggled to catch her breath. Her heart pounded as loud as the nearby thunder. Kasey ran into the kitchen. "Mom, are you alright? What was that noise?" Shane followed behind her, wide-eyed with excitement.

"Yes, I'm fine. The storm door broke, the wind gabbed it. Everyone's okay in barn." She blurted out between breaths. "All we can do now is wait out the storm."

"Mom, can I watch it from the family room?"

"No! Get into the hallway right now. I don't want anyone hurt by broken glass." The lights flickered and went out. She whispered to herself. "What *else* can go wrong?"

The storm raged for thirty-five minutes before it calmed enough for Brooke to go out and inspect the damage. The rain gauge on the porch showed that the storm hadn't just rolled in with thunder, lightning and wind, it also dumped almost an inch of rain—which Shane proudly showed to his mother. Brooke took in the rain gauge and the damage on the property. "Oh. . . my. . ."

"Look Mom, several pines broke their tops off." Shane pointed at the debris that littered the area, broken branches and shredded bundles of needles.

Kasey's focus was on the barns. "It looks like the horse barn, and indoor arena are okay. I hope the horses are too." Were they?

"Time for a closer inspection." Brooke said as she left the porch.

As they approached the hay barn, something was amiss. As they got closer, the roof seemed to be ajar. "Oh, No. . ." From the back side of the structure, they could see why: half the roof was missing and several of the rafters were broken in pieces or cracked. Brooke bit the inside of her lip to keep her emotions from spilling out in front of the kids. *Why Lord? Why?*

"Wow, Mom, those must have been some strong winds." Shane yelled back to his mother as he ran towards the barn.

"Get back here right now!" Brooke screamed after him. "I don't want you anywhere near that barn until we know if it's safe." The possibility of losing another family member ate at her soul.

"Oh all-*right*." Shane stopped in his tracks and sulked his way back to his mother.

"How are we going to get hay for the horses?" Kasey asked.

"I'll take care of it, until the barn is inspected and safe."

Brooke battled to remain strong. But on the inside, she felt weak and powerless. How could this be happening, only an hour earlier she was on a path to save the ranch from foreclosure.... Now? If there was any hope of proving to the bank that she could keep the repairs under control, it was teetering on the brink of despair. *Why God? Why are you letting me lose the ranch? Wasn't it enough for you to take my husband?*

Two hours later the power came on, and the kids had to get ready for bed. Once they were asleep and she was alone, Brooke finally allowed herself to breakdown, and she quietly cried into her pillow. *What am I going to tell the bank tomorrow? The property is supposed to be in marketable condition, and now it's anything but that. So much for all those assurances I gave them.*

The next morning arrived too soon and Brooke didn't want to face the problems in front of her. *What will the bank do about my loan when I tell them about the barn roof? I have to tell them, I'm sure they'll send*

a property inspector out before the new terms go into effect. She said a prayer and then resolved to face whatever lay in front of her. Brooke knew she had to move forward and trust God.

Later that morning she took a break from her training routine and went to review the property's insurance policy. Just what she expected; the house, indoor and the horse barn were fully insured but the other out-buildings had minimal insurance, just enough to cover materials. Cory was always handy around the property and could always make the necessary repairs. How she missed Cory and his cowboy knowhow.

That evening while Brooke was cooking dinner the phone rang. She glanced at the number, "Hello Amb –," before she could finish her greeting Amber broke in. "What happened today in your meeting at the Bank? Why didn't you stop by my desk afterward?

"I can't talk right now. The kids are in and I don't want them to overhear."

"How about later? Can I stop by after the they're in bed?"

Brooke hesitated. "Okay." She wasn't really in the mood for talking, but maybe Amber could help her think of a way through this nightmare that seemed to be getting worse with every day.

Dinner was over and Brooke sat at the table, aimlessly she leafed through her horse magazines, while Kasey and Shane finished up their homework. Half-way through her second magazine she came across the ad for the Mustang Holiday Challenge—and something caught her eye that she had skimmed over before. Her focus had been on a bonding activity to do with Kasey, not on winning.

$60,000 in prize money: $30,000 for first; $20,000 for second; $10,000 third. Not too bad. That prize money could help get the

mortgage caught up. This might be a way to save the ranch. A few minutes later Amber briskly charged into the kitchen. "What's going on, Brooke—what happened this afternoon?"

Brooke shot a look at Amber as she whispered, "the kids might still be awake. Let's go for a walk; I'll fill you in on the details while we're outside." Brooke grabbed a flashlight and headed out into the twilight alongside Amber.

"The storm last night took half the hay barn's roof off. Now the bank won't go ahead with the re-negotiation; one of the conditions they were putting on me was that the property had to be maintained in a saleable condition."

"I don't know what to say—I'm so sorry. What can I do to help?"

"There's nothing you can do."

"But. . . ."

"If I'm not caught up on the mortgage payments by December, the bank is going to start foreclosure on the property."

"But the process can take a long time, even more time if you're being evicted. You've got time. . . not a lot, but some."

"As a bank employee are you supposed to be telling me this?"

"Probably not, but it's the truth."

Brooke shined the spotlight on the barn roof. "There's the damage."

"Wow, it didn't just rip the sheet metal off—Are those broken rafters?"

"Yes, and I've gotta move the hay before the next rain comes. Fortunately, the damage occurred away from the bulk of the stacked hay."

"Will your insurance cover the repairs?"

"Cory only carried enough to pay for the materials, and I never changed the policy. The labor will be as much or more than the materials."

"You're sure in another tough spot—I hate to say this, but what about Ray?"

"He's not as handy as Cory was, and I think this job is more than he can handle."

Silence hung between them as they walked back to the house, the setback the storm had caused was taking its toll. Finally, Brooke broke the silence, "When you showed up, I was reading some horse journals and saw the ad for the Mustang Holiday Challenge. I had forgotten about the prize money. It would be enough to get the mortgage caught up. I wasn't entering to win, but now. . ."

"You've got the talent, and you're already entered."

Amber sat at the table and read though the ad while Brooke scooped some ice cream. They finished their snack and pushed the bowls to the center of the table. Amber looked at the ad again and then at Brooke. "Definitely worth trying to win, you have nothing to lose."

"I know, and now it looks like my only chance to save the ranch."

"Have you told Kasey yet?

Brooke shook her head. "Tomorrow."

"You have too. You've been putting it off for a while now."

"I know. We've gotta start getting things ready on the ranch for the mustang."

The next morning, Brooke started to tell Kasey about the mustang, but again put it off. She didn't want her carrying that distraction through the school day; it could wait until the afternoon. The delay gave her time to figure out how to break the news. She was unsure how Kasey would respond; the recent rift between them over showing still weighed heavily on her. *I need to emphasize that she will only be helping with the training and not doing the showing in front of the crowd.*

As the day marched on Brooke kept checking the clock, hoping that 3pm would arrive. But, at the same time she had deep apprehension about Kasey's response. She baked some cookies to pass the time and occupy her mind. Finally, the school bus bounced down the county road and stopped in front of the driveway. Five minutes later Kasey and Shane were sitting at the kitchen table eating fresh oatmeal cookies. After the normal conversation about the school day Brooke summoned her courage. "You know that we've been struggling to keep the ranch going. Even without the repair bills we've been having; it would be tight."

"Yeah, we know, Mom. What's up?" Kasey took a bite of her cookie.

"The recent repair bills from the storm have made it impossible. I've come up with a way that might allow us to get caught up on our bills. It's a long shot but it might be our last chance." Brooke paused for a long moment praying that the kids would be supportive.

Shane fidgeted in his chair while reaching for another cookie. "What is it, Mom?"

"There's a mustang training competition between now and January 1st and the prize money could get us caught up."

"Awesome."

"Cool."

Good so far. Brooke swallowed deep. *Here goes. . .* "I've entered it, and I'll need support from both of you. This will be an intensive training program and you'll have to help me with many of my chores."

"I'll do it," Kasey offered.

"Me too," Shane chimed in.

"There's more—the competition can be for teams of two. Kasey, I'd like you to partner with me."

Kasey's face went pale as her stomach did gymnastics. *A mustang. Having one on the property, I might be able to handle that, but working with it that's another thing. I can't do this! All those people. All those other horses."*

Brooke saw Kasey was uneasy. "Don't worry, honey, only one of the team members has to show the horse. The second person only helps with the training."

Kasey slowly let out a deep breath, her fear subsided a little. But her concerns still had her tense. *A mustang! Why does it have to be a mustang?* Since the loss of Sidekick, Kasey had not let herself get attached to another horse. She didn't realize it until now, but she was glad that none of the horses around the ranch were mustangs that would remind her of the loss of her best friend. Now, she would have to face fear and emotions head on when the mustang came. No longer would she be able to hide from them when the horse arrived on the property and she helped her mom train him.

After a long silence, Brooke asked, "Everything okay?"

Kasey stuffed her emotions deep down inside. "Yeah, everything is fine." She forced out the words along with a grin. She knew how important this was to her mother and the ranch.

"So, you'll help me with the training?" Brooke's eyes lit-up.

Keeping her smile big, Kasey pushed out an enthusiastic, "Sure Mom!" But deep down inside she was terrified of the emotions the mustang might stir inside of her.

"Okay kids, we have a lot of work to do to get ready for the new horse. There are several changes we will have to do around the property to have a wild mustang."

Shane looked puzzled. "Like what? We've had horses and mustangs on the property before."

"To adopt or train a wild mustang, the training area and the paddock which they are kept in must have a six-foot-high fence. Also, it's best if the training area is connected to their paddock.

"What are your plans?" Kasey asked.

"We'll build a paddock with some of the extra fence panels we have and attach it to the round pen. We'll move the portable shelter and make it part of the paddock. That will give him shelter and have everything in one functional space."

Kasey gave Brooke a hug. "Mom, you sure seem excited about this."

Brooke realized she was feeling better—not great, but at least a different feeling had begun to rise within her. *Hope.*

"Yes, I am excited. It's a long shot, but I think we have a chance."

CHAPTER

The week leading up to the mustang's arrival was beyond hectic with Brooke and Kasey working to prepare his temporary home. Brooke placed her arm around Kasey's shoulder as the afternoon sun beat down on them. "Well, we got the last panel up. Not bad for a couple of cowgirls." Brooke smiled.

Kasey climbed on top of the panels to get a better vantage point of their handywork. "Can some of my friends come over tomorrow when he gets delivered?"

"Sure, one or two, maybe three at the most."

"Thanks, Mom."

This wasn't the question that Kasey really wanted to ask; but she couldn't let her mom know how apprehensive she was about the mustang showing up at the ranch. Would he look like Sidekick and stir up old memories that she had buried? Would her mom spend too much time training the mustang? Brooke had her own set of questions. Did she tackle too big of a project? Would she be able to connect with the new horse and build the relationship she needed for the competition? And, could this mustang help save the ranch?

Early the next morning Brooke found Kasey in the family room curled up on the sofa with a pillow while watching an old move. "Couldn't you sleep either?" Brooke said as she stretched and yawned.

Kasey quickly glanced at her mother and then looked back at the TV. *I can't let mom see that I'm nervous about the mustang. She hasn't been this excited since before Dad died; I have to stay positive. Maybe if I keep busy I won't think about the new horse coming. . . Breakfast—that might help for now.*

"No, I couldn't sleep. . . Mom do you want me to make some breakfast?"

"Sure, thanks."

Shane came into the room as he rubbed his eyes. "When's he get here?"

"It's about a seven-hour drive from Ridgecrest, California, to here; so, I would guess he will get here anywhere from one to four this afternoon. They'll call when they're at the half-way point."

Kasey's friends, Josh and Maddie, arrived at two o'clock and the three of them disappeared into the family room to play video games. A few minutes later Amber pulled into the driveway with a Toyota 4-Runner right behind her. Brooke recognized the second car as delight and panic raced through her body. She quickly adjusted her hair and straightened her clothes. Amber parked in front of the barn and motioned to the SUV behind her. "Look what I found at the grocery store. I didn't think you would mind if I invited him out to see the mustang."

Brooke stuffed her emotions deep inside and fought to maintain a sweet smile. "Hi Tyler, I'm glad you came, please make yourself at home."

"Are you sure that I'm not imposing. Amber insisted that I see the mustang get delivered."

"It's fine—We'll be back in just a minute." Brooke seized Amber by the arm and led her into the barn. "Just what were you *thinking*—bringing Tyler here and not giving me any advance notice?"

"I didn't think you would mind since you've invited the home-group." Amber's eyes sparkled. "You said there is nothing between you two; so, what's the big deal. Besides, you always look great."

Brooke did tell Amber those things. If they were true, there shouldn't be a problem. The question remained—did she find herself attracted to Tyler? A question Brooke still was not ready to face. She shook her head. "Alright this time, but the next time give me some advance warning." Exasperation hung on her voice.

When they returned the women found Tyler inspecting the round pen. He shook one of the round pen panels. "This is a pretty sturdy corral you have here."

"Kasey and I put this together over the past week."

"You two are pretty handy."

"Ranch women have to be."

The three of them continued to talk as Brooke educated Tyler about mustangs and the competition.

At three o'clock Shane came running from the far end of the barn. "A truck and trailer are coming!" All heads turned towards the road as they watched the rig slowly make its way up the county road and turn onto the driveway. Brooke's heart pounded and her stomach danced as the moment drew closer. She realized how much was riding on the animal. The truck stopped in front of the group and out stepped a weathered beaten cowboy. "I'm a lookin' for Brooke Anderson. Which one of y'all would she be?"

Brooke stepped forward. "I'm Brooke."

"I've got this here mustang for you and the delivery charge is on this here paper."

"How should I make out the check?"

"To me, Cody Jones."

Meanwhile the group moved closer to the trailer, everyone tried to get a better look at the new horse. Cody turned toward the trailer. "I wouldn't get too close if I were you. He's still pretty wild. Ain't been halter broke yet." Some of the group backed away a few steps. Cody continued, "They tell me that the retired horse whisperer, Taylor Roberts, personally picked out all them mustangs for the competition. He wanted to make sure they all had a similar temperament and conformation so there'll be an even playin' field."

Kasey nearly jumped out of her skin. "You mean Taylor Roberts himself picked out this mustang?"

"Yup, that's what I've been told."

Brooke handed Cody his check. "What can we do to help get him unloaded?"

"If you can take down one of them panels from the round pen, I'll back partway into it and then we can unload him and then shoo him into the paddock right next to it."

A few minutes later Cody swung the back gate of the trailer open and out bolted a wide-eyed, 15-hand, dark bay horse. He flew to the far side of the pen, turned, lifted his head high and snorted as he checked out his new surroundings. Brooke moved closer and studied her new project. "Mom, he's gorgeous." Kasey muttered.

"Yeah, he's seems to be put together pretty well. I sure hope we can do him justice." Hope for the ranch rested on this mustang.

Tyler's eyes went back and forth from the mustang to Brooke. An intensity had enveloped her as she followed every movement of this beautiful creature—a side of Brooke he hadn't seen before—a side that intrigued him. Cody closed the door of the trailer and climbed into his truck. "Good luck, Ma'am."

As the truck and trailer started to leave the property the mustang ran at full speed from the paddock into the pen, bucking along the way, and just before he reached the panels on the far side he sat on his haunches and came to a sliding stop followed by a roll-back. He then reared and took off running back from where he came. He repeated these actions twice before he again sniffed and explored his surroundings.

"Wow Mom, he sure is fast."

"He sure is Shane." Brooke gave a satisfied smile as she climbed in his pen and walked into the center, where she stood quietly. The horse turned an ear toward her as he continued to explore while always keeping her in view with at least one eye. Gradually, both ears became locked on her and then both eyes. After several minutes, he carefully started to approach her. Each time he would step towards her, she would take a smaller step away from him, to show the wary horse that she was not a threat. Eventually, with his curiosity peaked and the distance between him and Brooke closed; he sniffed her outreached hand. Having achieved success, Brooke slowly backed out of the round pen.

Tyler was mesmerized by the whole process, never taking his eyes off the pair. "She's really good." He commented to Amber.

"That's what I've been telling you."

"Does she stand a chance of winning the contest?"

"I don't know. The competitions can be more about showmanship than pure training. The training part she's got down pat. Putting together a show—she may have some learning to do."

Tyler looked at the mustang and then back at Amber. "What about the mustang—he seems to have a lot of energy?"

"That he does, and he also looks to be smart and has a mind of his own. He'll give Brooke a run for her money. But the best performance horses always have some spirit."

Tyler walked over to Brooke. "I know you're going to be busy these next couple of months—but if you can find the time, I would still like to get some lessons from you. Both riding and natural horsemanship."

Brooke was caught off guard, taken back actually. "Sure, I can definitely find the time. When do you want to start?"

"Probably next week, I've got some traveling this week. I'll check my schedule and get back to you."

Shane who had been hanging around and watching the activities shouted to Brooke. "Hey Mom, take a look at this."

"What is it Shane?"

Shane was giggling. "The white on the mustang's forehead is in the shape of the Grinch."

Brooke grinned at Shane and then looked at the mustang. "You're right, the shape of his star and the way it connects to his strip, it does look like the silhouette of the Grinch. Hey Kasey, take a look at this." Laughter erupted from all three.

Sunday afternoon Brooke took care of some chores around the ranch while Kasey ran to the store to pick up a few items for dinner. On the way there she took a secret detour to stop at the McAllister's ranch.

"Hi Aunt Martha, do you have a few minutes?" She was more like a grandmother to both Kasey and Shane who had grown up calling her Aunt Martha.

"Sure Honey, I always have time for you. Does your mother know you are here?"

"Not really."

"I don't want you gettin' in any trouble now."

"I won't, and I really need to talk with you." Kasey was stretching the truth but wanted Martha's advice.

"I'll get us lemonade, and then you can tell me all about it while we sit on the porch."

Kasey couldn't wait, she followed Martha inside. "Mom's entered a mustang training contest and has listed me as her assistant trainer."

"Is that what's bothering you—I can see something is."

"Mom is so busy trying to save the ranch, she's now got this mustang and is entered in some competition that will get her the money she needs. She sort-of asked if Shane and I were okay with it, but she should have known I don't want another mustang around, not after losing Sidekick."

"Did she ask you about getting the mustang?"

"Sort of. . ."

"What did you say when she asked?"

"I guess I said it was okay. . . But I know she really needs the money."

"What's wrong with the competition?"

"Nothing, and helping her train the horse is okay, but why does it have to be a mustang? I'm afraid of getting attached to it. I've been afraid of getting attached to any horse ever since they put Sidekick down at the parade. Mom's got so much on her mind with the problems at the ranch I don't want her worrying about me and the mustang. I came to see you because I just needed to talk about it."

"You'll figure it out. And I'm sure your mom can handle it too. But if you need to talk, you can always come to me."

While they sipped the lemonade, Kasey told Martha about the argument she had the other week with her mother, and about her fear of riding in public. Martha listened while Kasey talked, and at the end gave her some simple advice. "Sometimes opening an old wound means it was never truly healed. It provides the opportunity for the wound to heal properly and allows us to grow. Just keep praying about it."

Kasey didn't think there was any reason to open an old wound. "I'd better be getting to the store and then home. Thanks for listening Aunt Martha."

When Kasey got home, Brooke was getting ready to start her second training session with the mustang. She had given him a day to settle in before starting his work, he needed to become familiar with his surroundings. Brooke's and Kasey's first task was to connect with the horse, each of them had to establish that they were his leader, and let him know that he can trust them.

After putting the groceries away Kasey went to the barn. "What do you want me to do, Mom?"

"Stand outside the pen and watch his body language and learn his signals."

Kasey grabbed a mounting block and put it next to the round pen. She crouched down on the block with her arms resting on a lower rail of the panel as she watched her mother work.

"Okay Kasey, your turn. After he accepts you, I'll go back in with him and try to rub his face with the rope halter."

Kasey went in and Brooke left the pen; the mustang started running back and forth between the round pen and his paddock, doing sliding stops before changing his direction. "Mom look at him go,"

Kasey stood perfectly still. The mustang stopped running and stared at her before walking in a spiral around her twice, getting closer to her with each loop. He stopped right in front of Kasey and watched her.

Brooke sat on the edge of the mounting block. Her jaw dropped slightly, she was seeing something special. In a soft voice she said, "Stay still and don't move; he's really interested in you."

He stood there for several minutes with his nostrils flaring as he took deep breaths trying to capture Kasey's essence. Finally, he took a step toward her and started to sniff her scent again. This went on for ten minutes until he was standing only inches away from Kasey, he then put his muzzle on her hand as if he were asking her to rub his face. She responded to his request and gently rubbed his nose and then his forehead.

"Whatever you're doing, keep it up." Kasey's heart pounded as memories of Sidekick flooded back. Could she risk starting a friendship with this new horse knowing that he had to be auctioned off at the end of the competition? "That's great Kasey, call it quits for now and slowly back out of the pen."

Kasey started to back towards the gate but with each step she took, the mustang followed. "Mom, he doesn't want me to leave." Finally, she reached the gate and squeezed out.

Brooke closed the gate and then focused on Kasey. "Wow, that was impressive in there." Kasey shrugged her shoulders, she was not going to bond with this horse.

"Let's try one more thing, before we break for the day. We'll both go in, one at a time, and get him used to the rope halter touching his body." This time Brooke held a rope halter in her hand for him to smell. After he sniffed it, she touched his muzzle with her hand and the halter to show him it was not scary. Brooke left the round pen. "Kasey, it's your turn." She handed Kasey the halter as they switched positions.

Several seconds later the mustang sniffed Kasey and the halter. She rubbed his face with it which he seemed to enjoy. Brooke shook her head. "I don't believe what he's letting you do. Let's call it quits for now. . . Why don't you see if he'll follow you into the paddock?"

Kasey walked through the open gate of the paddock with the mustang tagging right along. "Looks like someone has hooked on to you."

"Why me?"

"He senses something in you. Maybe he needs you or he thinks you need him."

Kasey didn't know what he needed, but she was sure she didn't need him. As they started to leave, the mustang started running at full speed and then did another sliding stop.

Brooke shook her head. "He sure does like to slide."

"Why not call him Slider?" Kasey offered.

Brooke smiled. "I like it. Slider it is."

Two days later, Brooke and Kasey were working with Slider whose training was a little behind schedule. He didn't like pressure behind his pole and was slow to accept the rope halter. He finally took to it just before it was time to leave for youth group. As they were putting their equipment away, Kasey asked. "Mom, tonight at youth group, can I invite them over for a small bonfire this Saturday? I'd like to show them Slider now that he's making progress again."

I don't want to squelch her enthusiasm. "Ok, but we can't afford to feed the group. They'll have to supply the fixins', I'll supply the fire."

Later that evening while driving home, Kasey announced. "Mom, it's all set. The youth group is coming out to see Slider. They also want to see you do some training with him."

Brooke glanced over at Kasey. "Wait a second, you can show him too."

"Mom, you're so much better than me." Was this the whole truth or was there something more?

"I hope they are not expecting too much; we just started working with him. How many are coming?"

"Fifteen or Twenty."

Brooke smiled at Kasey as her gut tightened. *That's a lot of kids and the ranch has to be tidied up. I just don't have the time... But on the other hand, Kasey is excited to show off the mustang. Their encouragement will be good for her. I'll just have to find a way to get everything done before the bonfire.* Brooke smiled, her outlook for the future was improving, the mustang had given her hope.

Word had spread throughout the church about the upcoming youth-group bonfire. Brooke's homegroup saw this as an opportunity to organize a work party to repair the barn and piggyback it with the event. Before Brooke knew what happened, half the church was showing up on Saturday to help repair the barn and property. The outpouring of support touched her heart. But she didn't like accepting help, it made her uneasy. How was she going to prove she could make it on her own? However, the thought of Tyler possibly coming to help grew a smile on her face.

The men arrived with a trailer full of lumber, rafters, and corrugated metal roofing. Scott Sena led the crew. "Good morning Brooke. Can you show us the storm damage?"

Brooke nodded as she counted the cars in her driveway. She then gestured to the area behind her. "As you can see the storm did more damage than to just the hay barn. Several trees had their tops snapped off, some of which also damaged the fence. The wind also broke the back door."

"Wow, you sure took a pretty good hit here." Sena slowly shook his head.

"Yes, we did."

"The carpenters from the church will tackle the roof. I'll make sure we have enough materials. The rest of the men will clean up the trees and fix the fence."

"What can I do to help?" Brooke pressed.

"Well—you can make a list of any other repairs or maintenance that needs to be done around the property. Then get back to your normal chores and train that mustang I've heard about. And stay out of the kitchen; my wife and the other ladies are going to take care of feeding us lunch and dinner."

Brooke paused, "I don't know what to say."

"Don't say anything. We'll call this an old-fashioned barn raising."

Most of the men had parked their cars and started to gather around Scott Sena; when Brooke spotted Tyler getting out of his SUV, her pulse jumped for a moment and then a smile returned to her lips. *He did show up.*

The morning sped along as Kasey and Brooke did their first session of the day with Slider before they exercised the other horses. Tyler had helped clear trees during the morning and after lunch sought out Brooke. "Hi, the trees are almost cleaned up. What else is on your list?"

Brooke looked at Tyler's new sneakers and almost new jeans as her eyes made their way up to his mostly clean long sleeve polo shirt. He definitely looked out of place on the ranch. "Let's see what we can find for you to do that will keep those new sneakers clean." Brooke smiled and laughed to herself. *Is he really capable of doing ranch chores by himself?*

"I'll have you know that my work clothes are in L.A. . ." Tyler returned the smile.

Brooke now laughed out loud. "Don't you mean your three-piece suits?"

Tyler played along. "Well, they do come in handy for the formal yard work." They laughed together as Brooke showed Tyler the list. He caught her scent as she moved close to him. *She even smells nice out here on the ranch.* "How about the tractor maintenance? I used to work on a farm as a kid and did a fair amount of work on tractors."

Brooke did a slow reappraisal of Tyler. *He's full of surprises.* "Okay. . . The tools for the tractor are in the hay barn. It needs to be greased and have the oil changed. If the filter and oil aren't there, I've got an account down at the Western States Ranch Supply, just outside of Hollister." Tyler's hand brushed Brooke's arm, electricity raced up her spine and caught her by surprise. And it somewhat unnerved her. Tyler waved goodbye as he headed to the tractor.

"Don't worry about it I'll take care of everything."

Tyler watched the two girls train the mustang while he worked on the tractor. He observed them playing horse games with Slider. When a saddle was taken into the pen, he took a break and moved closer. *I've gotta see this. It looks like they've made a lot of progress.* "Are you going to ride him today?"

"No—we're just using an old saddle to get him used to the idea of having something on his back. We won't get on him for almost another week. Before getting on his back, I want to do everything on the ground that I'll do in the saddle."

"That makes sense."

Tyler watched as they placed the old saddle and pad out in front of Slider and allowed him to explore the equipment. He sniffed every inch of the saddle and then picked up the pad with his teeth and shook it around. When he lost interest and dropped the pad, Brooke rubbed his body with it before placing it on his back. She handed the lead rope to Kasey. "Can you hold him while I get the saddle."

She picked up the saddle and balanced it on her right hip. Slider didn't pay much attention to Brooke as she walked up to his right side. He was preoccupied trying to put the lead rope into his mouth and playing tug of war with Kasey. "Don't let him put the rope in his mouth."

"But it keeps him busy."

"I know, but it's a bad habit." In one smooth movement Brooke swung the saddle up and gently placed it onto Slider's back. He moved sideways a few steps before going back to his game of tug of war with Kasey. Their prep-work had paid off.

Tyler's eyes were riveted on them as he walked over to the round pen. "I can't believe the progress you two have made."

"Thanks, but he's a quick learner." Brooke's eyes brightened as she returned a soft smile. The fact that he took the time to watch them train Slider warmed her inside.

Tyler finished up the oil change as Ray arrived and parked his farrier's truck next to the tractor. Ray surveyed the activity around the ranch which was starting to wind down. "What's going on around here?" he demanded of Tyler.

"The men from church pitched in to help Brooke recover from last week's storm. Are you here to help?"

"No, I'm here to shoe a horse... And what are you doin' to that tractor? I do the maintenance on it." Ray gruffly replied.

"It seems very well maintained. It was one of the items on Brooke's chore list, and I got the job of changing the oil and greasing the fittings."

"Where's Brooke?" Ray barked.

"She and Kasey just went into the barn. They just finished working the wild mustang." *Who is this guy? He's got some attitude.*

"Mustang! What mustang?" Ray's eyes widened. Then he spotted Slider peering out from his shelter.

Ray marched to the barn as Brooke was leaving the tack room. "What's this I hear about a mustang? You didn't tell me that you're gettin' a new horse, let alone a wild mustang."

Ray's voice thundered into the tack room where Kasey stopped in her tracks and retreated back to the saddles and bridles, where she lingered. Brooke snapped back. "For one thing, I didn't know I had to tell you. And for another, I meant to tell you, but I kept putting it off."

Ray's tone softened. "Why would you put off talkin' to me?"

"I didn't want to hurt your feelings."

Ray stepped back and cocked his head. "Why would that hurt my feelin's?"

Brooke spoke fast and in one breath. "Because I entered the Mustang Holiday Challenge with Kasey as my partner. It was a last-minute decision. And, if Kasey and I do well, we can put all the prize money toward the ranch." She took a deep breath.

Kasey remained in the tack room. *Boy, am I glad I'm in here. Ray's going to blow his top.*

"Didn't I ask you to be my partner a couple of weeks ago?"

"Well—yes, but things have changed."

"Like what!" Ray's tone became soft.

"I need the prize money for the ranch, and Kasey and I are going to work together as a team."

"I'm not sure it's a good idea—you two girls workin' that mustang alone."

"Why don't you watch me work him after you're done with Diablo's shoes. You'll see, it can work."

"Okay, I'll be there to watch you. Remember, Cory wanted me to look after you, so I'm just concerned about your safety."

Ray went to get his tools, and Kasey stepped out from the tack room. "Mom, did I just hear right? You told Ray about the mustang and he didn't blow his top?"

"You heard what I heard; he took it pretty well."

Brooke started her demo after the men had finished with the roof and the other repairs. "This is Slider, our new, three-and-a-half-year-old mustang project." Brooke opened the gate between his paddock and the round pen while Kasey shooed him into the round pen.

Inside the little arena, Brooke increased her bubble and asked Slider to canter to the left. After two loops around the paddock, Brooke explained. "I'll now lower my energy bubble and slow him to a trot and then to a walk." With no words, she had him trot, walk, stop and then turn toward her. "I'll now draw him towards me using just my energy." Once Slider came to her, she gave him a short rest and then massaged his poll before she pushed him away using her bubble and had him change directions. They repeated the process again going the opposite direction. The demonstration concluded with Brooke and Slider playing the horse games.

Her friends from church were giving Brooke their praises of Slider when Ray approached. Brooke swallowed deep as Ray began to talk. She was waiting for all the reasons that this was not a good idea. "He's a fine lookin' animal." Ray nodded.

"Thanks. Kasey and I think so, too."

"He's got a smart look about him."

"Sure does, he's demonstrated his intelligence and has a huge play drive to go with it."

Ray shifted his eyes toward the ground. "I'm sorry for raisin' my voice earlier, you caught me by surprise. . ."

"It's okay. . . I'm sorry for not telling you sooner." Brooke gently touched Ray's shoulder. *This is a big step for Ray. . . apologizing.*

Ray looked up at Brooke. "You two will do well with him."

"We hope so."

"Well, I better be goin'."

There was a genuineness to Ray's comments. Brooke was glad everything was finally out in the open. "Why don't you stay for dinner and the bonfire? They've made sloppy joes and are roasting hot dogs over the fire."

A smile came across Ray's face. "Thanks, that would be great."

After Ray went to his truck, Kasey approached. "Mom, did I just hear right? Ray apologized?"

"I'm as surprised as you are. Maybe Ray's changing."

The teens had eaten dinner and went off to explore the ranch before roasting marshmallows and making s'mores. Kasey and Maddie went to look at Slider, they leaned against the paddock panels and watched him chew his hay.

"He's a good-looking horse; you and your mom are doing a great job with him."

"Thanks, but I'm still not sure about him; he reminds me of Sidekick."

"What do you mean?"

"He has some similarities, and I'm afraid I could get attached to him."

"What's wrong with that?"

"I haven't let a horse get close to me since I lost Sidekick. . . Plus he's gotta get auctioned off at the end of the competition."

Slider came over to Kasey and Maddie. He stood in front of Kasey and stared at her.

"Looks like you've got an admirer." Maddie teased.

"Yeah, and I'm not even trying." Finally, Kasey gave in and reached through the panel and rubbed Slider's forehead with her hands. Confusion welled up inside of her as a tear trickled down her cheek. It felt good to connect with Slider, but it also hurt. Thoughts of Sidekick flowed back as Slider continued to rub against her.

A few minutes later Josh showed up. "Hi Kasey, Hi Maddie, want to go look at the barn repairs?"

Kasey needed to put some distance between her and Slider. "Sure," she replied.

Maddie winked at Kasey. "I'm going to go see if they're ready to roast the marshmallows. Y'all go ahead without me; I'll catch up with you at the fire."

They got to the barn, inside it was lit by a single lamp near the side door. Josh ran to the hay pile. "I'll race you to the top," he yelled back to Kasey as he scampered up the mound of stacked hay. At the top he sat down and smirked at Kasey as she made it to the top. "What took you so long?"

"No fair, you cheated and took a head start." Kasey collapsed to catch her breath.

"It sure is quiet up here; do you ever come up here by yourself?"

"No—not really."

"How about with other boys?"

"Josh Sena, how can you say such a thing?"

"You're here with me, aren't you?"

"Well. . .Yes, but that's different."

"Why?"

Kasey really didn't know what to say. *Should I tell Josh that I think he's cute? I can't just say nothing, it's too quiet, I have to say something.* Before she knew it, words were coming out of her mouth. "Because I like you." *I don't believe I said that.*

Josh reached over and took Kasey's hand. Her heart beat faster. *Should I pull my hand back? Should I stay here?*

"Kasey, Josh where are you?" Maddie called from below.

"We're up here." Kasey yelled back as she pulled her hand away from Josh.

"Come on, they're starting to roast the marshmallows."

The night air had a chill to it and the fire warmed Brooke to the core as she sat on a bench near the flames. She watched Shane roast his marshmallows when Tyler approached, "Mind if I sit down?"

"Not at all." Brooke slid over and smiled inside. A new feeling of warmth blanketed her, it did not come from the fire.

"You've made a lot of progress here today."

"Yes, we have. Getting the barn roof fixed is a Godsend. Everyone has been so generous with their time, *and you a city boy,* helping with the trees and the tractor."

"It felt good to help out. This type of thing doesn't happen very often in L.A. . ." Ray watched from a distance as Brooke's face lit up when Tyler sat down. "When's a good time for me to take my first lesson?" Tyler asked.

Brooke laughed. "You're really serious, aren't you?"

"Yes—I'm really impressed and want to learn more about natural horsemanship and talking the horse's language. It really intrigues me."

Brooke started to roast a marshmallow. "Do you want to ride too or just do groundwork?"

"Well. . . I've heard so much about reining since I've been here; I'd kind of like to see what it's about."

Brooke offered the hot golden-brown snack to Tyler and then began the roasting process once more. "Do you have any riding experience?"

"Yeah, a little, we had a horse that I played around with when I grew up."

Brooke started to make a s'more. "When would you like to start?"

Tyler poked the fire with a long stick and then looked at Brooke. "I'd like to try taking a lesson later this week when I get back from my trip. That's if you have the time—I know you're busy with your new project."

Brooke smiled. "I have time; and I still have a business to run—like giving riding lessons. . . When do you get back?"

"I should get back in time for Wednesday evening's choir practice."

"Then, how about Thursday afternoon?" Brooke offered the chocolate marshmallow treat to Tyler. "If you have flexibility with your schedule, how about 2pm?"

"I can make that work. . ." Tyler smiled. "Can I get you some hot chocolate?"

"Thanks, that would be nice."

While Tyler was getting the hot chocolate, Ray quietly sat down next to Brooke. She looked to her left expecting to see Tyler, surprise overtook her smile. "Ray, where'd you come from?"

"I've been around. . . That's a fine lookin' mustang you got."

"You said so earlier."

"Who's that city slicker hangin' around?"

"That's Tyler. He started coming to church around Labor Day."

"You trust a city boy around your tractor?"

"He was only changing the oil and greasing the fittings. Just basic stuff."

Tyler returned with two cups of steaming hot chocolate and handed one to Brooke. "Here you go." He then turned to Ray. "Hi, we met earlier today, but I don't think we've been formally introduced."

Brooke jumped in. "Ray, this is Tyler a friend from church. Tyler, this is Ray, an old family friend and my farrier."

Tyler offered his hand. "Nice to meet you. Would you like this hot chocolate?"

Ray didn't get up or offer his hand in greeting. He smiled and took the hot chocolate. "Thanks, don't mind if I do."

Tyler wasn't going to get any more time alone with Brooke that evening. His inner voice told him Ray wasn't going to leave Brooke's side. "I didn't realize it was this late. I need get going."

Brooke pouted. "Do you have to leave so soon?"

Tyler shrugged his shoulders. "Paperwork to get caught up on."

"If you must... Remember you're on for a riding lesson this Thursday at 2:00. Right?"

"I won't miss it." Tyler shot her a grin. Brooke smiled back.

"What's that about?" Ray asked.

"Tyler wants to learn about natural horsemanship; so, I'm giving him a lesson."

"The city-slicker wants to learn natural horsemanship. Fat chance."

"Some people like to expand their interests."

CHAPTER

The bonfire slid into history as the weekly routine started once again. Monday afternoons were Brooke's time to take care of paperwork once the morning training sessions were done. Today was no exception, but her focus was not on the stack of bills piled in front of her. It kept drifting to Slider and to the ranch. Could she and Slider do it? Could they win enough money to help save the ranch? *Can Slider and I win the competition and prove to everyone that their efforts weren't in vain?* Then a wave of despair flooded over her. Would luck be on her side? It hadn't been for some time. She forced the negative feelings aside and tried once again to focus on her paperwork.

It was late afternoon when the backdoor slammed. In a moment, Kasey leaned against the office door. "Hi Mom, Shane and I are home. What time are we going to work Slider this afternoon?"

"After I get through a little more of this accounting." The task that Brooke dreaded the most.

"Do you need me to work on anything between now and then?"

"Yes. . . Can you please drag the arenas?"

"Sure. . . ." Kasey's voice trailed off.

"What is it? I know that tone in your voice."

Kasey hesitated, "I used to love that job before I got my license."

"Now it's a chore, is that it?" Brooke smiled.

"Not exactly. But. . ."

"But what?"

"Never mind. I'll go change."

Brooke sat back for a moment. *Kasey wanted to tell me something. What is it? She'll tell me when she's ready.*

Brooke was finishing up with her paperwork when Kasey reappeared. "That was fast. Are you done already?"

Kasey bit her lip. "Mom, we've got a problem. . . The tractor died."

Brooke sank in her chair. "Not another expense!"

"I was dragging the indoor arena and it just stopped. It won't even turn over."

"Okay, I'll come out and take a look at it before we work Slider."

"I'm sorry, Mom. I don't think I did anything wrong."

"Don't worry about it. I'm sure you didn't. You just happened to be the one driving it when it happened."

"Are you sure?"

Brooke stood up and put her arm around Kasey. "Yes, I'm sure."

Brooke put her cell phone back in her pocket. "No one from Hollister Tractor Supply can come to pick up the tractor until tomorrow afternoon. I need it out of the arena before then so I can train tomorrow."

"Mom, can Ray help us get it out of here?"

"Good idea. I'll give him a call." The call was short, and her frown was gone. "Ray will be here in an hour or so... Let's work Slider while we wait."

"What do you want to do with him today?"

"Let's get him used to loping with a saddle on. Then we can hang some ropes off the saddle to get him used to something touching his side."

"Why?"

"It helps prepare him for people moving around on his back and their legs rubbing against his sides."

When they finished up with Slider Ray walked up to the paddock. "How's he workin' out?"

Brooke looked up. "He's doing great, but we still haven't asked much of him."

"Glad to hear it, you be careful with him—Are you ready to look at the tractor?"

Ray walked around the machine inspecting it, then he climbed up behind the steering wheel and turned the key. Nothing happened. Brooke then explained everything she knew about the tractor dying. "Can you fix it? I need to get it started—or at least get it out of the arena."

Ray turned the ignition switch again and got the same clicking sound. "Sounds like you still have electric power to the solenoid. But if the starter was goin' bad that wouldn't cause it to die." Ray got off the tractor and checked fluid levels. "Hydraulic fluid looks okay. Let's check the oil." A few moments later he shook his head. "This don't' look good."

Brooke moved closer to Ray; a lump grew in her throat. "What doesn't look good?"

"I'm not seein' any oil on the dip stick."

"How bad is that?" Brooke's voice wavered.

"I don't know how bad, but it sure ain't good."

"We won't have a chance to look at it for two or three days," the man from Hollister informed Brooke the following morning.

Frustrated by another looming large expense, Brooke called Amber. "I'm almost ready to quit. It seems like someone doesn't want me to succeed."

"You might be right. Every time it looks like you've got things starting to go your way something else happens. . . Only the storm damage doesn't fit the pattern. Everything else has been something breaking."

"What are you getting at?"

"What we've talked about before—isn't that land company after your property?"

"Yeah."

"Maybe. . ."

"Maybe *what*?"

"Just keep a sharp eye out." An uneasiness settled into Brooke's gut; she didn't like the implications of this discussion.

Tyler was back at his headquarters in L.A. taking care of loose ends. At mid-afternoon Bob arrived and summoned Tyler to his executive suite. Bob motioned to one of the armchairs in front of his large window. "How are things going in Flagstaff?"

"Slower than I had hoped." Tyler slid into the soft leather seat.

"In what way?"

"Getting a handle on the source of the problems isn't as straight-forward as I had hoped. And I've yet to hear a positive assessment of our company."

Bob sighed. "That's not good."

"No—and Hal Greer hasn't made us popular in the region either. He's not been careful, and some of his techniques can hurt our image."

"Should we get him out of there?"

"Not yet... Give me a little more time to assess the circumstances." The situation didn't sit well with Tyler. His instincts were telling him it was deeper than Hal.

"Do you think you can get things moving there?"

"I'm confident, and I've got plan in mind to gain the trust of the community."

Bob stood up and moved over to his desk. "I've heard enough, do whatever it takes to get the project going. I'm sure you've got things under control out there. I need to take care of some other urgent matters."

Tyler was caught off guard by the sudden end of their conversation. "If you say so."

"I want you to come over to my place for dinner tonight. Charlotte wants to see you." Bob ordered.

"But—I have other plans for this evening."

"Change them. You know how Charlotte can be."

"Okay, I'll be there." Tyler didn't argue, he figured Ryan knew the routine and would take it in stride.

On his way back to his office, Tyler had Emma cancel his evening dinner reservation while he unsuccessfully tried to reach Ryan. That evening while driving to Bob's, he finally reached Ryan. "Hey, son, I'm glad I finally got in touch with you."

"Why, we're supposed to have dinner tonight."

"About that. . ."

Ryan cut his dad off. "Let me guess, you're going to cancel, *right*?"

"I don't want to, but Bob is insisting that I come over for dinner. . . And he's the boss."

"Dad—you always have an excuse for putting your work before me. You set things up all the time, and then have to cancel. . . Maybe next time, if you can fit it in. . . See ya, Dad."

Tyler figured wrong, he felt angry and deflated. The conversation stung. *It's not my fault, things get in the way. I try to get together with Ryan, but my schedule is out of my control.*

The dinner was delicious, and Charlotte played the perfect hostess. Bob smiled through dinner as she monopolized the conversation and tried to learn the entire social goings on in Flagstaff. The topic of Tyler's ex-wife's and Dale's upcoming wedding was noticeably absent from the conversation. Tyler tactfully deflected all questions related to his social life and even if he hadn't, he wouldn't admit to himself that Brooke sparked his interest.

Charlotte was clearing the dessert dishes from the table when Bob stood up. "Come on Tyler, let's go for a walk."

"Sure," he forced a smile, *oh here it comes*. He'd been down this path before. It usually meant that Bob had something he wanted to get off his chest. They walked down to the stable as dusk advanced. Bob leaned against the fence and watched two horses graze in the irrigated green pasture.

"You know, I didn't bring you out for dinner so Charlotte could dote on you."

Tyler moved alongside Bob and rested against the fence. "I figured."

"I'm concerned about what's going on in Flagstaff."

"We've had issues like this before when starting up projects."

"I know. . . But there's something different—you've alluded to it, something deeper that you haven't uncovered yet."

"Why all the secrecy? Why did you want to talk about it here?"

"Just a feeling I have, and I've gotten hints of similar irregularities on some of our other projects. . ."

"But why meet here?"

Bob faced Tyler. "I don't have any proof, but I just feel like someone inside our company is trying to harm the business."

"That's ridiculous!"

"There's nothing concrete that I can put my finger on—it's just a feeling I have. Some things just don't add up."

"What do you want me to do?"

"I'm not entirely sure. . . That's why I wanted you out here tonight so we can talk freely. For one thing, continue to keep your profile low in Flagstaff and keep digging. Only Emma knows you're there and we will keep it that way. The rest of the office thinks you're doing advance work for a job in Seattle."

"How'd that rumor get started?"

"Don't ask. . . just go with it." Bob walked over to close the barn doors and then continued. "Until I tell you otherwise any conversations about this topic are only between you and me and they should not occur anywhere near the office."

Brooke had finished working Scout and was starting to get ready for Tyler's riding lesson, when her phone rang. "This is Hollister Tractor and we've got a preliminary estimate on your tractor."

"And. . .?" Brooke held her breath. She knew deep inside the news wasn't going to be good.

"The engine seized up due to a loss of oil."

"How could that happen? The oil was just changed." She watched Tyler do the oil change.

"The bolt on the oil pan was not tight, and the oil drained out."

"But why didn't the oil light go on?"

"That's the strange part. . . The wires to the pressure sensor were disconnected. Whoever was driving the tractor couldn't have seen the problem in time to turn off the tractor."

Brooke legs went weak. "Could this have happened accidentally?"

"I guess so, anything is possible, but the wires aren't anywhere near where you change the oil."

Brooke paused for a long moment. "How much is the repair?"

"Can't say for certain till we tear it apart and see how bad the pistons, cylinders and valves are. Minimum of $4,000 up to $8,000. Just depends."

"Thank you. I'll get back to you. By the way, don't say anything to anybody about the disconnected wires."

"Okay, whatever you say."

Brooke sat on a bale of hay and put her head in her hands. *How could this happen. Tyler doesn't seem like the irresponsible type. Why would he disconnect the wires to the oil gauge? But he is the one who changed the oil. It doesn't make sense.* And then her thoughts carried her down another track. *Was Amber right? Is someone trying to force me to sell?*

Brooke was still sitting on the bale of hay when Tyler walked into the barn. "I'm ready for my first lesson."

Brooke looked up with wet eyes. "You're here already?"

"Yeah, I'm a few minutes early. . . Are you alright? Is everything okay?"

"Not really, the tractor broke, and I just got the estimate to repair it. I can't afford to get it fixed and I can't afford not to get it fixed." Thoughts she didn't want flooded her mind. *Could Tyler be responsible? Why would a lawyer want to break my tractor?*

"What happened to it?"

"The engine seized. They say it lost its oil."

"How'd that happen?"

"The mechanic said the drain plug wasn't tight."

"That can't be. I know I tightened it before I put the oil in."

"That's what Hollister Tractor tells me."

Tyler had to think fast, this could hurt his company's plans, or he could turn it around and use it to his advantage. *It's a tightknit community. I don't want any negative attention. If I take care of the repair, it could put me in good with the community and might keep people from nosing around and finding out who I work for.* "Do we have time to go there? If I'm responsible I want to make things right."

"You what?" Brooke's mouth remained open.

"Yes, that's what I said."

Brooke was still taken aback by Tyler's offer. "Well, I guess so, as long as we're back by 3:30 when the kids get home." *He's willing to take care of things—that means he didn't do anything intentionally.* But on the heels of that thought came another. *But did someone else do it?*

The service manager explained the range of repairs that might be required once they got everything apart and saw the extent of the damage. He avoided any mention of the disconnected wires.

"Okay, let's make sure I understand," Tyler said. "The engine seized, and if it's just cylinders, we're talking around $4,000. Worst case is around $8,000."

"Yeah, you got it right."

"What's the replacement cost of the tractor?"

"New—about $30,000. If you can find a used one, they run from around $20,000."

"It's definitely worth the repair. When can you get started on the work? I'll cover the costs." Brooke's eyes widened.

"We should be able to start on it in two days. It'll take a week, maybe a little longer depending on what parts are needed."

Brooke couldn't believe what she was hearing. Tyler didn't even flinch at the prices. He turned to her. "Can you make do without a tractor until the repairs are done?"

Brooke stammered. "The work will pile up, but I guess I'll have to make do."

Tyler looked at the sales manager. "Do you have an equivalent rental tractor Brooke can use until the repairs are done?"

"Yeah, we have one."

"Can you have it delivered to Brooke's ranch this afternoon or tomorrow morning? I'll cover that cost also."

"Sure can, might be able to get it there by the close of business today." Brooke's heart skipped a beat. Tyler took care of the paperwork and the deposit while Brooke wandered the store trying to comprehend what she just heard.

Brooke was quiet on the short drive back to her ranch. She was perplexed about Tyler's generosity and didn't quite understand how to read it. As they got out of the SUV she finally asked, "Why are you doing this? You said you tightened the drain plug."

"I'm 99 percent sure I tightened it. But I was the last one to work on the tractor, right?"

"Yes."

"So, that makes me culpable and responsible for the repair. I have no evidence that I tightened the drain plug."

"You're sounding like a lawyer."

"Well. . . ."

Brooke relaxed. "That's right, you are one." Any lingering doubts concerning Tyler and the tractor had evaporated from Brooke's mind. A burden lifted from her shoulders as they got to the barn. "Okay, let me make sure I understand what you want to get out of these lessons. You want to learn more about natural horsemanship, and you want to learn how to do reining. Is that right?"

"That covers it." Brooke was starting to realize there was a lot more to this city boy than his looks and charm.

"I'm glad that you want to do more than ride, and that you want to learn more about natural horsemanship."

"Why's that?"

"Most people are only interested in getting on a horse and making it go. But I believe natural horsemanship makes you a better all-around rider. It helps you to communicate with your horse and most importantly it helps you read your horse."

"What do you mean it helps you read your horse?"

"You learn to understand the signals your horse sends to you. The turning of an ear, the flexing of his neck—it all tells you something. Understanding their communication will help you stay out of unnecessary battles during your training."

"I think I understand what you're saying. Sort of like a good attorney reading the nonverbal cues a person gives on the witness stand."

Brooke smiled. *He's sharp. . . I never thought of it like that before.* She took him in again, his blue eyes and sand blond hair. Her smile turned to a crooked grin. "Do you have any boots besides those sneakers you're wearing?"

"No, this is all I have."

"Then we'll stay on the ground today and you'll have to get some riding boots before you get on a horse. It's a safety issue; you need a heel on your boot and a sole that will easily slide out of the stirrup in case of an emergency."

"Do you mind helping me pick out the right type for what we'll be doing?"

Brooke returned a smile. *This could be fun.* "Sure, I'd be glad too, how about this weekend so you're ready for next week."

Tyler felt at-ease with Brooke and sensed that she would be open to his next request. "Would you like to go out for dinner while we're shopping?"

"That would be nice." She was taken aback, not by his question but by the lack of hesitation in her response.

Brooke got Cowboy, her main lesson horse out of his stall. "I'm going to start you off as though you have no knowledge about horses."

"Good idea. It's been years since I've been around horses."

Brooke showed Tyler how to put Cowboy in the crossties and then they cleaned him up. She demonstrated the proper technique for brushing him and cleaning out his hooves. "We'll worry about putting the saddle on once you've got the proper equipment to ride. Let's head to the round pen and start doing some groundwork."

"Will the training we're doing bother the mustang?"

"I don't think so. But we'll find out. Either way it'll be good for him to have some horses worked next to him." Brooke led Cowboy into the round pen and Slider came over to the edge of his paddock to see what was going on. He stood and watched as Brooke showed Tyler the horse games.

Tyler kept shielding his eyes from the intense sun. "Do you have a hat to use when working outside with the horses?"

"Just my ball cap which is back at my apartment."

"We'll get you a western hat while we're shopping for boots."

Tyler grinned. "Sounds like a plan." He was actually looking forward to a weekend event that didn't involve work.

The lesson started. "Okay, take this stick and gently press it into Cowboy's chest while keeping your feet still. The object of the game is to see who moves their feet first, you or Cowboy. Slowly increase the pressure on the stick until he makes the slightest backward movement with his feet. As soon as he does, release the pressure and then gently rub him with the end of the stick."

Tyler did as instructed and Cowboy took a step backwards. "Wow, it doesn't take much pressure to make him move."

"He's well trained. An untrained horse or a horse with a high play drive will really lean into the stick."

They worked for another twenty minutes before they put Cowboy back in his stall. When they left the barn a large truck with an orange tractor on its bed pulled into the driveway. Tyler turned to Brooke and smiled. "I guess they were able to get it delivered today."

Brooke gave Tyler a quick hug. "Thank you. You don't know what this means to me and the ranch."

Tyler headed back to work, and Brooke lingered outside to watch the tractor get unloaded. A few minutes later Ray came down the road with a skid-steer loaded on his trailer. She watched as he parked next to the barn, just as the delivery truck from Hollister Tractor headed back to the store. Ray got out of his truck and studied the rental tractor as he walked over to Brooke. "Tyler rented it for me." Brooke reacted before the questions were asked.

"That city dude? What was he doin' out here?"

Brooke ignored Ray's question and asked. "What are you doing here with your skid-steer?"

"I figured you could use some help."

"Thanks Ray. But I wish you'd called. You would have saved yourself a trip."

"What do you know about that guy?"

"Ray, you're a good friend. But what goes on between me and him, is really my business."

Ray walked around the tractor and inspected it. "Why'd he rent it for you?"

"He felt responsible for my tractor since he was the last one to work on it. So, he's paying for its repair, and he got this rental for me while my tractor is being fixed."

"Doesn't that seem suspicious to you?"

"No. It seems nice."

"Why would some guy you barely know spend that kind of money to fix something you can't prove he broke?"

She laughed. "Don't go getting crazy about this, Ray. We've gotten to know each other at church and choir. And he said the facts made him culpable."

"What's that mean? That sounds like lawyer talk."

"It means the facts and circumstantial evidence point to him being responsible. And by the way he is a lawyer."

Ray rolled his eyes. "I'm just lookin' out for you, Brooke. What do you really know about him? Nobody spends this kind of money without a reason."

"I don't have time to argue about this. I have work to do."

As Brooke took care of chores, Ray's words came back to her like dark seeds that grew in her mind. *I really don't know much about Tyler. It made so much sense when he explained why he was paying for the tractor repairs. Could he have another motive for being this nice?*

CHAPTER

K asey sat on Brooke's bed, and watched her mother search through the closet. "Mom, why are you making such a big deal about what to wear? You're just going shopping."

Brooke had asked herself the same question a half-dozen times and didn't have a good answer. She rationalized it many ways but always avoided the obvious answer; she was attracted to the new guy at church. "I don't know who I might run into, and we always want to give a good impression for the ranch when we're in town."

"It's only shopping for boots. . . I don't know why you have to take that guy shopping anyway."

"He's a friend from church, and he wants riding lessons. As his trainer, I'm responsible for making sure he's got the proper equipment for his lessons."

"You've never done this with any of your other clients."

"I've never had such a greenhorn before."

"Mom, that's lame. But if you really want to go out with this guy, I'll give you a hand putting together your outfit." Kasey wasn't sure how she felt about her mom going out. She was glad to see her excited and smiling. She'd been sad for so long. *If going out with this guy makes her smile, I'll help Mom look good. Nothing will come of it, anyway—he's nothing like Dad.*

Tyler walked into Boot Ranch and hesitated. "I can't believe the number of boots in here. Where do we start?"

Brooke smiled and nudged him towards the men's section. After finding the aisle with Tyler's size they picked out several styles of boots. Tyler tried on the first pair. Brooke asked, "How do they feel?"

"They seem okay and look good with my jeans."

"I wouldn't go that far."

"What do you mean?"

"Your designer jean might be okay around town, but you'll need some true cowboy jeans if you're gonna show." Tyler looked puzzled.

Brooke smiled back. "I'll explain later while we're looking at some jeans."

At the Flagstaff Saddlery Brooke stepped back and inspected Tyler and his new jeans. She noticed more than the jeans. *Not bad—he's in pretty good shape for a lawyer.*

Tyler motioned to Brooke to look at the cowboy further down the aisle. "Why do so many people around here wear their jeans with a crease down the front?"

"I wasn't going to overwhelm you with that yet."

"What do you mean?"

"A real cowboy starches and creases his jeans. If you go to a show, I'll remind you to get it done."

"Why do they do it?"

"I'm not sure about the crease, but the starch helps keep the jeans clean. It makes it easier to brush the dust off."

Tyler shook his head. "Maybe for shows, but I'm not ready to do that every day."

Brooke found herself relaxing more and more as the evening went on. She enjoyed helping Tyler put together his outfit. She had forgotten what it was like to spend time alone with a man. She was at ease around him but didn't understand why. He wasn't a country boy. Tyler, on the other hand, knew what attracted him to Brooke. She was pretty and easy to look at; in fact, Tyler had to make an effort not to stare. But there was more, much more; Brooke had a warmth about her, and she didn't put on airs; she was the complete opposite of what his ex-wife had become.

They left the store with Tyler's bags in their hands and new boots on his feet. Tyler asked, "Are you hungry?"

"Now that you mention it, yes."

They had planned to get something to eat, but this was taking on a different feel. Brooke could go along with that, easily. Tyler chose an Italian restaurant—a finer one. "I checked it out, while you were talking to the last salesman, and I made a reservation."

Brooke smiled. "So, you had this planned."

"Well, we were planning on getting a bite to eat, and I wanted to thank you for giving me a hand with the shopping. I wouldn't have had the first clue what to buy."

Inside the restaurant, there were eloquent fixtures, linen tablecloths and fine china settings. A well-dressed hostess showed them to a corner table set for two. Tyler seemed to be in his element and acted with an easy air of confidence. Brooke was insecure. She hadn't been out to a nice restaurant since before Cory's accident. Tyler held Brooke's chair for her, then the waiter handed them their menus. "Good evening, my name is Angelo, and I'll be your server. Would you like some wine while you look at the menu?"

Tyler looked at Brooke. "Would you like some?"

"Maybe a little. But I don't know much about wine."

Tyler smiled, he inspected the wine list, and then looked at Brooke. "Would you like an appetizer to go with the wine?"

"Yes, that would be nice."

Tyler turned toward Angelo. "Bruschetta and bottle of Pinot Grigio, please."

Brooke picked up her menu and paused. "Tyler—there aren't any prices on my menu."

Tyler smiled. "They're on mine."

"Can you tell me what they are so I can order?"

"No—order whatever you like on the menu."

"I can't. . . ."

"I insist. This is on me. Don't worry about it." *Brooke deserves a special treat. She's opened my eyes again. There's more to life than work.*

Angelo returned with a bottle of wine and two glasses. He poured a small amount into the first glass and handed it to Tyler who lightly swirled it before smelling the aroma and taking a small taste. "Yes, its fine." Angelo proceeded to pour the wine into both glasses as another waiter arrived with the appetizer.

"Would you like more time with the menus?"

"Yes please, another five minutes."

Tyler looked at Brooke. "What are you hungry for?"

"Something with pasta. What about you?"

"I'm thinking of the Penne Al Salmone. If you like, we can share."

Sharing a meal. Sharing time together. Sharing friendship. . . . Brooke felt herself warming to Tyler even more. "I like that idea. The Linquine Alla Zingara sounds interesting. I'll try that."

After Angelo returned and took their orders, they continued a light-hearted discussion about music and the goings on at church. Tyler steered clear of any topics related to real estate. He did not want to get into discussions where he would have to sidestep parts of the conversation. As they shared their entrées, Brooke started to bring Kasey and Shane into the conversation. "As a parent the teenage years can be so frustrating and rewarding at the same time. . ."

"I know what you're talking about."

"What do you mean?"

"I have a twenty-year-old son. The frustration and rewards don't stop when they leave the teenage years."

She hadn't seen a wedding ring and had assumed he was single— though it was hard to believe an attractive, outgoing person like Tyler had never been married. "Tell me about him."

"He attends UCLA."

"Like his father?"

Tyler shrugged his shoulders. "I guess."

Brooke ventured further onto the new ground. "What about his mother?"

"My ex-wife?"

Brooke relaxed a little. "I know this is really personal but—what happened?"

"A little over two years ago. . . she claimed that I was married to my work. She went and had an affair with one of the partners at my office."

"That must have made things complicated."

Tyler shook his head. "Just a bit. That's a big reason I was sent here. To ease tensions in the office." There was another reason, of course, but he didn't want to venture there. "What about you? It must be difficult since you lost your husband."

"It's been rough, but God's been good and has gotten us through it. He takes care of us when we need it, just one day at a time."

"That's a pretty amazing outlook."

"It can be a struggle to maintain my faith and trust, but so far I haven't been disappointed."

"I wish I could say the same. I loved my wife, but to have an affair and leave me for another man; sometimes that's hard to put behind me."

Brooke sat back. *That's interesting—a man who's been burned by a woman. And I've been disappointed by men.*

They strolled out to the car in the brisk autumn air when Tyler suggested. "It's a nice evening. Why don't we take a walk under the stars?"

Brooke hesitated, and found her heart saying *yes*. . . and her mind saying *no*. "I would love to, but I really should get home to the kids. It's getting late."

"You're right, maybe another time."

Back home, Kasey and Shane appeared in the kitchen before the back door had closed. "What took you guys so long?"

Brooke took off her jacket and smiled at Tyler. "My keepers." She turned to the kids and held out a small, white box. "Relax. Mr. Alexander insisted on bringing some dessert home for you."

Kasey cautiously eyed Tyler and then focused on her mom. Shane's face lit up. "Thank you, Mr. Alexander."

"You guys can call me Tyler, if that's alright with your mother."

Tyler and Shane looked at Brooke, but Kasey stared at the floor. Brooke nodded in approval. She stepped closer and touched her daughter's shoulder. "What's wrong?"

"Nothing." Kasey muttered. She shot a momentary glare at Tyler. Then in a moment, Shane and Kasey were both seated at the table, stabbing their forks into the tiramisu. As he put his fork and plate in the sink Shane announced, "That was great. You can go out with my Mom anytime."

Tyler smiled. "Well, thank you."

Shane asked, "Will I see you at church tomorrow?"

"I plan on it." Tyler said as he headed for the door. "Brooke, thanks for helping me get my gear for the riding lessons and for the great company this evening."

"I should be thanking you for the wonderful dinner."

When Tyler was gone, Brooke sat down at the table with Kasey. "You're awfully quiet. Everything okay?"

"Yeah. . ." Kasey changed the subject. "Where did y'all go for dinner?"

"Luciano's, it was very nice."

"No way. I've heard some of the kids at school say that's one of the best restaurants in Flagstaff. And it's expensive."

"I figured that out when the menu came without prices."

Kasey's mouth opened for a moment. "You're kidding me. What'd you do?"

"I made a fool of myself and asked Tyler if his menu had any prices."

"What he'd say?"

"He said, don't worry about it, and to get anything I want."

"He seems to like you."

"He's a friend."

"Mom. . . really?"

Later, alone in her room, Brooke replayed the revelation about Tyler's son and ex-wife. For some reason, the ex-wife made her a bit uneasy. Her own uneasiness troubled her more than the fact that he had an ex-wife. *Why does this bother me? We're just friends and I don't want a relationship, not now.* Finally, she pushed it all out of her mind—his generosity, his taking her to a fine restaurant, the offer of a walk under the stars, being great with her kids—all of it. *We're just friends and that's all it going to be so, it doesn't matter.*

CHAPTER

A new week had begun, but Brooke continued to think back to her evening with Tyler. It had been a long time since someone had treated her special. Her spirits were high. Optimism flowed through her veins and she was excited about Slider's training. Today was going to be his first ride. She was waiting in the kitchen when the kids got home. After their snack, Shane went off to work on his Boy Scout project and Brooke put the dishes in the sink. She turned her attention to Kasey. "It's the big day for Slider. Are you ready?"

Brooke tried to sound upbeat, but her previous optimism had eroded away and was being replaced with apprehension. Was it because so much of the ranch's future was riding on Slider, or was it a premonition that something would go wrong?

"Why are you asking me, I'm not the one riding him."

"You know what I mean. Are you ready to help?"

"Yeah, I just need to get into my jeans. Do you think he's going to be an easy first ride?"

"I sure hope so; we need to keep his training moving forward. But you never know, I've had some of my worst first rides on the horse that you would least expect it from."

"Let's hope Slider isn't one of those." Kasey said, as she went to get changed.

Thirty minutes later, Slider's tack was hanging on the side of the round pen. He was groomed and tacked up using the routine he had become accustomed to over the past week. Everything was in its place. Or so Kasey thought.

"Mom, where's the bridle?"

"I'll stick with the rope halter for now. We'll take more time to get him used to the bit while doing ground driving."

They moved Slider to the side of the round pen, then Brooke climbed up on the panel next to him, just like they had practiced for the past week. Brooke put some of her weight on him while still hanging onto the top rail.

"Mom, he's staying calm."

"Not so fast Kasey, I still don't have my full weight on him. . . . There, I'm on him. . . . Let go of him, and slowly back away." Brooke shifted her body weight in the saddle and lightly tapped Slider's rump with her hand. He slowly walked off.

"Great job Mom! He seems a little unsure, but he's trusting you anyway."

Relief eased through Brooke. "Two times around the round pen each direction, and I'll call it quits for this session." She was still smiling as she faced Kasey. "Maybe I was nervous about nothing." Brooke did not see what was coming. Behind Slider's shed a small dust devil had formed and was heading straight for them. Brooke caught a glimpse of a swirling wind as it came by the shed. *Oh no, hang on. This is not good.* She stopped their walk and stood still as the twisting funnel of air and dirt passed overhead. Slider didn't seem bothered; he switched his tail nonchalantly. Then unexpectedly Slider exploded straight up and then forward, with three good bucks. Brooke did not make it past the second buck. She landed on her side. Kasey ran. "*Mom—Mom, are you all right?*" She shouted.

Brooke leaned on her elbow. "Yeah, I'm fine. Get Slider, and we'll try that again. Did you see what happened? The dirt devil didn't seem to bother him at first."

Kasey carefully approached the bay horse and took hold of his rope halter. "It wasn't the dirt devil. It was the black plastic bag that came afterwards. It blew onto one of his legs." Kasey said as she looked at her mother and shook her head.

"Guess we'll have to flag him with some plastic bags to get him desensitized to them. Just another training exercise to do." *I can live with that if that's all my premonition was about.* But was it?

Brooke walked with a slight limp to Slider. Kasey's eyes were still wide as she looked at the horse and then her mom. "Are you sure you're okay?"

Brooke rubbed her hip. "Yeah, just a little sore. It'll be gone in a minute."

Kasey handed Slider to her mother. "He sure has a strong *buck* in him."

Brooke nodded. "Yeah, there's still a whole lot of wild in him."

Once more they went through the routine, this time without the dirt devil or plastic bag. Everything went as planned; Brooke and Slider successfully walked around the round pen two times each direction.

After the tack was put away Brooke leaned up against Slider's paddock and watched him warm himself in the late afternoon sun. *I could really use Kasey's help showing some of the client's horses. Getting the word out that a teenager can win on an Anderson trained horse will sure help business.*

Kasey joined Brooke. "What'ya doin', Mom?"

Brooke kept her eyes on the horse. "Watchin' Slider."

"Are you looking for anything in particular?"

"Trying to figure out how to train him for the show. We need to find out what he's good at and what he likes to do."

Slider raised his head when he saw Kasey, and then trotted over to her. Brooke smiled. "Looks like he's really hooked onto you."

"He always wants my attention. Maybe if I ignore him. . . ."

Kasey turned her back to Slider and crossed her arms. Slider snuffled at her hair, then grabbed her hat in his teeth, and walked to the other side of the paddock. Brooke laughed, as Kasey chased after him; he didn't want to give her hat back. Finally, he dropped it in the dirt, and trotted off, only to return when she picked it up. This time she rubbed his forehead, and he stood contentedly.

"At least we know he likes to play."

"Look at the slobber all over my hat." Kasey groaned. However, inside she smiled. The horse chose her as his friend and leader. At the same time, she was worried. She knew that at the end of the competition Slider would have to be put up for sale. She struggled for a solution; *Mom and the ranch need him to do well at the show. Can I allow him to get close to me? Will it hurt when he gets sold? But, to help mom get him trained I may have to get close to him.*

Brooke looked at her watch. "Okay, let's quit the playing around and start to plan out what we're going to do with him at the competition."

"One thing, for sure. He likes to do sliding stops and roll backs."

"True. He's athletically built and is slightly uphill. That'll make it easy for him to do many performance disciplines. He already likes to do several of the reining elements."

"Why don't you just go that direction?" Kasey asked.

"It's not that simple. To do quality reining, cutting, jumping, or even dressage it can take months and years of training. But the training isn't just to teach them the maneuver. It's also developing their strength to properly do the maneuver. We'll never have the time to increase his strength even if he wants to do these things."

"I see what you mean. How do we work around that?"

"Well for one thing, everyone else is in the same position."

"True. What have past winners done?"

"I've started to look at some prior performances; they mix a lot of tricks into their routines. He's smart and likes to play; so that could work."

Slider made his way over to where they were standing. He lifted his head over the rails and pulled on Kasey's sleeve to get her attention. She started to rub his muzzle as he kept trying to nibble on her hand, which they turned it into a game. Brooke shook her head. "This is what I mean. He wants to play."

Kasey teased. "Oh, this would make an exciting show. Watch the pretty lady play with the horse's lips."

"No—I'm serious. We need to figure out some tricks for him to mix in with the riding. And at this point I'm leaning towards a simple reining pattern."

Kasey nodded. "I can definitely see that."

Brooke looked back at Slider. "I'm starting to feel comfortable with this plan." But there was still the matter of Kasey and horse shows. She wanted to put it off, but she knew it had to be addressed. "Kasey, I know you've been reluctant, but I really need you to compete at some horse shows."

"*I said I don't want to ride at shows!*"

"I know you did. But things have changed."

"How?"

"Even if I do well at the Mustang Competition, I'll need to bring in more clients, or we won't be able to keep the ranch. Having the horses I've trained do well with a teenage non-professional riding them will get more people sending their horses to me."

"Why *me*?"

"Because you're a natural and an excellent rider. I can't find a better rider."

"Well try. . . because I'm not going to ride in public."

"You need to overcome this fear."

"*Why?* Maybe I'll just give up horses all-together."

Brooke nearly shouted. "Because if you don't ride and I don't get more clients, we'll lose the ranch!"

Silence hung in the air; Kasey stared at her mother with a shocked look. "Lose the ranch? Is that what's going to happen?" Then she exploded. "Don't put all that on *me*. I don't want it."

Kasey stormed off and Brooke's spirits sank with her shoulders. *What am I going to do? I need her help, and she needs to deal with her fears.* She was powerless to help Kasey face the fear that had taken hold of her. *How can you change someone's mind and heart? I guess you can't. Only God can.* A tear formed in her eye. "Slider," she said, stroking the horse's mane. "The only thing left for me to do is give it over to God and pray."

Kasey was irritable and short with the family, especially Shane, as they got ready to go to youth group. Turmoil swirled inside Kasey as she struggled to deal with the blowup, she had with her mother earlier in the week. She needed advice from Lisa, but did Kasey want to share how she yelled at her mom?

Wednesday evening choir practice was finishing when Juan announced: "It's time to start rehearsals for the Christmas Eve Cantata. Who's planning on singing in it?" Everyone raised their hand, and Brooke smiled when she saw Tyler's hand go up. Juan continued, "one of the songs we're going to do is 'Mary, Did You Know', and I'd like it to be a duet. Any volunteers?"

Brian Edmonston offered, "How about Brooke and Tyler. They'd sound great together."

Juan looked at Brooke and then Tyler. "What do you say?"

Their eyes met and held contact long enough to see each other's approval. They replied almost in unison. "Sure."

When the group disbanded, Juan met with them. "Are you sure you want take this on. It will mean some extra rehearsals."

"I'm in."

"Me, too."

"I'll have the music next week. We only have six Wednesdays to practice between now and Christmas. That's why we need extra rehearsals."

"I'm willing, how about you Brooke?" Tyler looked at her.

She smiled at Tyler and then turned toward Juan. "Yes, I'm willing too."

"Ok then we'll get started next week."

Youth group had just dismissed, and Kasey stuck around afterwards to be alone with Lisa. "I had a pretty bad argument with my mom the other day about me riding in shows."

"I thought that was resolved?"

"I did, too. I thought my mom had accepted the fact that I don't want to ride in public. But now she's bugging me about it again."

"What changed?"

"Nothing really."

"I don't buy that," Lisa smiled. "What's different?"

"The pressures on the ranch have gotten tougher. Mom said the other night we could even lose the ranch. That makes me feel terrible. But. . . ."

"But what?"

"But I just. . . I can't compete. And my mom wants people to see me doing well on the horses she trains. She says it will help bring in more clients."

"Do you think it will help?"

Kasey slid forward on her chair. "It could, but I don't know for sure."

"Didn't you love competing?"

"Yeah, but that was before the accident."

"Do you want to overcome your fear? What if riding in shows can make a difference and help your mom hold things together on the ranch? Would you do it?"

"I want to but. . . When I've thought about competing, I start to get a panic attack."

Lisa opened her Bible. "What have we been studying recently?"

Kasey sighed. "Putting your trust in God."

"Do you think this is a good opportunity to test your beliefs in a real-world situation?"

"But this isn't a spiritual thing. . . ."

"Exactly. It's everyday real life and this is where we really need to apply what we learn. What the Bible teaches isn't just for 'churchy things'; it's for every part of your life."

Kasey focused on the floor, then she looked up at Lisa. "What do you think I should do?"

"Are there any laid-back, real easy-going shows that you could enter and practice in?"

"A few."

"Why don't you pray about it, and then if you feel okay with it, suggest to your mom that you might be willing to try one of those shows to see if you can handle it."

Kasey hesitated, then offered a weak reply. "I'll try."

Lisa added, "This isn't just about you learning to face your fears. It's also about you learning to trust God."

"I'll think about it."

"Maybe the youth group can help you out by watching you ride at home once or twice to give you a small crowd without any strangers."

"We'll see."

Later that evening as Brooke was reading in bed, Kasey timidly walked into her mother's room and sat down on edge of the bed. Brooke lowered her book. "Something wrong?"

"No." After a long pause Kasey continued. "I've been thinking about our conversation the other day."

"Yes," Brooke patiently waited for Kasey to continue.

"Well, I do want to help you. . . But when I think about riding in front of a crowd, I start getting all nervous and scared inside."

Brooke bit her lip. *Which direction is she going to take this conversation?*

"I talked with Lisa tonight and she said it would be good for me to try to overcome my fear. It would be a way of growing my faith."

"She did?"

"Yeah, she said the youth group could help by watching me practice and then come to a schooling show where most of the crowd will be people I've already ridden in front of."

Brooke tempered her excitement at Kasey's news. "That's really great news. Lisa has given you sound advice." Brooke smiled as Kasey went off to bed. Doubt then crept in. *Did I push her too much? Is she doing this out of guilt? Will she overcome her fear?*

mber's riding lesson was over, and her horse was on the trailer. Brooke wanted to talk to her before she left but wavered about bringing up the exchange she had with Kasey. Brooke longed for the sound counsel she used to get from her mother and Martha, but both of those options were gone. Her mother's steadily advancing Alzheimer's had taken its toll, and Brooke's bitterness had wounded her relationship with Martha. She was too proud to share those personal concerns with the homegroup. Amber didn't have children, but Brooke needed reassurance that she was doing the right thing by pushing Kasey to compete.

"Do you have a few minutes before you leave? I need to bounce something off you," Brooke asked, then wished she hadn't. *She's going to think I'm a horrible mother.*

"Sure, what's up?"

Brooke walked over to the flowerbed next to the visitor viewing area and sat down on a landscape timber. Amber followed and sat down next to her. "It's about Kasey." Brooke absentmindedly pulled some weeds while talking.

"What about her?"

"You know about her fear of riding in public since the accident." Brooke paused and pulled some more weeds.

Amber coaxed. "Yeah, and. . ."

"We had a blowout about it earlier in the week and I told her that I need her to show. I think I laid a guilt trip on her."

"What do you mean?"

Brooke stopped pulling weeds and quickly looked at Amber and then focused on the ground. "I told her that if I didn't get her help, I could lose the ranch."

Amber sat up straight. "That's pretty heavy."

"That's what I'm thinking.—What should I do?"

"How'd she react?"

"Not good. She stormed away and slammed a couple of doors. . . But a couple of days later she came to me and said she would give it a try at a small schooling show."

Amber looked puzzled. "So. . . What's the problem?"

"I don't want her doing it out of guilt."

"Does it matter why she rides and overcomes her fear as long as she does it?"

"Yes, it does. . . I don't want her thinking it's her responsibility to save the ranch."

"If it gets her to face her fear though. . . ."

"It's just not right."

"Why not let it ride for a little while and let her do a show or two. See how she does, then take some of the pressure off. It's already made her willing to get over her problem; so don't fight it."

"I don't know if I can do that."

"Watch how it plays out for a little while. That's my advice."

Brooke gave a heavy sigh. "That's not all."

"What else?"

"There are times she seems reluctant to be around Slider. It's hard to explain. It's like she's a little distant."

"Like how?"

"He's really connected to her, but she doesn't seem willing to connect with him. With some of the things he's done to get her attention I would have expected a different response from her."

Amber shrugged. "She knows he's gonna be sold at the end of the competition, and maybe she doesn't want to get too close."

"I think there's more to it than that."

"What makes you say that?"

"Mother's intuition."

It was an unseasonably warm Friday afternoon for early November, and Maddie had come over to help Kasey get Scout cleaned up for the show. They had a grand time washing Scout who stoically suffered the humiliation. They took turns taking selfies with him.

"Hey Maddie, get a picture of him with his mane moussed into a Mohawk."

"That's really cute, why don't you see you can make his forelock into unicorn horn?"

They both giggled at the sight. The final humiliation was when they used soap bubbles and mousse foam to make him look like a French Poodle.

"I've got to show these pictures to Mom."

They were busily washing off Scout's final disgrace, when Amber dragged Brooke into the barn to display her handywork at straightening Brooke's hair and how it accentuated her natural blonde highlights. Kasey did not see her mother or Amber on the other side of Scout, when she haphazardly went to rinse his back.

"Kasey! Watch out for your mother. . ." Maddie was too late with her warning.

Brooke and Amber were doused with a solid stream of water. Maddie's horrified look said it all. Kasey stammered. "Sorry, Mom. . . ."

Brooke wiped her face, her startled look turned to a weak smile. Kasey tried to contain the giggle that bubbled to the surface but couldn't. Water puddled around Brooke. "Do you girls know what this means?" Brooke winked at Amber.

"No." Kasey's voice quivered.

Amber nodded to Brooke who ran to the barn and returned with another hose, spraying water at the two girls. "This is war." And in a moment, the battle escalated, as Kasey and Brooke took on each other with the hoses. Amber and Maddie sloshed and pelted each other with soaking wet sponges. During the height of the battle Kasey turned her head and caught sight of someone at the barn door. "Mom!" She shouted as she dropped the hose and pointed. Tyler stood grinning. Brooke flinched. *Oh no, he can't be early.* But then she tried rationalizing that there was nothing she could do at this point other than make the best of it. So, she started to laugh. "You never know what you'll find here if you arrive early."

Tyler laughed. "I guess not, but now I'm convinced which one of us has the problem with water."

A half-hour later Brooke entered the kitchen, dried and changed.

Tyler was nowhere to be found. A few minutes later he showed up with Shane. Brooke's focus fell on Shane. "Where were you two?"

"I showed him some of my favorite places."

Tyler placed his hand on Shane's shoulder. "It was a good tour, and he's got quite the imagination."

Brooke smiled back. "I can only guess."

Shane continued, "Mom, can Tyler come to the show with us tomorrow? He's never been to one."

Brooke was glad Shane had made the suggestion. She looked at Tyler. "If he wants to and doesn't have any other commitments."

"It sounds like fun and it will be part of my equestrian education. Shane can show me what a man does at a horse show."

Brooke studied Tyler. *He looks good in those jeans and boots. Guess I did a good job picking them out for him.* Tyler noticed her eyeing him. "How do I look?"

"The outfit looks great. You look like you grew up around here."

He looked at his watch. "We'd better get going or we'll be late for practice."

Amber jumped in. "Get going, guys. I'll make sure the kids are set for the evening and that everything is taken care of here."

Brooke grabbed her jacket and headed out the door. Her thoughts were no longer on Kasey's show or the ranch's problems but on the evening ahead. She felt a connection with Tyler and a sense of peace; a welcome change from what had recently occupied her mind.

After they left, the two girls went to Kasey's bedroom where Maddie asked. "Who is that guy with your Mom? He's cute for an old guy."

"He's new at church."

The girls dropped onto the bed, and Maddie casually asked, "Is your mom dating him?"

Kasey's jaw tightened. "My Mom with that city dude? I hope not. He's taking riding lessons from her and they're in choir together. She says they're just friends."

"Do you buy that—really? I saw the way she looked at him."

"I'm not sure." I've noticed the way she looks at him, too. But she'd never be interested in a city guy, especially after Dad. He was so good around the ranch and the horses. I can't see her going for someone who doesn't even know how to ride yet."

"Yeah, but she's teaching him."

Kasey ignored the remark, she wished Maddie had never brought up the subject. "Hey, can you help me decide what to wear for the show tomorrow?"

At rehearsal, Brooke and Tyler's voices blended beautifully. As they finished, Juan smiled. "Wow, I can see how to pull so much more from your voices. Can I get you to come out for a couple more rehearsals? Please?"

Tyler looked at Juan and then Brooke. "I've got some business trips scheduled, but I might be able to fit them in. How about you?"

"I'm going to be really busy with the mustang."

Juan pleaded, "But you both need some diversion from your daily activities. . . Come on. . ."

"Okay, I'll find some time." Brooke conceded.

Fifteen minutes later, they parked next to the old railway station and walked through town toward a log and clapboard building. Tyler took in the eclectic collection of historic buildings that lined the street, noticing that most had been renovated to keep their old town charm. As they approached the Wagon Wheel he winked at

Brooke. "Looks like an authentic western saloon. What's the food like?"

"It's the best. Their bread pudding is to die for."

"That good?"

"Believe me."

Neither of them noticed Ray, who was driving by. He turned his head and then whipped his truck into the parking lot behind them, where he watched until they entered the restaurant. He then drove away, disappointment showed in his eyes.

As the evening progressed Brooke found herself being drawn to Tyler and his easy down to earth style. She couldn't believe he was a big city lawyer. It wasn't till after the dessert came, that Brooke glanced at her watch. "Oh-no!—I didn't realize it was this late. I told Kasey I would be back a half-hour ago."

Back at the ranch she rushed out of the SUV and then leaned back in. "I'd better go in alone. It might not be pretty in there, pre-show jitters and me being late. At least the desserts will be a little bit of a peace offering."

"Will it be like Daniel going into the lion's den?"

"Almost."

"Sorry about keeping you out so late."

"Don't be. I enjoyed myself and lost track of the time."

"Good luck." Tyler shot her a half-grin.

Brooke closed the door and realized she didn't want the evening to end; she tapped on the car window. As the it lowered, she leaned in, "Thanks again for the dinner. See you tomorrow?"

"Count on it."

Brooke found Kasey sitting at the kitchen table. "Sorry I'm late."

Kasey jumped on the comment. *"What took you so long?* I need your help to get ready for tomorrow."

"I'm sorry—time got away from us. I'm not that late, and we still have time to make sure everything is ready."

"When you're out with Tyler you're never back when you supposed to be."

Brooke smiled inside. *We do enjoy talking to each other.* "We had a lot to talk about. Besides I've only been out with him twice."

Shane wandered into the kitchen. "Where's Tyler?"

"He had to go home."

"Is he coming tomorrow?" Hope was evident in Shane's voice.

Kasey rolled her eyes. "Oh great, now he has to come to my horse show."

K asey's eyes opened wide; the damp sheets clung to her skin as she awoke in a cold sweat. She hadn't had a nightmare for months and this one came at the wrong time. It was hours before she would have to get up—Could she go back to sleep? Lying there her heart raced as she thought about the day ahead, and then a wave of nausea descended. *I can't disappoint Mom. I know she really needs my help. But I don't know if I can do this.* She tossed and turned for what seemed like hours as her thoughts jumped from the accident to the next day's show. Finally, exhaustion overtook her anxiety and she fell back to sleep.

At the showgrounds Brooke turned to Kasey on their way to get her show packet. "There were more people from your youth group who watched you the other day at the ranch, than are here. You'll do fine."

Kasey snapped. "Yeah, maybe in the ring it's okay. But there's only one horse and rider; what about the practice arena?"

Over at the practice arena, they leaned against the top rails and watched. "See," Brooke said, gently. "There are only two horses in that big arena. It's no different than the two of us riding at the same time at home."

"What if more riders show up?" Kasey could feel her heart starting to race again. "The footing stinks. It's too shallow, and it's hard."

Brooke took a deep breath. "The footing's not perfect, but it's safe.—And we showed up early so you'd have plenty of time to practice without a lot of riders around. If it gets too crowded, you'll take a break."

Kasey gave a deep, uneasy sigh. "I'm here. So, I guess I *have* to go through with it."

Back at their horse trailer, they found Josh and Shane sitting in the folding chairs. Kasey's eyes brightened "What are you doing here so early? I thought you were coming in the church van."

"I decided to come early and give you a hand in case you needed it."

Kasey shot a look to her mom. Brooke got the message. *Duck out.* "I've got some things to take care of in the truck; why don't you two get Scout ready? Shane, why don't you join me at the truck while you play your video game?"

"Why, I'm comfortable here." Shane mumbled.

"Because you can keep your battery charging in the truck."

Kasey smiled at her mother. *Thanks.*

As Brooke busied herself a measure of peace returned. She hadn't realized it, but she'd taken on some of Kasey's stress. Maybe the distraction of Josh's presence would keep Kasey from dwelling on the show ahead. Brooke wasn't concerned about Kasey's performance; she just wanted her to make it through the day without an emotional meltdown. A half-hour later, Scout was tacked up and Brooke was in the truck reading a magazine. She was startled by tapping on the glass and a loud, "Hey!"

Brooke turned to see Tyler looking though the passenger window. She smiled, and a wave of deep satisfaction came over her. Having him here—why did that make everything feel like it would be alright?

"Is this how you get ready for horse shows?" He winked. "Is that Josh, the pastor's son? Looks like Kasey is a million miles away from any kind of competition."

"Don't knock it. He's keeping her distracted."

Kasey was sitting on Scout and still chatting with Josh when she looked up, her smile faded when she saw Tyler talking to her mother. "What's wrong? Kasey," Josh asked.

"Nothing's wrong." Then she barked over at Brooke, "Can you stop talking, and help me warmup Scout?"

Brooke gave a resigned sigh as she glanced at Tyler. She foresaw a demanding day ahead as the time of Kasey's ride drew closer. "I'll be right there." She looked at Tyler. "Duty calls. We'll talk later."

"Hey, no pressure. I'm just here to watch and learn. Do what you have to do."

Thirty minutes before her ride, the rest of the youth group showed and stopped by to let Kasey know they were there. Lisa pulled Kasey aside. "Do you remember what we talked about?"

"Yeah, I think so."

"Then tell me what you're going to think about."

Kasey recited from memory. "Who's the most powerful being in the universe?—God. Who's watched every ride I ever made?—God. Who should I be riding for?—God. So, it doesn't matter how good or bad I do, He's seen me at my best and worst. I just want to ride to please Him, and I know He'll protect me."

"Perfect. Just repeat that to yourself. . . It will help."

The youth group headed to the bleachers, and Kasey did a little fine-tuning of Scout's grooming. But then her thoughts began to run wild—first to the nightmare and then to the accident. *In her mind's-eye she could see her father, that scene she couldn't stop replaying once it began—running to push her out of the way just before Slim's horses knocked him to the ground, their sharp, heavy hooves trampling him*. . . Kasey's palms and forehead broke into a sweat and her heart began to race. The nausea rolled over her; this time she had to run into the horse trailer to vomit. With her stomach empty the queasiness started to subside and none too soon, it was time to ride.

Kasey mounted and loped a few times around the practice area. She and Scout then walked to the show arena with Brooke alongside. When the gate was closed behind her, Brooke called out. "Good Luck." Brooke took a position next to Tyler to watch the ride.

As Kasey got ready to start the pattern, she repeated what she and Lisa discussed. *Who's the most powerful*. . . As she recited the words mentally, she took deep breaths and felt her body relax. Peace started to envelope her, not entirely replacing her fear, but partially overshadowing it.

The pattern started out a little shaky. Brooke could see Kasey's nerves affecting her position and timing. As Brooke focused on Kasey her nerves got the best of her and she grabbed Tyler's hand partway through the pattern. A little later in the pattern Kasey gained confidence and her riding improved, Brooke started to relax but continued to hold Tyler's hand. Tyler was pleasantly surprised, but then. *What am I doing? I don't want to get involved.* But something kept him from releasing her hand—a feeling of warmth and human connection he had yearned to feel for too many months. Or was it years?

Near the conclusion of the pattern, Brooke glanced down at her hand interwoven with Tyler's. She quickly released her grip and blushed as he turned toward her. Brooke offered, "Sorry. A mother's nerves."

"Glad to help." He smiled back and gently wrapped his hand around hers. Brooke's hand relaxed in his.

Ray, who had been working non-stop as the show farrier, took a break to watch Kasey. He was standing across the show ring with a friend when he spotted Brooke with Tyler, again. They were holding hands. Ray muttered to himself under his breath.

"What's that?" his friend asked.

"Some dude is trying to buy Brooke's affection. I'm sure there's something up with this guy."

"Maybe she likes him."

"No way. He's not her type." Ray turned abruptly and marched back to his farrier's truck.

After the judge had spoken with Kasey, Brooke met her at the gate as she walked out of the arena on a loose rein. "Great job! What did the judge have to say?"

Kasey smiled. "He said there were a few minor mistakes, mostly on my transitions between maneuvers. He told me to relax and then things would come together."

"Well, you should be proud of yourself; that was huge. Let's take a short break and then we'll get you ready for the next pattern."

"It looked great to me." Tyler added.

Kasey ignored the comment. When they got back to the trailer Kasey was greeted by Lisa and the youth group. Her friends encouraged her and infused needed energy back into her body. Lisa pulled Kasey aside for a moment. "Well? How did it go?"

"I was really scared, but then I did what you said."

"And. . .?"

"The fear didn't go away, but I was able to work through it, just like you said."

Lisa smiled and gave Kasey a hug. "It'll get easier as you learn to keep your eyes on God. . . I'm so happy for you and proud of you too."

"Thanks, and thanks for coming. Knowing that my friends were here really helped too."

Kasey's nerves danced on edge while preparing for the next pattern, but they didn't rise to another panic attack. The second ride went slightly better than the first. Progress was being made. With Kasey done for the day Brooke and Tyler decided to watch Amber ride while Kasey took care of Scout. After watching Amber, they ran into Lisa, and Brooke stopped to chat. "Thanks for all your help. I think it made a big difference for Kasey."

Lisa gave a warm smile. "Anytime—She did great. It's so rewarding to see the kids put their faith into practice."

Twenty minutes later Brooke and Tyler arrived back to the trailer to see Kasey bolt out of the tack room with her face beet red. Brooke shot a quick look at Tyler and made a beeline for the trailer's tack room door. Inside she found that Kasey had not been alone. "Josh Sena, what's going on here?"

"Nothing Mrs. Anderson." He stammered.

Brooke looked at Kasey and then back at Josh. "There'd better not be anything going on here."

Brooke winked at Tyler as she shook her head and walked away.

CHAPTER

17

Should I have accepted Shane's invitation to the trail ride? Am I getting too close to the family? I still have a job to do here and they might be impacted. Tyler wrestled with competing facts, and feelings. *But the ranch is more than Brooke can handle. Whatever I do will be in her best interest.* Struggling, he tried to justify this personal excursion. *I can learn more about the region and the wilderness area by actually exploring it.* One thing was sure. He'd keep the conversation away from AA Land Company and its acquisition of properties. He didn't want to mislead Brooke and hoped he could keep the two agendas untangled. If and when the time came, any dealings with Brooke concerning her ranch, would be in her long-term best interests.

Tyler had dismissed any lingering thoughts about the trail ride by the time he arrived at the ranch just after 11:30. He found himself looking forward to spending time with Brooke. His work had kept him from being involved in a family activity for years. The office had consumed all of his time for as long as he could remember.

"Come on in, the door's open," Brooke called from the kitchen, where she was preparing lunch. "In the future, don't bother knocking. Just come in. All our friends do."

"Are you sure? That's unheard of in L.A. . ."

"You're not in L.A. anymore."

"That's for sure. Is there anything I can do to help with lunch?"

Shane charged into the kitchen. "Hi! Wanna see the Scout project I'm working on?"

Tyler looked at Brooke. "Is there time?"

"Sure, I'll get you when it's time to go."

Out in the equipment barn, Shane pointed at some pieces of cut wood. "This is for my second-class merit badge."

"Looks like you're just getting started. What's it going to be?"

"A birdhouse for the Northern Flicker that lives in the Kachina Wetlands. Four of us are building them."

Tyler examined the wood. "Okay—now I can see how the pieces will go together."

"Thanks, but it would look better if my Dad was helping me. The other boys are getting help from their dads. My Dad and I built Pinewood Derby cars together, and in the house is a bench we built."

"I'd like to see them." Tyler thought back to when his father helped him with woodworking projects. And at the same moment a small stab of pain hit him in the stomach. How many opportunities had he missed to do something like this with Ryan?

Shane's voice became higher. "You *would*?"

Tyler took a deep breath. "Sure."

"Can I show them to you when we get back from the trail ride?"

"Yes—I would like to see them." Tyler smiled and nodded.

Tyler's concern about the outing was a waste of his energy. He enjoyed the trail ride and successfully avoided any work-related topics. After the ride Brooke and Kasey fed the horses while Shane took Tyler to his room.

"You really do nice work. These projects look great."

"Thanks, my dad and I worked on them together."

Tyler looked at the wall above the race cars. "Are all these ribbons from the Pinewood Derby?"

"Only a couple—the rest are from horse shows and rodeo competitions." Shane grabbed a ribbon and a picture. "I won this ribbon for taking first place in the mutton busting contest. Here I am"—he pointed to his image inside the metal frame—"and that's my dad holding me up after I won."

Tyler felt the small stab of sadness again. Shane's dad had done a lot with him and been there for him. "Your dad must have really been proud of you." His own father had played and worked with him, guiding him towards manhood. *Where did I go wrong? How did I miss this with my own son?*

"Yeah, he was great." All at once Shane became unusually quiet.

"Everything okay Shane?"

"I guess. I was just thinking how all the other boys have their dads to help them. Mom tries, but she doesn't really know how to do this kind of stuff."

Tyler was at a loss for words. They both remained silent, looking at the derby cars. In a moment, Shane said, "You told me your dad taught you woodworking. Could you help me?"

Tyler was moved, and his first impulse was to say yes. *He's a good kid, and he needs an adult male in his life.* But then it got complicated. *I don't want to promise him something I can't deliver on. My job has*

always come first. I messed up with Ryan, and this kid is already hurt-
ing. He doesn't need someone stepping into his life and then bailing out.

"Let me talk to your mother."

Tyler found Brooke in the barn and explained Shane's request. "What do you think I should do?"

"If you're serious about wanting to help, but you're concerned about having enough time, be straight with Shane. Just tell him you can't guarantee you'll be able to give all the time he might want, but that you'll help when your schedule allows."

"Are you sure? I don't want to disappoint him."

"If he knows the ground rules up front, he should be fine."

As Tyler was getting ready to head home, he gave Shane his answer. The boy's eyes lit up. "That's great! When can we start? Can you stay for dinner?"

"I'd love to, but I have to go home and prepare for a meeting to-morrow." Shane pouted. "But," Tyler continued, "how about Thursday after my riding lesson?"

Shane's eyes brightened again. "Great!"

Not long after Tyler's vehicle vanished down the road, Ray parked his truck by the barn and went to the house. Inside he found Brooke. "Was that city guy here again? I thought I passed him when I turned off the main road."

"His name is Tyler, and he was here for a riding lesson."

Shane came into the kitchen. "Hey Ray."

"Hi Shane, what's new?"

"We went for a trail ride with Tyler, and he's going to help me with my Scouting project."

In another moment Shane had disappeared, and Ray started with the questions. "What's going on Brooke? It seems I'm seein' you with this guy more and more."

"Nothing's going on. We're just friends from church, and we're finding we have a lot in common."

"You've gotta be kiddin' me. *You and some guy from L.A. have a lot in common?* What do you really know about him anyway?"

"Ray, I told you before—who I choose for a friend really isn't any of your concern."

"You'd be right if Cory hadn't asked me to keep an eye on you and make sure you're taken care of."

"That was over two years ago—I appreciate your concern, but. . ."

"I'm only lookin' out for ya."

Brooke half-smiled. "Oh, Ray." The tension eased out of the room.

"I was in the area," Ray redirected the conversation, "and thought I would see if you had any chores that needed to be done."

Brooke thought for a moment. "No, we're in pretty good shape right now.—You want to stay for dinner?"

He grinned. "Sure."

The next morning Diablo was tacked up and standing in the hot walker. Brooke turned it on, nothing happened. She turned it off and then on again. Still nothing. A jolt of despair took hold. *Not another repair. This walker has to work. What am I going to do?* With the new mustang she needed all the time she could get for his training. He had to perform at his best, she couldn't waste time warming up and cooling down horses.

Two hours later, responding to her frantic phone call, Ray was staring at the hot walker rubbing his chin and pondering the situation. "Okay, it's not the breaker—let me get my voltmeter and make sure the motor is getting power."

For the next few minutes, Brooke paced as she watched Ray work his way from the control panel to the motor that drove the hot walker. He stopped at the motor. "I think I found it. There's a loose wire nut. It must have worked itself free somehow."

Brooke went to look. "Worked itself free?—How could that happen?"

Ray shrugged and focused on the motor. "Who knows. . . Okay, that should do it. Try turning it on."

Brooke flipped the switch. The motor hummed and the hot walker started moving. Her face relaxed into a smile. "Ray, thank you so much. I don't know what I would do without you."

Ray grinned. "See?—you need a guy who knows what he's doin' around this place."

Brooke gave Ray a quick hug. "Thanks Ray."

That evening at the dinner table, Brooke told the kids about the day's events. Shane looked baffled. "Mom, it was working yesterday afternoon when I showed Tyler how to run it."

"You showed Tyler how to run the hot walker?"

"Yeah, he was looking at it and asked me what it was for and how it worked."

Looking at it? Brooke forced the thought from her mind.

Two days later, Brooke was hosing off Scout when she sensed someone walking down the aisle-way. She shutoff the water to listen, and then called out. "Who's there?"

No one answered, she stepped away from the horse to look down the aisle. Hal Greer was peering into Diablo's stall. Dread washed over her which was immediately replaced by smoldering anger. She briskly walked toward Hal. *What's he doing here? I told him to stay off the property.*

"Mr. Greer," she barked at him. "Why are you here?"

Hal touched his fingers to the brim of his hat. "Good afternoon Ms. Anderson. The last time I was here I gave you something to think about. Have you come to a decision?"

Brooke became stiff as another flood of anger surged inside. She wanted to scream at him and chase him off the ranch, but she willed herself not to do so. "Mr. Greer, I thought I made myself clear the last time you came on my property. I have no intention of selling. Not to you or to anyone. Now, is that *perfectly* clear?"

Hal seemed unfazed by Brooke's response. "I understand you don't have any intention of selling. But your intention and the hard reality of your situation are not the same thing." He lit a cigarette and dropped the burning match onto a small pile of swept hay.

"What are you doing?" Brooke shouted. "This place could go up in flames." She stomped on the match and glared at Hal.

"Sorry." Antagonism hung on the word.

"Put out that cigarette. There's no smoking in this barn." Hal took another drag on the cigarette. "So, is this some kind of threat?" Brooke demanded, as she moved toward the large sliding door.

"I would never do that, Brooke. I'm looking out for your interests. I don't want you losing everything. It could all go up in smoke like that." Greer snapped his fingers.

Brooke sensed his real intent—to scare her. She opened the barn door. "Mr. Greer, I have plans in motion to save this ranch. So, whatever you're thinking, you might as well forget it. I'm telling you to leave this property—*my* property—and stay off it."

Hal stepped out of the barn, then he turned back to look at Brooke. He flicked an ash off his cigarette. She saw evil in his eyes. "You know, through eminent domain many a person has lost their property when they didn't want to sell."

Brooke raised her voice. "You need to leave—Now—Before I call the Sheriff."

"I'm leaving. Just remember, I did try to help you." He headed to his truck.

Brooke watched him go down her long driveway and turn onto the county road. Then she stepped inside the barn and slid the door back in place. Closed. To shut out Hal Greer—along with the tangle of pressures her life had become since Cory died.

She was shaking. If only she could go back to the simpler times before Cory died. But if she stopped for even a moment and let herself be alone with her thoughts for too long, it felt like everything was poised to crash in around her. All at once, the strain of the past two years, the losses and struggles to keep this place—her home and her children's home—all the pressures threatened to engulf her. Why did Hal Greer have to show up and remind her? Things had been starting to go so well.

Taking slow deep breaths to control her pulse, she went back to Scout who was waiting patiently. She was so furious with Hal and his smug attitude; she couldn't focus on Scout's bath. It would have to wait until later after she had calmed down. As the anger subsided, doubts and fear crept in. *What did he mean, he tried to help me? I thought they needed a compelling reason to use eminent domain. What reason could they have to take my home and my ranch?* Brooke hands were shaking as she led Scout back to his stall. A pressure grew behind her eyes, it stung—but she willed herself not to cry. *I'll call Tyler. He's an attorney.* And with that phone call, Tyler was on his way. It was the first time she didn't ask, *what would Cory do?*

Thirty-five minutes later Tyler was approaching Brooke's ranch. He had never heard her distraught and couldn't tell if she was angry or, was she that upset. All he knew was that she needed someone to talk to, and she had called *him*. He pushed that thought aside and focused on the immediate situation. It sounded like something was wrong on the property. There was danger in talking to her, but he was willing to take that risk. He found Brooke in the kitchen making a pot of coffee. "Are you okay?"

She turned toward Tyler; her face was streaked from tears. "I've settled down some. You should have seen me an hour ago."

"That bad?"

"I was furious."

"Why?"

"That horrible man, Hal Greer."

Tyler stopped dead in his tracks and swallowed deep. *What did I just get myself into?* He was there, and now he had to stick it out. At least he might learn more about what Hal is up to.

Brooke sat down at the table with Tyler and vented about the encounter. Tyler struggled to remain calm. Inwardly, he wanted to throttle Hal Greer for threatening Brooke and for abusing his position at the AA Land Company. But he had to keep his cover and avoid giving Brooke any legal advice. All the while the voice in his head was shouting at him. *Great job. You let yourself get too close. This was the situation you needed to avoid. Now what are you going to do?*

As Brooke finished, tears started to flow from her eyes. "What should I do?"

Tyler twirled the spoon in his coffee procrastinating as long as he could before he answered. "I'm not licensed to practice in Arizona; so, you really should talk to someone who's passed the bar here."

"I'm not asking you to represent me. I just want to know—can Hal

Greer and his company claim eminent domain, and can I do anything to keep him off my property?"

Anger churned inside as he thought about what Hal Greer had done. Tyler leaned back in his chair and struggled to remain calm has he calculated an answer that protected him and his company. *Give her generic advice that anyone can find on the web—stuff that doesn't impact the company.* She was staring at him, anticipating and wiping the tears from eyes. This woman who was battling to save her property. Where was the line? How had he let himself lose track of it? *Okay. Give her the information she needs to file a restraining order against Hal.* He could tell her where to find that on the web. AA Land Company could then use the restraining order as a pretense to get rid of Greer since he is becoming a liability. . . . *This could work.*

Tyler blew out a long breath and began. "Here's the deal. You can get a restraining order against Hal Greer on the basis that he has harassed you and you feel threatened. That should keep him off the property. I'll show you where to get the legal forms to file."

Brooke did not let it rest there. "What about his threats of taking my land through eminent domain?"

Tyler picked his way carefully through this minefield. "That's more difficult to answer. In the past, the government had to show it was in the best interest of the community to enact this provision of the law. However, there have been some recent cases where special interest groups have manipulated the system to use eminent domain for their personal gain. I'd have to know what's going on at all levels of the government and who may be influencing them in order to rule that out completely.—I just don't have that information."

When he finished, he smiled to himself for dodging another bullet, but at the same time, guilt gnawed at him. He was in no-man's land, not being fully truthful with this woman who trusted him as a friend.

Brooke had become calm for the moment, but her fears lingered. She took their empty coffee cups to the sink and then wiped her cheeks with the heel of her hand. "Maybe I can save this place, and maybe I can't. I know I have to keep trying." She shifted the conversation. "Since you're here and I need a diversion" she said as her composure returned, "I guess we could get started on your riding lesson."

Tyler nodded as he headed for the kitchen door. Brooke intercepted him and wrapped her arms around him. "Thanks, Tyler, for taking the time to talk with me and give me good advice. I don't know who else I can really trust to help me now."

Tyler did not know what to say or do; he wanted to step back—but Brooke held on. At the same time, he wanted to hold her and comfort her, but that felt wrong. Or at least not right. Uneasiness rested on Tyler, he was not being honest with her. She *trusted* him, and he was not being completely truthful with her.

The screen door banged open; they turned to see Kasey was home from school—with Shane behind her, wide-eyed and staring. Brooke's arms were still wrapped around Tyler.

"Mom—what are you doing?"

CHAPTER

It had been a month since Tyler was at the corporate offices; there was much for him to catch up on. He spent the morning in meetings with Barbara and her staff going over some of his old projects. His mind kept drifting to the upcoming meeting with Bob; he respected him and didn't want to be a disappointment. For the past few weeks, he'd been vague about his progress in Flagstaff, but the issues couldn't be sidestepped any longer; he'd have to give Bob all the details.

The working lunch at Bob's country club was over, and Tyler, dressed in a pale blue short-sleeved shirt, teed off at the first hole. Even though it was the rainy season in L.A., it was a beautiful partly sunny day. And then it began—another dance around a set of questions, except that Bob was relentless. As they followed their first shots, Bob launched in. "What's going on in Flagstaff?"

"I don't know yet... It's complicated."

"What do you mean it's complicated? You've been there for months. You should have some idea of what's going on by now."

They reached Tyler's ball, which lay on the edge of the fairway. "I have some ideas, but I can't substantiate them yet." Tyler planted his feet and swung his five-iron, sending his ball toward the green; it landed in the bunker in front of green.

"Good swing, but tough luck, Tyler." Bob smiled and started walking toward his ball. "Then tell me what you think—I need information."

"I've been checking the courthouse records, and many of the properties we're interested in have recently been purchased by the same group of individuals. After a lot of digging, it appears that most of them can be traced back to two dummy corporations. But I haven't been able to track down who owns them."

They reached Bob's ball in the middle of the fairway. He leaned against his seven-iron and looked at Tyler. "We need find out who's behind this without tipping our hand."

Bob swung—his ball landed on the green. "What about Hal Greer? Is he with us or against us?"

"My gut tells me he's against us. But I don't have any hard proof."

Bob let a few expletives fly before Tyler cut in, "I have an idea. We can put pressure on Hal without him knowing it's us. We can then use it as a pretense to fire him if we have to."

Bob looked confused. "What are you talking about?"

"That woman I told you about, Brooke. . . . Hal's been harassing her, and she's asked me for advice."

"I thought I told you to be careful."

"I've been. . . . This is the first time she's asked me for serious advice, and she's really helped me understand the community. Don't worry, I only pointed her to info she could find on the web. I kept it clean."

They started walking toward the green. "What do you propose?"

"That I use Brooke and have her get a restraining order against Hal. If need be, the restraining order can be the reason we fire him. He'll have no idea that we're on to him, so he'll be more likely to continue working with whoever is behind the operation."

"Will you be able to get her to do that without compromising your cover?"

The phrase, 'get her to'; there was that line again. Do you 'get' someone you care about to "do" things for you without them knowing you're pulling strings? What if pulling those strings helps them? "Yeah," he said. "I believe so."

Several holes later, Bob brought their conversation back to Flagstaff. "What's going on with the Forest Service discussions?"

"The Southwest Region is open to our proposal, but they have to vet the idea through headquarters."

"How much longer before we get some feedback?"

"We should have a preliminary response right after Thanksgiving."

"That's all well and good. But if we don't find out who's behind buying up those properties soon, we'll have too much money invested in this project to get out of it without some serious damage. Get some answers soon."

"I'll do my best."

"I don't need your best. I just need you to *do it*. Soon. We're starting to have similar problems on another project, and I don't want two messes on my hands."

The golf was over, and Tyler drove to Ryan's volleyball match with a voice pounding in his head. *Did I just say I was going to use Brooke? Am I doing it for her good—or for the good of the company?*

After fighting L.A. traffic, Tyler slid onto the lower row of bleachers at Ryan's volleyball match. If it hadn't been for the bumper-to-bumper mess on the freeway he would have arrived at the beginning instead at the end of play. As he took his seat, Ryan made eye contact with him. There was the usual look of frustration followed by mild disgust. Tyler knew that he had disappointed Ryan once again and wanted to make amends. His time with Shane made him long for something more with his own son. While watching the last few points he wondered how they could get past their rocky history. The match was over, and Tyler was waiting outside the locker room when Ryan came out. "Great match. You and the team looked great."

Ryan stared at him. "Oh really? How would you know? You only saw the last few minutes."

"Bob had me in a meeting."

"As usual—work comes first, right Dad?"

"I have responsibilities."

Ryan went silent, and Tyler changed the subject. "You've gotta be hungry. Let's get some dinner." Ryan nodded.

A short while later they were standing in line at Sal's Kosher Sandwich Shop, known for serving up the best hot pastrami sandwiches in L.A. . . . With their orders in hand, they found an outside table decorated for Christmas with colored lights wrapped around the umbrella. Hoping to break the ice, Tyler brought up the holidays. "So, Ryan—will we be getting together for Thanksgiving here in L.A. or in Flagstaff?"

Ryan studied his plate. "I'm spending Thanksgiving with Mom. Don't you remember?—She's getting married that weekend."

A knot formed in Tyler's gut. The impending marriage had been blocked out of his mind. He had forgotten how it would impact his Thanksgiving holiday with Ryan. But he rallied, he was not going to show how much he hurt. "Right. Then we'll get together for Christmas."

Ryan was less than enthusiastic. "We'll see."

The rest of the meal was just as awkward, with both men avoiding meaningful conversation. After dinner Tyler dropped Ryan off at his apartment. "Sorry about getting to the match late. Can I make it up to you?" Tyler opened his wallet and pulled out two one-hundred-dollar bills and pressed them into Ryan's hand.

"Dad!—I don't want your money. You can't buy me. You just don't get it." He threw the money on the passenger seat as he slipped out of the car. He slammed the door and headed into his apartment.

Tyler was dumbfounded for the second time that night. *How can I have the kind of relationship with Ryan that Shane had with his father?* Maybe it was too late for that.

Tyler was back in Flagstaff the next day and took care of a few business matters before he headed out to Brooke's for another riding lesson. He convinced himself that using Brooke to get rid of Hal was in her best interest. He rationalized that getting a restraining order against Hal couldn't hurt her. On the other hand, it seemed obvious that she really needed to downsize. The amount of work required to keep the ranch going was overwhelming. She couldn't possibly keep the ranch going as a single parent.

An hour later, Tyler was mounted on Cowboy, while Brooke stood in the middle of the arena. She held one end of a long rope attached to the horse's bridle. As Cowboy and Tyler went around her, she called out instructions. "Sit tall. . . Relax your lower back. . .Allow your hips to flow with the horse. . . That's it, now pick up the trot."

After a few circles of loping at the end of the lunge line, Brooke brought Cowboy back to a walk. "Are you starting to feel that when you relax and allow your body to move with the horse it gives you a much more comfortable ride?"

"Yeah. And you having control of the horse allows me to focus on getting the rhythm with Cowboy, which also makes it a lot easier."

"Are you ready to start again?"

"In a minute. I wish we had done this lesson before that long trail ride. I don't think my backside has fully recovered yet."

Brooke laughed. "There's no substitute for time in the saddle."

Tyler stood in the stirrups to get relief. "Thanks. I never realized how many muscles you use when riding. This is good exercise."

Brooke walked up alongside Cowboy. "As long as you're doing more than walking it's a great form of exercise."

Tyler sat back down in the saddle. "Have you given any more thought to what you want to do concerning Hal Greer?"

"No, I've kept that horrible man out of my mind."

"That won't keep him off your property."

Brooke looked down and kicked the dirt with her boot. "I know." She looked up at Tyler. "What should I do?"

"To start with, you can get that restraining order and keep him off your property, and away from you."

"I can't afford a lawyer to do that."

"You don't need one. You can do it yourself, and I can guide you."

Brooke's face brightened. "You're serious?"

"You bet."

Brooke's smile was broad. "If you weren't on Cowboy, I'd give you a big hug."

The riding lesson was over, and it was time to rehearse their duet. Brooke placed the music on the piano. "The Christmas concert will be here before we know it. I think we need to start focusing on our song." Brooke said. Tyler nodded as he sat down next to her on the piano bench.

In her room, Kasey put down the novel she was reading and listened to the voices in the other room. *That can't be Mom and Tyler. They sound really good together.* There were things she liked about him. . . Mainly that her mother smiled when he was around. But how could anyone replace her father? And Kasey noticed that Ray didn't trust him for some reason, which left her uneasy.

After Tyler and Brooke finished singing, he was getting ready to leave and pulled out his wallet. "That's $65 for the lesson, right?"

Brooke shook her head. "With the legal advice and help you're giving me, it's on the house."

"I can't accept that," Tyler protested.

Brooke smiled. "You'll have too." Her eyes showed determination.

"Okay then if you won't take the cash, I'll treat your family to dinner tonight."

Kasey and Shane, who had meandered into kitchen became active participants in the conversation. "That would be great Mom, can we?" Shane pleaded.

Kasey chimed in. "Mom, I'm tired of the same old things for dinner. A change would be nice."

Brooke was outnumbered. "Okay, this time." She then turned to Tyler and whispered through her smile. "That wasn't playing fair."

"I was taught to always get the jury on your side." They both laughed.

Tyler focused on Shane and Kasey. "Okay kids where do you want to go? Someplace fancy? Chinese? Italian, or something else?"

"Chinese?" Kasey urged.

Brooke looked at the three of them and everyone nodded in

agreement. Kasey whispered to Shane. "I guess there are some benefits to having Tyler around."

Tyler saw an opportunity while they waited for the kids to get ready. "I don't see how you do it. . . Get all the chores done around here, take care of the family, and run your business?"

Brooke slowly exhaled. "Quite often not everything gets done that needs to be worked on."

"Do you expect it to get better?"

"If I can get the mortgage caught up it will take some of the pressure off, but the responsibilities will remain the same."

Tyler pressed. "Is there anything I can do to help?"

"No, you're doing more than enough. But. . . ."

"But what?"

"I don't know. This place does get overwhelming."

Tyler was satisfied. *Next time mention that she would be better off with a smaller, more manageable property.*

The next day's training with Slider was going to be intense, with three training sessions planned. Brooke and Kasey were starting to feel more pressure; they had a little more than a month to go before the competition and Slider still had a tendency to be a bit willful. Brooke felt tentative about Slider's progress and was becoming uncomfortable with the lack of clarity she had about the performance direction. She knew some decisions had to be made about the routine—soon. But what direction should she go? They headed toward Slider's paddock in the brisk morning air under a cobalt blue sky, "It looks like a beautiful morning for training. Can you record my ride on him while I work on his flying lead change? I'd like to see how he looks—I know how he feels." Kasey pulled out her cell phone and got ready to record.

"Sure thing, Mom. But I've never seen you do lead changes on such a young horse before. Why with Slider?"

"We've got to push the limits if we're going to have a chance of winning this thing. With Slider's conformation, the lead change should come easy to him."

"Anything else you want me to do?"

"Later today I'd like you to take him through his groundwork. He likes doing that with you. He enjoys it so much that I think we may want to incorporate some of it into his performance."

Kasey's voice went up an octave. "Not with me showing him!"

"No, I'll show him after you help get him trained." Brooke gave a small sigh. *We've got such a long way to go before she'll be comfortable showing again.*

Just before lunch, Brooke was sitting with Kasey in front of the computer analyzing the video of her and Slider. Brooke pointed to the screen. "He's definitely balanced in his transitions. We should be able to put flying lead changes in his reining routine by the end of next month. The big question is, how testy is he going to be when this is no longer new and fun?"

"You're right, Mom. He does great the first couple of times we try something new. Then he seems to test you to find out if you are really serious about what you're asking of him."

Brooke shrugged. "There are worse quirks. We just have to figure out how to get him through that testy stage faster."

Kasey navigated to the Heritage Mustang Competition website where she and Brooke viewed some past winning performances. They noticed that all of the winners had some type of trick or gimmick. "You know, Mom, you've done a great job with the compulsory portion of his training and I would put him against any of the horses we've seen for that part of the competition. But we need something really special for the freestyle performance."

Brooke tilted her head. "I know... It has to be unique to us. But it hasn't come to me yet."

Kasey offered. "I've been playing with him and he's starting to do some basic tricks. I can push him to do more."

"Yes, I've seen you two playing and it's looking good. That'll be a great help."

Kasey studied the videos as Brooke stared out the window at the barns—then suddenly she turned back toward Kasey. "Reining is such a large part of our business. We have to be true to ourselves and keep that as part of our signature performance. But it needs something more; maybe we should try to see what he'll do bridle-less and with no saddle."

Kasey's eyes widened. "We could add bits and pieces of other disciplines, to show he's an all-around horse."

"Definitely! That's part of the reason for this competition, to showcase the versatility of the mustang."

"We could add a few jumps."

"That's a good idea, exactly the type of variety we need."

Kasey shook her head after watching several more performances. "It's amazing what they've done in 100 days." She turned and looked at Brooke while letting out a heavy breath. "At least we've been building on the basics that are needed to get there."

"You're right. Let's keep working with him. We'll revisit our progress on a daily basis until we completely figure out our final routine. You keep teaching him tricks. I know we'll need them."

And what they really needed was a great gimmick—which still seemed to elude them.

The recent intensity in Brooke's life had consumed all her time and she had not found the time to visit her mother. Guilt was planting its seeds in her mind that she wasn't being a good daughter. To lessen her regret, she adjusted her schedule and took the evening off to visit Alice at the nursing home. On the way there her cell phone rang; Brooke glanced at the incoming number. "Hi Amber."

"Can you talk?"

"Sure for a few minutes. We're on our way over to see my mom, and Kasey's driving."

"I was just checking to see if I can bring anything for Thanksgiving Dinner tomorrow?"

Brooke paused. "It would be great if you could pick up some wine and sparkling cider."

"For how many?"

"Four adults and two kids."

"Who'd you invite."

"You, Tyler, and Ray."

Amber's voice became sullen. "Oh, you didn't!"

"What do you mean?"

"Do I have to explain it to you? Two men who are attracted to you sitting at the same dinner table with you. It's a recipe for disaster." Amber was one to over exaggerate, but in this case—Brooke suddenly realized, Amber might have hit the mark.

She shifted in her seat. "I can't un-invite either of them. Any suggestions?"

"Prayer."

They pulled into the parking lot. "We're at the nursing home, and I've gotta go. We'll have to keep our fingers crossed about tomorrow."

Brooke bit her lip; her stress had now gone up another level. She'd have to be on her toes. *I love Ray like a brother, but sometimes he can be protective. How could I have been so blind?* The relaxing Thanksgiving with friends she'd planned might be anything but.

Her mother's small room was decorated for Christmas, and mementoes of Alice's past were prominently displayed on the wall. Brooke, Kasey, and Shane slipped off their jackets, and walked toward the elderly woman—who did not look up. She paged through an old scrapbook, fully engrossed. Brooke was surprised to see her mother looking at a book but recalled previous conversations with the nursing staff. One nurse had told her, "Dementia patients sometimes can have periods of lucidness and remember the past, or even on rare occasions be cognizant of the present."

"Hi, Alice," she greeted her mom, "what are you looking at?" Brooke was hopeful that her mother was having a good day and would remember them.

"A scrapbook of my trick riding days." Then her mother looked up, straight at them, there was no recognition in her eyes. "May I help you? Are you here to see me?"

Brooke's heart sank when it was clear that she and the kids were strangers to her mother. She forced a smile and was thankful that she was interacting. "Yes, we're here to visit you. I'm Brooke and this is Kasey and Shane." Brooke motioned to the kids and continued. "Can you tell us about what's in the book?"

Alice turned the scrapbook so everyone could see the pictures and the newspaper clippings. Kasey and Shane stepped forward, and in a moment their grandmother started to turn page after page, engrossed in the past, reciting story after story about her trick riding days.

As Alice turned one of the pages, Kasey's eyes widened. "You were in a bad accident?"

"Oh yes. It kept me from riding for quite some time."

Shane bent down to peer at the yellowed pictures. "What happened?"

"Well—I was doing a 'death drag' when my horse stumbled and went down."

Shane stared at her with amazement. "Wow, you did some cool stuff. Were you hurt bad? What's a 'death drag'?"

"It made the papers—as you can see here—and I was in the hospital for six weeks. . . . A 'death drag' is when you hang off the side of your horse by your legs, with your head only an inch or two from the ground."

Shane couldn't believe what he was hearing from Granny. "That sounds awesome. . . What'd you hurt?"

"I broke my leg, arm, and collar bone. I also had a concussion and was in a coma for six days."

Kasey's heart raced; she was caught up in a flashback of her own terrible accident. It was as if she was back on the street that night. There he was standing between the charging horses and her, looking at her just before the horses trampled him. . . . She shuddered. *What is it with our family? We seemed jinxed with bad accidents.*

Shane was completely taken in. "Did you ride again?

"Not for a long time. The doctors didn't want me on a horse again. They said it was too dangerous, especially if I had another concussion. They also said the damage to my leg would prevent me from ever doing trick riding again. But me and my friends, we had different ideas."

"Did you compete again?"

Alice smiled. "Not for over two years. It took me one whole year to get strong enough to ride. It took me almost another year until I was brave enough to do many of the tricks I used to do, especially the 'death drag'."

Kasey's need to know finally overpowered her reluctance. "How'd you get over being afraid?"

Alice looked at Kasey. "I didn't."

"Then how'd you ride?"

"That's when I became a Christian. I trusted God and rode in spite of my fear." Kasey was silent. "At first my fear almost paralyzed me, and I would get sick in the stomach before I rode. But when I became a Christian and learned that God has all things under his control, it made it easier for me to face my fear. I knew that whatever happened to me I would be where God wanted me, and he would use it for good. The more I rode the easier it got. . . I never completely lost my fear but with God's help I refused to let it control me."

Kasey remained still. *This is the second time I was told how God helped someone control their fear.* Then a small rush of doubt returned. *No. Granny is much stronger than I am. . . . I can't. I just can't.*

Alice closed the scrapbook. In another moment, her eyes clouded with a faraway look. She became quiet once again as she sat and stared out the window.

Thanksgiving morning arrived with a full list of tasks that still had to be done on the ranch. The horses had to be taken care of and Slider needed attention to keep his training moving forward. Amber's comment from the night before nagged at Brooke throughout her chores. *How could I have been so blind to miss Ray's attitude toward Tyler. All I wanted was to have my friends around me today. Why does everything have to be a challenge?*

As the morning progressed her mind drifted to Tyler. *I don't know why his coming around here is such a big deal. There's nothing between us but friendship.* Deep in her heart she knew something different—the feeling she had tried to ignore but could not shake.

Amber arrived early to help with the dinner preparations. She was slicing bananas for the fruit salad when she looked toward Brooke. "Did the loan officer call you this week?"

"Yes, he wants to meet with me next week to review my file. It seems someone told him about the progress I've made on maintaining the ranch and that the church pitched-in to fix the roof... Who could have given him that information?" Brooke flashed a grin at Amber.

Amber shrugged. "I don't know who it could be."

"Really?"

"Well—are you ready for the meeting?"

"Just about. I'll finish the paperwork over the weekend."

A short while later, Ray moseyed into the kitchen. "Hey ladies, I'm a bit early, is there anything you need me to do?"

"We're good in here. Why don't you watch some football with Shane? He's in the family room."

"I never really liked that game, but I'll keep Shane company for a bit. Holler if you need me."

As Ray left the kitchen, Amber complimented him. "Ray, you look nice today."

"Thanks Amber, so do you."

Brooke relaxed a little. They're trying to be nice to each other. . . *Maybe it's a good omen for the rest of the day.*

After his fourth visit to the kitchen, Amber whispered in a low voice, "Can't you think of some chore for him to do to keep him busy for the rest of the afternoon? He's driving me crazy."

"It's not that bad."

Amber stared at Brooke. "Not that bad—yet. Just you wait. It's gonna get really interesting."

They heard the back door open, and Tyler walked into the kitchen. Amber raised her eyebrows and glanced at Brooke again. "Here we go."

Tyler looked at Brooke. "Did I just miss something?"

Brooke shook her head. "No, just something that's happening in Amber's imagination."

They chased Tyler out of the kitchen and into the family room— just in time for him to hear a huge roar from the television. "What happened? What's the score?"

Shane jumped up from the sofa. "Hi, Tyler. Do ya wanna watch some football with us? It's the second quarter, and the Cowboys are walloping the Lions 21-3. They just scored again."

Ray looked away from the TV and stared at Tyler. "You here for dinner?"

"Brooke was kind enough to invite me. She said she didn't want me having Thanksgiving dinner at a restaurant."

"Oh." Ray returned his focus back at the screen.

Halftime came, and Shane was on his feet. "Tyler if we have enough time before dinner can you help me with my Scout project?"

"Sure, if your mom says it's okay."

Out at the barn, Shane picked up two pieces of wood and showed them to Tyler. "Do you have any ideas on how I can get the pieces together?"

Tyler carefully studied the wooden parts of the birdhouse spread across the workbench. "There's a trick my Dad showed me." Tyler stood three of the sides in formation, using some extra pieces of wood as braces. "There, you should be able to do this again, but with some glue at the joints and then add a few nails to help hold it together."

"That was slick. I'll try it after dinner. . . . Can you come and watch and make sure I'm doing it right?"

"I'd be happy to."

While Tyler and Shane were at the barn, Ray stalked into the kitchen. "You didn't say anything about that dude coming for dinner. . . ."

"I didn't think it was important."

"*You didn't think it was important?* Haven't I been telling you to be careful around him? You don't know much about this dude."

"Well, this is an opportunity to learn more. . . Ray, go get cleaned up. Then come back here and help us get dinner on the table."

The dining room was decorated for Thanksgiving with autumn colors in the tablecloth. To make room for the dinner, Brooke had moved the cornucopia center piece to the buffet, next to the "Tree of Thanksgiving." The tree was constructed from an Aspen branch, with prayers of thankfulness written on its paper leaves.

With everyone at the dinner table, Brooke asked each person to say something they were thankful for; she asked Tyler to go last and then give the dinner blessing. They all bowed their heads, except Ray who kept his eyes focused on Tyler. The meal was cordial enough, with small talk being the main topic. By the end, however, Ray's questions started to get more pointed.

"So, Tyler—who do you work for?"

"I'm not at liberty to say."

"Why's that?"

"I can't say."

"Well then, what kind of lawyer are you?"

Something about Ray irritated Tyler and he was not going to give him any satisfaction. "A good one." Amber choked back a laugh. Dread descended upon Brooke; what Amber had warned her about seemed to be starting.

Ray's ears turned pink. "So, do you represent banks or corporations?"

"Really that's a private matter. Attorney client privilege you know."

Ray changed directions. "Did you grow up in L.A. or someplace else?"

Tyler was still was not going to give Ray any meaningful answers. "Someplace else."

"Where'd you go to college?"

I've already let people at church know where I went to college, but I'll continue to play with this guy, something about him rubs me the wrong way. "In California."

Ray voice got louder. "Where in California?"

Ask me vague questions and I'll give you vague answers. "Southern California."

Brooke felt the peaceful dinner spiraling out of control, she had enough and stepped in. "Why don't you men let us clear the table? Tyler, can you help Shane with that trick you showed him for putting his project together? Then in an hour we'll have dessert."

Brooke paused for a moment, she needed to come up with something for Ray to do. "Ray, can you take a look at Slider's feet and give me your opinion if he should get shoes? Kasey will give you a hand." Kasey didn't say a word but looked at her mother and rolled her eyes.

Once everyone had left the house and the disaster averted, Brooke took a much-needed rest and slumped into a chair; Amber sat next to her.

"I'm impressed. You handled that situation like a pro."

"Yeah, but I wished I'd talked to you earlier. I might have avoided the whole situation. It really got stressful, didn't it?"

Amber gave a small laugh. "True, but it was kind of fun watching Tyler play with Ray."

"Amber!" Brooke paused and thought back to dinner as a half-smile passed across her face.

Everyone had gathered back at the table for dessert. Brooke took great care to steer the conversation away from Tyler. "So Ray, what do you think of Slider's feet?"

"You're gonna want to put shoes on him soon."

After that, it was clear that Brooke was keeping the conversation focused on Ray and horses and preventing Ray from trying to grill Tyler. At the conclusion of dessert, Tyler pushed away from the table. His presence had caused tension at Brooke's holiday dinner. Excusing himself was the best solution, but deep inside he really wanted to stay.

"Brooke, it's been a terrific meal and I enjoyed everyone's company. But I have some holiday phone calls to make. So, I'll head back to my apartment." Tyler walked to the kitchen door and Brooke followed.

She regretted that they'd never had even a moment alone. "I'm so glad you were able to make it. . . Duet practice tomorrow?"

"Definitely, we still need it. What time works for you?"

"Why not late afternoon? Then you can stay for leftovers."

Tyler grinned. "I'd love to. . . ." His eyes went to Shane who had followed them. "Shane, we can work on the next birdhouse then."

Later that evening after Amber left, Ray lingered around the kitchen as Brooke put away the last of the dishes. "Did you see what I've been telling you? You don't know nothing about this dude. And did you notice how evasive he was every time I asked a direct question?"

Ray hit a nerve, but Brooke held a calm façade. *Doesn't he realize that Tyler was just playing with him.* "Ray your behavior today was totally inappropriate."

"What do you mean? I think those questions were fine."

"It was the tone you used and your body language. They conveyed a lot more than the questions. That, and the way you kept after him. Didn't you see how uncomfortable you made everyone? Especially *me*?"

"But that dude is hiding something from you."

"Not everyone can tell everything about their job."

Frustration rose in Ray's voice. "You don't believe me. . . . I'll show you."

While sitting in bed, Brooke's thoughts circled around Tyler. Ray's words had hit their mark. *I really* don't *know very much about him. And he definitely doesn't offer much information about himself.* But he had become such a good friend. And Shane had warmed up to him. She pushed Ray's words from her mind.

Brooke left the loan office lighthearted and smiling but at the same time bewildered. Her grin was still ear to ear when she stopped at Amber's desk, "What a roller coaster of a week this has been. The stressful Thanksgiving Dinner with Tyler and Ray, then the hot water heater broke on Friday, and now this!"

"Don't keep me in suspense, tell me what happened in your meeting."

"They're going to re-work my loan."

"Why? How? Tell me the details?"

"Slow down Amber—I have to get going, but here are the quick highlights. It seems some respected members of the community vouched for me at the bank. They won't start foreclosure right now. And they are giving me until January 15th to start making my mortgage payments in full. They are then giving me until June 15th to get caught up on my payments. However, there is one catch. If I don't make every payment in full, they will start the foreclosure process immediately.

"That's great girl, it buys you some time and gives you a chance."

Tyler hadn't been Christmas tree shopping for years; the scent of freshly cut evergreens lined up in precise rows; it was going to be fun. Tyler was glad Shane had asked him to join them on the excursion. The fresh snow from the night before added to his anticipation for the journey. As he drove to Brooke's he wished Bob hadn't ordered him to work undercover. He knew Brooke could be trusted and regretted not being able to tell her the real reason he was in Flagstaff. *Maybe I should just tell her. But when?*

Tyler arrived at the ranch and found no one in the house. He headed to the barn where Cowboy was already saddled, and everyone was tacking up their horses. Tyler looked at Brooke. "I thought we were going to get a Christmas tree. Why's everyone getting ready for a ride?"

Brooke smiled. "We are going for a tree. We just do it differently here."

"What do you mean? I thought we'd take your truck and put it in the bed."

Shane stepped out from a stall. "We go out to find the tree on horseback and then drag it home."

Brooke's eyes were bright. "This is an Anderson family tradition. We go out to the forest and find a lonely pine which we cut down and bring home. We've been doing it since the kids were little."

A half-hour later, they were walking their horses single file through the fresh snow. The air was still, the only sounds were the muffled hoof steps plodding though the white powder and the heavy breathing of the horses as jets of steam shot from their nostrils. Tyler called to Brooke. "What kind of tree are you looking for?"

"A tree with lots of imperfections."

"Did I hear you right? You're looking for imperfection?"

"Yes, and you'll find out why." Tyler shook his head. *She does surprise me.*

A mile into the ride, Shane yelled from his position behind Tyler. "Mom, I see one over to the left."

Brooke rode closer to examine the seven-foot-tall pine. Everyone got off their horses and inspected the tree. Kasey put her hands on her hips as she stood next to her mother. "I think it can work. We've had worse looking trees and few that looked better."

Shane joined in. "Can I cut it down?"

Brooke looked at Tyler. "What do you think of our tree? Give us your honest opinion."

Tyler studied the tree. *This is a really pathetic looking tree. I don't want to offend them if they think it is the right tree for them.* "Well, it's a good height. It's green." *But it's so scraggly.* Tyler walked around the tree again. "It's got room for decorations." He struggled to find more positive things to say. "The needles look nice, and there won't be a lot to clean up when they start falling off."

Brooke and the kids fidgeted while watching, biting their lips to keep from laughing. Finally, Brooke rescued him. "Would you find it on a Christmas tree lot in L.A.?"

Tyler hesitated a moment. "I don't think so."

Brooke smiled. "Then it's perfect, let's cut it down and drag it home."

Tyler looked baffled, then Brooke came alongside of him. "You'll understand—soon."

Tyler held the tree steady while Shane cut it down with a bow saw. He then demonstrated his Scouting knots to Tyler as he tied a rope to the tree using a clove-hitch and handed the other end to his mother. Kasey led the way home, followed by Brooke with Shane and Tyler bringing up the rear. For most of the trip home, Shane told Tyler about many other Christmas tree hunting expeditions. Tyler started to appreciate all the memories that this ranch held for Brooke and her kids.

Back at the ranch they put the horses in their stalls and gathered around the tree. Brooke explained that she had to get a few things ready before the tree could come into the house. Then Shane threw a snowball at Kasey but hit his mom. She dusted the snow off her coat and bent down, grabbed a large handful of snow as she formed it into a firm ball. She zeroed-in on Shane and threw the frozen ball as he took cover behind Tyler—which meant, she hit Tyler squarely in the stomach.

Tyler grinned and looked at Shane. "Does this mean war? The guys against the girls?"

Shane nodded and laughed. "Yeah!"

They both grabbed handfuls of snow. Tyler hurled a snowball at Brooke, while Shane aimed at Kasey. The girls took cover behind the truck, while the boys hid behind a lone ponderosa pine.

Tyler let Shane command their team. "What should I do? We don't get a lot of snow in L.A. . ."

"Make lots of snowballs and stack them next to the tree. We want plenty of ammunition."

The skirmish took off in earnest, with only a few direct hits being scored by either side. As Shane and Tyler replenished their snowball supply, Tyler paused and looked at Shane. "How badly do we want to win this war?"

Shane grinned. "I don't know. I'm just having fun fighting it."

"If we want a nice dinner and good time putting up the tree, we may want to make this fight a draw or even consider losing the war."

"You've never fought my Mom or sister before. They. . . ."

At that moment, Brooke and Kasey launched a surprise attack on the boys, charging their stronghold, destroying their arsenal, and pelting them with snowballs.

Shane shouted. "We surrender!" Then fell back into the snow and played wounded.

Tyler was taken captive by the women who gathered their prisoners and told them to get the tree into the house. Brooke started laughing. "You've never been in an Anderson snowball fight."

"Yeah, the girls cheat," Shane insisted. "They don't stay over on their side."

Kasey teased. *"Who won?"*

The tree was set up in the family room with boxes of decorations scattered around the floor. Brooke sat next to Tyler as she started to go through the boxes. As Brooke carefully retrieved the ornaments, she had to push back the melancholy that was trying to invade her Christmas. She explained the history behind each decoration as the kids put them on the tree. By the time most of the decorations were in place, Tyler started to understand how the ranch, Cory, and the family were intertwined.

Brooke looked at the tree and then at Tyler. "Do you notice anything about the tree?"

'I sure do. It looks fantastic."

Brooke smiled. "Remember how forlorn this tree looked? We picked this tree to remind us how God has taken us who are broken and hurting and undeserving of his grace. It reminds us if we believe in Him, He will in His time cover our bodies with fine clothes worthy of a king and then bring us into his presence." Tyler nodded.

The kids had gone off to do their chores, and Brooke turned to Tyler. "Can you help me put the star on the tree." Tyler steadied the small ladder as she stretched to set the star in its place. Brooke came down the ladder and misstepped; Tyler instinctively reached out to steady her as she jumped to the ground. She landed in his arms, her face inches from his.

Tyler looked gently into her eyes, the impulse to move closer grew. But something inside stopped him. *What am I doing? Is this the right time and place to get involved with someone—especially Brooke?* Brooke's emotions surged, along with confusion. Warmth embraced her as he held her secure in his arms, their eyes remained fixed on each other. *Is this moving too fast? He's from a different world. But somehow it feels right.* She waited for Tyler.

Leaning forward Tyler succumbed to the power that drew him in and gently kissed Brooke. She kissed him back. And then reality surfaced, they stepped back from each other. Brooke blushed and moved further away. "Kasey and Shane could come in here at any time."

Tyler picked up the ladder. "I'm sorry if. . . ."

"Don't be."

Later that evening as Tyler was leaving, he whispered to Brooke. "Shane asked me to come with the family and watch him in the Christmas Parade next weekend. Is that okay with you?"

"Sure, it would be great."

He put on his gloves. "I wasn't sure how Kasey would take it—if I'm there—the Christmas Parade and all. . ."

"She'll be fine."

Brooke and Kasey had just finished the afternoon session with Slider and were walking back to the barn. The sun's angle had dropped, and Brooke shivered as the temperature fell. As she put on her winter coat, she asked Kasey. "Could you please help me for a little bit longer and video a couple of the roll-backs I'll be doing with Diablo?"

"Sure, Mom."

Brooke moved with a spring in her step for the first time in months, maybe years. Since the meeting with Ramos at the bank, she was confident about her chances to save the ranch. Even if she didn't win the mustang competition the ranch wasn't lost. It was as though a heavy burden had been lifted from her shoulders. Her life had finally turned the corner. . .

She hoisted the saddle onto Diablo. "Kasey, it was your week to inspect the tack. Is there anything we need to take care of? I'll be going past Jake's tomorrow, and can drop off anything that needs to be worked on."

"Everything looked fine.—Remember, we have some training boots that need to be repaired."

Twenty minutes later Diablo was warmed up and Brooke was ready to start the sliding stops and rollbacks. Kasey strategically positioned herself where the judge would sit, so the camera would capture the judge's view. Kasey called out. "Okay, Mom, I'm all set up here."

"I'll start slow and controlled, then work up to doing it full speed." Brooke called back.

The first two sliding stops and rollbacks were done with precision. Diablo stayed straight as she slid and remained square while coming to a complete halt, he then pivoted 180 degrees on his inside hind leg while keeping it planted.

"Okay, I'm going to increase the speed." Brooke started the lope along the rail and turned to go down the center of the arena as she picked up more speed. Two-thirds of the way down the middle she and Diablo executed a proper maneuver.

"It looks great Mom."

Brooke rode over to Kasey and took off her winter jacket. "Can you hang this on the rail? Now that I'm working, I've gotten too warm—I'm going to do two more. This next one I'll try to get a little more distance with the slide and try to keep his shoulder from falling in during the roll back."

"Okay, I'll get it recorded."

Brooke picked up speed along the outside rail and headed down the middle, this time faster than before. They started their sliding stop at the designated spot and had an exceptional slide which immediately went into the rollback, then Brooke's and Kasey's lives changed forever. Diablo executed the rollback flawlessly, but Brooke and the saddle did not stay with him; he turned left but Brooke and the saddle went straight.

What's happening? I'm falling . . . Everything went black as Brooke's head hit the ground—hard. She landed on her side with her shoulder taking the brunt of the impact. She slid ten feet before lying motionless on the ground. Kasey stood frozen next to her camera. Images of her dad trying to wave off the chuck wagon returned. *No, not Mom, too. This can't be happening.* She bolted toward her mother as fast as she could run. "*Mom, Mom . . . are you alright?*" There was no reply. Her stomach churned and her mouth went dry as she ran to Brooke and knelt down by her side. She yelled at her mother half in fear and half in anger.

"*Mom, Mom—wake up, talk to me!*"

Her mother could not be doing this to her. God could not be doing this to her. Not another parent. Sobbing uncontrollably, she called 911.

CHAPTER

A mber rushed into the waiting room at the trauma center to
find Kasey pacing the floor next to a montage of Santa and
his eight reindeer. Shane sat next to an artificial Christmas tree, focused on the TV that was mounted high on the wall. "Where's your
mother? How serious is she? What happened? When can we see her?"
She finally took a breath.

"She's in x-ray." Kasey's eyes were bloodshot, and her face was
pale and strained. "She hit her head really hard when she came off.
They think she has a concussion and maybe some broken bones. At
least she's conscious now and talking a little. It's. . . ." Kasey's eyes
filled with tears.

"It's what?

"It's all my fault."

"What do you mean?"

"The saddle broke, and it was my week to inspect the equipment. I must have missed something."

"You don't know that."

"Yes, I do! I saw it. The broken latigo on the saddle. It's my fault."

Amber put her arm around Kasey. "It could have been fine when you checked it—And I'm sure your mom is going to be all right."

They sat down in the corner of an almost empty waiting room. Kasey cradled her forehead in her hands. "What are we going to do? What's Mom going to do? How's the ranch going to keep going? Mom's not going to be able work." She paused and wiped her eyes. *"What about the mustang?"*

"Don't worry about those things right now. Let's see what the doctors have to say. The good Lord will take care of everything."

A half-hour later, Ray burst into the trauma center. He fixed his eyes on Kasey. "Is she going to be all right? What happened?"

Amber put her hand on Kasey's shoulder and stepped forward to shield her from Ray's angst. "Calm down, Ray. She's in x-ray, and we'll know more shortly."

By the time Ray had settled down a nurse motioned for them to follow her. Inside the sterile examination room, they found Brooke lying on a gurney and connected to an IV and several monitors. A doctor followed them into the room as he read the radiology report. He took off his glasses and looked at Brooke. "You've banged yourself up quite a bit."

She opened her eyes and struggled to focus. "How bad is it?" She fought to keep her eyes open.

The doctor repositioned a monitor and pointed to her radiology images with his pen. "You've got a cracked rib and a fractured collarbone." He then pointed to another image. "Here you can see a greenstick fracture of your left radius." Moving to the last set of images he continued. "There's no skull fracture, but it is too soon to know if there is any swelling of your brain. Based on how your eyes are reacting and that you were unconscious for several minutes, we need to keep you here at least overnight for observation."

Brooke went paler than she already was. "How long 'till I can work and ride again?"

The doctor turned towards her. "Once your arm is in a cast, you'll be able to do a lot of your activities after about a week. That's not the case with the rib and collarbone. They'll slow you down for a bit longer. With the broken collarbone, I don't want you driving for six to eight weeks, and no heavy lifting for twelve to sixteen weeks. Otherwise, you could re-injure the break and have to start the healing process all over again. The discomfort from your rib will give a good indication of what you can and can't do."

Brooke was stoic. "Do I *have* to stay here overnight? How much will that cost?"

"I don't know what they charge, but I highly recommend you stay. If swelling starts inside your cranium it can get serious pretty fast, and it's not wise to put the responsibility of monitoring you on someone who's not trained," he looked at Kasey and Shane.

Brooke bit her lower lip. "Okay."

Forty minutes later the group had migrated to Brooke's new location in the general-care ward. Kasey and Shane were silent, Ray seemed restless and uncomfortable. "Brooke I've never liked hospitals. So, I'll head over to your place and get started on the evening chores."

"Thanks, Ray. Amber's here with me, plus the pain medication has me tired. I won't be good company. . . I appreciate your help." Then she looked at Kasey and Shane. "Why don't you two head home, get something to eat, and help Ray with the chores? After you get your homework done, give me a call or come back here if there's time."

Amber moved closer to her bed. "I'll stay here with you, then I'll head over to the ranch to spend the night with them."

When Ray, Kasey, and Shane were gone, Amber placed her hand on Brooke's arm. "Brooke, everything's going to be okay."

"Right. I'm a mess, I can't work, and you say everything's going to be 'okay. *Sure,* it is." Sarcasm hung on each word.

"Brooke, listen to me. . . ." But she didn't want to hear anything. Was it the grim reality of the situation, exhaustion, or the effect of the drugs? In fact, her future was bleaker than ever.

"I can't talk about it anymore; I can't even think about it." She gave her friend's hand a weak squeeze. "Thanks for staying with the kids."

"Is there anything else I can do?"

Brooke paused. "If the kids come back here, can you send my cell phone with them? Also, can you let Tyler know where I am." Brooke ached to hear Tyler's voice and feel the comfort of his presence.

"Sure, and I'll also get you on the church prayer chain."

"Thanks." *Like that will do any good. They've prayed for me and the ranch for two years and has it made any difference?*

After the kids' second visit, the initial shock from the trauma had started to wear off, and a blanket of exhaustion descended. Brooke was just starting to doze off when her phone rang. "Hello," her voice was weak and hoarse.

"Is. . .Brooke Anderson there?"

"Yes, this is Brooke."

Tyler didn't recognize her voice, and when he did, dismay descended upon his heart. *This can't be Brooke. Amber said she was just banged up a bit. How bad is she really?* "This is Tyler. I hear you gave everyone a scare today."

Brooke's voice and spirits picked up a little. "Not really, just a fall from Diablo. Everyone is just being really cautious."

"What happened?"

"I don't know. The last thing I remember is we were doing a sliding stop and roll back, next thing I remember is, I was on the ground with Kasey next to me."

"You were *unconscious*?" Tyler hated that he couldn't be with Brooke, he was concerned that she was hiding the severity of her injuries.

"Only for a little bit."

"Brooke, I really want to be with you, but I'm out of town and I can't get back until tomorrow evening. I'll try to catch an earlier flight."

"Don't worry about it. I'll be fine. Your call brightened my evening. . . . Anyway, I'm really tired, and I'm supposed to rest. Why don't you call me tomorrow when I have a little more energy?" After the call, Brooke settled back into the pillows and closed her eyes. She softly pressed her lips together and a tired smile appeared. *He called. I hope I'll see him tomorrow.* She was too tired and groggy from the pain medication to worry much about the ranch.

On the way home from school Kasey replayed her mother's accident over and over again in her mind, examining every detail as if she were studying the video she recorded. Shane jolted her back to the reality. "Hey, watch out for that car." He yelled.

"Mind your own business. I saw the car." She snapped back. But did she see the car while she was deep in thought?

"Hey, who's going to train Slider now that Mom is busted up?" Shane asked.

"Mom is not busted up." She wanted to believe that. But in fact, Brooke was injured– and as that reality was taking hold, Shane's comment shoved another ugly fact in her face. Someone had to train Slider. A vice tightened in her stomach at that realization. *What am I going to do? If Mom can't work for a while, how is she going to make the mortgage payment. . . . She needs Slider to win the competition. How is she going to do that now?* There was only one way for Slider to win the competition, which landed on Kasey like a lead weight. She needed to talk to someone, a confidant, someone who would give her sound advice.

At that moment, Shane yelled, "Hey! This isn't the way home. Where are you going?"

"Aunt Martha's. And if you say anything to Mom, I'll tell her it was your idea."

Martha was ecstatic to see them. "What are you two doing here? I'm so glad to see you. Does your mother know you're here?"

Kasey dropped eye-contact. "Let's not go there."

Martha pursed her lips. "That's what I thought. Well, I heard through the church prayer chain that you mother was in an accident yesterday. How's she doing?"

"She has a concussion and a couple broken bones. She'll be off the horses for at least six to eight weeks."

"How's she handling it?"

"Not well. And I don't think it's completely sunk in yet."

Shane interrupted. "Where's Uncle Slim?"

"He's out doing some maintenance on the wagon. Why don't you go out and say hi?"

As soon as he had banged his way out the back door, Martha got back to her questions.

"So, what brings you here?"

"The accident and the mustang. I need some advice."

Kasey proceeded to pour out her heart to Martha—about how she inspected the tack and that she was responsible for the accident. She explained how Slider was her mom's best hope for saving the ranch and she's ruined that chance. "The only way out is for me to compete on Slider, and I'm too scared to try."

Martha sat quietly stroking Kasey's hand. After several minutes of silence, she spoke. "If you inspected the tack as thoroughly as you said, there's no way the accident can be your fault. If there was a problem with the leather that was not visible to the eye, you can't hold yourself responsible. With that being said, you can't take on the responsibility of saving the ranch. You can help, but it's not your obligation. We've had a similar conversation before—right?"

"Yeah."

"Who's got everything under control?"

"God."

"And what are we supposed to do?"

"Seek his direction and learn and grow from every situation."

"That's right. . . I can't tell you what to do, but I can help you seek God. I'll be praying extra hard for you."

"Thanks, Aunt Martha."

Tyler landed at the airport and rushed to the ranch. He focused on one thing, Brooke. *She's been teetering on the brink of financial insolvency. How is she going to pay the bills when she can't ride? With all the chores to do and the number of horses to ride—it was too much for her before. The best thing for her to do is down-size and get herself on a firm financial footing, and then move forward.*

By the time he turned down the road to Brooke's ranch, he had convinced himself beyond a shadow of a doubt that downsizing was exactly what she needed to do. What he hadn't figured out was the best way and time to broach the subject. He entered the kitchen to find Kasey cleaning up. She motioned to the family room where her mother was resting. *Does he always have to be here? Mom needs her rest; she doesn't need him coming by and disturbing her.*

Tyler was determined to raise Brooke's spirits. He found her resting in the recliner and shot her a half-grin. "I know you've wanted to find a way to take a vacation, but isn't this carrying things a little too far?" Tyler was taken back by what he saw when she turned towards him. Brooke's lined face revealed her exhaustion and how deeply she was hurting. The black eye only made the picture worse. He wanted to take her in his arms and comfort her, but with Kasey in the next room he resisted the urge.

Her heart beat a little faster at the sound of Tyler's voice then she gave a tired smile. "Don't knock it until you've tried it." She longed for his warm embrace but knew it was not the place.

Tyler sat on the sofa next to Brooke's recliner as she described the events of the past couple of days. The conversation moved to the ranch and how it would operate for the next couple of months. "The fact is I don't know how I'm going to do it." Defeat rang in her words. "I was barely able to meet the conditions of the bank when I was able to work. Now what am I going to do?"

Tyler simply nodded as he struggled to compartmentalize his thoughts and feelings. Was this the right time to bring up downsizing, or did she simply need comforting?

"Maybe I should just give up and sell before the bank does the inevitable and forecloses. What other options do I have?" She let out a deep sigh that matched her mood.

Tyler could not let the opportunity pass and transitioned into lawyer mode. "You're probably right. It would be better *not* to have a foreclosure on your record when you try to put things back together." Where was this coming from? Wanting to do the best for her, or wanting to do what was best for the company? He shook off the guilt. *She's in bad financial straits after all. I'll do my best to get her a good price for the property.*

Brooke was not consoled, not in the least. She sank deeper into her recliner. She wanted to sink out of sight. While she knew the reality of the situation, deep down inside she longed for encouragement and hope not sound legal advice. Tyler saw the effect of his words, and backpedaled. "But maybe there's something else that can be done. I was just thinking out loud. Why don't you get some rest? I'll check on you tomorrow and we'll talk some more." Brooke nodded; her face was ashen. Her hope was almost gone.

Tyler's and Ray's eyes locked as they passed each other on Brooke's driveway. In a moment, Ray was inside, sitting next to Brooke. "What was that guy doing here?"

"Ray, I'm too tired for this."

"I'm just trying to look out for you.—You're not always a good judge of people. Remember that hand you hired a couple of years ago. He stole a couple hundred dollars of tack from y'all before Cory fired him." Brooke slowly shook her head.

"There's something about that guy I just don't trust."

Brooke stiffened slightly. "He goes to church. And yes, he's a bit private about his work, but that goes with being an attorney."

"I know a lot of people who go to church who I would not trust any further than I can throw a horse."

"Ray, I appreciate your concern, but we're just friends and he's also a client. I can take care of myself."

"Okay, but you be careful." He stood up. "I'm gonna check on the horses. Is there anything else you need me to do before I head on home?"

"No, I think we're good for the rest of the evening. Thanks again for your help."

"That's what I'm here for. You take care and get some rest."

Brooke moved slowly the next morning, she had a lot more aches and pains than the previous day. The pain medication provided some relief but left her groggy, a feeling that made her uncomfortable. The saddle failure kept infiltrating her mind. Wanting to put those thoughts to rest she went to inspect the tack; she had to make sure nothing else was about to break and injure Kasey. Inside the tack room her saddle was where Ray had set it—sitting on a rack in the middle of the room. She closely examined the saddle. *I just don't understand how the latigo could have failed. We inspect the critical pieces of equipment every single week.* She ran her hand from the cantle to the horn, where the broken piece of the latigo still hung attached to the cinch. Turning it in her fingers, she looked at every detail. Then she froze. Her heartbeat faster as she clenched her teeth, and her face turned red. Her aches and pains had disappeared. The outside of the latigo had broken, but the inside—the leather against to the front rigging dee, looked like it had been cut almost the whole way through. *This was no accident. My saddle was sabotaged.* There's no way that Kasey would have found this during a routine saddle inspection. She would have had to take apart the saddle to find this. And even then, only if she was looking for it. *Who could have done this?—Hal Greer.*

Brooke called Tyler. "Call the police. I'll be there as fast as possible." Was Tyler's immediate response.

A sheriff's deputy was there by the time Tyler arrived. And while Brooke explained to them what she had found, a detective arrived. "I'm Damon Lopez from the Investigative Unit of the Coconino Sheriff's Department," he said, showing Brooke his identification. "Are you Brooke Anderson?"

"Yes."

He looked at Tyler. "And you are?"

"Tyler Alexander, a friend."

Brooke interjected, "He's also a lawyer and I want him here."

Tyler politely smiled. *So much for keeping a low profile.*

Detective Lopez did not appear impressed and turned his attention back to Brooke and looked at his iPad. "I see from our records we were out here a couple of months ago."

"Yes, someone drove through our fence."

"I also see the case is still open."

"That's right, I'm still waiting for them to find who did it."

"Hmm, let's talk about what happened today. Can you tell me what happened?"

Tyler stood next to Brooke as she explained. "Today I found that someone sabotaged my saddle. It could have happened the other day or earlier. My saddle failed the other day when I had my riding accident, or so we thought it was an accident. That is, until I was inspecting the saddle and found the latigo had been cut." Brooke pointed toward the saddle.

Detective Lopez moved closer to the saddle and started to inspect it without touching it. "Who's handled this saddle since the accident?"

"Probably just my daughter, Kasey; Ray, and a friend; and myself."

"We might be able to pull a partial print off the metal pieces. We can't get anything off the leather." He continued to examine the saddle.

"Do you have any idea when the latigo could have been cut?"

Brooke shook her head. "It's been a week or two since I took the saddle apart to give it a thorough cleaning. I wouldn't have found the cut unless I took the latigo off the rigging dee." Brooke picked up the leather latigo and showed the detective where it had been cut. "See the clean slice on the underside of the leather, but on the outside, it's torn." She awkwardly bent the leather back using her good hand. "You can also see that the cut goes almost three-quarters of the way through the leather."

Detective Lopez took several pictures of the latigo and handed it back to Brooke. "Can you bend it for me, so the cut is visible in the picture?"

Brooke fumbled with the piece of leather, trying to keep her hand out of the way of the camera. "Let me take care of that," Tyler offered.

After the two men finished with the pictures, the detective started to look around the room. "Who has access to the tack room, and is it kept locked?"

"It's open when we're around, usually from the morning feeding until the last check at night. Pretty much anyone who comes to the ranch has access to the room. It's kind of a meeting place."

"That won't help narrow down who had access to the saddle."

"Sorry."

"Do you have any idea who may have wanted to cause the accident?"

Brooke looked at Tyler and then back at Detective Lopez. "Yes, Hal Greer, he's been threatening me. He wants to buy my property for the AA Land Company."

Tyler cringed. *Oh no, please don't bring the company into this.*

Detective Lopez wrote in his notebook and then looked at Brooke. "Did Greer have access to this room?"

"I guess so—but I didn't see him near it. I'm on a horse more than I'm in the barn."

After forty-five minutes of questions and pictures Detective Lopez packed the saddle in his unmarked SUV. "I'll take the saddle to headquarters for further investigation. Here's a receipt. If nothing more is found on the saddle you should be able to get it back in a couple of days." He then looked at Tyler and then back at Brooke. "Have your attorney give me a call to see if it's ready."

Tyler stiffened slightly. "I'm not her attorney, I'm just a friend."

"Okay—Anyway you may want to keep quiet about the damage you found on the saddle for a little bit."

Brooke seemed confused. "Why's that?"

"If the latigo and the incident with your fence are related the person who did it may become much more cautious if they know we're looking for them, and then we may never find out who did it. But, on the other hand if they think they are in the clear they are more likely to slip up and make a mistake."

Tyler jumped in. "But if they think no one is on to them, they may try something else."

"I thought you said you weren't her lawyer?"

"I'm a friend who's concerned about her safety."

Detective Lopez was indifferent. "If you want to catch who did this you may have to take that risk."

Twenty minutes later Brooke and Tyler were back in the house seated in the kitchen. "What do you think; should I keep quiet about the cut latigo?"

"Well—to be honest, if their motive was to cause you to lose the ranch, they may have succeeded. You're in pretty bad shape."

"Do you mean physically or financially?"

"Both."

"That's for sure." Brooke nodded.

"So, they probably won't have any reason to try anything else."

"True, if the ranch is the motive. But what about Kasey and Shane? I don't want them in any danger. They should know."

"That's your decision. But I would advise against it. You can accomplish the same thing without scaring them."

"How?"

"Tell them you want all your tack thoroughly inspected every day. Tell them, that with the bad luck you've been having and all the accidents around here, you want them to be extra careful. They'll just think you're being a paranoid mother." As Tyler finished his sentence, a look of concern grew on both of their faces. *Have all the previous accidents really been accidents?*

Brooke broke the silence. "About those other events, were they really. . ."

Tyler finished her sentence. ". . .accidents? I know what you're thinking. But let's not rush to a conclusion. We need to think this through."

They went over the list of things that broke over the past year. Acts of nature like the windstorm were immediately ruled out. A few other items like the dishwasher which had been acting up for weeks before it died were also ruled out. That left several incidents that were seemingly random, but all impacted the ranch's operations, such as Zoomey, the hot walker, the water pump, the hot water heater and the tractor.

Brooke's stomach twisted again. "Do you think this is all about forcing me to sell?"

Tyler held his tongue, as his anger grew. *This better not be related to Hal Greer. I know this is potentially a key piece of land for the project, but we don't resort to criminal activity to get it. There are legal ways of accomplishing our goals. Take a deep breath and think quick about how to get out of this mess. If Greer is behind this, it makes me look bad, considering the way Brooke and I have become friends. I could easily be implicated in the events by circumstantial evidence. I have to distance myself from Hal Greer and protect myself and AA.*

"This could very well be about forcing you to sell," he then added. "Have you started the paperwork to get the restraining order against Hal Greer?"

Brooke sank back in her chair. "No, I haven't taken the time. I really didn't think it was necessary."

"I suggest that you do it immediately, as a precaution. Also, tell Shane and Kasey to be extra careful around the ranch. Tell them you're just really concerned that no one else gets hurt right now, while you're laid up."

"Do you think he will try anything else?"

"I doubt it. Your accident has pretty well doomed you to foreclosure. Only an act of God could keep you afloat until you're able to work again."

"Thanks for the optimistic assessment."

"Right now, an honest assessment is what's needed."

"You're right. It just stings to hear it put so bluntly."

Tyler moved next to Brooke and put his arm around her. "I didn't want to say it. But. . . ."

"I know."

"You should call Detective Lopez and tell him about the other accidents on the ranch. It could be important to his investigation."

"You're right."

Brooke wandered into the family room and sank deep into the recliner. She picked up the TV remote but did not turn on the set. Despair and anger fought for control of her. There was little she could do to save the ranch. Only God could help her now.

Seething anger for Hal Greer arose. The need for vengeance that had grown in her since Cory's death now flooded her with full force. *I want the book thrown at that man and his company. His actions not only endangered me, but they also endangered my children. He's got to pay.* She flung the remote across the room.

CHAPTER

*E*xhaustion reappeared and diffused Brooke's smoldering anger. She fell asleep in the recliner and awoke to banging in the kitchen when Shane and Kasey got home from school. Shane charged into the family room. "What's for dinner?"

Brooke paused. *Dinner?* "I've been too tired to even think about it. Kasey, you may have to take care of it for a few days."

Kasey forced a smile. "Sure Mom."

Brooke saw that Kasey was getting overwhelmed. She couldn't put all the demands of the ranch on Kasey and Shane. When they'd left the room, she summoned what little energy that remined and went to her office, then pulled up the spread sheet for the ranch and home expenses. It took only moments for the hard reality of her finances to crash in on her. The clients she'd built up over the past year would very likely leave if she couldn't train their horses for the next 8 to 12 weeks. *Dear God, help us.* Without divine intervention, there was no way out of her mess. *But if you didn't intervene to save Cory, why will you help us now?*

The next day at Tammy's Diner, Kasey slid into a booth across the table from Lisa.

"Thanks for meeting me." Kasey said as she picked up a menu.

"Does your mom know we're talking?"

"Maybe."

"Does that mean, you didn't tell her?"

"Why?"

"Well, it somewhat affects any advice I might give you." Kasey looked bewildered as Lisa continued. "For one thing, it tells me where you're coming from, and it gives me some idea of how much to involve your mother in any suggestions I might have."

"Oh." Kasey fiddled with her napkin. "You've heard what happened to my Mom?"

"Yes, I'm sorry about the accident. It's on the church prayer chain."

"Even though she isn't pressuring me to do anything, this changes everything."

"How's that?"

"Well—she definitely needs my help training the horses, and I'm fine with that. And she should be riding again by the time the show season really starts up."

"So, what's the issue?"

"The mustang." Kasey paused and let out a deep breath. "If we don't show him next month at the competition there's no chance of us winning the money that's needed to get the ranch back on its feet. My mom isn't asking me too, but. . . ." Kasey's voice trembled slightly. "But I feel I have to step up and show Slider. I want to do it for my Mom. I just don't know if I can."

Lisa reached across the table, touched Kasey's hand, and smiled. "Wanting to is a big step. Have you prayed about it?"

"Yes, and that's why I'm here talking to you. After praying about it I still feel like I'm supposed to do it, but I don't want to get my Mom's hopes up and then chicken out. That's why I haven't told her I'm meeting with you."

"If it's God's will, I know you can do it.—I've had to overcome similar fears."

"*You did?* You've never talked about it at youth group."

"It's in the past, and I don't want to get attention because of it. I want to be known for what I'm doing now. So, what I'm going to share with you has to stay between us. . . Okay?"

Kasey's eyes were riveted on Lisa. "Sure." *What could it be?*

The sodas and fries they'd ordered arrived. Lisa took a sip of her soda and began as she moved her long brown hair behind her ear. "Right after high school I was given a full scholarship to college to be on their aerial ski team. My goal was to make the U.S. Olympic Team; it was partly my dream and partly my Dad's. Toward the end of my sophomore year, I had a serious accident which should have ended my career. After the accident, I became afraid to do my signature jump, the Back Double Full-Full-Double Full."

"Wow, that even *sounds* dangerous."

"It's one of the most difficult jumps to do. I had my Dad wanting me to push on through rehabilitation and my team mates were counting on me. I didn't let anyone know about my fear. I was the team's top ranked skier and we had just taken second place in the collegiate championships. They needed me back on the team if they were going to have a chance at the National Championship the following year."

Kasey's eyes were wide and riveted on Lisa. "What happened? What did you do?"

"During my lengthy rehabilitation, I started attending the Fellowship of Christian Athletes. I got counseling and support from our college leader. She taught me that God had given me these gifts and I should use them to glorify Him. It didn't matter what happened to us on a day to day basis in the way of trials and troubles. These problems weren't about us; they were just opportunities to glorify God. The horrible things that happen to us in our lives can still be used to glorify Him; and in the big picture that's what it's all about."

Kasey became distant and sat quietly for a few moments. "Do you mean like those people who committed their lives to God at my Dad's memorial service?"

"Yeah, that's part of it, but it's also about how many people he touched throughout his life just by the way he lived."

Kasey took in Lisa's comments. "So, how'd this work out for you?"

"It took six months of hard work at rehab before I was able to get back on skis. I wanted to compete but didn't know if I could ever attempt that trick again. There were too many memories."

"Did you ever compete again? Did you ever do the trick?"

"Yes, and yes. I applied the principals I told you about before your schooling show. But at the same time my relationship with God grew and so did my trust in Him. It got to the point I skied for Him, I felt like God smiled when I skied."

"How'd you do when you started skiing in competitions?"

"I made the U.S. Ski Team and competed in the Olympics."

Kasey's eyes widened. "You're kidding me. How'd you do?"

"I took fourth place. It was a great experience."

"You're not that old. Why'd you stop?"

Lisa chuckled. "I still ski; I just don't compete. As my relationship grew with God, I wanted to spend more time studying His Word and sharing it with others. I ended up sharing my new-found faith with the others on the ski team. I found it exhilarating watching some of my teammates come to know God. That became more important to me than anything else. I didn't have the time to train and be in the Word as much as I wanted. So, I made the decision to go in the direction of my biggest passion."

"So how does this apply to me?"

"Pray about it and ask God where He wants you to grow. Then go that direction and be willing to make changes as you sense Him guiding you. If you feel you're supposed to trust Him more and put your total trust in him to overcome your fears, then maybe going forward to show the mustang is the right choice. Only you can make that call and then you have to take ownership of your decision. Otherwise, when things get tough you might second guess yourself and want to quit."

Kasey again sat quietly while she twirled her fry in some ketchup. *I can see a lot of truth in what Lisa's saying. But what do I do if I have a panic attack? But maybe it's not all about what I do; maybe it's about trusting God to take care of it.* Kasey looked up from her plate and poured out her new revelation to Lisa.

Lisa's face brightened. "You're getting it. And as you develop your relationship with God, it will go from being head knowledge to something that you routinely put into practice."

Later at home, Kasey found herself teetering. It was one thing to be sitting across a table from Lisa, hearing reassurances. It was another to be on Slider in the middle of a crowded arena. *Will I lose control? Will I have another panic attack? But if I can keep it in my mind that I'm riding for God and no one else, I might be able to keep my fears from growing. If I'm riding for God it doesn't matter who else is watching. Who is more powerful than Him?*

Tyler closed his door of the SUV and sat next to Brooke. "Are you sure you want me to take you to the parade?"

"Yes, I'll be fine, and you're helping me out."

"Shouldn't you stay home and rest?"

"It's more important that I support Shane and Kasey. If I get tired you can take me home. If I went with them I'd be stuck there until the parade was finished."

"Okay if you say so."

This was the first time since Cory's death that Brooke seemed excited about going to the parade. Was Cory's accident behind her along with the bitterness that was born in the past? The temperature had dropped below freezing by the time they reached the parade route, and the crystalized snow crunched beneath their feet as they walked along the sidewalk. Brooke pointed to the colorful food truck. "You should try one of the *biscochitos*. Juanita Mendez makes the best in the area."

Tyler bought half dozen, and continued down the street, exploring the Christmas displays in the store windows. He spotted a hot chocolate stand in front of the Baptist Church. "Would you like some, to warm yourself up? You look cold."

"Thanks. . . . I guess I'm shivering a little."

"We need to keep you warm."

I like this. Someone who notices and cares. . . Brooke smiled. As they walked a little further down the street their hands met and their fingers wove together. Their hands were now firmly in in each other's grasp. Brooke suddenly froze when the parade began. The lead float this year was Martha and Slim's chuck wagon. Every muscle in her body became rigid at the sight of the wagon and then a slight release of tension worked its way to her hands. *I'm glad to see Slim has given up the driving job to Kyle.* "It's about time," she half-muttered.

"What was that you said?" Tyler asked.

"Oh, nothing."

Thirty-seconds later the wagon passed in front of her, the exact spot that Cory. . . And then suddenly her hand went limp in Tyler's as that nightmare of a Christmas rushed in. *What am I doing here with another man?* Then guilt, regret, and loneliness flooded in.

"What's the matter Brooke?"

"I need to leave."

"Sure, whatever you need." *That's strange,* he thought; *she seemed fine just a minute ago.*

Twenty minutes later Tyler was parked next to Brooke's house. "Are you alright?" He reached over and touched her hand. "Was this too much too soon?"

Brooke drew back. Was she ready to share this part of her past with him? It was so deeply personal, and at times still so raw. Then she made her decision. "Something happened at the parade several years ago, and it rushed through my mind as we were standing there. It brought back feelings I thought I'd dealt with."

"Do you want to talk about it?"

A release came, Tyler's concern gave her peace and comfort. "If you really want to hear about it."

And for the next few minutes, she told him what happened at the Christmas Parade three years earlier. "When the same chuck wagon passed the place where the accident occurred it was more than I could take."

"You've been through a lot."

Brooke studied him. All at once she realized something had changed inside her. Was it because she'd bared her soul about the accident and its effect on her? Maybe that was why she now felt so much closer to Tyler. She wanted to know more about him. Brooke took Tyler's hand in both of hers and gazed deep into his eyes. "This is why I've been avoiding relationships. . . What is it that makes you so cautious?"

All at once, Tyler found himself tangled in his own web of secrecy. Right up to this moment, he'd justified what he was doing, insisting that he'd never directly lied to Brooke. But now, from deep inside, a voice was shouting that his lack of candor could easily be considered lying—this was a moment when only the full truth was demanded.

He waffled, then decided—at least for now—to stick to the facts about his personal life. "I truly did love. . . and I guess still do love my ex-wife at least to some degree. I didn't seek the divorce. And, there was a lot of truth to what she said about our marriage. I failed at being a good husband. I provided financially but got so wrapped up in supplying her with material things that I neglected the more important parts of the relationship. So, I threw myself into my work even more. I'd never failed at anything in my life until then, and I guess I don't want to take a chance of failing again. Since then, I've kept my distance from relationships and. . . ." Tyler paused, his usual confidence started to fall apart. *Should I go any deeper?* It was risky to share on a personal level. He decided he needed to allow Brooke to see a little deeper into his soul. "You're the first woman I've allowed to get close to me since the divorce. I've built a wall around me and used work to keep anyone from getting close."

"You seem to have made friends since coming here."

"Not really, just acquaintances. For some reason, you're the only one I've let get close."

"That's a good start," she smiled.

"Is it really?—Will work eventually take priority and destroy everything for me like it usually does?" *Yes, you're using her,* the voice inside shouted again. She was intertwined with his work and she didn't even know it. *Anything I do will ultimately be in Brooke's best interests. Will it? Really? Are you sure you know what that is?*

Brooke squeezed his hand. "You've seem to be balancing work with the rest of your life now."

Tyler's heart ached. He wished—how he wished!—he could tell Brooke *everything* about why he was in Flagstaff. "But can I keep doing it when the pressures of work build?"

Brooke kept smiling and squeezed his hand again. "I'm sure you can." She tried to slide closer to Tyler, but winced in pain.

His desire for Brooke grew. He slid closer to her and put his arm around her.

A few minutes later Brooke pulled gently away from his embrace. "Can we go into the house? I think we'll be more comfortable there." Inside Tyler helped Brooke get out of her winter jacket. When she twisted to avoid moving her shoulder, she came close to him again. As their eyes fixed on each other their emotions rose. He moved closer, until their lips touched. Brooke did not resist and closed her eyes. Then headlights shown through the family room window, signaling the arrival of Kasey and Shane. Their brief time together ended.

Behind his steering wheel Tyler headed home alone to his apartment. *What's the matter with me? Why am I letting myself fall for this woman? I've always been able to compartmentalize work and pleasure. What is it about her that makes me drop my guard?*

Alone in her room, with the kids asleep, Brooke lay awake late into the night. *When I'm with Tyler everything feels right. Maybe—this is a man that I can trust, a man who won't let me down.*

CHAPTER

Around the church it was called 'Operation Brooke' and within 24 hours it had taken shape. The church community signed up to provide dinners for the next two weeks and there was a list of volunteers who agreed to ride the horses that needed training. This took some pressure off of Kasey, but she was still unsure if she should show Slider. Would she get her mom's hopes up and not be able to deliver? The deep fear that she might panic during the performance was enough to paralyze her. She couldn't put off talking to her mother much longer. A decision to show Slider had to be made soon. There was still much work to do before the competition, and time was running out. Only a little more than three weeks was left before New Year's Day.

The afternoon chores had started, and Maddie came by to help Kasey. As they rode the Gator to the hay barn, Maddie asked. "Have you decided if you're going to show Slider?"

"I think so. . . My talk with Lisa really helped me. But there are still a few things that I'm not certain about."

"Like what?"

Kasey started loading bales on the UTV. "Like, do we really have a chance to win? And is it really worth all the time and effort if we still don't have a gimmick for the competition?"

"What kind of routine are you planning to use with him?"

"Mom wants a reining theme which makes sense, but I think we need something more than reining. She was thinking of doing part of the pattern bridle-less."

Maddie pushed another bale toward Kasey and paused to catch her breath. "Do you have anything else in mind?"

Kasey grabbed the bale and threw it on top of the others, then she leaned against the Gator. "Well. . . I have been thinking of something."

"Yeah, what is it?"

"You know I've been teaching Slider tricks?"

"Right."

"I've taught him to lie down, and you know how he likes to take his own saddle pad off." Kasey paused.

"Okay. . . and?"

"Mom wanted some liberty groundwork to be included in the show. So, at the end of the show I'll ask Slider if he's tired and he gives me yawn. I can teach him that. Then I'll take off his saddle, and he takes off his saddle pad, I then fold it into a pillow and place it on the ground. I then sing a lullaby to him, and he lays down and puts his head on the pillow. After that I'll sit down and lean against him. . . . What do you think?"

Maddie rolled her eyes. "That would be neat if you could do it, but I think you're nuts. Can you really train him to do all that in the next three weeks?"

"I've got most of the individual pieces done, it's just a matter of putting them all together in one big trick."

"If you can pull that off, that would be great."

As they headed back to the stalls with the load of hay, Maddie changed the subject. "Kasey, I know you're real busy, but do you want to come to my sister's dance recital this weekend? It's not too long, and it would be fun to have some company."

"I'll try. It depends on what my mom has scheduled."

Kasey's indecision had her stomach twisted into a knot; she couldn't put it off any longer. She had to talk to her mom. Brooke was already in bed; the injuries had taken their toll on her body and the exhaustion forced her to bed early. Kasey carefully sat on the footboard of her mother's bed and focused on Brooke who was reading.

Brooke looked up from her book. "What is it, Kasey?"

"It's the competition." Her voice was soft and timid.

Brooke's heart jumped. "Yes, what about it?"

"You obviously can't show Slider, not in your condition."

Brooke nodded. "True."

"That leaves me as the only option to show him. But that will still take a lot of money to get to L.A. for the competition... Right?"

"Right."

"We should only spend all that money if we have a good chance of doing well."

Brooke remained silent for a moment. "You're making good sense." *Where is she going with this conversation?*

"I don't want you to spend all that money and then me be a

disappointment to you. We need to make sure we have a routine that will knock 'em dead. But we've been missing something."

"Yes, we've talked about this before."

Kasey started talking faster. "I have an idea." In a rush, she explained the routine she'd shared with Maddie, but going into greater detail. She ended with, "what do you think?"

Brooke leaned back into her pillow. "I've seen you play with most of these elements. If you can put it all together into one routine, it could be a great ending for the performance." Brooke's heart raced as she paused and looked into Kasey's eyes. "Does this mean you're going to show him?"

"I guess so. . . I know how much we need the money and what this means to you and the ranch. I just don't want to fail you."

"Hold on. I don't want you doing this because you think you have to save the ranch. I don't want you taking on that responsibility. You should only compete Slider because you want to show him."

"That's part of it; but I also want to overcome my fears, like Granny did." Kasey moved closer to Brooke and gave her a gentle hug.

The next day on his way to his riding lesson Tyler kept thinking about all the memories Shane had of his father. The phone call earlier that afternoon with Ryan reminded him how strained his relationship with his own son had become. Failure was not in Tyler's vocabulary, but that's what his relationship with Ryan was, a colossal wreck. And then there was Shane—and the way the two of them had clicked. *I blew it with Ryan. Do I have anything to offer this kid?* Maybe he did have something to offer, they seemed to have a connection.

Tyler found Brooke in the tack room going over a list of instructions for her temporary help. "You're looking better today; the black eye is barely noticeable. How are you feeling?"

Brooke looked up from her papers. "A whole lot better as long as I don't move certain ways."

"How's the church help working out?"

"It's more work than I realized doing all the coordination and planning for the different riders and helpers—I kind of enjoy it." Brooke put down her papers and continued. "Are you ready for your lesson?"

"I am. . . Are you sure you're up to it?"

"Most definitely. As long as I can sit though most of it."

Tyler gave a half grin. "That's okay, I will too."

"Funny." Brooke rolled her eyes and grinned.

After the lesson and Cowboy was put away, Tyler asked. "Where can I find Shane?"

"In the equipment barn. He's getting things ready for you."

"I'll be there until you're ready to practice the duet."

It's nice that the two boys have taken to each other. "Thanks for taking the time to help him."

Tyler paused. "We're helping each other." Brooke was confused by the comment.

Shane saw Tyler walk into the barn. "Hi Tyler, how was your lesson? Did my mom work you hard?"

"Not too hard. . . I think I can still sit." Tyler said as he rubbed his backside. Shane began to laugh. Then Tyler carefully examined the pieces of wood laid out on the table. "So, where are you with the project?"

"One bird house is done except for painting it, there are three more to go." Shane said proudly.

Tyler started working with Shane and they continued until all three bird houses were done. As they carried them into the house Tyler decided to try to learn from a kid. "So, Shane, what is it that made your dad so special?"

Shane thought for a moment. "I don't know. . . We just always did things together and he was never too busy to talk to me or help me."

The one thing I never seemed to give Ryan. Time. "What do you mean?"

"Well. . . The night of the accident I was supposed to be getting dressed and Dad found me playing with my trucks. I was using them to move my clothing that I was going to wear. Instead of getting mad at me, he got down on the floor and started helping me move my shoes from the closet to the bed. That is—until he ran into mom's foot halfway to the bed. She was standing over him with her arms crossed. She didn't look very happy; I think we were late. Dad managed to keep us both out of trouble by explaining we were getting dressed, just using a different way.

"It sounds like he was a really great guy and dad."

"That's what everyone said at his memorial service."

The one thing I never gave Ryan, my time with no distractions. Was Ryan right? Have I always tried to buy his love?

Kasey awoke in the middle of the night to the sound of her dog whining. She got out of bed and rubbed her eyes as she looked out her bedroom window. A faint orange glow hung over the equipment barn. As Jake's whine persisted, she scanned the rest of the property. When her eyes came back to the barn the glow seemed brighter and terror took hold.

She yelled as she rushed to her mother's room and roused Brooke out of a deep sleep. "Mom, Mom wake up the barn is on fire!"

Brooke sat up abruptly at the word fire, only to feel her ribs and collarbone violently object. She winced in pain. *"Kasey, call 911."* Kasey gave the details to the emergency dispatcher, as Brooke struggled to put on clothes.

"Mom, they're on the way."

Brooke was now wide awake and feared the worst as she took a deep breath. "Which barn is it?"

"The equipment barn."

Brooke slowly exhaled. "Good—not the horse barn. . . . We need to go check on the horses and make sure they're okay. We'll let the fire company deal with the fire."

A few minutes later the whole family was in the horse barn checking the stalls. The horse looked tired, blinking their eyes as they adjusted to the bright lights in the aisle. Brooke sighed. "Thank God the smoke is blowing the other direction or we'd have to deal with a barn full of anxious horses."

"What should we do?" Kasey asked.

"There's not much we can do except wait." Brooke said, as the first fire siren neared, and the emergency vehicle tuned into the driveway. Brooke kept a tight hold on Shane to keep him out of the way as the firefighters went about their business. With the initial adrenaline rush fading, Brooke connected the dots to the previous mishaps. *Another accident? Why me? Why my family? We don't deserve another tragedy.* Despair rained down on Brooke like the water from the hoses that drenched the fire. With the kids huddled around her she fought to remain strong and not show the anguish that grew inside.

Fifteen minutes later the fire was out, and the bright lights of the vehicles were shining on the smoke that rose from the corner of the barn. The fire chief came over to Brooke. "You're lucky you called us when you did. Otherwise you might have lost the building."

When the last fire truck left, Brooke and the kids checked the horses one more time before heading into the house.

Back inside the house Shane asked, "Mom, can I watch some TV? I can't get to sleep."

"You two can stay up for a half-hour and then you need to try to get to sleep."

Brooke understood their inability to sleep, her mind raced as she tried to figure out how the fire started. She wanted to call Tyler but willed herself not to—not at this hour and besides, the crisis had past.

The next morning Brooke woke up at seven, after only three hours of sleep. She decided to let the kids sleep in and go to school late; sitting in class half asleep didn't seem like it would accomplish anything. Later, when the kids were off to school, she sat down in the recliner to get some rest. She took the opportunity to call Tyler, something she wanted to do all morning.

Tyler arrived shortly before noon with two sandwiches and an assortment of sides from Isaac's Gourmet Deli. He found Brooke in the family room. "Thought you might be hungry for something different."

"How'd you know?" Brooke said as she tried to get out of the recliner.

"No, you stay there. I'll bring everything to you. Save your energy for when your workers show up this afternoon."

Brooke relaxed back into the chair. "You don't have to convince me to stay here."

Partway into his sandwich Tyler paused. "Tell me what happened last night? How did you discover the fire?"

"Jake woke up Kasey and she saw the fire."

"Lucky for you."

"Yeah, we were able to save the structure because the fire company got here quickly."

"What started it?"

Brooke wiped her mouth with a napkin. "We don't know yet. The Fire Marshall should be out here sometime today to inspect the damage and look for the cause."

Tyler took a drink of his mineral water. "I hate to ask this. . . But is there any chance it's related to your accident?"

Brooke froze. "Oh God, I hope not."

As they finished lunch a red and white SUV came down the driveway and parked next to the equipment barn. Brooke and Tyler went out to observe and offer their assistance. On the side of the SUV, Coconino County Fire Department was printed in bold golden letters. Brooke walked up to barn where the man was inspecting the debris. "Hi, I'm Brooke Anderson, the owner; is there any information you need or anything I can do to help?"

The man who was inspecting the damage around the electrical box stopped what he was doing. "I'm Brad Phillips, the Fire Marshall." He extended his hand to Brooke, "Mrs. Anderson I presume." He then reached for Tyler's hand. "And you are?"

"Tyler, a friend of the family." And she quickly added. "He's also an attorney."

"I'm here to determine the cause of the fire. Can you tell me what the barn is used for and is anything continually plugged into an outlet?"

"It's the equipment barn where we park the tractor and other farm equipment. It's also used as a woodworking and repair shop."

"I see. . . And, how did you discover the fire?"

"My daughter looked outside and saw it. She woke me up and we called 911. The first truck arrived ten minutes later."

"Thanks, I'll let you know if I need any more information."

"When will I be able to get the tractor out of the barn?"

"I'll let you know when I finish my inspection."

An hour later, Brad knocked at the backdoor and Tyler led him into the kitchen. "Mrs. Anderson, I've completed my inspection and you are now free to move your equipment out of the barn and clean up the damage."

Brooke was relieved and gave a soft sigh. "Thank you. Do you have an idea what started the fire?"

"It looks like it started with an extension cord running to a space heater. The wires in the cord appeared to be damaged and overheated. It then spread from there through the sawdust on the floor, over to scraps of wood and the rags next to the workbench. You shouldn't leave a space heater plugged in when you're not in the area. Another piece of advice for you, don't leave oily rags lying around. They should be kept in a metal container."

Something wasn't right. "We never leave the space heater on. And, the barn was just cleaned up. We keep this place very clean and orderly."

"I know what I found."

Brooke was agitated. "Is it possible this didn't happen by accident?"

"Why do you ask?"

"We *only* use the space heater when we're working on equipment in the barn. Otherwise, it very rarely gets plugged in."

Tyler remained quiet and let Brooke take charge. Brad pulled up some pictures on his camera and showed Brooke. "If someone was trying to burn down your barn, they did a bad job. There's a fifty-fifty chance the fire would have burned itself out; maybe in twenty or thirty minutes. The building is steel framed and steel sided, and there probably wasn't enough fuel to get the fire hot enough or to do a huge amount of damage. If someone wanted to burn down the barn they would have started the fire at the tractor where there's a fuel tank and lots of combustible material, like next to the hay."

Tyler stepped in. "If a fire had started, say, at the tractor would it be a little more obvious that it was arson?"

Brad thought for moment. "I suppose so. . . Why do you ask about arson?"

"Because I never leave anything plugged in at the barn," Brooke insisted. "Especially not a space heater."

"All I can say is, be glad the fire didn't do a lot of damage."

"Yeah, except maybe to my business. When my clients hear there was *another* mishap on my ranch, they'll start to leave."

When Brad left, both Brooke and Tyler sat down at the table. Brooke shook her head. "Shane told me he turned everything off when he was finished in the barn."

"I was there with him. We never used the space heater, and I thought he did a good job of cleaning up after himself."

Brooke bit her lower lip. "Then what explains the fire marshal's report?"

Tyler hesitated. "Is someone trying to scare you?" *It better not be Hal Greer. If it is, I need to distance myself and the company from him, and fast.*

Brooke narrowed her eyes. "You mean Hal Greer?"

Tyler shrugged. "Yeah."

"But why try to damage the barn and not burn it down?"

"We don't know whether or not he was trying to send a message or trying to burn it down. But you'd better get a restraining order against him as soon as possible. I'd also let the detective know about the fire."

CHAPTER

K asey's decision to show the mustang meant she would have to step up her game if she was going to have a chance of winning. Up until now she had gotten the job done and managed to keep an emotional distance from Slider. A deeper connection with Slider was needed, something she had worked hard to avoid. Her nerves were on edge, can she bury the memories of losing Sidekick? Could she let go and allow herself to feel again? She couldn't afford to shut Slider out.

The afternoon had wound down when Kasey went into the kitchen. "Mom, I'm heading out to the barn to mess with Slider."

"I thought you were done with him for the day."

"I was—but I decided to go spend some more time with him. If I'm going to show him, I need to really build his trust in me." This was Kasey's first attempt to break down her barriers.

"We'll be eating in forty-five minutes, don't be late."

As Kasey left the kitchen, a small smile appeared on Brooke's face. *Maybe the healing is starting to happen. I hope this goes well.*

Out at the barn, Kasey went into Slider's stall which had now been moved into the barn from the paddock, a true indication his training was progressing. Taking a soft currycomb, she started to make tiny circles on his neck and withers, talking gently to him. "Hey buddy, it looks like it's up to you and me now. I know I haven't been that good of a friend to you, I kind of kept you at a distance. I didn't want you close to me. A couple of years ago I had a mustang named Sidekick who was my best friend and then there was this accident. It was at the Christmas Parade and some kids set off fireworks that spooked the team of horses pulling Aunt Martha's and Uncle Slim's chuckwagon. The noise also scared the 4-H horses, I got knocked of Sidekick and broke my leg. The wild team was charging right for me when my dad jumped in front of the team and got them to turn, but not before they ran over him. During the commotion, Sidekick broke his leg in a storm grate. Ever since then I've been afraid to ride in public or let another horse become my friend and get close to me. Anyway, now my Mom is in trouble and needs our help. We're going to have to become a team that can read each other's thoughts; we'll have to work as one. I can't be an island anymore; I need you to get close to me."

It was as though Slider answered Kasey as he twisted his head back and started nibbling on her arm with his lips. She smiled and a tear trickled down her cheek as she wrapped her arms around his neck. "Hey buddy, let me get you a treat." Kasey returned with a handful of peppermint candies and found Slider lying down in the middle of his stall with all four feet neatly tucked beneath his body. She shook her head and smiled as she knelt beside him. "Here you go, Slider."

Back at the house, Shane bolted into the kitchen. "Mom, what time is dinner?"

"Soon, everything that was dropped off by the church is warmed up. We're just waiting for Kasey. She was supposed to be here ten minutes ago." Brooke didn't let it show, but her angst was rising. *Why did I allow Kasey to go out to the barn alone? With all the accidents around here, is it even safe for these kids to be here anymore?* "Shane, I'm going out to get Kasey. You stay in the house." At the barn, she found the aisle lights on and the tack door open. She called out, *"Kasey!"* There was no reply. Looking down the aisle, she saw that Slider's halter was missing from his stall door. *Where could those two have gone?* She checked the indoor arena. No Kasey. Outside she called again, but still no reply. Her anxiety was rising. *Where are they? If anything has happened to her. . . That Hal Greer will pay.*

Brooke forced herself to take a deep breath and slow down her thoughts. She ran through all the possible scenarios as to where they could be or what they could be doing. *I didn't check Slider's stall. Maybe Kasey's injured, and didn't hear me calling her. . . Oh no, Lord, please don't let it be that.* In spite of her injuries, Brooke was in front of Slider's stall within seconds—and she stopped dead in her tracks. Lying in the sawdust was Slider, with Kasey leaning up against his back with her earbuds in and the music was blasting. Brooke heaved a sigh of relief. *At least she's not hurt.* "Kasey—Kasey, it's dinner time." Finally, Brooke yelled loud enough to be heard above the music.

Kasey looked up. *"What,* Mom?"

"Take out your earbuds."

Kasey pulled one out. "You want something?"

"Yes, it's dinner time."

Kasey looked at her watch. "Oh, sorry. I lost track of time."

"Let's get into the house."

Brooke made her way back to the kitchen. Her panic was gone, and some peace had returned, she smiled. Kasey and Slider were starting to bond.

"I'll be out in a minute." Brooke called to Tyler who had just entered the kitchen. He surveyed his surroundings. *It seems unusually quiet around here this evening.*

A few minutes later, Brooke appeared, with a winter coat in hand. "Do you mind helping me with my jacket? The collarbone still makes it difficult to get it on."

"Sure." Tyler took her coat. "Where is everyone."

"Shane's spending the night with some friends, and Kasey went with Maddie to her sister's dance recital."

After Brooke slid into her coat, Tyler let his hands slide down her side—then slowly wrapped his arms around her waist. She leaned back into Tyler's chest as he let out a deep breath. "Seems like a shame to let an evening like this go to waste."

Brooke rested her head against Tyler's chin. "I know, but I have to get some Christmas shopping done without the kids along, and you're my driver tonight."

"As you wish, my lady. Your carriage awaits."

By the time Tyler parked in the Old Town District of Flagstaff a light snow had started to fall. "Do you want to shop first or have dinner? Your call."

Brooke looked at her watch. "The restaurants stay open later than the stores. Let's do the shopping so we don't run out of time."

"Where to first?"

"Stacy's Western Boutique."

As they strolled down the sidewalk past the bright-colored Christmas displays, Tyler glanced at Brooke. "Will you help me pick something out for Kasey and Shane?"

"You don't need to do that."

"I insist. It might help me break the ice with Kasey."

When they went inside Stacy's, Tyler stopped at the jewelry counter. Beneath the glass counter tops were necklaces and earrings that had a western flare. "How about these?" he said, pointing to pair of Navajo turquois and silver earrings.

"Those would be nice."

Tyler watched Brooke's eyes go the necklace that was next to the pieces he suggested for Kasey.

Brooke picked up a sweater and held it up in front of her for Tyler to see. "What do you think of this for a teenage girl?"

Tyler cocked his head slightly. "I don't know about a teenage girl, but it would look great on you."

"Stop. Be serious."

"I am. It would look great on you."

Brooke laughed. "That settles it. . . I'll get it for Kasey—and then I'll borrow it."

When they arrived at the cashier, a wave of cold reality overtook Brooke. What she had considered to be extravagant, was for Tyler a casual expense. *What am I thinking? We're from two different worlds.*

As the clerk gift wrapped the earrings for Kasey, Tyler asked Brooke. "Where to next?"

"A sporting goods store."

Out on the street they walked hand in hand back to the SUV. Just enough snow had fallen that the wreaths attached to the light poles were frosted, and small swirls of snow had eddied into the corners of the store entrances. Further down the street, they saw the multicolored Christmas decorations softly glowing through the white mist that filled the air. For the first time this season, the Christmas spirit had come upon them. As they turned, Brooke and Tyler gazed into each other's eyes, and Tyler slipped his arm around her waist as they walked down the street.

At the sporting goods store, they looked at rugby jerseys and shoes. Brooke was overwhelmed by the range of choices. After a brief discussion with a salesclerk, a conversation in which Brooke only understood bits and pieces, Tyler showed Brooke a regulation rugby ball. "If Shane's going out for the rugby team it would be good for him to have this to practice with."

"Are you sure."

Tyler nodded. "I'm sure."

The next stop was a quick dinner at a franchised restaurant. The empty house beckoned them, and they wanted to get home quickly. While waiting for their orders to arrive, Tyler's face became serious. "I need to bring this up, and I hope it doesn't spoil your evening. But I'm concerned about your safety. Have you gotten the restraining order yet?"

"I wish you hadn't reminded me of that man and his horrible company."

Tyler leaned back and let out a slow breath. *Okay, so maybe tonight isn't a good time to tell her who I work for. . . . I'll save it for another time.* Tyler pushed on. "I want to make sure that you, Kasey, and Shane are protected."

"No, I haven't done it yet. I plan to Wednesday when I go for my doctor's appointment. Any chance you can give me a ride?"

"I wish I could, but I've got meetings all day. If you can do it Monday, I'll help you file it."

Brooke pretended to pout—then grinned. "That would be nice."

"Okay, then Monday it is." *She needs to get it done soon so Bob and I can move forward with our plan.*

They were back at the house by 9:30 and relaxing on the sofa. Brooke nestled against Tyler's side with his arm wrapped around her. Their conversation drifted from the duet, to Kasey working with Slider. Then Brooke leaned back into Tyler's body, and rubbed her head against his cheek. She tilted back and met his eyes with hers. Tyler moved closer to her lips. Then the kitchen door banged. "Mom, I'm home," Kasey called out. Brooke sat upright, winced with her collarbone aching and then let out a deep breath.

"I'm in the family room." Brooke called back.

Kasey charged into the room—and stopped dead in her tracks when she saw Tyler sitting next to Brooke. "Oh, you have company."

Tyler stood up. "I was just visiting until you got home. Now, I've gotta head out."

He looked down at Brooke. "See you tomorrow?"

She returned a soft smile. "Count on it."

Back at his apartment, Tyler made a call. It was late in the evening, but things had to be discussed—soon. Bob wasn't happy; things were supposed to have improved a month ago.

"I need some more time Bob. I just got word from the Forest Service that they will approve the plan with some minor revisions."

"What about those protestors?" Bob pressed him. "You were supposed to have dealt with that situation. We need results now!"

"I have a meeting scheduled with their leader tomorrow. I couldn't make a deal with them until I was sure the Forest Service was on board with our plan."

"The property, the one your lady friend owns. Have you gotten that taken care of?"

"Partially. A restraining order against Hal is being filed Monday. Then we can move to fire him. That'll buy the company some good PR in the community. As for the property itself, I'm working on some ideas, and I'll present them to you soon."

"Don't disappoint me, Tyler."

The next morning, Tyler went to the Back Country Outfitters for a prearranged meeting with Amy Jones and the other leaders of the protest movement. Entering the store, Tyler saw Amy at the counter. "Hi Amy, I'm Tyler Alexander from AA Land Company and I'm here for our meeting."

Amy's eyebrows narrowed. "We've met before, haven't we?"

"Yes, a couple of months ago, when I bought some hiking boots."

Amy pursed her lips. "I remember now. You led me to believe that you supported our protest against AA."

Tyler shot her a relaxed smile, hoping to put Amy at ease. "I agreed with many of your positions and was here to get an honest assessment of what your movement was trying to accomplish. The only fact I didn't tell you was that I worked for AA Land Company."

Amy relaxed her clenched jaw. "Did you say that you agreed with some of our demands?"

"Yes. But I think you'll do better to refer to them as concerns. The term demand tends to put off some of the higher-ups in my company and in the government."

Amy cocked her head slightly. "Why are you telling me this?"

"Because I'm here to help you and hopefully create an alliance with you and your group."

"This doesn't sound like the story I got from the people in your Flagstaff office."

"I'm from headquarters, and I have the power to negotiate and work with you and your group. Do you have a room where we can meet? I have a presentation to show you."

"We have a small meeting room in the back."

Three others joined Tyler and Amy. Tyler turned on his laptop and a small video projector and aimed it at the wall. "Here is a map of the proposed development. As you can see, it's not anything like you've been told. After talking with Amy, the other month"—he glanced at her, and she returned a half-hearted scowl—"we've made some modifications to the original design in order to address your group's concerns. A buffer zone in the way of recreational fields will be located between the community and the forest land."

Tyler went on to explain the other details about the community, emphasizing the ecological green nature of the plan. He also made sure he addressed the fire concerns, the overuse of the wilderness areas and the plan which the Forest Service had agreed to. "We have their full cooperation," he concluded.

Amy leaned forward with her elbows on the table and her fingers intertwined. "It all sounds very good, and if I do say so, very slick. I've seen these types of presentations before. They're designed to placate us until it is too late to stop the project. . . So, forgive me if I'm a bit skeptical."

Tyler leaned forward and pulled some papers out of his computer bag. "Your sentiment doesn't surprise me."

He handed Amy and the others several sheets of paper. "Here you'll find a summary of my discussions with the Forest Service and my contacts there. You're welcome to contact them with any questions you may have. There's also a list of future meetings. You can have two of your representatives attend the meetings to make sure your concerns are addressed."

Amy and her three colleagues gave each other questioning looks. "Why are you doing this?" Amy asked once again.

"The whole purpose of this project is to establish a pilot development that demonstrates high-tech communities can be established and operated to be ecologically friendly. We concluded that our best chance for success was to get groups like yours on board."

Tyler stepped out of the room for a few minutes while they discussed his presentation. When he reentered, Amy continued to act as their spokesperson. "Tyler, you present a compelling case. I'm personally a bit skeptical, but I'm willing to give you a chance to prove you're a man of your word. We'll definitely participate in your meetings and be a watchdog for the community."

Tyler started putting his computer away. "That's great. I look forward to working with you." He paused for a moment. "What I've read online, and from my previous conversation with you I see that you and your colleagues don't advocate violence."

"That's right."

"Do you know who is vandalizing our properties and creating disturbances at your protests?"

"I wish I did. They're creating bad press for us. We want to be known as a peaceful group."

Tyler continued gathering his things. *Well, one out of two isn't bad. I sure wish I could find out who is behind the vandalism.*

The project was starting to fall into place. Now that some people in the community knew who he worked for, he more than ever had to tell Brooke about his job. Sooner than later, he needed to lift his veil of secrecy.

While they sat in the auditorium waiting for Shane's play to begin, Kasey worked on how to use what she saw at the dance recital. The lightshow performance that the dance troupe put on was amazing. They appeared on the dark stage dressed in black, the only thing she could see were the LED lights outlining their bodies. The dancers' stick-like appearance accentuated all of their movements. Could this be incorporated into Slider's routine? Because he was a dark bay it might be easier to pull off. Could they get the arena dark enough to use for the light show?

She turned and looked at her mother. *Can I pull this off without telling Mom? It sure would be a great surprise for her. I know; I'll see if Amber can help me. With Mom being laid up, it will make perfect sense if I get some help from her. Mom will never suspect.* As she waited for the show to begin, Kasey settled deep into her chair with a secret grin.

Brooke and Tyler sat next to each other throughout the performance, both desired to let their hands become intertwined, but fought the urge with Kasey sitting next to Brooke. After the performance, Shane walked into the lobby with a smile that went ear to ear. "How did I do?"

Brooke was the first to respond. "You did great!"

Kasey smiled. "Yeah, you didn't fall off the stage."

Shane looked at Tyler.

Tyler walked over and put his hand on Shane's shoulder. "That was one of the best 'Ghost of Christmas Pasts' that I've seen."

"Really?"

"You bet. I'm glad you asked me to come and see the play." A wave of regret overwhelmed Tyler, he had missed so many of Ryan's events.

CHAPTER

25

Now that the Forest Service and protestors were on board with the project, it was time to start moving forward. But there were still problems to resolve. How had he let his business and personal life become intertwined? Tyler had to tell Brooke about his job. He couldn't put it off any longer with the protestors knowing his identity. And, now with the meetings he was having at the bank, more people would know that he worked for the AA Land Company. How would she take the news? Would she understand that he was ordered to be secretive about his employer? It wasn't his choice. Who he worked for didn't change who he was or that he was concerned about her future.

Bob had flown into Flagstaff for the day to meet with Tyler and the local retail bank officers. They had investment banking support but wanted a community bank involved to help solidify public support.

Placing a branch of the Flagstaff National Bank in the development would help. Could they entice the bank to participate? Tyler and Bob walked into the vice president's office and found Clifford Johnson's assistant working at the filing cabinet with her back to them. "We have a 10:00 appointment to see Mr. Johnson." Tyler announced.

The assistant turned around. *"Tyler!"* Her eyes were wide open and her jaw dropped.

Tyler flinched and turned pale. "Amber." *The cat is really out of the bag now. I've got to talk to Brooke.*

She stared. "You work for AA Land Company?"

"Yes." He motioned to Bob. "And this is our president, Robert Alexander."

Amber's face was motionless with her eyes riveted on Tyler. "Mr. Johnson is waiting for you in the conference room."

On the way to the room, Tyler turned and found himself face to face with Amber's sullen glare. "Amber, we need to talk before you call Brooke. . . It's important."

Amber followed him into the room. "I don't know what you have to say, but it better be good."

"When we have a break in the meeting, I'll explain." During the lull, Tyler charged out of the room and followed Amber to her desk. "Please let me explain what's going on."

"I don't think anything you can say will make a single bit of difference. You've been lying to my friend."

"During today's discussion, you've heard what the project is about, and it's not like any of the rumors you've heard—Right?"

"I guess."

"What you *didn't* hear in the meeting was that there were issues with the project moving forward. I was sent here to find out what the problems were, and I was ordered not to let *anyone* know who I worked for." Amber continued to hold her scowl. "By keeping my identity hidden I was able to find out that Hal Greer was working against the company—he was the guy pressuring Brooke, remember?—And now we've started the process of firing him."

"Why couldn't you tell Brooke? She. . ."

"That's right, she's too close. I couldn't take the chance of something slipping out. We needed to find out who was involved. Once I knew Hal was the guy I had to make sure we had solid evidence about what he was up to."

Amber shook her head. "I saw the drawings in there. . . How are you going to explain to Brooke that your company still wants her ranch?"

Tyler took a deep breath, glanced over his shoulder to see who was nearby, then he spoke in a hushed tone. "No one knows yet, but I have an idea that should allow Brooke to keep the ranch. You can't say anything about this to anyone—not until I get it cleared through our board of directors."

"And suppose you *don't* get it cleared."

"I promise you; I'll go down trying even if it gets me fired."

Amber's face started to soften. "Then you really do care about Brooke and her family?"

"More than you know. For a while I thought that selling the ranch was the most sensible thing Brooke could do—so much to manage for one person. Then I started to see what it means to all of them and how their past and future are intertwined with the property."

Amber looked at him, as if gauging his honesty. "So, you're going to try to help Brooke keep the ranch? *Really?*"

"Yes, that's what I said."

"Tyler, people say a lot of things in business."

The meeting went well into the lunch hour, and Tyler kept glancing at Amber, knowing he now needed her as an ally. *Can't she see that the AA Land Company was trying to work with the community and has a conscience?* As the meeting broke for lunch Mr. Johnson looked at Amber. "Could you go down to Magnolias and hold a table for six?"

"But there are only five of you?"

"I want you to join us and keep taking notes. This is going to be a working lunch. We need to figure out how the bank can be part of this."

Bob looked at Tyler. "Why don't you go on ahead with Amber. I'll walk down with Cliff. There are a few things I'd like to discuss."

Amber seemed much more relaxed after getting a different perspective of the AA Land Company, and Tyler. She and Tyler talked and laughed as they walked down the street to Magnolia's. Amber lightly hung on Tyler's arm, she returned to her normal vivacious personality by the time they reached the restaurant. They talked about the riding lessons they both had gotten from Brooke. As they approached the restaurant door Amber leaned over and kissed Tyler on the cheek. "Thanks Tyler for what you're trying to do for Brooke."

Ray held the door of the truck as Brooke climbed in. "Thanks, Ray, for giving me a ride to the doctor. I hate bothering you in the middle of the day, but everyone else was busy."

Ray grinned. "Glad to. You've had so many people around your place lately it's been hard to get any time alone with you."

Brooke's recovery was going as expected, she was still on schedule to get her cast off in four weeks. They stopped for lunch at a drive-thru and then cut across town on the way back to the ranch. At a traffic light next to Magnolia's, Brooke saw Amber flirting—and Tyler smiling, seeming to enjoy it. And then, the kiss on the cheek. *So, you weren't able to drive me to my doctor's appointment. You had important meetings to attend. And you—Amber! I thought you were my friend.* Jealousy and resentment churned inside of Brooke.

Ray noticed Brooke's glare. "Hey, isn't that Amber and that lawyer dude?"

Brooke seethed. "Yes."

"What are they doing together?"

"That's what I'd like to know," she muttered to herself.

By the time they reached the main road, Brooke had worked herself into a fit of resentment. Her thoughts went to the other men who had disappointed her—and now Tyler had to be added to that list. She dwelled on what she saw for the rest of the trip home. *How could Amber betray me.* And then, she remembered Ray's warning.

Brooke wanted some good physical activity to vent her anger. But her current limitations made that a challenge; she opted to brush Scout. Initially the brushing was hard and aggressive but with time it became gentle and melancholy as tears streamed down her cheeks. Forty minutes later the tears still flowed, and she couldn't decide who had hurt her more: Tyler for using her, or Amber for betraying her. She heard Kasey calling for her and looked at her watch; it was time for Slider's training session. Could she put the earlier events behind her and focus on Kasey and Slider? What happened was personal, too personal, and she didn't want Kasey knowing how she'd been hurt. She kept stroking Scout and tried to put on a brave face.

"Hi Mom, are you ready to help me with Slider?"

Brooke paused, took a deep breath and turned around. "Sure, you can get him tacked up." She quickly looked away so Kasey wouldn't see her red eyes.

"Okay—I'll be ready in fifteen minutes."

Brooke went back to her brushing. *I really don't want to be doing anything right now. But I promised Kasey. The other riders will be here soon. I've got to pull it together.*

Kasey was mounted and warming up Slider when it started. "Kasey you're slouching. Sit up."

"Okay, Mom."

A minute later. "You're spending too much time warming up at the trot. Get him loping."

"Yes, Mom."

"Stop messing with his head."

Kasey tried to explain. "I'm trying to get him to stretch down."

Brooke snapped back. "He doesn't need that now."

Kasey bit her lip to keep from replying. *What has gotten into her? She's really cranky.*

"Start working his lead changes then we'll work on his stops."

Kasey dutifully followed her mother's directions. Then three minutes later she heard. "Why are you doing flying lead changes? He needs more loping to warm up."

After ten minutes of the conflicting directions, Kasey was confused. "What's going on? You keep changing what you want me to do."

"Nothing's the matter. Just follow my directions." Came the order.

Kasey had all she could take. "Mom, I'm done with this session. I'm gonna hack him out for a few minutes and then take a break before I work on ground schooling. . . Alone."

Brooke stood there stunned. *Kasey sure is moody today.* She thought back to the training session and realized it wasn't Kasey. *I'll need to be careful with the other riders. I've got to get my act together.*

Kasey avoided her mother for the rest of the evening; she didn't want another confrontation. When she had some time, alone, Kasey called Amber. "Hi Amber, I talked with the engineer you told me about. He said it will be easy to put those light strips on Slider."

"That's great."

"Can you give a hand with it later in the week? I may need someone to occupy mom so she doesn't find out about the surprise."

"Sure, glad to do it."

Kasey paused. "Mom seemed really out of sorts this afternoon. Do you know what's bothering her?"

"No, not really. . . Only thing I can think of is her doctor's appointment which was earlier in the day. Maybe she's frustrated that things aren't healing up fast enough."

"Could be. . . But she said things are healing on schedule. Maybe that's longer than she wants it to take."

They both dismissed it.

The next morning Brooke tried to be productive in her paperwork; however, she continued to brood about what she witnessed the day before. *Can I forgive Tyler for lying to me and then going out with Amber? He told me has was busy and couldn't give me a ride. It sure looked like he was busy, but not with the type of work he implied.* Could she put this latest disappointment of a man in her life, behind her? If past history was an indicator, the answer was no. Brooke had never been inclined to forgive. A trait she inherited from her mother.

A woman, let alone a friend, had never betrayed Brooke like this before. Yes, she'd had petty squabbles, disagreements she could put behind her. But this? This was a whole new level. She knew Amber was a flirt but this had gone too far. *Why would Amber betray me like this?*

Her thoughts became tangled, the betrayal, the anger, all added to the confusion. At 11:00 she had enough, she pushed herself away from the computer, put on her coat and went outside to get some fresh air. On her way to the barn her cell phone rang, she checked the incoming number, Tyler. Brooke shoved the phone back in her pocket and kept walking. After checking on the horses she left the barn, going somewhere, anywhere but back into the house. Then she noticed Ray's farrier truck heading down the driveway. He parked next to the house, and she headed over to meet him. "What brings you here at this time of the day?"

Ray jumped out of his truck. "I've got some big news for you."

"I hope it's good."

"I don't know about good, but it's definitely important." Ray let the words hang in the air.

"Well. . .?"

"After I saw how that lawyer hurt you yesterday I knew I had to do something. So, I talked to a friend of mine in the Sheriff's Department who sometimes does detective work on the side." Ray paused again.

"Yeah, go on." Brooke urged him on.

"I asked my friend to check out that lawyer."

"Oh Ray!" But Brooke's curiosity was peaked. She wanted to hear more.

"I knew that dude wasn't any good. Guess who he works for? *The AA Land Company.*"

"What?" Brooke's heart sank, crushed in fact. She felt weak and leaned up against Ray's truck. It was one thing to betray her with

Amber, it was something else to have deceived her for the past three and a half months. "How could I have been so blind?"

Ray walked over and put his arm around her. "You were lonely, he was slick. And, you've never been the best judge of people."

Brooke forced out the words. "Does Amber know who he works for?"

"I bet. . . She works for the bank. They've probably got some big deal goin' on."

Ray continued. "You've had all these accidents around here; didn't they pick up after he showed up?"

Still confused by the news about Tyler Brooke nodded. "I guess so."

Ray walked her into the house and stayed with Brooke for the rest of the afternoon. Brooke was too shocked and hurt to be angry. That would come later.

Later that afternoon Tyler knocked on Brooke's door and started to enter the kitchen as had become his routine when he was met by Ray, who stood just inside the room. "You're not welcome here." Ray's voice boomed.

Tyler stopped. "What do you mean? Where's Brooke? Is she okay?"

"She doesn't want to see you."

Kasey glared at Tyler from the kitchen table.

"Excuse me. . . I want to hear that from Brooke."

"I said she doesn't want to see you."

Tyler did not want to escalate the situation and create a scene. Ray was not going to move, and it would require a physical altercation to get past him. Nothing added up, and it didn't seem he was going to get any more information. A tactical retreat was in order.

He got to his car but changed his mind, one more attempt was needed.

Ray met him at the back door again. "I told you she doesn't want to see you. Now get off the property."

Tyler tried a different approach. "Tell her I need to talk to her about Hal Greer." Their voices had become elevated.

This struck a nerve, Brooke, darted from the family room. *Still trying to look like the good guy and save me from Hal. Hah, some joke. Hal Greer works for him!*

She stormed to the kitchen door. "You have some nerve showing your face around here. You lied to me you filthy ##**@#! Hal Greer works for you! You put my children in danger with your power games. All for what? Your precious money?" Tyler tried to speak but she cut him off. "If you ever step foot on this property again, I'll have you arrested for trespassing!" Brooke slammed the door.

Bewildered, Tyler went back to his car and made a call. "Amber, this is Tyler. Do you know what is going on with Brooke?"

"Why?" Amber replied.

Tyler explained what had just transpired at the ranch.

Amber was uncharacteristically quiet and then replied. "I haven't talked to Brooke since the other day. I have no idea what's going on. I'll call her and get back to you."

Amber called Brooke and she ignored the call. A few minutes later Amber sent a text message. *B, I need to talk to you. Amb.* Brooke decided to reply. It was different than talking. She gave a one-word reply.

No!

Amber stared at her phone and then called Tyler. "Tyler, she won't talk to me."

"Why? What is going on? She now knows that I work for the AA Land Company, but to be this angry."

"I don't know. But based on what you've said, I bet Ray is involved. . . I'll call Kasey later this evening and see if I can get some information."

A couple of hours later Kasey looked at her incoming caller ID: *"Amber". Should I answer it? Mom's not talking to her, should I?* She thought for a moment and asked, what would Dad do. Then she cautiously answered the phone. "Hello, Amber."

"Hi Kasey. Do you know what's going on with your mom?"

"You haven't heard?"

"No, what is it."

Kasey thought for a moment and decided it couldn't hurt. "Well, Mom saw you and Tyler going into a restaurant for lunch yesterday. She said you kissed Tyler."

Amber shook her head. "Is *that* it? It was a business lunch, and I was thanking him for something important he's doing for your Mom."

Kasey's tone remained sullen. "That's not all."

"What else."

"Did you know that Tyler works for the AA Land Company? Ray just found out and told Mom."

"Yes, I know. Tyler told me yesterday at the bank meeting and was going to tell your mother later in the day. How'd Ray find out?"

"He hired a detective."

"Oh, that Ray—causing trouble again." Exasperation hung on every word.

"He's got Mom all worked up about you and Tyler."

"I need to talk some sense into your mother."

"I know, but I don't know how you're gonna do it. You know how she can be when she's been hurt. . . . Good luck."

Kasey put down the phone. She was now more confused than before the call. The man who she didn't trust may not be as bad as

Ray was saying. Amber seemed to have some good answers. But Ray had some pretty damning facts. Who should she believe? Again, she thought about what her father would do. Let everyone explain their side of the story and then check the facts. She decided to talk to her mom.

Kasey found her mother in the office staring at a spreadsheet. "Mom." She paused and then started to repeat herself. "Mom. . ."

Brooke finally turned. "Yes, Kasey."

"You know I'm not a fan of Tyler. But do you have any facts that support what Ray has told you?"

"I saw them together going into the restaurant. And Ray found out he works for the people who want our ranch—something Tyler didn't bother to tell me. What more do I need?"

"Is there any chance that what you saw wasn't what it looked like?"

Brooke thought for a moment. "No!"

Kasey let out a deep breath and left the office. *She's in one of her moods. Just like with Slim and Martha, Mom's made up her mind about the facts and won't listen to anyone.*

Tyler got back from his run, still angry at himself. *How could things have spiraled out of control so fast? Maybe if I had told Brooke sooner?*

Then his phone rang. Brooke's home phone. Tyler smiled. *She's finally calling, giving me the chance to explain.*

"Hello, Brooke."

There was silence on the other end of the line. "No. This is Shane."

"Shane what are doing calling me at this hour?"

"I have to know. Did you do what they say you did?"

Tyler took a slow deep breath. "I don't know what you've been told. So, all I can tell you are the facts. I care about your Mom very much and wouldn't do anything to hurt her. Yes, I do work for AA Land Company and I wasn't allowed to tell anyone that I work for them. And, I didn't come here to take the ranch away from your mother."

"So, you didn't try to hurt Mom."

"No. . . I've been trying to help her."

"I'm glad. . . . How can we make Mom understand?"

Tyler ran his hand through his hair. "Shane, we need to pray."

CHAPTER

T yler had an emptiness inside, with it came pain and confusion. For one of the few times in his life, he was not in control. During the Sunday sermon Tyler scanned the sanctuary for Brooke as his stomach tightened into a knot. He didn't realize how much Brooke meant to him and that she had found a special place in his heart. Was she right? Was there any truth to what she said? Maybe in the past. But this time he was trying to do right by her. Nevertheless, her words still stung. They reminded him of the words his ex-wife used when she filed for divorce. He couldn't lose Brooke; she had brought meaning back into his life.

Tyler found Amber in the foyer after the service; his face spoke volumes; it was strained and tired. "Have you talked with Brooke yet? Can you get her to listen to me? I've got to explain everything."

Amber frowned. "No, she still won't answer my calls."

Tyler continued, "Ray was at the ranch when I stopped by the other day. How much of this is his doing?"

"I suspect a lot. Kasey told me that Ray got someone to check you out. That's how Brooke found out you work for the AA Land Company and to make matters worse she saw me kiss you the other day in front of the restaurant and let her imagination go wild."

"You've got to be kidding, that was all about her. I could really kick myself for not telling her last week about my company like I had planned."

"Why didn't you?"

"We were having such a pleasant evening. I didn't want it to stop. Just the mention of Hal Greer's name soured her mood. So, I put it off. Who knew?"

"I don't know what to tell you. Brooke is not one to forgive and forget. Maybe if she hears the facts she'll listen to reason."

"That might take care of what she thinks she saw outside the restaurant. What about me working for the AA Land Company?"

"You did hide it from her for three months." Amber shook her head, her disgust showed.

"True, but I didn't have any choice, and it was for a good reason."

"That won't matter. Your best chance to put this behind you, is to follow through with whatever you're doing to let her keep the ranch. That will prove what you are saying. Remember actions speak louder than words."

"I'm going to LA this week to work on that. I have a meeting with the company president to sell him on the idea. If you're able to talk to Brooke before I get back, don't mention any of this to her. I don't want to get her hopes up until I have it approved."

"Ok, and I'll also do a little digging to see if I can find out exactly what Ray told her. It'll be good to know if we are dealing with fact or fiction."

"I'll keep trying to get in touch with her. I've gotta talk to her."

The next day while Tyler was in L.A. he kept trying to reach Brooke, still no answer. He struggled to keep his focus on the project as he prepared for his meeting. *Will Bob go for the plan? I've got all the details worked out and the stats show it will be a good use of the land. But will he balk at my connection to Brooke? I can show him it makes sense no matter who runs the operation.*

Tyler knocked at Bob's front door and Charlotte answered. "Hi Tyler. I'm so glad you were able to meet Bob here; he's waiting for you in his office," she beamed. "I've wanted to show off my new Christmas decorations."

Tyler politely smiled, but his Christmas spirit had been torn away. "I'd love to see them," but his heart wasn't in it.

A few minutes later Bob and Tyler got to work in his den. Tyler explained why a horse stable was needed in the development. Bob probed. "Why an equestrian facility and not ball fields?"

"We'll still have the same number of ball fields; we just won't be using this property for them. Besides, my research shows that we will lose the horse owner demographic if we don't provide these facilities. You're a horse owner. Wouldn't it be nice to have a facility that your kids could ride their bike to, and one that also takes care of all your horse's needs? Think of the savings if you didn't have to buy any extra land, maintain a barn and fencing, worry about feed."

Bob slowly nodded his head. "I see your point." He paused and then looked over the top of his glasses at Tyler. "Just who is going to own and operate this facility?"

"I suggest we get someone who already has a good reputation in the community."

"And who is that going to be?"

"Brooke Anderson."

"Is that the woman you've been getting to know?"

"Yes, it is. And after getting to know her I think she would be the perfect person to run the operation."

"Didn't you say she was having some problems keeping her ranch going?"

Tyler slowly let out a deep breath. "That's a long story. But the cliff note version is, Hal Greer may have been involved in sabotaging her business and forcing her books into the red. I don't have any hard facts yet, just circumstantial evidence. In other words, she wouldn't be in her present position if someone wasn't hurting her business."

"You're sure of this?"

"I'm sure of it. I've seen some of the results myself. If she didn't have community support, she would have closed her doors already."

Bob thought for moment. "I guess it could be good PR if we worked with a local business person who's well-liked. We may also have some image rebuilding to do after what Hal has done there." Bob paused and swirled the ice in his drink. "Have you fired Hal yet?"

Tyler shook his head. "I'll do it when I get back."

Bob's tone changed. "Have you gotten a handle on who's causing our problems?"

"Not yet. They've been careful to cover their tracks. I'm hoping Hal can shed some light on the issue."

"Keep probing. I want to know who's behind this, especially if they're tied to our company."

Kasey had driven herself and Shane to youth group. Brooke stayed home to work on paperwork, or so she told the kids and herself. She wasn't ready to encounter Tyler or Amber and attending any church activity increased that risk. The bills and invoices stared back at her. *How could my two best friends betray me?* A war raged inside, one that *forgiveness* wasn't winning. The facts that Ray presented were so damning; could she ever forgive either of them.

Frustrated, she made herself a hot cup of bold Columbian coffee, hoping it would provide some comfort. As she poured her beverage, Ray came through the kitchen door. "Hi Brooke. Thought I might find you home."

"Evening, Ray. What brings you here?"

"Just checkin' up on you. . . Any coffee left?"

"Yes, help yourself."

Ray poured himself a cup of coffee. "Have you decided what you're gonna do about Amber and that lawyer?"

Brooke looked puzzled. "What do you mean what am I going to do?"

Ray took a gulp of his coffee. "I thought you might have them arrested for what they did to you and your ranch."

Brooke's face went blank. "I hadn't thought about that."

Ray pushed. "What do you mean you hadn't thought about it? Messin' with the water pump, the hot water heater and disconnecting the wires to the oil sensor; that was criminal."

Brooke started to reply—then froze. *How does Ray know about the wires being disconnected? Only the mechanic at Hollister Tractor knew about that. . .* Her heart pounded and her stomach tightened as the hairs on the nape of her neck stood up. *No—it can't be. But it has to be. . .* Inside she was confused but outwardly Brooke forced herself to remain calm. *Do I confront him? I'm here alone; can I trust him? If he's been sabotaging things around here, if he set fire to my barn, what else is he capable of? But I need to know.*

"Do you think Tyler was responsible for the accidents at the ranch?"

"I'd bet my last dollar."

"You think he tried to burn the barn down with the tractor in it—which he'd just paid to fix?"

"What better way to shift suspicion away from yourself?"

"How'd he do it? The Fire Marshall didn't find any sign of arson?"

Ray thought about the question. "He could've damaged an extension cord and had it going to a space heater that was set to turn on when the temperature dropped."

That's the basic idea that the Fire Marshall explained to me. . . . No, not Ray. Another man disappointing her. She had to know more. "He wouldn't hurt me; do you think he's responsible for the saddle accident too? The leather just failed. How could Tyler do that?"

"Brooke, you're too trusting. There're lots of ways to cause leather to fail. He could have weakened the latigo with acid or scored the area with a knife. Maybe he didn't want to hurt you; maybe he just wanted it to break while you were mounting, you know, to scare you."

That settles it; Ray is too close on all accounts. But why would he do it. The pieces started to come together. His advances that she rebuffed, the new friend she had in Tyler. Ray was tired of waiting for what he'd never get, so he took matters into his own hands. Rage grew inside of her. This was a dilemma she'd never foreseen—Now, what to do about Ray. He had to be confronted, but how and when? Definitely not now, not when she was home alone. Anger continued to boil as Brooke's face turned red, she avoided looking at Ray, afraid her eyes would betray her new knowledge.

"Ray, this new information has hit me hard. I'm feeling very tired. Do you mind letting yourself out? I need to rest."

Ray gently placed his paw on Brooke's hand. "Sure, you get some rest. But don't you go and do something rash. Let the police take care of that dude." Cringing inside, she wanted to stand up and slap him. But she willed herself to sit still as her temper boiled, she bit her lip to keep from saying anything. Finally, he took his hand away.

She forced out a friendly grin. "Thanks Ray." *And I may just take you up on your advice.*

Once Ray's truck disappeared out of sight Brooke went back into the kitchen. Her fury exploded, she slammed her coffee cup on to the counter shattering it into pieces; she was enraged at how Ray had used her. Then, the emptiness came. She had pushed away all of her closest confidants, Martha, Tyler, and even Amber. Who could she talk to? Who would give her sound advice? The hollowness she felt was almost as painful as the fact that another man had failed her.

Morning arrived for Brooke after a long night of restless sleep. Shortly after Kasey and Shane had left for school Brooke called Detective Lopez. Twenty minutes later he was at the ranch interviewing her. "What makes you believe Ray Harris is responsible for your injury and the other incidents that have occurred around your ranch?"

"He knows things that only I know about the accident and the other mishaps."

Lopez looked up from writing his notes. "Like what?"

Anger still smoldered inside of her. "He knew that the wires had been disconnected between the oil sensor and oil gauge on the tractor. Only I and the service manager at Hollister Tractor knew about that, and he said he wouldn't share the information." Brooke paused and waited for Lopez to catch up with his notes. "When Ray suggested how the fire started, he gave the exact scenario that the Fire Marshall described. He also said that my saddle could have been damaged by scoring the leather with a knife. Only you, I, and Tyler know that's why my latigo failed."

Lopez finished typing and looked up from his iPad. "Could Mr. Alexander have told Ray about the saddle?"

"No way! They don't talk and Ray's been suggesting Tyler is responsible for the accidents."

"So, you really don't have any hard evidence to show that Ray is responsible?"

Brooke shook her head. "No. And how are we going to get hard evidence? Ray's around here all the time and always has access to the equipment and saddles."

"I'm sorry to say, but you're right. Short of him telling someone what he did, or confessing, there's not much we can do to actually prove it."

"Should I confront him?"

"It has some risk. If he's been doing these things, he may not be stable. On the other hand, it could put him on notice that he's being watched. It could put an end to the incidents."

Brooke didn't even pause. "I want him stopped."

"You'll need a witness."

"I agree, I didn't want to confront him last night, not when I was here all alone. But will he open up with someone around?"

"Good point... We could wire you and be hidden nearby for your protection."

Brooke's eyes were hard and cold. "Let's get it done."

"When?"

"Now!"

"You can get him out here that quick?"

"Trust me."

Phone calls were made, and Brooke was taken to the Sheriff's office where she was fitted with a wire. Early in the afternoon she arrived back at her house in Lopez's unmarked car along with two other detectives. After Brooke's wire was checked and the deputies were ready, she called Ray. "You said some things last night that made me rethink our relationship."

"Yeah?" Anticipation hung in Ray's reply.

"We need to talk about it, can you come over?"

"I just finished up Garrison's horses. I'll be there in fifteen."

Brooke took a deep breath and put the phone on the table. Lopez looked at her and nodded. "Nice job. Let's get into position. I and two other deputies will be in the bedroom and two more will be down the street. When they hear that Ray's arrived, they'll park at the end of your driveway as backup. If the situation gets tense and you want me in the room, just say my name."

Brooke nodded. "Okay."

Ray arrived, walked into the kitchen with a large smile and saw Brooke sitting at the table. "You want to talk about our relationship?"

"Yes, I'm not sure it's been going in the right direction. But first, I want to put some other matters to rest concerning Tyler."

"Like what?" Ray said as he sat down across from Brooke.

"You've made some pretty serious accusations against him, and I want to make sure they make sense before I take action."

"Which ones?"

"How about the tractor. What makes you think Tyler purposely damaged the tractor?"

"He was the last one to work on it."

"That doesn't mean he did it on purpose. Last night you said he disconnected the wires. . . How can we know that for sure?"

Ray did not immediately reply but got a glass of water. "I saw the wires disconnected when I inspected the tractor."

Brooke furrowed her forehead. "Why didn't you tell me then?"

"I didn't want to worry you."

I was with you the whole time. You never looked inside the tractor. You tried to start it and checked the oil, and that was all. "Okay. What about the saddle. What makes you think he's responsible for that?"

"He's been hangin' around here a lot and has had access to your tack."

"So have a lot of other people. . . Even you."

Ray stiffened slightly. "But he's got motive. He wants your ranch."

"Why would he risk doing that? He knows the odds of me being able to keep the ranch are pretty slim."

Ray took a drink of water. "I don't know. . . Maybe he got tired of waiting."

"What makes you think the saddle was sabotaged. . . What was it you said—a knife scored the latigo?"

"It's what any knowledgeable horseman would do to damage a saddle."

Brooke's voice became slightly elevated. "Ray, Tyler is not a knowledgeable horseman. He doesn't even know what a latigo is. . . You're telling me details that only me and the police know about. How do you know them?"

Ray squirmed in his chair, and then stood up. "I don't *know* about them. I'm just guessing."

"You're guessing right on every instance. That can't be a coincidence."

Ray picked up his glass. "I thought I came here to talk about us finally getting together."

Brooke had enough. "Not a chance—Didn't you say the accidents picked up once Tyler showed up? Well, you were around the whole time too. I believe you're the one who's been damaging things around here!"

Ray's face turned into a mask of rage. "Why in the hell would I do that? How can you even accuse me. . .?"

"You hate Tyler and ever since he showed up, you've been trying to get rid of him." Brooke's heart raced along with her mind. She tensed as she saw Ray's anger start to boil over. She was ready to call Detective Lopez.

"He's a city dude and ain't no good for you!" Ray's voice got louder.

Brooke's own anger flared, and she shouted back, "Ray, you've been trying to prove I need you ever since Cory died. And what better way than to make me think I'm just a helpless woman. Well, let me tell you. . . ."

Ray squeezed his glass until it shattered in his hand spewing blood onto the table. "If you hadn't ignored Cory's dying wish, and let me take care of you, I wouldn't have had to *make* you need me."

"Oh. . . Ray! He didn't mean for us to get married."

"Yes, he did!"

"Ray, there's no way Cory would want that. He would never want me married to someone who doesn't believe in God. That would go against everything he stood for."

Ray's face went red and his eyes became wild. "You've always needed me, and I've never gotten anything back. It's about time. . .And I'm gonna take it one way or another."

He started toward her.

Brooke's face went pale. She'd never seen Ray so enraged. She backed away. "Ray, you're scaring me!"

The deputies waiting in the other room entered the kitchen with weapons drawn and aimed at Ray. *"Put your hands up! Get down on your knees!"*

"What's this?" Ray shouted.

"Face down on the floor, put your hands behind your back." Detective Lopez ordered.

Several minutes later Ray was up on his feet being led outside to a waiting squad car. As he was placed in the vehicle he looked back at the house with a defiant glare.

CHAPTER

*B*rooke struggled for the past couple of hours to keep her focus on the volunteer riders. With the horses exercised and the riders gone, Brooke went to the tack room and gazed at her saddle. The facts didn't add up. Ray had been responsible for the accidents. But she strove to understand where Hal Greer and Tyler fit into the picture? Nothing made sense.

There was no one Brooke could talk too, she had shut out all of her confidants. Brooke desperately needed to bare her soul to someone. Who could she turn to? Finally, she went into her bedroom to pray. Her anxiety started to fade as the first inklings of peace appeared—along with a mild urge to go see her mother. Though her mom might not be able to hold a conversation, she would be able to listen. That was what she needed most—an unjudging ear.

Kasey dropped Brooke off at the sparsely decorated nursing home. Inside, Brooke found the staff was much less inhibited with their Christmas spirit; they had made numerous additions since her last visit. An artificial tree now lit up in the foyer along with displays of Santa and his elves. Brooke found her mother sitting in her room, paging through an old photo album that she had dropped off earlier in the month. "Hi Alice, what are you looking at?"

Alice raised her head. "Your wedding pictures."

A jolt of surprise flashed through Brooke. *But she's looking at my picture. Makes sense she'd know I'm the woman in them.* She returned a smile. "That was a long time ago. A lot has happened since then."

Alice studied Brooke. "You look unsettled. What's bothering you?"

Brooke was taken back by the observation. "Thanks, it will help to get it off my chest." She sat beside her mother, took her hand, and let it all out—Cory's accident, the mishaps around the ranch and Tyler's deceitful action. The pain, hurt and anger spilled out. And then Brooke was finally silent.

"Dear, dear Brooke," her mother said, "I sense bitterness and un-forgiveness in your spirit. Let it go. Don't hold on to it like I've done for all these years. It will eat you up inside and destroy you and your health. You need to forgive."

Brooke was startled by her mother's clarity. She'd witnessed moments of it before, but now her mother seemed so present. She was talking to the mother she'd known ten years earlier. "How can I forgive them for what they've done to me? It hurts so much." Tears started to flow from her eyes.

Alice took her hand. "By yourself you can't, but with God's help you can. Remember, he forgave us all for our sins."

"But he's God. He has the power to forgive. I'm just a woman who's been hurt and disappointed by every man who's come into my life. Even Daddy abandoned me."

Alice's expression changed. "No, he didn't."

Brooke stared at her. "What do you mean? You told me he left us for another woman and was never coming back."

"I know... but it's time I told you the truth. I hope you can forgive me."

What was her mother saying? Was it the dementia—or....

"I made up that story to protect myself from the truth."

"Then why did he leave us?"

"I kicked him out because of his drugs and cheating."

"You kicked him out?"

Alice paged through the photo album as though she were refreshing her memory. "Your father came back from Vietnam hooked on drugs and suffering from wild emotional swings. We didn't know then how much the war had affected so many of those poor guys." She looked up at Brooke. "A couple years later you were born. That seemed to help him for a little while. He truly loved you. But then he lost his job and started to slip into a dark, dark place. He wouldn't go near you. God knows, he wouldn't touch me. The drug use got worse. I suspected he was stealing to buy drugs." Alice closed the photo album.

"I was angry. Angry at what the war did to him. Angry at him. He started staying out all night. Whole weekends he'd disappear. I held every single misdeed against him, and all the hurt I felt kept building up. I couldn't forgive him. The final straw was when he started seeing another woman, or so I thought. I was just looking for an excuse to push him away. So, I kicked him out and never saw or heard from him again."

"Why didn't you tell me the truth?"

"You were so young, just four or five, and I got tired of answering your questions about 'where's my daddy?' I wanted him out of our lives; so, I told you he died after he left us. I figured that would stop your questions. Put it all to rest. . . I didn't want you blaming me for him leaving."

Brooke's heart was pounding. This revelation was coming so fast. . . so much to take in.

"Much later I learned that he wasn't with that woman; but the damage had been done, and my pride was not going to allow me to try to make things right. Too many people had believed my lie. . . By then, your father was gone." Her mother's chin fell to her chest, and tears came.

Brooke's jaw hung open. What was she hearing? *All those years. All that time lost. My reason for judging all men as abandoners was based on a lie.* She put her hand on her mother's shoulder. "Why are you telling me this now?"

Alice looked up, deep into Brooke's eyes, tears streaming. "I don't want you making the same mistake I made by letting bitterness and regret wreak havoc on your life and health. Forgive those who've hurt you and ask forgiveness from those you've hurt."

"But what about Daddy. If he didn't die, what happened to him?"

Alice stared at the wall in front of her and didn't answer.

"Mom. Mom!"

Her mother's hands went limp, the photo album fell from her lap. She vanished into the mental fog again. Brooke rushed for a nurse. When they returned her mother was still staring at the wall. "Mrs. Anderson, on rare occasions we've seen this happen before. They have a brief period of lucidity and then immediately return to their previous state."

Brooke followed the nurse back out into the hallway. "But I need her back. She was telling me something very important. I need to finish talking with her."

"I wish I could help you. But I can't. There's nothing anyone can do to bring her out of the state she's in. You were lucky to have a few minutes with her."

Luck? Or. . .

Almost in shock, Brooke went back to her mother's room and watched and—hoped. Brooke resigned herself to the fact it was over. But what her mother said had penetrated her soul and started a transformation. *Forgiveness.*

Brooke leaned over her mother and whispered. "You did what you thought was best. I forgive you." She couldn't believe she uttered those words as she gave her mother a gentle kiss on her cheek. Maybe God was touching her life. As she passed the nurses' station the duty nurse stopped her. "I hope your time with your mother was meaningful."

Brooke paused and thought. "Yes. . . it was."

Dumbfounded by the revelation about her father, more than that, it was as though the conversation had contained a divine message. How else could she explain the events of the evening? Perhaps, this was her Christmas gift from God. As they drove out the parking lot Kasey asked. "You're really quiet, Mom. What's going on?"

Brooke was not ready to tell her all she had just learned. She needed time to absorb what had happened. She simply replied, "Grandma was. . . clear. She talked to me a little. Said some things that I need to ponder."

"I've been thinking about some things, too. Mom—when are you going to talk to Amber and hear what she has to say?"

Brooke looked out the car window and watched the nursing home fade into the darkness. "Soon—real soon."

The Lakers and the Spurs were tied, with three minutes remaining in the fourth quarter. The matchup was electrifying, and Ryan was really into the game. Tyler thought the courtside seats at the Lakers game would help repair the connection with his son. Tyler smiled, there was his son, sitting next to James Holahan, the newest late-night TV host. A primo seat. *After the game, I'll see if he has made up his mind about Christmas yet. He didn't seem that interested in getting together during my last trip. Hopefully tonight will help change his mind.*

When the game ended, Tyler leaned over to Ryan. "Great game—right?"

"Sure was. How'd you ever get courtside seats on such short notice?"

"I called in a favor from a friend."

"Well, tell them thanks."

Tyler reached for his phone. It wasn't there. He checked all of his pockets. Gone. "Ryan, do you remember when you last saw me with my phone?"

"You were checking some messages when we came into the building. I haven't seen you use it since then. Why, don't you have it?"

"No, and I need it." They searched around the seats, and finally went to the lost and found. Still no phone. The great mood he'd been in was gone; he'd have to take time in the morning to get a new phone.

In spite of the issue with his phone, Tyler was confident that the evening was going well. He parked outside Ryan's apartment and decided to push for that holiday visit. "That car of yours is a couple years old now. If you drive out to Flagstaff to visit me over Christmas, I'll upgrade it to a brand-new model."

Ryan shook his head; and got out of the car. "Dad! You just don't get it. All this stuff is great—but why do you keep trying to buy my love?" He slammed the door and left.

Tyler watched his son retreat to his apartment. Then sat in solitude, still feeling the sting of Ryan's words. He knew he blew it. Again. Nothing he did resembled what he knew about Shane's relationship with his father. *What I want is time with my son. Everything I try seems to fail. I don't even know how to start.* His head slumped to his chest. *Lord help me.*

Brooke tossed and turned all night, the conversation with her mother was embedded in her mind. She sought council from Pastor Sena the next morning. He advised Brooke that the conversation with her mother may have been a message from God. After that meeting Brooke took the first hard step and texted Amber and asked to have a meeting. She wasn't quite ready to talk on the phone. She needed some time to think. A couple of hours later Amber tentatively walked into Brooke's kitchen. "Brooke, what's going on?"

The late-morning sun poured light into the kitchen as Brooke stammered. "Have you heard about Ray?"

"Yeah. It's pretty much all over town."

"It's still so hard to believe he was behind all the accidents on the ranch. The Sheriff is also going to check the vehicles on Ray's property to see if they contain any evidence tying them to Zoomey's accident."

"Wow! How'd you find out?"

Brooke's nerves were on edge. This was new ground for her. "First, I have a confession."

"You do?"

"Ray was feeding me lies about how you and Tyler were working together to take the ranch."

Amber's jaw dropped open. "And you believed him?"

"I am so ashamed of myself now. But the evidence he fed me was pretty convincing, and then I saw you kissing Tyler the other day. It all kind of made sense. Tyler, you, the bank, and AA Land Company. . . ."

Amber shook her head and sighed. "Oh, Brooke. Girl, sometimes you do let your mind go to crazy places. I guess I understand it. But if you had just talked to us. . . ."

Brooke nodded. "You're right. It was crazy. I want to say I'm sorry. I want to ask for your forgiveness for thinking the worst of you and not believing in you. Will you forgive me?" Brooke finally took a breath.

Amber moved over to Brooke and threw her arms around her. "Yes, absolutely. Just don't do that again!"

Tears were in Brooke's eyes. Then she started to smile. "I won't. I promise." The conversation shifted. "I've been trying to reach Tyler, but he won't answer my calls."

"He was pretty frustrated when I saw him at church before he left for L.A. . ." Amber offered.

"Do you think he's washed his hands of me? I left a pretty nasty message on his phone when I found out he worked for the AA Land Company. I was irate that he'd hidden that from me."

"He said he was coming back to finish some business and will be here for the Christmas Eve service. I wouldn't be too hard on him for being secretive. From what he told me; he was under orders. I can't tell you about it. Maybe he can explain it to you."

"I'll listen, but I'm still angry about him lying to me."

For a few moments silence hung between the two friends, then Amber spoke again. "Can I be honest?"

"Sure."

"This isn't like you—to forgive and seek forgiveness. What's changed?"

Brooke stared at her cup before looking back at her friend. "I think God sent me a message, telling me I need to forgive."

Amber stayed focused on her. "What do you mean?"

Brooke poured out the story of what happened the night before at the nursing home. Every detail. Amber sat back; astonishment blanketed her face. "It sure does sound like you've had a message from God."

"Yeah. It does."

"What about your dad? Are you going to try to find him?"

"I don't know. He hasn't contacted me in all these years." A tinge of hurt lingered on her words.

"What about your mom. Have you forgiven her?"

"Surprisingly, yes. And I have a peace about it."

After a long morning at the cell phone store Tyler sat in his seat on the plane, scrolling through a long list of messages and missed calls on his new phone. There were six missed calls from Brooke. *I'm surprised she's trying to reach me.* Taking a deep breath, he called her back. No answer. *She probably wants to tell me she never wants to see me again.* The door of the plane closed; any more attempts to call Brooke would have to wait. As soon as the wheels touched down Tyler connected to a mobile network. *Another missed call from Brooke.* He tried calling her again, this time there she answered. Awkward silence hung between them until Tyler offered. "Have you been trying to reach me?"

"Yes, I'd like to talk to you. Can you come over?"

He tried to read the tone of her voice and couldn't. "I've just landed in Flagstaff, and I need to take care of one urgent business matter. Is it okay if I come over after that?"

"Yes, that would be fine."

"Is everything okay with you?"

She hesitated. "I think so."

Now that his business affiliation was no longer secret Tyler arranged for his meeting at the Flagstaff offices. The man he needed to see was sitting at the table in a small conference room. Tyler entered carrying an envelope in his hand, sat down, and slid it across the table. Hal Greer looked at it but didn't touch the document. "What's this? Who are you?"

"I'm Tyler Alexander, Vice President of Alexander and Alexander Land Company."

Greer momentarily squirmed in his seat before a smug look reappeared on his face. "Why do you want to see me?"

"There are some pretty serious allegations against you. And a restraining order has been filed against you by one of the local property owners." Greer was expressionless. Tyler continued. "With the damage you've done to this company's reputation we have every right to fire you. I've also looked into the records at the courthouse and found that you've been involved with several other transactions in the area, beyond those you did for our company. These types of allegations could easily cost you your realtor's license."

"Hey, wait a minute!" But Tyler shut him down. "I will finish what I was saying. If you provide me the names of the individuals you're working with, we might not file a complaint with the Arizona Real Estate Board. If the information is valuable enough, I may include some type of severance package."

Tyler's skin crawled when he made that offer, but Bob insisted he wanted the information and was willing to pay for it. The company had to find the inside person. Hal glared at him. "I don't have to tell you anything."

"Is that your final answer?"

"Final and only answer."

Tyler stood up and walked toward the door. "Consider yourself terminated. There'll be no severance package."

Hal shot up from his chair. "You'll be hearing from my lawyer."

The sky was overcast and threatening to snow as Tyler drove to Brooke's. Was the dreary day an ominous sign of what lay ahead? Twenty minutes later he pulled up next to her house and noticed something had changed. Christmas lights had been strung along the eaves. He knocked on Brooke's kitchen door. It wasn't right, just walking in anymore, not after the events of the past week. A faint voice came from inside. "Come on in, the door is open."

Brooke was on the far side of the kitchen when he stepped inside; an uncomfortable silence hung between them. Tyler offered. "You seem to be moving better."

"Yeah. Each day gets a little easier." Brooke paused, not sure how to deal with her battling emotions. She wanted to hug him, but at the same time she wanted to scream at him. "You've been to L.A.?"

"Yes, some business matters to take care of before Christmas." After that—what to say next? "The Christmas lights look nice on the outside of the house. When did you put them up?"

"Shane and Kasey did it this morning. It's the first time they've been up since we lost Cory."

"Oh, what's the occasion?"

"Time to move on and start a new chapter in our lives."

Tyler was uneasy. Why did she want to see him and where she was going with the conversation? "Are you still planning to sing at tonight's Christmas Eve Service?"

Brooke's mouth went dry. "Well. . . are you?"

"I'm planning on it. . . . So, is that why you wanted to see me?"

"Not exactly. Please. Have a seat."

Facing each other across the table, Brooke began. "This is not easy for me to do so please bear with me as I find the right words." Tyler watched her hands tremble. "I was told lies about you and Amber. I'm ashamed to say I believed them."

"Really. What lies?"

"Ray said you were behind the accidents on the ranch, and that you and Amber were working together with the bank to take the ranch away from me. Then he showed me that you work for the AA Land Company and I saw Amber kissing you in front of the restaurant—it all seemed to make sense."

"But it wasn't what it looked like."

Brooke held up her hand to stop him. "Let me finish. I know now. Amber explained all that the other day. And it turns out that Ray was behind a lot of the so-called accidents."

"How did you find out?"

"He let it slip while he was trying to implicate you."

Brooke went on to explain what happened with the Sheriff's deputies, and how they got Ray to confess. When she finished, she reached across the table, and laid one hand on top of Tyler's.

"I need to apologize for thinking the worst about you and not giving you a chance to explain."

Tyler smiled. "Apology accepted."

"But –" Brooke continued. "I am really disappointed in you. You hurt me when you weren't honest about who you worked for."

Tyler slowly let out a long sigh. "You're right. I should have told you. But I was under orders from the home office to keep my affiliation with AA Land Company hidden. I wanted to tell you and tried to a couple of times. But it never seemed like the right moment."

"You did?—when?"

"The evening we went Christmas shopping, I wanted to tell you at the restaurant. But when I saw how the mention of Hal Greer upset you, I couldn't bring myself to let you know who I worked for. I didn't want to ruin the evening."

"It did upset me. But you should have told me even if it did kill the mood. You should have told me and taken the chance on our relationship."

Relationship. Why did he have such difficulties with them? Tyler's eyes softened. "Brooke, please forgive me for not telling you who I work for. I truly am sorry. I hope you can believe me."

The earlier conversation with her mother and her message from God hit Brooke hard. Sure, she'd been told to forgive, and yet in that moment she realized it was a choice she still had to make. A decision that in the past she chose to ignore. However, if she was going to move forward, she had to change. Brooke looked steadily into his eyes. He was open. Remorseful.

"Yes, I forgive you." Tears formed in her eyes, and she could no longer hold back the torrent of emotion that had been building inside of her. "I've missed you so much. I thought I lost you."

Tyler rose and moved to her side. With his hand firmly grasping hers, he guided Brooke to her feet—then wrapped his arms around her as she laid her head against his chest. "I've missed you too. I haven't been able to focus on my work. All I can do is think of you."

Brooke's tears turned to sobs. Clinging to Tyler, burying her face against him, she felt as if a great barrier had fallen. There was a oneness with him, something that hadn't existed with anyone for years, not since Cory. There was no more guilt. Tyler gently cradled Brooke's cheek in his hand, as he lifted her face, and looked deep into her eyes. He moved his lips closer to hers until they met. This time there was no holding back.

CHAPTER

28

On his way back to Brooke's to get ready for the Christmas Eve concert Tyler made a quick stop at Stacy's Boutique. For the first time in years, he wanted to do something besides work, and Brooke was responsible for that change in his life. However, in spite of this peace, something still nagged at him. He still had not figured out how to connect with Ryan. When he arrived at the ranch, Shane was waiting for him in the kitchen. "Hi Tyler, Mom said I should hang out with you until she and Kasey are ready."

"Okay, what do you have in mind?"

"I can show you my new Scout project."

"Sure, what is it?"

"It's a collection of pictures of me and my dad all put in one picture frame."

"You mean a collage?"

"Yeah, that's what they called it"

A few minutes later they were sitting in front of a computer screen while Shane navigated to his project. Shane pointed to the screen. "For this part of the project they want us to take a bunch of pictures and put them together to tell a story."

"What's the story that you're going to tell?"

"About how my Dad taught me to ride."

Tyler studied the screen. There were at least fifteen to twenty pictures, the majority with Shane and Cory in them. The images touched a nerve with Tyler and brought into focus how much of Ryan's life he missed. *Could Ryan have put together a collage like this when he was a kid? Are there any pictures of me and Ryan just having fun?* The sad answer was—very few. Tyler was good at volleyball but instead of teaching him the game, he sent Ryan to volleyball camp. Most of his family pictures were staged and posed. It hit him like a cement block that he really didn't spend much time with Ryan. *If only I could go back.*

Brooke entered the family room. "You boys ready to go?"

Tyler stared. Brooke looked spectacular in a long black skirt with black boots. Her deep red sweater balanced the outfit perfectly. "A-yeah. We're ready." He couldn't take his eyes off her.

At the Christmas Eve service, Tyler longed for the type of relationship Shane had with his dad. Was it too late for him? The choir started the singing with several carols and then performed a short cantata. The chorus then left the stage; all except Tyler and Brooke who stayed for their duet. They walked to center stage and stopped at their marks, the lights dimmed in the sanctuary, except for two spotlights that shown down on them. The instrumental track started softly as they smiled at each other. . . and began.

Mary, did you know that your baby boy
Would someday walk on water?
Mary, did you know that your baby boy
Would save our sons and daughters?
Did you know that your baby boy
Has come to make you new?
This child that you've delivered
Will soon deliver you.

The words and music flowed together, their eyes met, and the song was filled with an emotion they'd never achieved during any of their rehearsals. Many in the audience were moved to tears.

Mary, did you know?
The blind will see, the deaf will hear
The dead will live a-gain
The lame will leap, the dumb will speak
The praises of the Lamb.

As they concluded, Tyler looked at Brooke and put his arm around her and then gave her a hug. She responded by turning to him and wrapping both arms around his waist and returned a quick embrace. Shane smiled. Kasey looked the other way. She still wasn't comfortable with the idea of someone replacing her father.

Pastor Sena started his message. "This is not a traditional Christmas Eve sermon, where I focus on the birth of the Christ child. Instead, I feel in my heart we need to delve into the bigger implications of what this event means. The key to Christmas is John 3:16, *For God so loved the world that he gave his only begotten Son, that whoever believes in him should not perish but have eternal life.* This is why the Christ Child came into this world. He was the perfect example of unconditional love. Even though mankind rejected Him, he took on our sins so that we might spend eternity with him."

Tyler sat there, pierced to the soul. *This guy has done it again. He's talking straight at me. How'd he know what I've been struggling with?* The words landed on Tyler, as if they were spoken just for him. Sena didn't know that he was struggling to have a better relationship with Ryan, or that he'd just been wondering how to bridge the gap between them. . . But God knew. Tyler's love had always been manipulative, not pure. What Ryan had said earlier suddenly made sense. Ryan was looking for unconditional love with no strings or conditions attached. A deep remorse gripped Tyler, all the times he'd tried to buy Ryan's love or when he expected something in return for what he considered love. The tears that formed in Tyler's eyes started to stream down his cheeks, as the full realization of his actions came into view. Brooke noticed Tyler's tears, leaned close to him and whispered. "Are you alright?" Tyler nodded. She placed her hand on his.

At the conclusion of the sermon the lights were dimmed once more. Everyone lit the candles they'd been given, and their voices rose.

Silent night, holy night!

All is calm, all is bright. . . .

Tyler thought. *I see it all now. I can see what I did, and what I failed to do.* He once more put his arm around Brooke, and she leaned her head against his shoulder. This felt right. Neither one fought what was drawing them together.

Inside Brooke's home there was Christmas music and laughter as they ate hors d'oeuvre and drank punch while "It's a Wonderful

Life" played in the background. Kasey couldn't help to notice the joy on her mom's face, an emotion that had been missing for a long time. She wasn't crazy about Tyler, but at least he made her mother happy again. That counted for a lot. *He'll never come close to Dad. But I'll try to give him a chance.*

While basking in the warmth coming from the fireplace, Tyler enjoyed the family time, especially the few moments he could steal alone with Brooke. Still, something tugged at his heart. It was that message earlier in the evening, and what Shane had been telling him. Then there was Ryan's comment during their last encounter. It was no coincidence; God had to be the one trying to get his attention. *But what am I supposed to do? I've messed up every other attempt of trying to connect with Ryan.*

Brooke looked at Tyler. "You seem far away."

"Just thinking."

She put her hand on his shoulder. "The same thing that touched you during the sermon?"

It's scary the way she can read me. Tyler sighed. "Yeah, family things."

"Your son?"

"I was hoping to spend Christmas with him." Sadness touched his words.

"It's a short notice. But why don't you invite him here? We'd love the extra company." Kasey shot her mom a look.

"No. No—it would never. . . ." Tyler stopped. *It's a crazy idea, one so crazy it will only work with the aid of divine intervention.* He looked at Brooke. "Are you sure?"

"Yes, I mean it."

"It's a long shot that he'll be able to come. But I have to try. I've gotta go and see if I can pull things together."

Shane groaned. "You have to go already?"

"Yes Shane, he has to go." Brooke got up and went with Tyler to the door. "I'll pray for you."

"Thanks."

Her smile warmed him as she blew him a parting kiss.

All the way back to his apartment Tyler rehearsed what he'd say to Ryan. Nothing sounded quite right. What would convince Ryan that he was sincere about changing. At his apartment he shut off the engine. . . and prayed. *God, I believe you've sent me a message, and I truly want to change. I'll need your help to make this happen. I don't have the power to do it myself. But I especially need your help to reach Ryan. Please give me the right words to let him know that you are changing me. Please, give me a chance to repair our relationship.*

Tyler wiped a tear from his eye as he got out of the car and left a trail of solitary footprints in the fresh snow. He threw his coat on the back of the overstuffed chair, plopped down in it and then took several minutes to work up the courage to make the call. He shook his head in disbelief. *This phone call shouldn't be causing me so much angst.* But it was if everything was riding on the conversation, it was so important for him to reconnect with Ryan. Finally, he dialed the number.

"Dad?—What's up?"

"Son, I need to apologize to you for not being a good father."

"Dad, you don't have to. . . ."

"Ryan, please. I need to say this. I know I was not there for you, and when I was, I really wasn't. I thought I could buy your love. I thought I was doing the father thing right. But I wasn't, I see that now."

Tyler paused; there was dead silence on the other end of the line. "Ryan, please forgive me."

Again, there was silence.

"Dad, Robyn's here. We're kinda just enjoying Christmas Eve—alone."

Tyler almost spoke but held back. *Please, God.*

In a moment, Ryan offered. "Well, it's a step. . . . It's good that you see what you've done."

Tyler heard the skepticism. "I don't know how to prove to you that I'm trying to change. But everything that I think to do, could end up being interpreted the wrong way."

Ryan muttered. "Probably."

Tyler let the comment slide. "Here's what I'm going to do. I'll have a roundtrip airline ticket to Flagstaff delivered to your apartment first thing tomorrow. It'll be fully refundable and transferable. You can use it, get the money back for it, give it away. Do whatever you want with it. My car will be waiting for you at the Flagstaff airport. The keys will be hidden at the usual spot. I'll text the parking lot location." Tyler's heart was racing and his hands were damp.

"You were right. It sounds just like before."

Tyler's heart sank. "Maybe it does. But, there are no strings attached. You can stay as short or as long as you like. I'm trying to leave you options, so you're in control and not me."

"Maybe you are."

"They're some people here that I'd like you to meet. I'll text you the address where I'll be."

"We'll see."

"Whether you decide to come or not, the ticket will be delivered tomorrow morning, and everything else will be in place waiting for you."

"Dad, I've gotta go. Robyn and I have plans for this evening."

Ryan hung up and Tyler slumped in the chair. His gut had tightened into a knot, and he felt spent. He'd never been one to get anxious but letting go of control was new ground for him. He made several phone calls and had the tickets purchased and a courier delivering them in the morning. The rest was up to Ryan.

Ryan sat on the sofa and stared at his phone. Robyn snuggled closer to him. "What was that about?"

"It was a strange conversation with my dad. He was trying to get me to go see him tomorrow in Flagstaff."

"Why's that so strange?"

"He apologized for not being a good father, and he's buying me a plane ticket to get there. He said there were no strings attached."

"Maybe he's got the Christmas Spirit?"

"It was weird. . . It actually sounded like he meant it when he said there were no strings attached. In the past, he would have tried to bribe me. But this seemed different. . . It seemed like he was really trying to let me be in control."

Robyn sat up and looked into Ryan's eyes. "Kinda cool. What are you going to do?"

"I'll think of something."

The next morning Tyler dropped off his car at the airport and picked up a rental. Would his efforts be in vain? Promptly at ten he knocked on Brooke's door and went in. "Anyone here?" He called.

"Yes, we're in the family room." Brooke called out.

Tyler walked in to see a pile of presents still beneath the tree and torn wrapping paper spread about the room. His smile broadened. "Looks like you've been busy."

"Brooke laughed. "Just the stocking stuffers. There's more to go."

"I thought you'd be done by now."

"Never, taking care of the horses comes first. We worked Slider and then we read the Christmas Story before we started opening the stocking stuffers. I purposely held off on the packages under the tree until you got here."

"You shouldn't have."

Brooke shot Tyler a stern look. He got the message and grinned. "If that's the case, can I get Shane's help to bring in some packages from the car?"

Shane jumped up. "Sure."

Once all of Tyler packages were in and next to the tree, they settled down in the family room. Kasey and Shane flanked Brooke on the sofa as Tyler sat forward on the recliner and observed. This was the first time either Shane or Kasey could remember someone outside their immediate family being part of a Christmas morning. Shane was fine with it, but Kasey still had reservations about the situation. She still remembered her father sitting in that same chair just a few years earlier.

Brooke looked at Tyler. "You sit back and relax. Kasey's in charge of passing out the gifts. You're our guest." She winked at him when the kids weren't looking.

Tyler pulled out his cell phone and leaned back in the chair and started snapping pictures. The smiling, joking, and family love he witnessed warmed him inside. For a time, he was so caught up in the moment that he forgot about the possible arrival of Ryan. They were down to the last few packages, the ones brought in from the car, and the one leaning up against the wall. Brooke motioned for Kasey to give it to Tyler. He pulled off the paper and a silly grin spread across his face. Tyler read the card out aloud. "We thought it was time that you had your own horse to ride." He then held up the Palomino stick horse and laughed. Shane then handed Tyler a much smaller package that jingled softly. He opened it up to find his first set of spurs.

"Aren't they neat?" Shane said while pointing at the rowels.

"They sure are. I didn't think I'd get these for a while."

Brooke grinned. "Congratulations, you've graduated to spurs."

"Thanks. It means a lot to me that you think my riding has improved that much."

Kasey pushed the four small heavy boxes in front of Shane along with one oddly shaped box. He slid down on the floor in front of the boxes, eyeing the oddly shaped box first and then he ripped off its paper. "Neat, a bar bell. I've been needing one of those. I've gotta put on some muscle for rugby." He then attacked the rest of the boxes and put the weights on the bar.

Brooke looked at Tyler and nodded. "Okay Kasey, you're next."

Kasey picked up her much smaller package and carefully removed the paper. Her eyes brightened when she read the store name on the box, and then. "Ah, they're gorgeous. . . Thank you, Tyler." She took earrings out of the box and held them up to show Brooke.

Brooke smiled. "They'll look really pretty with your new sweater."

There were two packages to go, both for Brooke. She pulled the paper off the larger one revealing the name of the store. Her eyes went to Tyler before opening the box to find the skirt and blouse ensemble she kept admiring while at the Stacy's. "It's beautiful. You shouldn't have."

Kasey looked on. "Can I borrow it sometime?" Brooke laughed.

Tyler sat in the chair snapping pictures of the activity. He put down the camera. "One more package to go."

Kasey handed Brooke a much smaller package, expertly wrapped. Anticipation showed in her eyes as she carefully unwrapped it to find the same store name branded on the box. *He's got good taste but he really shouldn't have.* She couldn't wait to see what was inside and opened the box to find a necklace. The one Tyler had looked at for

Kasey, a simple elegant western silver cross on a silver chain. She looked at Tyler as a tear trickled down her cheek.

Tyler shrugged. "It seemed the outfit needed something to finish it off."

"But it was so expensive."

"Don't think that. Compared to what your family has done in my life, it's nothing." Brooke moved over and gave Tyler a hug. Shane laughed as she wrapped her cast around his back. Kasey turned away.

After their brunch, Brooke and Tyler went for a short stroll around the property. Part way into their walk Tyler took Brooke's hand. "It sure is pretty around here. The frosted Ponderosas, the snow-covered mountains in the background. . . So, peaceful."

"Yes, it is. I hope I can keep it."

Tyler wanted to tell Brooke about his plans but didn't want to get her hopes up. Not until he had a final decision from the board.

"Any word from Ryan yet?"

Tyler shrugged his shoulders. "I don't know. He didn't commit to it last night. I called the ticket courier this morning and they said no one answered the door."

"I'll keep praying."

The girls were working on dinner preparations as Tyler sat at the kitchen table scanning his smartphone. Brooke picked up on Tyler's apprehension. "Why don't you and Shane go for a ride?"

Tyler started to say no. But, it came to him. *What am I trying to change in my life? It's not just Ryan I have to make time for. It's everyone who's important to me.* "Sure." Tyler looked at Brooke. "When should we be back?"

"Dinner is at four. Try to be back by three in case there's anything we need help with."

"Call me if he shows up before we get back."

Kasey looked at her mom. "What's that about?"

"Didn't I tell you? Tyler's son, Ryan, may be joining us for dinner." Brooke shook her head and smiled as Kasey flew around the house picking up the Christmas Day clutter.

The boys came back on schedule to find Brooke, Kasey, and Amber, who came for dinner, putting the final touches on dinner. Brooke gave Tyler an inquisitive look. "Hear anything?"

Tyler shook his head. "No, not a word."

"There's still time." Brooke sent Tyler and Shane to the family room where they watched some football.

Amber nudged Brooke. "What was that about?"

"Tyler's son might be joining us for dinner."

"A son, how old?"

"In college."

Amber smiled as she looked at Kasey. "Hm, a college boy. Does he look like his dad?" Kasey shook her head and rolled her eyes.

"Is that the only thing on your mind?" Brooke teased.

Amber shot back. "Men and horses. . . Yup, that just about fills it up." They laughed.

Four o'clock was nearing and the table was set. Tyler checked his watch between every down of the game. He had given up hope when the front doorbell rang. His heart jumped. *Could it be Ryan?*

"Shane, could you get the door and see who it is?" Brooke called.

Shane raced to the front door. "It's some guy," Shane paused. "He says his name is Ryan and wants to know if Tyler Alexander is here."

Tyler exhaled. *He did come—Maybe there's hope.* Then he almost ran to the front door. "Come in Ryan, Merry Christmas. I'm so glad you made it." He motioned to Shane. "This is Shane who you've already met."

Brooke took off her apron and went into the living room. "Hi I'm

Brooke, I'm glad you could come." She took him in. "You are the spitting image of your father."

"That's what they tell me. And, thank you for inviting me to dinner."

Tyler inquired. "Everything go okay? Your flight should have been here hours ago?"

"Yeah, I decided to drive. Didn't want to be tied down to a flight schedule."

Brooke shook her head. "But such a long trip to drive."

"I found it relaxing."

"Okay. . . We're just about ready to sit down for dinner, let me take your coat." She handed the coat to Shane.

Kasey and Amber were placing food on the table when the trio entered the dining room. Brooke motioned to Kasey. "This is my daughter Kasey and this is my friend Amber."

Kasey tried not to let it be obvious, but her eyes interrogated the new visitor. *Definitely a city boy. Cute, undeniably cute.* Then it hit her. *He looks like Tyler.*

Amber caught Brooke's eye and raised her eyebrows. Brooke smiled back as they sat down for dinner. Throughout dinner the usual questions about where you live, school, work, and so on were casually exchanged. After dessert Brooke inquired. "How long will you be visiting?"

"Just this evening. I need to leave by seven so I can get back at a reasonable hour."

Brooke protested. "That's too much driving for such a short visit. Do you really have to go?"

"There are some things going on back in L.A. tomorrow and I'd like to get back for them."

Brooke looked at Tyler. "Can you change his mind?"

"I'd like to, but I promised Ryan I wouldn't put any constraints on his visit."

Ryan gave his dad a surprised look. A half an hour later they accompanied Ryan to the door. Brooke gave him a polite hug as did Amber. Kasey simply gave a shy smile and handshake while Shane heartedly shook his hand and said. "I hope you come back soon. I'd like to hear more about where you live and your volleyball team."

Tyler walked out to the car with Ryan. "Thanks for coming. It meant a lot to me."

"It was fun; they're nice people. Plus, it was an interesting road trip."

"If you get tired on the way back, don't push it. Find a hotel and call me to take care of the bill; many places have a minimum check-in age you know."

"Dad, I think I'm past that age now."

"Anyway, if you run into a problem just give me a call."

Ryan drove away and Brooke walked out to Tyler and put her arm around him. "He came."

Tyler sniffled a little. "Yes, he came. Maybe it's a start."

By the time he reached Flagstaff Ryan was on his phone. "Hi Robyn, I miss you.

"I miss you too." Came Robyn's reply.

"How's your Christmas going?"

"It's been typical. How about you? How did it go with your dad?"

"Surprisingly good. He didn't try to keep me there, and there were no bribes. He even offered to help me get back, no strings were attached."

"Then why are you leaving? I'll be stuck up in Santa Barbara until New Years. Why don't you stay and test things a little more with your dad?"

Ryan pulled into a gas station. "You mean hang out with my dad for the week?"

"Sure, you've got your wheels, so if it gets bad you can leave at any time."

"That's true and they've got some good skiing here in Flagstaff."

"What about your dad? Just don't ski, spend some time with him"

"I'm skeptical, but it could be an interesting test. He's burned me so many times before, it will take more than a week to convince me that he's changed. I've had a whole lifetime of playing second fiddle to his work."

"Do you have anything to lose?"

"I guess not."

Ryan turned around and drove back to Brooke's. They were still lingering at the dinner table talking about the upcoming adventure to L.A. when there was a knock at the backdoor. Brooke looked at Kasey and then Tyler. "Who could that be at this hour? On Christmas?"

She went to the back door and after a brief conversation, called out with a smile. "Tyler, it's for you."

CHAPTER

Tyler and Ryan were able to get in two days of skiing before Brooke and Kasey had to leave. Ryan noticed something different about his dad. Since he had been burned in the past, he did not readily accept that his father had changed. As their final activity together, Tyler and Ryan had stopped by Brooke's to help load equipment into the truck and trailer the evening before she and Kasey were to leave for L.A. . . Brooke sat at the table with a mug of hot coffee in front her, frustration showed on her face as she placed her phone on the table. Tyler walked over and put his hand on her shoulder. "What's wrong?"

"I blew it. I really blew it." Brooke shook her head.

"What do you mean? How?"

Brooke stood up. "I've been so busy with the preparations that I forgot to make the hotel reservations. The Rose Bowl and the

Tournament of Roses Parade have every hotel booked in the area. There aren't any rooms left that I can afford and that are within an hour's drive of the show grounds. What am I going to do?".

Ryan offered. "Dad, what about your condo?"

Tyler smiled at Ryan. "It's the right price, but it's a bit too far. You can use it as a last resort."

Brooke sighed. "Thanks, its good knowing I've got something to fall back on."

Ryan watched carefully. He wasn't used to seeing his father get involved in the lives of others.

"I've got to make some phone calls." Tyler started to leave the room

"That's more like the Dad I know." Ryan muttered.

"What's that you said?" Kasey queried.

"Oh, nothing," Ryan gave a weak smile to Kasey.

Ten minutes later Tyler returned to the kitchen. "I've got good news." They all looked at him and waited. "I've found a place for you that's five to ten minutes from the L.A. Equestrian Center, and it's free."

They gave a unified look of disbelief. Brooke went further. "How and where?"

"My Uncle Bob has a small place not too far from the Center. He said there's plenty of room for you. There's also a stall for Slider, if you need it."

Ryan shot a disbelieving look towards his dad as Brooke ran to Tyler and wrapped her arms around him. "We won't be imposing, will we?"

Tyler smiled. "Trust me, my aunt will be in seventh heaven being a hostess to you. There's even room for Amber."

"You'll be there to introduce us?" Brooke questioned.

"Absolutely. After your packed and on your way, I'll catch a flight and meet you there and help get you settled in."

Kasey turned to Ryan. "Is this really going to work out?"

Ryan reassured her. "If Uncle Bob agreed to it, I'm sure it will work out. My Dad's right about Aunt Charlotte."

Kasey breathed a sigh of relief as Ryan shook his head and muttered. "I can't believe he just did that."

"Did what?" Kasey asked.

"Oh nothing. Doesn't matter." Ryan became quiet and continued to observe.

The drive to L.A, was uneventful with Kasey and Amber sharing the driving duties. Brooke watched the scenery and was surprised by the knot that was tightening in her gut. It wasn't the upcoming competition; it was meeting Tyler's aunt and uncle. Meeting Ryan was one thing but staying at his uncle's house was something else. *What kind of impression will I make? These people are from L.A. and I'm just a country girl. Will they like me? Will I feel out of place in their home?*

Traffic didn't cooperate; it took an extra hour before they drove through the main gate of the L.A. Equestrian Center. Kasey's eyes became large as she scanned the area. "Wow, this place is huge."

Brooke chuckled softly. "What'd you'd expect in L.A.?"

Amber followed the small signs directing the Mustang Competitors to the stabling and the registration office. She stopped behind a blue BMW that was parked next to the show office. Brooke got out of the truck and her face lit up when Tyler got out of the BMW. He was dressed for L.A... "You made it already?"

"Sure, no problem."

Her eyes examined him, every detail. "I see you're back in your element."

Tyler shrugged. "I'm not so sure about that... How was your trip?"

Brooke laughed as she took his arm. "Pretty uneventful... I didn't believe you when you said how bad the traffic would be. I thought between Christmas and New Year's it would ease up."

Tyler grinned slightly. "It never dies down around here."

Brooke, Kasey and Tyler went into the event office with Kasey remaining a respectable distance from Tyler. She still wasn't comfortable around him, especially in public. A few minutes later they came out of the office with their show packet and stall assignment. Kasey continued to take in the surroundings. "Mom, it's so busy here. Do you think the commotion will bother Slider?"

"He's pretty laid back; I think he'll be fine."

The temporary stall was a ten-by-ten box with little light, except for what the door let in. Kasey's voice sounded worried. "I was hoping for something a little bigger and maybe—nicer."

Brooke let out a deep breath. "This is typical for temporary stalls. I overheard in the show office that they are packed. Many of the parade horses are staying here."

Tyler whispered to Brooke. "Does he have to stay here, or can he stay off the grounds?"

"I don' t know... Why?"

"Remember, he can stay at my uncle's. Why don't you see if you like that barn better?"

Brooke checked with the show office and then talked with Kasey. "They say there's nothing in the rules requiring the competing horses to stay on the show property overnight. The Mustangs must be on the show grounds from 10 am to 4pm on the days of competition...

Anyway, we'd have to trailer some of those days anyway to get to the parade and to the final event venue."

Kasey whispered. "Mom, let's check out the other stall. I'd much rather have Slider stay where we're spending the night. Then we can keep an eye on him."

A short time later they had Slider in his stall and the trailer un-hitched as they drove to check out their accommodations, and maybe Slider's. Tyler took over the driving with Kasey in the passenger seat and Brooke in the middle, tight up against him. Amber and Shane were squeezed into the backseat with some luggage and supplies. As they drove down Riverside Drive, Tyler glanced over at Brooke and winked. "I hope nobody sees me driving this rig. I'll never live it down."

She elbowed him. "Oh—stop it." They laughed.

A few minutes later Tyler turned onto Country Club Road. They wound up the narrow tree lined road until Tyler entered a gated drive-way. After pushing several numbers on the keypad, the gate slowly opened. Tyler parked in front of a Spanish style house. "Wow! What a gorgeous place. I love the red terracotta roof." Brooke exclaimed.

"They've lived here for years. I used to play in the yard when I was Shane's age."

"They let you play in this manicured lawn?"

"They're just normal people, you'll see."

After absorbing all the surroundings, Brooke looked at Tyler. "I thought you said a little place... I had no idea."

"It's really not that big; it just seems it from the outside."

At the front door, they were greeted by Charlotte. "Welcome, please come in. I've been expecting you... Tyler, just don't stand there; introduce me to your friends."

Tyler smiled. "Yes, Aunt Charlotte." He motioned to Brooke who was next to him and then started the introductions, after which they all politely shook hands and exchanged greetings.

Charlotte had started to transition into her hostess mode when Tyler interrupted. "Aunt Charlotte, we're on a tight schedule until the mustang gets settled. Is Uncle Bob around? The show stalls over at the Equestrian Center are kind of small and I'd like to make sure Slider can stay here."

Charlotte waved her open hands at Tyler. "Oh, no reason to bother Bob with that, and he's not here right now. The horses and barns are my thing. Most definitely he can stay here; I've got two empty stalls you can use. . . Let me show you the stable."

On the way to the Slider's stall, they zigzagged through the house and out the patio doors past the swimming pool. Shane was transfixed on the pool as they walked by it. "Is the water warm?"

Tyler pointed to several black panels hidden behind some bushes. "You bet, see it's heated."

"Man, wish I had brought my swimming suit."

Charlotte jumped in. "No problem young man, we keep extra suits around for such occasions."

Shane smiled broadly. They went out through a gate into the stable area where there was a four-stall barn, tack room, wash stall, feed room, and small lounge. Behind the barn was a 100 by 200 foot covered but not enclosed arena which had two green paddocks along the one side and a dry lot along the other side.

Brooke looked at Charlotte. "Do you ride?"

"Just a little."

Tyler interrupted. "Don't be so modest. I've heard that you've competed at some big shows."

Charlotte beamed. "That was with my retired horse. I have a trainer who does most of the riding now. My new horse isn't at that level yet. . . Let me introduce you to them."

Inside the barn, she proudly showed one of her treasures. "This is my retired friend, Rooster's Double Take. He's taken me far. Now it's time to for me to look after him."

The group peered into the stall. Brooke took in his confirmation. "He's a handsome boy."

Charlotte's eyes glistened. "In the stall, next to him is Risky's Special Blessing. He just got back from a training tune-up. I'll be showing him at a local show at the end of the month. There's one more who's being ridden and shown by my trainer at his facility."

Brooke appreciated the quality of the horses and the care with which they were obviously showered. "They are lovely horses, and this is a beautiful place you have here."

"Thank you. . . Across the aisle-way are two empty stalls that you are welcome to use. There's a wash stall at the other end of the barn. Please make yourself at home and use anything in the barn or the arena."

Brooke turned to Kasey. "What do you think?"

"It sure would be nice to have Slider close during the night. I'd still like to take him over to the Equestrian Center for some familiarization rides so it's not too new for him. But we could do most of the rehearsals here. We only have two days before the competition starts."

Brooke turned to Charlotte and Tyler. "I think it's settled. Slider will stay here with us."

"I'm so glad we're able to help.—Let me show you to your rooms so you can unpack before going back to get your mustang."

Tyler and Brooke lingered at the back of the group as they headed to the house. Tyler loosely took hold of Brooke's hand. "I told you my Aunt was the consummate hostess."

"She's sweet."

Tyler grinned. Brooke playfully elbowed him. "Hey, you never told me your Aunt was into reining horses."

"It never came up. It's always been her thing, my family never really got involved with it."

"She seems passionate about it."

"It's in her heritage. Her family have been ranchers in California since the mid 1800s and horses have always been an important part of their culture."

Back in the house Charlotte took the group to the family room. "This is where we spend most of our time; the rest of the house is for entertaining. Please feel free to use it and make yourself at home."

Shane looked out the window. "Wow, look at the view of the city!"

Charlotte gently touched Shane on the shoulder. "Yes, we enjoy it too."

The room had an old west warmth, furnished with wood and leather furniture. The decorations displayed her family's western heritage. The Christmas decorations in this room had a decidedly cowboy flair. The group headed to the bedrooms and Brooke turned toward Tyler. "I like your Aunt."

Later that evening after Slider was taken care of, Charlotte had a down-home meal waiting for Brooke and her team. They sat around a large dark rustic pine table to a meal of burgers and assorted sides. Bob who was back from his golf match joined them for dinner. "So, Brooke, I hear you've had a good effect on my nephew. You've gotten him to think about more than just work."

"I hope that's a good thing."

Bob laughed. "Absolutely, that's one of the reasons I sent him to

Flagstaff. He needed to get a life." Tyler cringed.

Brooke's curiosity was peaked. "He works for you?"

Bob gave Tyler a look. "Just like his father, never saying much. . . Yes, he's a Vice President and my top attorney."

Shane couldn't contain himself. "Tyler, you're really a Vice President?"

Tyler nodded his head and kept quiet. He knew more was coming. Brooke was intrigued. "And I assume you're the president of AA Land Company. . ." The pieces of the puzzle started to come together. "And AA stands for?"

Bob proudly replied. "Alexander and Alexander. My father and his brother were Orange Grove farmers back during the depression and saw the future growth of the region. They started buying properties that the banks had foreclosed. This eventually expanded into ranching and other types of farming. When the building boom hit, they strategically started selling land. At that point, the business started transitioning into a land development business more than farming and ranching. And, here we are today."

Shane didn't miss a word. "Do you still do ranching and farming?"

"Yes, but that's now a much smaller part of the business."

Brooke murmured to Tyler. "We need to talk later."

Bob saw Brooke's face as she whispered to Tyler. "I'm sorry if Tyler kept quiet about this. But he was under my strict orders to keep his association with AA secret while he did his research."

Brooke looked at Bob and then back at Tyler. She didn't like being kept in the dark. But being reminded that Tyler was under orders, softened her slightly. Kasey quietly observed. She wasn't sure how to process what she was hearing. She saw how her mother and Tyler were connecting and now, all the ties he had to L.A. . . If they got more serious, what would this mean to her and her friends?

After dinner Brooke wanted to talk. "Tyler, can you come check on Slider with me?"

Tyler took a deep breath. "Sure." *Judgment time is here.*

On the way to the barn, Brooke became animated. "You could have told me whose house we were staying at, and that you were more than *just* an attorney for AA Land Company."

"I didn't think it was important. He's only my uncle. We're just regular people."

"Regular people, my eye... You own half of Southern California."

"Did you see anything pretentious here today?"

Brooke paused and thought. "I guess not... But you didn't tell me you were a vice president."

"It's just words. I report to people like everyone else. The title just gets in the way and I never cared about it anyway. For me, it's about the job and closing the deal."

Brooke sighed as she took Tyler's hand and walked back to the house. *He continues to be full of surprises.*

CHAPTER

30

The Holiday Mustang Challenge opened with all the participants and their mustangs lined up in the center of the covered arena. While the teams were waiting to be introduced the big screen scoreboard played interviews with the spectators. The announcer asked one little boy, "which mustang do you like?"

"The Christmas Mustang." He quickly replied.

The announcer laughed. "And which one is the Christmas Mustang?"

"The one with the Grinch on his forehead, you know, from the Christmas cartoon."

The camera then panned across the lineup of mustangs and stopped on Slider's head. "There you have it folks. This young man is rooting for Slider, the Christmas Mustang and his trainer."

The crowd erupted in laughter as the special effects people super-imposed a Christmas hat on Slider's Grinch marking. Kasey looked up at the screen and wanted to hide. Brooke took it in stride and smiled.

The announcer got the program back on track and started to introduce the teams; Bobby McFay and Eric Gold, Hank Cooper and Scott Sewell, Katy Grant and Linda Powell and the list went on. Horror showed on Kasey's face as she looked at her mother. "What did we think we were doing entering this competition? All the big names are here. We don't stand a chance. I'll end up making a fool of myself. They're already laughing at Slider."

Brooke had similar thoughts, but she couldn't share them with Kasey. She had to remain strong and supportive. "Somebody thought we were good enough. Not everyone who applied was selected to compete. All the applications went through a review panel."

Kasey's voice quivered. "I'm sure they made a mistake with us."

The next participant's name they heard was, "Brooke Anderson and Kasey Anderson with Slider the Christmas Mustang, they're our only mother-daughter team competing this Holiday Weekend. And we have a note here. Due to Brooke's injury, Kasey will be showing their mustang. . . Good luck Kasey."

Kasey's knees went weak. She wanted to run out of the arena, but her legs wouldn't carry her. She had to pull herself together. She needed to do it for herself. She needed to do it for her mom. Could she put the past behind her?

When the introductions were over, Brooke saw apprehension in Kasey's face. "You'll do great today in the compulsories. You and Slider are a team; you've got a real connection. There's something between you and that horse that nobody else here has with their mustang. Use it; go show what Slider can do. Show them how special he is."

The pep talk helped. "You're right Mom. I've gotta do it for Slider, to show everyone how special he is."

The first day of competition was the pattern class, in which the rider had to demonstrate the mustang's ability to walk, jog, extend the jog, lope, and extend the lope. They also had to demonstrate the ability to do a simple or flying lead change, turn 360 degrees, and stop. These were all elements that Kasey and Slider had been working on for the past three months. Their hard work and effort paid off. Kasey was in fifth place at the end of day one with two points separating Kasey from the leader.

Day two of the competition arrived with Kasey more relaxed than the day before, where her nerves may have cost her that point or two. The trail portion was now the focus; it had leading elements and riding elements as part of the test. This type of work was a natural strength of Kasey's. She'd always been able to read a horse and knew instinctively when to release pressure. They demonstrated their ability as a team; Kasey and Slider moved up to second place. There was one day left in the competition. Could they move into first place?

A sizable contingent from Flagstaff had made the trek to L.A... They came to support Kasey and to watch her and Slider perform. After her ride, Kasey searched the crowds for Josh, but did not see him. Twenty minutes later Maddie and her family had stopped by to say hi, but Josh still hadn't appeared. She kept checking her watch as her apprehension rose. Finally, she spotted his dad heading her way. She walked toward him, forcing herself not to run. "Pastor Sena did Josh come with you?"

"Yes, we watched your routine today. Excellent job."

"Do you know where he is? I need to talk to him about moving the props tomorrow."

"He disappeared an hour ago, I thought he was heading over to see you."

Kasey breathed a small sigh of relief. He was at the show grounds. But on the other hand, she was infuriated. If he was here, why hadn't he stopped by?"

Forty minutes later he showed up at Slider's stall. "Hi Kasey, you looked awesome out there today."

Kasey was still agitated. "Where've you been? I needed to talk to you?"

"I've been lookin' for a gift for you." He pulled a small string bracelet out of his pocket and handed to Kasey. "I hunted all over for this."

Kasey's anger melted as Josh helped put it on. "You went out and got this for me?" Josh gave an awkward half grin.

Kasey held her hand out to admire the bracelet. "You're coming to the New Year's Eve party tonight? Right?"

"Sure, I was planning on giving you your gift then."

"Ok, I'll see you then and talk to you about tomorrow. We've gotta get Slider back to his stall before the party."

The New Year's Eve Party was held at the Equestrian Center with festive lights covering the trees that lined the area. It didn't attract the typical L.A. crowd but brought out those who were socially minded and wanted to support the wild mustangs and burros. The event was packed with several big-name stars who used their draw power for the charity. It had been advertised as a casual western event. Brooke found out this had a different meaning in L.A. . . .

"Tyler, I can't believe the way some of these women are dressed."

Tyler laughed. "Around here if you put on boots and wear a cowboy hat, it makes it western."

Brooke's family hung together and took the opportunity to thank their friends for making the trip to support Kasey. Josh found Kasey proudly wearing her string bracelet and then asked her to dance. He draped his arms around Kasey's waist. "Do you want to ride back to Flagstaff with me and my Dad?"

She leaned her head against his shoulder. "I'd like to, but I have to help drive the trailer back. My Mom's still not allowed to drive."

"Oh—I forgot that you're here to help your mom."

Tyler used the dance floor to his advantage. He held Brooke firmly in his arms. "I didn't think I'd get a chance to be alone with you."

Brooke glanced around and then looked back into Tyler's eyes. "You call this alone?"

"Can anyone hear what we're saying to each other?"

Brooke continued to look into his eyes. "Probably not."

Tyler gave a small sigh that ended with a smile. "Then we're alone."

Brooke leaned her head against his shoulder as they slowly swayed to the music.

After the party and when they were back at the Alexanders' ranchette, Kasey went to check on Slider while everyone else settled down for the night. Brooke was pouring a glass of water when she answered her phone. "Mom! Get down here right away. Slider's cast in his stall."

Brooke shoved the phone in her pocket and ran. "Tyler, Shane, we need you at the barn. NOW! Slider is cast."

Tyler watched Brooke fly by and then followed. "What?" Moments later, he found himself standing outside Slider's stall.

With panic in her eyes Kasey looked at Brooke. "He's not thrashing too much right now. We need to get him up."

Brooke barked out orders. "Somebody, get some rope or long lead lines."

Tyler and Shane were back moments later handing Brooke a collection of ropes.

"Kasey, see if you can loop the rope around his rear leg and then hand it to Tyler."

Brooke watched on as Kasey maneuvered close to Slider while she tried to calm him with her voice. She slipped a loop over his leg and handed the rope to Tyler.

Brooke continued. "That's great. Now do the same with the front leg that's against the wall. Then you and Shane hang onto it. When I say pull, you and Tyler gently try to pull Slider's legs away from the wall."

Kasey wiped a tear from her eye as she got close to his front legs and looped the rope around his leg. Brooke said a two-word silent prayer to herself, *please God,* and the gave the order. "Okay pull."

Adrenaline surged through their veins as they pulled with all their strength. Slider struggled, and persistence won out. He flipped away from the wall and fought his way back to his feet where he shook the sawdust from his body. He limped slightly as he circled around his stall. They moved out of the stall and breathed a sigh of relief. Brooke looked at Kasey, Shane and Tyler. "Good job guys." She then focused on Kasey. "Let's check him out."

Tyler looked on. "Do you need a vet?"

"At this hour on New Year's Eve? You've got to be kidding. Who's going to be available? And we don't know anyone here."

"I'll get my aunt and uncle and see who they know." Tyler disappeared to get his phone.

Brooke and Kasey ran their hands over Slider's body and found no cuts, but when they jogged him down the aisle-way he still seemed slightly off on his left hind. Kasey's heart raced as she bordered on being frantic. "What are we going to do? He's got to show tomorrow. There's so much riding on it. The world has to know how good he is."

Brooke's heart also raced, but then the harsh realities hit her hard. This also will impact her chances of keeping the ranch. Her stomach teetered on nausea as all the stress poured down. She struggled to remain strong. *I'm the mother; I need to be there for her. I can't let my emotions take control.* "Let's take it one step at a time. We don't know what's wrong with him yet. Maybe he'll be okay by morning?" Brooke wished she fully believed her own words.

Tyler got back to the barn as he finished with his call. "Uncle Bob and Aunt Charlotte are coming home now. She's calling her vet."

Kasey looked towards Tyler. "Thanks."

Two hours later Dr. Jim Berry finished his exam. "He's not too bad. His left hip was out, and I manipulated it back into position. He may be little sore for a couple of days. Nothing a few days off won't cure."

Kasey looked at Brooke and then at Jim. "He's supposed to be in the Rose Parade tomorrow morning and then compete in the freestyle competition at the Holiday Mustang Challenge. . . What will happen to him if he competes?"

Jim paused, looked at Slider and back at Kasey. "No permanent damage. He might just be sore and maybe a little off, but that's all." Jim thought some more. "Can he skip the parade?"

"No, it's a required part of the competition."

"He is borderline. Maybe he can do it and won't be lame. Let's see what tomorrow brings."

Kasey's expression softened; she had a glimmer of hope.

"I'll give him some Phenylbutazone for tonight and come back before the parade and check him over again."

Brooke jumped in. "**No**! The competition rules specifically prohibit drugs."

"Okay." Jim replied. "We'll just keep our fingers crossed and see what he's like in the morning."

Jim left and everyone headed to the house, hoping they could get some sleep. Brooke caught up to Charlotte. "Thank you so much for calling your vet; is there anything I can do?"

Charlotte shook her head. "No, don't be silly. It was my pleasure. Just get some rest, you have a big day in front of you."

Brooke went back to Tyler and took his arm. "The more I'm around her, the more I like your aunt, there's something special about her."

"Yes, she's special." Tyler looked at his watch. "We missed the ball dropping at midnight."

Brooke gave a tired smile. "There's always another year."

Tyler took her in his arms and whispered. "Happy New Year." She closed her eyes and waited for the kiss that followed.

Meanwhile, Kasey sneaked back to the barn and grabbed some blankets out of the trailer and made a nest in the empty stall next to Slider. "Goodnight boy. No more scares... You hear."

CHAPTER

In the wee hours of the morning Brooke tossed and turned in bed. The injury to Slider brought with it an avalanche of bad memories; mostly, the past year of bad luck and sabotage. With Ray in jail, she thought it was all over. But was all of her misfortune gone? Tonight's episode in the barn made Brooke question her future once again. Now wide awake and her mind chasing down all the bad scenarios, Brooke decided to check on Slider. Outside his stall, she stopped, smiled, and slowly shook her head. There she found Kasey sound asleep, buried in a pile of horse blankets. *Twenty years earlier I would have done the same thing... Who am I kidding, I almost did it myself.* Brooke let Kasey sleep; she needed all her rest for the big day ahead. Brooke then looked in on Slider who was standing in the middle of the stall, slowly chewing his hay.

The vet would be back in another two hours, and they'd have their first answer. Would it be safe to ride Slider? Then the second question; will his injury affect his way of moving, and his placement in the competition? Brooke and Kasey faced some difficult decisions in the next few hours, ones that would affect the rest their lives.

As dawn arrived, Kasey was up and getting ready for the day ahead long before Charlotte's vet arrived. Slider was already bathed, and Kasey was checking the props for the afternoon's performance. Brooke who was waiting outside, called to Kasey who was in the barn. "The vet's here, it's time to get the verdict on Slider."

Kasey took a deep breath and willed herself to go over to Slider's stall. She wanted to hope for the best but was afraid it would jinx the examination. Jim went into the stall and ran his hands over Slider, giving him a thorough checkup. He then led him out of the stall and handed the lead rope to Kasey. "Can you jog him out for me?"

"Sure."

Kasey jogged him down the driveway for twenty yards, stopped, turned around and jogged back. Jim carefully watched the process and then asked Kasey to do it one more time. When Kasey and Slider returned, he pronounced his verdict. "He's jogging out fine, but I was able to detect just a little muscle tenderness in his back, near his left hip. He should be able to ride in the freestyle this afternoon. He'll need a slow and good warmup."

Kasey relaxed a little but was still anxious. "What about the parade; can he be ridden in the parade?"

"If you want to ride him in the afternoon, I'd advise against it, the long parade with you on his back might get his muscles sore." Jim paused and thought for a moment. "Could you lead him instead of riding him?"

Kasey looked at Brooke. "What do the rules say?"

Brooke shrugged her shoulders. "I don't know, I'll check."

Before she could get the show packet out of the truck, Kasey had rules pulled up on her cell phone. "It doesn't say anything about riding; it just says the horses have to be in the parade."

Brooke looked through her documents. "You're right. But we'd better check with the show steward."

As Jim wrote up his bill, he offered. "If anyone at the show needs to talk to me about Slider, have them give me a call; here's my business card." He wrote a number on the back. "That's my personal cell on the back; I can be reached at it anytime today."

As he handed the bill to Brooke, Charlotte intercepted it. "They're my guests; please put it on my account."

Brooke began to protest but Tyler who'd been observing from a distance, stepped in. "Don't waste your breath Brooke. When Aunt Charlotte makes up her mind, you're not going to change it." He winked at Charlotte.

Two hours later at the parade staging area, Brooke and Tyler came back from a meeting with the Show Steward and the Show Committee. They found Amber holding Slider.

"Where's Kasey?"

Amber motioned to the back of the trailer. "In there."

Brooke looked in the trailer and found Kasey kneeling in the sawdust vomiting up her breakfast. She went to Kasey and gently touched her shoulder. "What's the matter?"

"When we got here, I was feeling fine. But then all the floats, the people, the parade. I had a flashback to Dad's accident. . . Then I had trouble breathing and felt sick to my stomach."

Brooke knelt while she rubbed Kasey's shoulder. "We've been so busy that we never thought about how the parade might affect you. How are you feeling now?"

"A little better. I think the worst of it's past, at least for now." Kasey stood up, "Can I get a drink of water?"

"Sure." Brooke asked Shane to get a bottle of water and then put her arm back around Kasey. "We've got the ruling from the Show Committee."

Kasey became motionless. "Yeah, what is it?"

"I explained everything to them, and they were very understanding. But they said that it was implied that you had to ride. Tyler took the legal approach and explained that rules can't be implied; they have to be specific. . . He was good."

"Did he change their minds?"

"Partially, they were still adamant that you were supposed to ride. If you didn't ride but walked the parade with Slider, you'd have a five-point reduction in your total score."

The wind came out of Kasey. "But that'll take us out of the running for first place."

"Yes, but you're still close enough to the leaders that anything can happen during the freestyle."

The walk along the parade route went off without a hitch. Slider seemed to enjoy the attention and was relaxed the whole time. His eye remained calm; it almost seemed like he was smiling at the crowd. After the parade, they had a couple of hours to get to the Staples Center and get ready. Temporary stalls were setup on the ground floor, beneath the stands of the arena. Once Slider was in his stall and the props were all positioned for the performance, Kasey and her team explored the arena. They walked into the immense, dimly lit stadium and gazed at the empty stands.

Kasey was awestruck. "It's so big!"

Brooke turned in a circle to take in the panoramic view. "Wow! It's impressive."

They finished their tour and got back to the business of making sure everything was ready for the performance. The spectators started to trickle into the arena, and some of their friends from Flagstaff came by to wish her luck. Kasey's youth group leaders, Lisa and Daniel, made the trip to support her and were among the first to visit. Lisa found a moment alone with Kasey. "How are you holding up?"

"A bit overwhelmed. . . And this morning, I had a small panic attack just before the parade."

"That's not surprising. Many athletes get sick before a major competition. Remember, everyone gets scared. It's what you decide to do with the fear that makes the difference. Right?"

"Yeah."

"And what are you going to do about your fear?"

"Give it to God."

"And who do you ride for everyday?"

"The most powerful being in the Universe."

"So, the few extra people in this building don't add much to that, do they?"

Kasey smiled. "I guess not."

Lisa called Daniel over, and the three of them held hands and said a short prayer. It was time for the competition to get underway.

All the competitors were in the arena being introduced one by one and then they reached Kasey. "Here we have number 25, Slider the Christmas Mustang, a 5-year-old mustang gelding from the Fort Sage

Herd Management Area in California. He's been trained by Brooke and Kasey Anderson, the only mother-daughter team in the competition. They are carrying on the family tradition started by Brooke's late husband, Cory Anderson, who won the original mustang competition many years ago and went on to become a top reining rider. As you can see by Brooke's cast, she's had an accident, unrelated to training the mustang; so, Kasey will be the exhibitor today. Let's hear it for Brooke and Kasey."

The introduction was bittersweet for the pair. Having Cory acknowledged gave them a sense of pride, but at the same time it reminded them of their loss. After the introduction, they went back to their stall and made final preparations. Brooke and Tyler went back and forth between a viewing area and the stall to keep abreast of how the other riders were doing. The performances were living up to the big names that were showing. There were just two riders before Kasey when Amber motioned to Brooke. "Why don't you and Tyler go and watch from the competitors viewing area. Shane and I have everything covered back here."

Brooke hesitated. "But. . . ."

Amber cut her off. "Tyler, please take her there; Brooke's nerves might rub off on Kasey. Anyway, we've got things covered here." Amber winked at Kasey.

Brooke and Tyler settled into some seats and waited; Brooke fidgeted. "I need to be down there."

Tyler took her hand. "They said they've got things under control. There's not much you can do anyway." Brooke reluctantly and unsuccessfully tried to sit back and enjoy the show.

It was now Kasey's turn to compete. Slider was warmed up and had his LED lights put on as Kasey's crew drove out in the truck and placed all her props at the correct locations. Amber made sure the beacon lights, which allowed Kasey to navigate in the dark arena, were in the proper locations and turned on. It was time to begin and Kasey nodded to the sound crew who started her freestyle music. Amber motioned to the technical crew to kill the lights. Kasey started into the arena at a gallop as she whispered to herself. "Here you go God; I'm riding for you."

Brooke's heart nearly stopped when the lights went out. "What's going on? Kasey's supposed to be riding!"

Tyler's heart raced with Brooke's. "I don't know. . . Look, there's something moving."

Just then Kasey flipped the switch and the stick figure image, Slider, instantly appeared. They raced down the middle of the arena, executed a sliding stop and roll back. She then turned on her own lighted outline and repeated the maneuver going the other direction. They then completed two figure eights with a flying lead change in the middle. Brooke sat there totally awestruck, unable to utter a sound. Kasey came down the middle one more time and did another sliding stop followed by a spin each direction. At end of the second spin Amber signaled for the arena lights to come back on and Kasey turned off the LED lights. The audience erupted into cheers.

As the arena lights gained intensity, Kasey repeated part of her pattern with the addition of the serpentine jumps which she and Slider executed flawlessly. She again stopped in the middle, leaned forward and removed Slider's bridle and repeated the routine bridle-less. She came to one final sliding stop and hopped off Slider as the music transitioned to Brahms Lullaby and the voice over of her asking Slider if he was tired. Slider laid down and put his head on the pillow as rehearsed. The crowd exploded with whistles and cheers at the conclusion.

Brooke was the first to scream and whistle as she turned to Tyler and grabbed his arm. "Do you believe that girl! She was amazing. She totally surprised me... Did you know about this?"

Tyler looked at Brooke and shook his head in amazement. "Not me, I had no idea."

Brooke bolted from the stands dragging Tyler behind. She had to see Kasey.

The competitors were lined up in the center of the arena for the competition results. Brooke watched Kasey sit tall on Slider. "I'm so proud of what she's accomplished no matter what the results."

Tyler became slightly agitated. "What do mean *no matter what the results*. With that performance, she's got to win."

"If she had ridden in the parade, I'd have to agree. But that five-point reduction, and some of the performances those other riders turned in, first place has to be up for grabs."

They were down to the final two, Kasey and Cody Hardcastle. The question was, who would be in first and who would be in second. Brooke was beside herself with excitement. *Can it be? Did Kasey really pull this off?* Her mind was a rush of activity. In less than a moment her thoughts went from getting the bills paid off to what the competition could mean to her business, as well as their careers. Most importantly she realized that Kasey had conquered her fear of riding in public. She squeezed Tyler's hand so tight that the blood stopped flowing to his fingers. He didn't mind; he smiled as his eyes went back and forth between Kasey and Brooke.

Kasey, shaking from the surge of adrenaline, sat on Slider, still not fully believing what was happening. She almost pinched herself to make sure it wasn't a dream. *How did this happen? I shouldn't be here, not with everyone else who is around me.* Then the announcement came. "And in second place with 143 points it's. . . Kasey Anderson on Slider, The Christmas Mustang. And, in first place with 144.5 points is Cody Hardcastle. The judges want me to say that if Kasey had been able to ride Slider in the parade, they wouldn't have had to give her the five-point mandatory reduction in their score, and she would have won this competition. For those of you who are planning on purchasing a mustang at today's auction, Slider wasn't ridden in the parade today because he got cast in his stall last night and ended up with a slightly sore back. To do what he did today was truly amazing. For those of you bidding, make sure that these first and second place horses bring record prices at the auction."

Brooke beamed with pride for Kasey as she turned to Tyler. "Let's get back to the stall and give her a hand."

They helped Kasey remove Slider's saddle and hung his sec-ond-place ribbon around his neck. Kasey led him back to the arena entrance and froze at the gate. Dread showed in her eyes. She pushed the lead rope to Brooke's hands. "I can't do it. I can't take him into the auction." She bolted back to the stall, tears streaming down her cheeks.

Brooke's heart was crushed as she led Slider into the arena. *Such a wonderful day—does it have to end on such a sad note. I wish there was something I could do for her.* Brooke led Slider around the perimeter of the arena to show him off to perspective buyers. Halfway around she looked up into the stands and saw Slim and Martha. She momentar-ily stopped in her tracks. The conversation she had with her mother flashed through her mind, and she felt guilty for not doing what she knew she had to do. *I can't put it off any longer. I've got to talk to them.* She started walking again and picked up her pace; she had to get back before they left. Her eyes eagerly search the stands, there was no sign of them, they had left.

"Brooke. . .Brooke," She looked up to see Martha calling her name. "Tell Kasey she did a great job."

Relief rushed over Brooke. "I will. Please don't leave until I get a chance to talk to you—it's important."

Bidding started on Slider and quickly passed the point where Brooke could have any hope of buying him back. The price went to the point where their portion of the proceeds would pay off the back payments to the bank and make a sizeable dent in next year's mortgage. At the conclusion of the auction it was announced that both the first and second place mustangs fetched record bids with Slider exceeding all expectations at thirty-thousand dollars. Brooke handed Slider off to the show attendant and made her way back to Kasey. Tears formed in her eyes as she fought to maintain her composure.

While leaving the arena, she spotted Slim and Martha. She could no longer contain her swirling torrent of emotions. Tears now streamed down her cheeks. Kasey, Slider, and now Martha, it was more than she could handle. She ran toward Martha and wrapped her arms around her. "I'm so sorry for how I've treated you two for the past couple of years. Please forgive me."

Martha was bawling, too. "Yes, I forgive you."

Brooke looked at Slim with questioning eyes that invited him in. Slim wrapped his arms around them both. "I forgive you too." He said in between sobs.

In between sobs Brooke pushed out words. "I've missed you two so much."

As the tears subsided Brooke told them about her conversation with Alice. Martha was surprised. "I knew a little of that, but I didn't know your father might still be alive."

They filled each other in on what they knew, until they reached Kasey at the empty stall. She was sitting on a tack trunk. The tears had stopped, but her cheeks were flushed, and her eyes were bloodshot.

"Is Slider sold?"

"Yes, he brought a record bid."

Kasey smiled; it was some consolation. She knew her buddy was priceless. Tyler watched from a distance as reunion unfolded. He smiled and took them in. There was a steady flow of well-wishers from Flagstaff who came by to congratulate Kasey and Brooke on their excellent work. When Uncle Bob and Aunt Charlotte showed up at the stall, he and Tyler exchanged a few words and then Tyler quietly disappeared.

Bob pulled Brooke aside. "Tyler's been filling me in on your situation up there in Flagstaff. He's also told me that our development has been missing an important piece of local culture."

Brooke was confused. "Like what?"

"He's said the development needs a riding center, and he'd been trying to convince me that you should operate it from your ranch."

Brooke's jaw dropped. "He never said anything to me."

"He didn't want to get your hopes up until the board or I approved it... From what I've seen this week, the professionalism from you and your daughter, I now know what Tyler's been trying to tell me. I don't need to wait for the board's approval. I'll make you the offer right now. What do you say?"

Brooke's jaw opened further. "I—a—don't know what to say..." She looked but could not find Tyler. "What are the details?"

"Will work them out later. Are you interested?"

"Yes! Absolutely yes."

Maddie, Josh, and Kasey were in their own little group while Brooke and Bob finished their conversation. Josh hung his arm over Kasey's shoulder. "You sure looked great out there today Babe."

"Thanks"

"Let's ditch this place and go for walk." Josh took Kasey's hand and started to leave.

Kasey was torn and it showed on her face. "I'd like to, but I can't. All these people are stopping by. . . I really need to stay."

"It's your mom's thing not yours. They won't miss you."

Just then Brooke walked over and interrupted their conversation. "Kasey, have you seen Tyler?"

"No Mom, not since you got back."

As Brooke continued to look for Tyler, a silhouette of a man and horse moved down the corridor towards them. Something about the man's walk caught Brooke's attention and she watched as they approached. Her heart raced as she nudged Kasey and motioned toward the two figures. Kasey shifted her focus to the horse. No words passed between mother and daughter as something riveted their attention to the pair. They'd seen lots of horses being led before and at this competition they'd expected to see this sight. But some invisible force drew them towards the pair. Kasey's heart now raced to keep up with Brooke's. The horse and man passed beneath a light and their outline transitioned into a recognizable form. Kasey's heart no longer raced; it jumped out of body as she cried, "Slider", and she bolted toward her friend.

Tyler smiled. "He's all yours." He held out the lead rope to Kasey who grabbed it and wrapped both arms around Slider's neck.

Tears of joy ran down her face as she tightly held her friend in her grasp. "You bought him?"

Tyler nodded. "For you."

Brooke didn't try to hold back the tears as she swiftly moved over to Tyler and wrapped her arms around him. "Thank you. . . But how?"

"Uncle Bob, he took care of the bidding for me."

"But the price he went for. . . You shouldn't have."

"I needed to. It was important."

Kasey unwrapped herself from Slider and gave Tyler a hug. "Thank you."

Tyler smiled broadly.

The group of well-wishers now swarmed around Kasey and Slider and congratulated her on getting Slider back. Josh slipped away and watched from a distance before going off to explore.

Tyler and Brooke started to take a few items to the trailer. "You really shouldn't have. He was too expensive. And you've done so much already. . . Bob told me how you've worked to put a riding center in the plans, and you want me as the operator."

"It makes good business sense."

At the trailer, Brooke wrapped her arms around Tyler again and came nose to nose with him. "How can I thank you?" Her smile grew.

Tyler ached inside. He didn't want to utter the words he was about to say. It was the hardest thing he'd ever had to do. He pulled back slightly. "I wanted to talk to you about that." Brooke was confused; she was sure he would take the hint. Tyler continued. "I want to talk to you about taking a break."

Brooke's shoulder slumped forward she was totally caught off guard. 'What do you mean?"

"I've always bought and manipulated my relationships. I don't want to do it anymore. Our relationship needs to move forward on something stronger, not just me helping you keep the ranch and buying Slider for Kasey. I needed to do those things, but I don't want them to buy your love." Brooke sat down on the running board of the trailer, she was blindsided. Tyler continued. "There's one other thing. . . You know I've been trying to build a relationship with Ryan."

Brooke nodded, still in shock.

"It looks like I have a chance to make it happen. It could mean many of my weekends will be spent back in L.A. getting involved in his life. I can't commit to anything with you when I know I've got to put my priorities somewhere else for now."

Brooke looked up at Tyler. "So, what does this mean?"

"It means I really do care about you and—I love you—but if we're going to become something, it needs to start out right. I don't want to stop seeing you. I need to back off and give you your freedom. While I'm focusing my time on Ryan, you should have the freedom to see other men. Our relationship has to start off on the right foot. Building a future with you can't be based on gratitude; it won't last, it has to be built on stronger ground."

"I see your point. But I think we do have something more."

"So do I, but let's make sure we go forward for the right reasons. If it's God ordained, we'll know it in a year or so." Brooke stood up and wrapped her arms around Tyler and put her head on his shoulder as he rested his head against her. They just stood and embraced.

Tyler was pained inside; he didn't want to leave Brooke, not now. But he had an appointment. Reluctantly, Tyler broke the silence. "I want to stay, but I have to meet Ryan and his girlfriend."

Brooke sniffled a little. "I think I understand."

Brooke slowly walked back to the stall. Her mind agreed with Tyler, but her heart said something different. The stall was now illuminated with bright lights and there was a flurry of activity. A strange man was talking to Kasey in front of where Slider once stood. Kasey pointed. "That's my Mom over there."

"Mrs. Anderson, since your daughter is still a minor, we need your permission to interview her."

"Wait, tell me what this is all about?" Brooke was confused; she was caught off guard.

"This is for the Rural Horse Network's show, 'The Nations Horse'. We've been covering the Mustang Competition and we want to interview Kasey and talk to her about the super job she did."

Brooke relaxed as a smile started to appear. "Sure, what do I need to sign?"

The interview took thirty minutes but was edited down to a ten-minute slot in the show. They asked Kasey how she came up with the idea of doing the ride in the dark with just her and Slider lit up. They had her show off Slider and do a few tricks with him. Kasey smiled and joked with the crew; she seemed at ease in front of the camera. Brooke sneaked a peak at one of the monitors. The producer stood next to her. "Your daughter is a natural in front of the camera."

"I can see. I can't believe how relaxed she is."

The interview was over, and the crew was packing up when the producer came to talk to Brooke and Kasey. "I'm Steve Johnson, the producer. Thanks for taking the time to work with us."

Kasey's smile still hadn't left her face. "It was great fun."

Steve handed them his business card. "Kasey, you're great in front of the camera. You just might be who I've been looking for."

They both looked at him and then at each other. Brooke asked. "What do you mean?"

"I've been wanting to pitch a program to my managers, one that is geared to the teenage rider. I think you could be the perfect host."

Kasey laughed. "Who me? You've gotta be kidding."

"No, really. It's a long shot but are you interested?"

Brooke started to answer when Kasey blurted, "Yes!"

Brooke pushed on with her thought. "There are a lot of questions that need to be asked. Where would this be done? How much time is involved?"

Steve nodded. "All good questions and those are things that can be worked out later. I just want to know if you have any interest."

Kasey looked at Brooke with pleading eyes. Brooke sighed. "Yes, we're interested in finding out more."

CHAPTER

T yler sat drumming his fingers on the steering wheel. He looked in his rearview mirror, then he looked at the cars around him. The traffic still wasn't moving. He was on the I5, the 24-hour news station reported a major accident ahead. He looked at his watch and then the knot in his stomach reappeared. *I can't miss this meeting with Ryan, or even be late.* His tapping became more agitated. Fifteen minutes later he'd crept far enough along to get off at the next exit. He picked his way along back streets, praying he'd make all the traffic lights. He looked at his watch again and knew there was no way he could make it on time. At best, he would be five minutes late. He called Ryan, no answer. The knot got tighter.

Ryan and Robyn arrived at the restaurant early and took seats at their table. It was a new upscale Italian restaurant; Ryan had picked one his dad would enjoy. Ryan played with his napkin. "It'll be interesting to see if my dad actually shows up."

Robyn gave a hard look to Ryan. "Why would you say such a thing?"

"Because for my whole life he's either missed my important events or he's been so late it wasn't worth showing up."

"It can't be that bad?"

"You don't know my dad; work is everything."

"A workaholic?"

"The worst kind, then he thinks he can buy your love... He claims he's changed, but I doubt if it will stick."

"You spent a couple of days with him; you said you noticed a difference."

"A little, but that's one reason we're here. I set up a test for him."

"A test?"

"Yeah, I knew he'd be at that Mustang Competition with his girlfriend this afternoon and probably would want to go out with them this evening. So, I purposely set our meeting up to conflict with it. That way I'll know if he's really serious about me or just mouthing the right words."

"Ryan. That's not fair. From what you've told me, this competition is a big deal, they came all the way from Flagstaff to compete. Asking him to leave his friends, especially if they did well; that's just not right."

"Maybe, but it will tell me what I need to know."

Ryan checked his watch. "He's got five more minutes."

Every minute Ryan checked his watch until the appointed time that his father was supposed to be there. Then he stood up. "Let's go Robyn. He's not going to show up."

"Give him a few extra minutes."

"He's had a few extra minutes my whole life. Besides he could've called." Ryan insisted and almost dragged Robyn out of the restaurant.

At the car, she complained. "You rushed me so much I left my handbag back at the table."

Irritation flashed across Ryan's eyes as they headed back to retrieve her purse. While they were leaving the restaurant the second time, they met Tyler at the door.

Tyler was breathing hard after running from the parking lot. "Good, I got here before you left. There was an accident on the interstate; I had to go through town."

"Why didn't you call?"

"I did, several times. It immediately went to voice mail each time."

Ryan checked his phone. It wouldn't turn on. "Oh. . . I forgot to charge it last night."

Robyn cleared her throat—and then glared at Ryan.

Ryan tried to ignore the look. "Dad, this is my girlfriend Robyn."

"It's a pleasure to meet you." Tyler smiled as he shook her hand.

She smiled back. "Should we go to our table?"

The conversation was slightly awkward through the appetizers. Then Ryan asked how the competition went. Tyler told him about the placings and that Kasey and Slider should have won except for not riding in the parade. Ryan wanted more. "How'd she deal with having to give him up for adoption?"

"Not well, she couldn't even show him during the bidding. Brooke had to take care of that."

"That doesn't surprise me from what I saw in Flagstaff."

Tyler's smile went wide. "You should have seen her face when I handed her Slider after it was all over and told her he was hers."

"You bought him?"

"Yeah, it was the right thing to do."

"I'm sure the company will get some good publicity out of it, also."

"No, it's strictly a private matter. The firm has nothing to do with it at all."

Tyler went to the restroom. Ryan looked at Robyn. "Maybe he's changing."

"He seems very nice."

He took her hand. "Did you really *forget* your purse?"

She smiled back.

Everyone was trying to wind down after a rewarding and exciting afternoon. Shane finally got a chance to get into the pool as Brooke and Amber watched him from their spot next to the fire pit. Amber took in her surroundings. "Can you believe this place? It's like we're at a five-star resort."

"Yes, it's nice."

"Is that all you have to say?—Okay Brooke, you've been quiet all evening. Level with me, what's going on?"

"It's Tyler."

"What do you mean, it's Tyler?"

"We had a discussion before he left to meet Ryan."

"Yeah, why's that got you so down."

"He thinks we should cool our relationship down for little bit. He wants me to have my freedom."

Amber sat up and faced Brooke. "You're not making sense."

"Tyler's always bought love in the past. And with all he's done for me and Kasey, he doesn't want any hint that I'm coming to him because of what he's done. He trying to break that cycle. He's also going to focus on improving his relationship with Ryan."

"Is he crazy?"

"No, truth is I know where he's coming from and I agree with him. But that doesn't change the fact that I wish he were here right now."

"Let me get this straight. You agree with him?"

"Yes, we're still going to see each other and be friends, just no commitment tying me down to him. After a year or so, if we still feel the same about each other; maybe then we'll move forward."

Amber slouched back into her chair. "You two are crazy. I've seen the looks you two have given each other. No amount of money could buy those looks. I give you three months, six tops; and you then two will be inseparable." Brooke smiled.

A few minutes later Charlotte came and sat down next to Brooke. "I wanted to say something earlier today but just couldn't find any time alone with you."

Brooke looked at her. "What is it?"

"Did I hear the announcer correctly this afternoon? Were you the wife of Cory Anderson?"

"Yes, why?"

"I heard about the terrible accident. I'm so sorry for your loss."

"I've finally come to terms with it."

Charlotte touched her hand. "I'm glad. . . There's one other thing."

"Yes?"

"That horse I told you about, the one that's in training and being ridden by a professional."

Brooke nodded.

Charlotte swallowed deeply. "You should know it's one of Cory's horses that was sold after the accident."

Brooke's eyes lit up. "Which one?"

"Moonlight Dancer."

"I'm so glad you have him. He couldn't have gone to a nicer person."

The three ladies talked horses and riding for the rest of the evening. Brooke had found a new friend.

The holidays were long past, and winter had started to blossom into spring in the high meadows around Flagstaff. Ray was still in jail and had confessed to causing most of the accidents around the ranch. He would not admit to causing Zoomey's death. He was adamant that he was not involved. With no accidents occurring to interrupt the flow, activities on the ranch had gotten into a smooth rhythm.

It was a brisk Saturday morning when Shane ran out to the road and brought in the mail. He dropped it on the kitchen table as he ran back outside. Just beneath some other letters, but barely visible, was a letter addressed to Kasey from the Rural Horse Network.

ACKNOWLEDGMENTS

Nancy Reppert—My wife and partner who encouraged me throughout the writing and editing process, who through her numerous
test reads provided me with valuable insights for the story. I also
thank her for carrying the extra load at home to provide me with
the time to write.

David Hazard—My writing coach who saw potential in my writing
and worked to develop this talent. Thanks for your help and all
the wise advice.

Hannah and Samantha—For putting up with a dad who hid in his writing room for hours at a time and for helping their mother hold
down the farm.

Heather Rutherford—My copy editor who did an amazing job in turning the manuscript out in record time.

Stephanie Jennings—One of my first test readers who took the time to
open her house to David and me while we saught her impressions
of the story. I also thank Stephanie for sharing her knowledge
about the reining world.

Sara Newcomer—The final proofreader before the story went to copy
editing. Thank you for the insights that you provided.

Beta readers—Damon, Brian, Paula, Shannon, Esther, Caroline, Linda,
Heather and Bill. Thank you all for your encouragement and valuable feedback.

PHILIP M. REPPERT has used his experiences in the horse industry and living in the American Southwest to craft this first novel in the Sweetwater novel series. He has extensive knowledge of the horse industry with 25+ years of experience and has been professionally trained in natural horsemanship with 15 years of experience. He has also been a certified natural horsemanship instructor.

Throughout his riding career, he has successfully competed in Eventing, Dressage, and Jumping, and has also successfully trained numerous green and feral horses. His family currently runs a horse boarding and training facility in Western Pennsylvania.

In addition to training horses, Philip has a B.S. in Electrical Engineering and a Ph.D. in Geophysics from the Massachusetts Institute of Technology. He has two grown stepdaughters and two grown daughters. His wife has homeschooled their daughters, and also works in the horse industry.